AMAZON EDITOR'S PICK

AMAZON #1 PARANORMAL BESTSELLER

"An eerie tone permeates the entire story, with even mundane events feeling off-kilter. The whole cast seems to have multiple personas, all tinged with darkness."
—*Foreword Clarion Review*

"… a Spiritual roller coaster ride! *Harry Potter* meets the *Exorcist*!"
—*American Online Radio*

"At times an intriguing mystery, at others a chilling thriller…Jack's development throughout is an adventurous, if spooky, coming of age story that will thrill and at times scare readers of classic urban fantasy and YA series."
—*Booklife Reviews*

THE BOOK OF SOULS

SERIES

KEVIN MOORE

ISBN: 978-1-953865-68-7 (Paperback)

Library of Congress Control Number: 2022919117

Any references to historical events, real people, or real places are used fictitiously. Names, characters, and places are products of the author's imagination.

Books Fluent
3014 Dauphine Street
New Orleans, LA

Dedicated to Pat, my wife and Soulmate.

BOOK I

THE BOOK OF SOULS

KEVIN MOORE

PROLOGUE

It's dark. We climb through a broken window to get into the abandoned boarding house. The feeling of being watched rolls over me like a wave. The hairs on the back of my neck stand at attention. Our eyes meet; before I can see a face, the floor crumbles with a loud crash beneath me.

The shock of the impact takes the breath from my lungs. I lie on the floor paralyzed, liquid pooling around my head. Blood. I gasp for air. Darkness. Complete silence except a small voice in the distance. Someone is calling my name. "I'm down here!" Only, there is no voice with which to yell; my body can't move.

This is where you die.

Click, click, click–something is crawling on the floor, the walls, the ceiling. Rats? No, it's something much larger. I look up at the collapsed ceiling above me. A skeletal horse head with a deformed skeleton human body crawls through the hole. This creature is able to cling onto the ceiling above me, which freaks me out. It makes a guttural sound, revealing its nasty teeth. I hear sounds of people talking; whispering fills the room. I can't make the words out initially, only noises, movements. Shadows circle me.

"Give me his thoughts."

"Give me his breath!"

None of their mouths move, but their words are clear. "I want his soul!" barks the creature crawling along the ceiling.

Never have I been more terrified. I've fallen into the bowels of hell! Shadows descend upon me, closing in enough to touch me before a soft voice breaks through the darkness.

"Step away from the boy!"

A light in the form of a woman illuminates the area. An angel? My dead mother? No, she is dressed as a nun. She moves toward me, bringing light with her.

I hear a chorus of voices. "Don't listen to that bitch!" "Witch!" "Poisoner!"

Her light opens a portal to another time and place. Suddenly, we are all in a large kitchen. My body lies still on the floor. Yet, I am also sitting at the dining room table. The most frightening, surreal feeling washes over me, the feeling of watching one's lifeless body on the floor while being completely aware of it. Sitting with me at the table is a very large man, a pregnant woman, and two shadows. One of the shadows has beady yellow eyes, but the other one lacks facial clarity. The woman at the table is extremely docile, her head down, like she is filled with shame. Maybe fear—like me?

The nun is dressed in full habit—a uniform from an earlier time. She stands with her back to us, cooking or brewing something on the stove. The skeletal creature immerses its nails in the ceiling; it is watching, waiting. "Be careful, Jack. She's a witch!"

Really creepy laughter follows. There are shadows all over the room, jumping on and off the walls. Two more demons crawl through the hole in the ceiling. My body is on the floor between the table and the nun. Several of the shadows slide along the floor toward my lifeless body. Clearly, I'm dead. How else can I observe this madness? Surely, this is hell. The nun's head spins one hundred eighty degrees. "Leave that boy be!" The sound of her neck cracking as she speaks gives me the fucking willies. I have never been more alone. Shadows slide away from my body and jump back on the walls.

Two of the demons crawl down the wall onto the ground. Their bony tails swinging back and forth. One of them stands up straight and eyes me; it must be seven or eight feet tall. I avert my eyes. Another one drags its body close to the ground, inching toward me. The creature is aggressive, now very close, smelling me. Its tongue moves in and out like a serpent; it is the only part of its body not made of bones.

I piss myself. It comes out of my body lying across the room, not the me sitting at the table. The creature puts its mouth to my ear, speaking in a foreign language. It smells like burnt flesh. She does not speak but moves at warp speed. Grabbing the creature by its tail, she swings it off the wall. Its bones shatter all around the room.

The nun leans down to me and whispers without moving her lips. "It can only live off fear; if you don't allow it to seize your fear, it will starve." All of our communication is done mind to mind.

She then turns to the two remaining demons. "You don't know if you are a horse or a human? So, I'll treat you like a dog. Lay down!" They do as instructed.

"Where am I?" No answer. "Am I dead?" I ask.

This gets the creatures up, roaring like it's feeding time. The shadows begin to run and jump on and off the walls like they are riding a carousel. Music begins to play a disjointed melody.

"I'll make you some tea," the nun says calmly.

"She's a witch, Jack!" "That's a potion! Don't drink it! She'll poison you!" "You will end up like us!" More creepy laughter.

My body has shown no signs of life since wetting itself. I'm sure that it will never move again. The big fat man stands up at the table, exposing himself. The nun's head spins again with the same cracking, bone-chilling sound. I'm no longer sure of who or what I am more afraid of, only that I am afraid of everything.

I shiver. Ice cold—must be to keep the dead from rotting. Although it doesn't help with the nasty smell. I thought hell was supposed to be hot!

"Sit down and put that away!" the nun demands. "Until we clean you, you will be staying put!" Then in a much softer tone, she says, "Don't you want to go home? Back to your creator?"

The man sits, shrinking exponentially smaller, until he is the size of a doll. "There, there, you must feel better now," she says in her soft voice.

"She's a witch!" the shadows yell. "Stand up and whip it out! Show her your dick!"

The nun ignores them and brings me a cup of tea. "It's very hot; let it sit."

Looking up at her, I ask, "Is this hell?"

A choir of voices screeches at me. "It's hell! You're dead!" "Dead, Jackie boy!" "Horrible boy you are!" Creepy laughter follows.

The two shadows sitting at the table begin pounding on it so hard that it makes the table come off the ground, scaring the pregnant girl. "You belong in hell! Hell, Jack! Don't fight it, boy! It's much warmer there!" they shout at me. The nun grabs hold of the beady-eyed shadow like it is a rag doll, shaking it. She throws it against the wall. The splattered shadow becomes nothing more than a giant ink spot.

The nun bends down to speak to me. "They feed off your thoughts, your memories, your worries. Don't give them anything to eat."

I am so frightened I can't control what I'm feeling, thinking. My thoughts run wild; is it too late to catch myself? My father comes to mind. How will he handle my death? "You're going to hell, Jack, for what you did to your father!" yells the other shadow at the table.

"Splat!" The nun fires him off the wall. Another chorus of "Witch! Witch!" begins. "Drink your tea. It will calm you till they get here." Her voice is hypnotic.

I am so confused. Who's coming? Angels? More demons? Creatures? Is this purgatory? Am I going to hell?

Erase the thought, Jack. Don't think!

A stampede of people run through the abandoned boarding house. "Where is he?" Flashlights. "Don't go upstairs; the floor's not safe." "I found him; he's in here!"

Firemen and paramedics come into the kitchen, but they are in the deserted part of the room where my body has landed. The living stand in that empty room in a condemned boarding house. The dead, however, are still in the old kitchen, where a battle is raging. The nun stands by me at the table. "Witch!" Shadows jump off the wall in a threatening fashion. "She's a no-good fucking witch!" they yell.

"Go back to your body, Jack," she says firmly. She does not move her lips, but the command clearly comes from her.

"Isn't the body dead?" I ask.

"It is somewhere in the in-between. Now, go back to your body." She speaks with a sense of urgency.

I get up from the table. "Am I going to die?"

4

"That's between you and God. Go."

Standing like a baby fawn, I wobble—can't trust my legs. "Can you come?" I beg her. My trust is completely in her now.

"No, I need more time with these three." Looking around the table, I see the woman has given birth to her baby, which appears to be stillborn. The man remains as small as a doll sitting in the chair. Shadows have circled my motionless body. "We will never let him go!" they yell. "Never!"

I walk forward, dizzy as a drunkard, afraid to let go of the table. I call out to the nun as I stumble. "They'll get me!"

"Yea, though I walk through the valley of the shadow of death, I will fear no evil! For Thou art with me," the nun intones. "Go, Jack. Call on the Holy Spirit to light your way. They will move."

Shadows continue jumping on and off the wall to their carousel of dizzying music. "Don't let them touch you, attach to you," the nun adds.

I move back to the chair filled with fear. What does that mean? Attach to me?

"Pray it with me, Jack," she says firmly. "Yea, though I walk through the valley of the shadow of death, I will fear no evil for Thou art with me."

I grab hold of the table and get up, using it as a crutch, taking baby steps toward my body. This is my mountain—my Everest. If I don't get back into my body, I fear I will be lost. "The Lord is my shepherd I shall not want..." Closer. "Though I walk through the valley of the shadow of Death I will fear no evil."

My body is in complete darkness as I repeat the lines from Psalm 23 over and over. It becomes my mantra. Finally, a soft light leads me. It is coming from inside me...my light...God's light.

Shadows step back into the darkness, away from my body. The nun disappears into the astral plane. Sounds of sirens float somewhere in or above my head.

I can't stay awake. I close my eyes.

THE BOOK OF SOULS

It is a typical morning in the Kelly house. Katherine is up first and has all the kids' lunches ready. I make coffee and finish scrambling eggs. We are both dressed and ready for another action-packed day. We love it and feel blessed—but of course we complain like every other married couple in America with children and full-time jobs. All we want is another hour of sleep, or to finish reading the books on our nightstands.

Stevie, my oldest, comes bouncing into the kitchen dressed for school, fresh from a shower. Now twelve, he has decided he is too old to shower at night. He wants to look good for a girl at school, I think, but when I say that he rolls his eyes and says, "Dad—really?" He spent the summer in soccer camp determined to "rule" the soccer season. Katherine and I have to peel off his uniform at night. "Mom, you remember I have practice today at 4, right?"

Katherine points to the white board on the kitchen wall with the schedule for September 19. Today. Topping the list in Stevie's handwriting is "Steve— Soccer practice—4 p.m."

Katherine is the most organized person I know. After dinner she gets out her smart phone where she keeps her schedule, and has each of our three children write down everything they need. Cookies for bake sale, soccer practice, piano lessons…

Mike, my youngest, comes into the kitchen looking for his backpack—not a surprise. I point to the coat rack where it is hanging. "No, I switched that one out with the new one grandma gave me." I shake my head and put some eggs on a plate for him. "Where did you leave it last?" This helps no one. Katherine, Stevie, and Mike all speak at the same time: "If I knew where I had it last, I wouldn't be looking for it."

Lilly comes bouncing into the kitchen, her ponytail swinging behind her. "Dad, the bird's back. He's tapping on the window again."

A couple of weeks ago, the same bird started tapping at the top of our living room window. The windows are long and wide, designed to bring the outside landscape inside the house. It looks like a robin, but I'm no bird expert. Every night at dinner—tap, tap, tap. Really annoying.

I shoo it away, but it keeps coming back, on a mission, like a carrier pigeon with a message from a long-lost friend.

"Mom, can I have the keys to the car?" Mike asks. "Maybe my backpack is there."

Mike goes out to the car, leaving the front door open. Our tapping bird flies into the living room like a kamikaze pilot. "Dad! The bird is in the house!" Lilly yells.

"Mike!" Stevie yells. Just like that, our typical morning is no more.

Chaos ensues with the bird flying all around the living room. It quickly becomes a circus. Mike comes back in with his backpack, closing the door. "No! Open the door!" we all yell.

We scatter about, opening doors, taking the screens off the windows. Katherine has a broom but won't actually whack or threaten the bird with it. Stevie's idea is to play music very loud so he blasts music like the bird is a prisoner of war and we're trying to get him to crack. His music is so loud it reminds me of the the "Ride of the Valkyries." The bird keeps dive-bombing us to the blaring music. It seems to have an intention.

"Turn the air conditioner on—no the heat!" I yell, hoping the heat from the vents will make the bird fly lower and realize it has multiple escape routes.

The boys are yelling "Get him!" to which Lilly replies, "How do you know it's a him?"

"We don't care what sex he is—we just want him out of the house," Stevie replies.

8

Lilly decides she is going to Google how to tell the sex of a bird. Katherine concludes the music may be disorienting him or her, which may be why the bird can't find the open door or window.

Our next-door neighbor is standing in the living room, which we don't realize until we shut the music off. She startles us all. Apparently, she has been trying to get our attention over the music.

"What's wrong? What's happening!" she yells. Then she sees the bird flying around the room, shakes her head in horror, and steps back toward the open front door, like she may run.

I take the broom from Katherine and try to get the bird out of an open window without hurting him. He's not having any of it and flies directly at me in attack mode. Our neighbor begins to recite, "Birds crashing into windows, houses, or cars are supposed to bring news of death. They are omens." Without taking a breath she adds, "Birds looking in the windows or tapping at windows can also mean someone from the other side is trying to contact you."

"Maybe it's Grandpa," Mike says.

Everyone stops, including me. "What?"

Our neighbor and Mike start to talk at once, but Katherine stops them. "It can also mean that the bird has simply wandered in. Let's drop this silliness and get the bird out of my house."

Our neighbor heads out the front door. "Good luck," she shouts ominously.

"Hey, she didn't tell us what it means if the bird is in the house," Stevie says.

Finally, I catch the back of the bird with the broom, sending him or her out the rear door. It lands in a tree and eyes the house, as if to say, "I'm not done with you guys." We put the screens back on, close all the doors, and laugh.

The bird doesn't leave. It comes back to the living room window and begins tapping. "You need to squirt him with the hose, Dad," Lilly says. "A bird in the house can also mean death, according to this website."

We are running late, so I hold the front door open as everyone files out. Katherine gives me a kiss. "Don't forget to pick up the Midrin; the pharmacy called again."

Yes, I keep forgetting because it's been a while since I had a migraine headache. I'd like to believe these killer migraines of mine are not coming back, but it may be false hope. As the kids get in the car with Katherine, she turns to look at me. "You still want to have the Midrin just in case you get one. You know how nasty they can be." The woman reads my mind.

"I'll get it."

We go off to our separate lives, where we are known and judged individually, not as the Kelly clan. At the end of the day, we will take turns talking about our days at dinner. Katherine always starts the dinner conversation by going around the table: "Tell me about the best part of your day." We always start with the youngest, Mike. Then she'll ask, "Does anyone have a problem they would like the family to help with?" Communication. We want them to be able to rely on one another.

Katherine is an only child. I had a brother, Brick, who suffered a very bad accident that almost killed him as a kid. He survived but died a young man in the first Iraq War. My dad, God bless his soul, always said it was God's will. Whoever's will it was, it left me brother-less and basically an only child.

My morning at work is uneventful, but the afternoon takes a turn for the worse, as if this morning's conversation was foreshadowing. The afternoon begins with the start of a wicked migraine. No amount of Tylenol will help. Damn it, I should have picked up the Midrin. This one comes with such a vengeance that it immobilizes me. I ask my secretary not to disturb me, close my office door, and pull down the shades. I fall into a deep sleep, trading this headache for an afternoon dream.

Music plays, but I can't make out the tune. I dream about my father—how happy we all were when he moved to California. We are walking on the beach, and then somehow, we become separated by the water, he on one side, the rest of us across from him on a different beach. The water grows wider and wider between us. He continues to call my name, but I can't get to him. I begin to panic. Opening my mouth to yell, nothing comes out. He's gone…

I sit around a table with ten people in my conference room. At first, I am not sure if it is a dream or if it is real. I am leading a client meeting, which I typically do. A bird slams into the window, embedding itself into the glass, startling all of us. More birds begin slamming into the window, creating a panic. My clients stand up, looking at me, wanting me to do something.

Again, I try to speak, but the sound of the birds hitting the glass drowns me out. People begin to rush out of the room, leaving their folders and briefcases behind. I try to stop them but I am too tired. So, I continue to sleep—to dream.

My brother Brick and I are laughing and running down 2nd Avenue in New York like we always did as kids. Brick has not been in my thoughts in such a long time. Someone calls our names. I turn to see who is calling us, but no one is there. When I turn back, Brick is gone and I'm left standing alone on 2nd Avenue—no people, no cars.

An explosion of ringing phones makes me stir, but I incorporate them into my dream. They won't stop: The office line rings, and my cell phone keeps going off in an urgent fashion. I wake up. I'm still in my office, my feet up on the desk. I look around, clear my head, and pick up my cell phone, which has blown up with multiple missed calls and texts. Text after text tells me to come home. They're all from Katherine.

My heart races. I call home. "Where are you?" she asks, highly agitated. "You need to come home!"

"What's wrong?" My voice, like me, is groggy.

"Stevie came home from soccer practice not feeling well; he has a temperature."

"Maybe he caught something at school," I ramble—something I do when I can't concentrate.

"Come home. He's never sick; you know that." She speaks in a worried tone I have not heard since my father's heart attack.

I look at my watch and think the time must be off; it reads 7 p.m. "Is it really 7 o'clock?"

She pauses. "Jack, are you okay?"

"I'm fine, I'm fine. I just lost track of time." Katherine doesn't need to know I've been asleep in my office for the past five hours with a migraine.

Here's the thing: you never know how happy you are in your mundane everyday life until it changes for the worse. By the time I get home, Stevie's fever rages at 103. He is vomiting. It worsens. A convulsion? Maybe a seizure?

Before the night is over, we rush him to the hospital. The hospital is worse than the DMV. We wait.

The doctor is keeping him for observation. Observation? He's sick, damn it. Do something! We wait for a room, but soon the whole situation goes upside down. They're sending him to ICU immediately. He's twitching, convulsing, they think he may be bleeding internally. Intensive care requires constant; close monitoring and support from special equipment and medications in order to ensure normal bodily functions.

Critically ill? How can a normal boy who when I left this morning was healthy as … as what? He was the picture of health. The doctor in ICU asks us the same questions as the doctors in the ER. "Did he fall? Did he get hit with something in the head? Have you been out of the country? Were you camping recently? Did you notice any kind of bug bites?"

No. No. No. No.

Sitting in ICU amidst the sound of machines breathing for your child is as scary, as haunting a sound as you will ever hear. Everyone and everything has a smell. Including me. Katherine and I touch his feet because that is the only part we can touch. ICU doctors and nurses are swarming him. They move in and out of our room in a constant procession, running tests and taking blood. All his numbers are crazy bad—off-the-charts bad. He is under attack. A bacterium? Maybe a virus? No one seems to know.

They start talking about quarantine and decide he needs to be isolated. "Quarantine?" I ask. Katherine holds on to me tightly.

"It's just a precaution," the doctor says. "Until we figure out what's wrong here."

At first, they tell us we can't go in his room. I get crazy. "Give me gloves, give me a mask. I'll sign a disclosure but let me in with my kid! This is bullshit! You don't even know what's wrong with him."

- - -

October begins the way September ended, with Stevie deathly ill. He's off the respirator, which is great, but his skin color is gray, and he doesn't recognize us most of the time. His eyes roll back in his head, and his body is limp. Turns out Stevie may have contracted some kind of bacteria that attacked his brain, and he is now fighting for his life. Katherine and I are the only ones allowed to see him. We play music, read to him, speak to him, plead with him to fight. "Stevie, don't give up, baby; we're here waiting for you!"

It began here. All those things you think don't really exist. Ghosts, spirits, demons—they come calling.

After Katherine drives home to be with Lilly and Mike, I take the night shift, sitting next to the bed, holding Stevie's limp hand. His grip tightens intensely as his eyes open. "Dad, don't leave me. Don't let go of me."

It is the first time in weeks he's spoken. His voice is weak, but clear. His eyes look straight at me.

"I'm here," I whisper. "I'm not going anywhere."

He blinks. I turn to bring the chair closer, but his grip won't let me move. "Good," he says, "because they keep trying to take me out of here."

"It's probably just for tests," I say, brushing his hair back.

Stevie looks up at me, frightened, and shakes his head. He can't keep his eyes open. "Don't worry; I'm not going anywhere," I add.

We hold hands all night. Once in a while, he tightens his grip, and I gently squeeze back. I think of my father. Brick had fallen through the ceiling in an abandoned building when he was a kid in New York City. The fall almost killed him. My dad wouldn't leave his side. We had no mother; she died of cancer when we were four and six. Dad never really spoke about it until I was an adult. So, it was my dad alone with Brick in the hospital. I've built up five weeks of vacation at work and another three weeks in personal/sick time. I take it all.

When Brick started to improve, Dad would come home, sit with a cup of tea or a Scotch, and just stare. "Jack," he said, "you need to pray. He may never walk again."

Brick did walk again because Dad would not let him give up. Now, I have to make sure Stevie doesn't give up.

- - -

Tonight is the first time they come to visit. My head snaps forward, startling me awake. The room is dimly lit. Something is not right. It takes me a bit to focus but I see shadows moving slowly along the wall, moving quietly around the room. Hairs on the back of my neck stand at attention. No one but Stevie and I are in the room. He tightens his grip. I'm not sure what I'm seeing. I stand up, and the shadows begin to pulsate. There is some kind of force in the room. They start to make sounds like cicadas, like the humming of a high-tension power line. Matching the electrical feedback, the room starts to spin like a carousel, faster and faster. Suddenly, the shadows begin to jump off the walls in three-dimensional form. Not people—shadows.

Stevie's eyes pop open. Fear washes over his face. "Don't worry," I whisper. "You're not going anywhere." Dear God, what is this? Keep them away from him!

One or two jump back onto the wall, but one stands close to the bed. He has no eyes—well, not human eyes. No face or body features, either, just a dense shadow that changes form in front of me. I'm too frightened to speak, to breathe. How can I protect my boy from this?

The lights come on, chasing them from sight, but they leave a chill in the air. The temperature in the room is much colder. Looking around, I can sense they are still here, hiding.

"Are you all right?" the nurse asks.

Sweat forms on my lip while I shiver from the chill in the room. "Yes. He opened his eyes, spoke to me; that's good, right?" I speak with a cotton mouth.

She looks at me strangely, rubbing her arms. "Why is it so cold in here?" she asks.

Still scared, I shrug. The nurse walks over to the controls and turns the air down. "It must be broken; I'll have maintenance take a look."

You know the saying "time stood still?" Well, it doesn't; it actually moves faster. It flies by without Stevie showing any real improvement. The doctors are now pretty sure it is bacteria in his system. They tell us it may cause him to hallucinate, which is why he keeps thinking someone is after him, trying to take him. What is my problem? Am I hallucinating? I felt and saw the same thing but I told no one. Not even Katherine.

The shadows come back the next two nights. I start leaving the lights on, which the nurse opposes. "He needs to rest," she says. That's all he does, I think. I resort to watching a movie on my iPad and sipping tea.

Suddenly, everything in the room goes dark, including the iPad. Music starts to blare, but it isn't just one song; it's like someone keeps turning the radio dial, so you hear one or two notes. Lights in the room flick on and off.

The warped figures of shadows slide down the wall and across the floor —big ones, small ones, distorted ones. Heat permeates from the walls and floor. I grab the iPad to take a picture of what I am seeing in order to show Katherine, but the screen pulsates; it's so hot it burns my hands, and I drop the iPad to the floor. Stevie shoots up in bed, startling the crap out of me. I knock everything off his bed tray onto the floor. One of the shadows jumps off the wall and moves toward me, growing larger and bolder, forcing me to back up.

Stevie grabs hold of my arm. I climb onto his bed and try to protect him with my body. "Don't let them take me, Dad," he whispers as the sounds in the room get louder and louder.

The room goes quiet. As quickly as they arrived, the shadows disappeared, leaving me exhausted but unable to sleep.

- - -

Stevie shows some improvement over the next two days. He is confused a lot but is awake much more often and for longer periods of time. He takes drinks of water, although he rarely speaks. He is still very weak. Katherine and I barely see each other; she handles the day shift, then goes home to Lilly and Mike at night.

Katherine is standing at the nurse's station. Behind her, a nurse comes out of Stevie's room, dressed differently from the other nurses. I run my hand across Katherine's back to let her know I'm here, then head down the hall to his room. Stevie is moaning and squirming. Holding his little body, I say, "Dad's here. Are you in pain?"

He doesn't answer me.

"What was the nurse doing?" I ask Katherine, as she walks wearily into the room a minute later.

"Oh, as you know they keep ruling things out; he's plateauing. They want to send him home."

"Home?" I ask. She sits in the chair with the weight of a very heavy woman, which she is not. "He just needs to get a little stronger." Katherine adds.

Stevie opens his eyes like he did that first night, with fear shining from them. Katherine sees it. He mouths the words more than he speaks them. "They were back."

Katherine looks at me. "Who was back?"

I shake my head. "No, Stevie, that was a nurse who was just in here."

"What nurse?" Katherine asks.

"No," Stevie says, gripping my hand like he is hanging from a cliff.

"A nurse came out of his room when I was walking down the hall," I say nonchalantly.

They both speak at the same time, although Katherine is louder and more forceful. "There was no nurse in this room," she says.

Stevie just says, "Nooooo."

Katherine looks at me. "The nurses on duty were all doing their end-of-shift paperwork. I was standing right there."

I hold Stevie's hand; I don't want to frighten him. I take a long breath. "Well, I saw a woman dressed as a nurse come out of this room, just moments before I walked in," I tell her. "Actually, she wasn't dressed quite like the other nurses, but it was a nurse's uniform."

Katherine stares at Stevie, and the look on her face makes me turn back to him. His eyes are wide, and he is shaking his head. Katherine gets up and leaves the room, and I turn my focus back to Stevie. Moments later, she returns with Stevie's nurse. She is not the same woman I saw. No one—not her, not any of the other nurses on the station—have been in his room during the last twenty minutes. No candy stripers or any volunteers are on this floor.

Katherine gets her things to go.

- - -

Stevie rests through a quiet evening. The nurse comes in to take his vitals and blood for more testing. Every night is the same; they come in, poke him for blood, and tell us the same thing. Nothing. While he is resting, I take a walk. Then I see her. That nurse again, walking toward Stevie's room. She stops. Turns into another room when she sees me coming. Glancing into Stevie's room, I see our nurse is finishing up her charting.

I decided to look in the room where the other nurse entered. She is not

16

in there.

Settling into Stevie's room, I play music he likes, read him some positive quotes. No shadow people. No mysterious crosses or nurses. Just us two. I've brought rosary beads and holy water and I place them on the little night table, returning to the spiritual comforts of my youth to help me fight, help me stay strong.

All hell breaks loose in the hall—a full-on code blue in the room next door. Sounds of hospital staff running in and out get me up, and I walk slowly toward the door.

Stevie's voice stops me. "They're coming."

Behind him on the wall is a shadow. Pulsating. Bigger and bigger Running back to his bed, I turn the lamp to face the wall, hoping to prevent the shadow from forming. It continues to pulsate. Then the wall becomes a merry-go-round of shadows. A low murmur or humming begins, almost like a Gregorian chant.

"You can't have my son!" I yell, grabbing the rosary. It explodes in my hands, the beads shooting across the wall and bouncing along the floor. I drape myself over Stevie as if I can prevent the spirit world from intruding on this one, and I begin to pray.

They come with force and power. One, then two, then ten are jumping on and off the wall. Faceless. Making gurgling sounds. Pulling his sheets down and grabbing at his arms, his legs. Stevie is frightened but too weak to fight them off.

"Look at me, Stevie. Look at me! They can't hurt you!" The sound of my voice is drowned by the screams and wall banging next door. "What do you want?" I yell. "What? What do you want?"

"Him!" they say in chorus. "Him!"

I stand up. "You can't have him!" They circle me, but it is not me they want.

A lot of noise follows in the hall outside our door. I reach for the holy water and throw it at the shadows on the wall. It runs down the wall, staining it with blood.

Silence follows. The kind of quiet you can hear. The screams that previously filled the air have left their echoes behind.

I turn on all the lights in the room and look around at the walls. No blood. Stevie sleeps with deep breaths, a slight whistle in his exhale. As I keep vigil next to his bed, I watch a man and woman walk past our door in obvious grief. Our nurse comes in later and tells me that the teenage boy next door had died. That was the source of the commotion. All the noise and screams came from him coding, but they couldn't save him. All I want—need—is sleep, but I don't get any.

As anxious as I am to see Stevie and have some time with Katherine before we exchange shifts, I've begun to dread and fear the night in his room. It terrifies me. Still, I have not been able to tell Katherine about the nightly assaults that Stevie and I have endured. Nor how exhausted we are.

It's raining, a rarity in southern California in October. The kind of rain that tap dances along the sidewalk. There's lightning, thunder.

Lulu is the night nurse. She is new to us, nice, but ditzy. She tells me about her boyfriends, how tired she is because she's always working. Three days at this hospital, three days at another, she says. She has two boyfriends to keep happy. Looking at her, I smile. She must be sixty—good for her. Lulu has no problem telling me how much both men are in love with her. Her stories are a nice diversion. I follow her to the door, trying to prolong her stay.

Tonight is unusually quiet except for the sounds of the storm. The halls in the hospital are empty. Lulu does not return; I wonder if she found a spare bed to take a nap. Which is what I involuntarily do while reading my book. When I wake up, the room is freezing. Frost has covered the windows; I can actually see my breath. There are not enough covers on Stevie's bed to keep him warm. The temperature says 70, but that is not possible. I ring for Lulu, or anyone really.

Lulu appears after a good ten minutes, looking very tired. She immediately tries to warm herself upon entering the room. "What did you do?" she asks, heading to the thermostat.

"Nothing."

"That can't be right."

"Look at the window."

We both walk to the window. There literally is frost on it; it has to be thirty degrees in the room. Now very much awake, Lulu leaves and returns with her supervisor and several blankets. She checks on Stevie, picks up the phone, and calls maintenance. The room becomes a circus of a different kind.

Maintenance people come in and out, trying to figure out what's wrong. They all say and do the same thing: "Geez, it's freezing in here. It must be broken."

You think?

I'm thankful for the diversion. It is freezing, but there will be no haunting tonight. People walk in and out, more blankets, more supervisors—and then an executive decision.

"We need to move you to another room," Lulu says. The cold room enlivens her.

The new room is smaller, but warmer. Stevie and I settle in. If I could just sleep. Lulu comes into the new room to make sure we are comfortable. She walks over to me. "This is a better room. That room has a ghost." Her tone is very conspiratorial.

"Ghost?" I'm almost happy for her acknowledgment, maybe that is what we are seeing, but if it is, we are seeing more than one. "As in haunted?" I ask.

Lulu looks at me. On a different day, before Stevie got sick, I would have thought her batshit crazy, but not after what we've seen.

"Yes, a ghost. And not a friendly one," she adds.

I'm finally able to breathe. I think we're going to be fine. A weight comes off me. "Do you think I can get a cup of tea?"

"Sure," she says, and leaves the room. Within minutes the sounds start: electric humming, the cicada bug sound. When she returns the room has gotten noticeably colder. Not nearly as bad as our previous room, but colder than it was when we moved in. The sound stops—waiting for her to leave?

- - -

Stevie has plateaued. That's hospital and insurance talk for "he isn't improving, and we don't want to spend any more money trying."

It's been six weeks in the hospital, and we're finally going home! Trust me when I say we are happy, but he is not out of the woods. There is nothing left for them to do. They are not exactly sure what happened; they blame some kind of bacteria. We are in the Middle Ages, but it is not the Black Plague, because Stevie is the only one who contracted it. It is random.

Stevie is still weak. He needs his mom and me to nurse him back to health. A real nurse will come by several times a week as well. They'll send a physical and occupational therapist. There might be some brain damage, which might cause problems with his motor skills. Time will tell. Still, they have no name for the bacteria that almost took his life and left him like a rag doll.

I just want to be in our house with my wife and children.

Katherine sets up Stevie's bedroom with an additional cot and a lounge chair, so one of us, including Lilly and Mike, can spend long periods of time with him. Our first night home, a few very close friends and Katherine's mom come to visit. They bring food. We even open a bottle of wine. Okay, two bottles.

Sitting in the living room, I try hard to follow the conversations, longing for the ordinary things in my life to return. Ordinary things that appear really extraordinary to me at this moment. I want them back. Like Katherine and I getting dinner on the table. Stevie dressed in his soccer uniform. Lilly in a ponytail making us laugh. Mike, always the last one at the table. Always needing to do one more thing before he sits down.

"Is that someone at the door?" I don't know who asked, but it brings me back to the now.

"What?" I ask.

"More wine?" Katherine offers.

I shake my head and get up to see who is at the door. We have a small porch between the wood door and screen door, like an old-fashioned mud room. Turning on the light, I see the screen door tapping against the door frame.

As I lock the screen door, a movement outside catches my eye. I walk off the porch to get a look. Nothing. No one. Several papers lay in the driveway; I pick them up and throw them in the trash can. That is when I see the shadow of a woman. Her outline reminds me of Mary Poppins. It looks like she is standing on the side of my house. Anger overtakes my fear, and believe me, I am afraid.

"I see you!" After yelling, I walk to the side of the house where she was standing.

No one is there. The shadow is gone.

"Oh my God! Stevie!" I run back into the house, making a commotion that gets everyone's attention, but I don't care. They followed us home. I swing open the bedroom door to find Mike and Lilly on the cot talking to Stevie.

"Billy keeps asking me when you are coming back to school. Hi, Daddy," Lilly says. "We're just telling Stevie how much his friends miss him."

Katherine comes in with a look on her face that says, Jack, what's going on? "Everyone okay?"

"Yes," Mike says. "We're just encouraging him—like you told us to."

Katherine turns to me. "Let's say goodbye to our guests. It's been a long day."

I don't move. Katherine touches my back, the way only she can. It speaks volumes. You are not alone. I'm here; the kids are here. It will get better.

Everyone leaves except Katherine's mom. They talk quietly in the living room. The lights are soft. While putting glasses in the sink, the sound of the screen door swinging open gets my attention. I'm glad I never greased that door. It shuts as if someone is trying to muffle the sound. I wait. Katherine looks over at me. She hears it too. Our front door opens very slowly. A woman's footsteps echo through the door. Reaching quietly for the flashlight under the sink, I watch as this female—shadow? spirit? ghost?—slides through the front door. It becomes clear to me that we are in some kind of spiritual warfare. Is it over death? Was Stevie supposed to die? I will fight and steal him from the clutches of death because I cannot let that happen.

The shadow is in the kitchen. I turn the flashlight at its center. It divides into two and seems to retreat; the divided shadows climb onto the wall in my living room.

"Stay there!" I command, as I back slowly down the hall, holding the flashlight like a gun.

My mother in-law wears a look of complete horror. Finally, someone other than Stevie and I see them. Katherine begins to walk toward me, but I keep backing up until I make it to his room. Stevie is alone and awake. "They're here, aren't they, Dad?"

I nod.

"They followed us."

Katherine looks at Stevie, and then me. "Who? Who followed us?" she asks anxiously. Neither of us answers. "Jack," she says sternly, "What is happening? You ran everyone out of here." She looks at Stevie and lowers her voice. "What is this?"

"Come with me," I finally say.

Using the flashlight, I outline the divided shadow on the living room wall. "You see them?" I ask. Katherine moves around the room to view the wall from different angles. "You see them, right?"

"Yes, but you know how people see Jesus or Buddha on the wall of a building—or piece of cheese? You said in the past that you think they want to see it, or need to see it. Is that what you're doing here?"

"No." Stevie says. He holds onto the side of the wall weakly. "They want something from us, Mom."

Katherine rushes to him. "Don't worry, Mom and Dad will take care of this. Let's get you back to bed."

She puts her arm around him and starts walking him back to his room. I look at the wall. It is clear to me that I see two shadows looking like the opposite sides of the same coin. We tell Katherine everything that has happened—all the shadows in the hospital, the freezing room, the noise. "I'll take the first shift," I say.

Stevie falls asleep. I read everything I can on spirits, sightings, people who have come close to death, or in some cases have been dead for seconds—or minutes. At some point I fall into a deep sleep until that low humming and hissing sound disturbs me. Someone—something—is in the room with us. When I open my eyes, shadows are jumping on and off the walls.

Stevie sits up, frightened. One of the shadows towers over him. I jump out of the chair, leap onto his bed, and wrap him in my arms. I yell but don't recognize the sound of my own voice. Katherine rushes in first, followed by Lilly, then Mike. Looking into the shadow's face, I see tiny, yellow laser-like objects that I think are eyes.

"What do you want? What?" I yell.

"Him," it whispers as its eyes brighten. "Him!"

It screeches, leaps at us, and grabs hold of Stevie's arm.

"No, you can't have him! You can't have him!"

All of us are in bed, wrapping ourselves together.

"It's you they want, Dad," Stevie says. He is the Stevie of old, healthy. "What?"

"You have to decide. It's not fair to grandpa and it's not fair to us."

The shadows hold their positions on and off the wall. I'm less afraid at the thought of them wanting me than wanting Stevie. I stand up and move away from the bed; the shadows move with me. My confusion of why they want me is fueled only by how healthy Stevie looks.

"Why is it unfair to grandpa? He's dead," I say.

My family looks at me with so much love that the reason doesn't matter. As I move farther from the bed, my mind begins to race. Did I have a stroke or an aneurysm in Stevie's room that night? Was that the code blue?

I look at Mike, who is sitting at the edge of the bed. Mike loved to be chased around the house before his bath, naked, when he was a toddler. I want to pick him up and toss him in the air like I did when he was a baby, just to hear him squeal with delight.

"Mike…"

He smiles at me and disappears. It feels like I've been punched in the solar plexus.

"Dad," Lilly says.

I gaze at her. "Lilly?" Lilly who always makes me laugh. Lilly in her ponytail saying, "Dad, let me paint your nails. I'll paint them clear."

My mind is jumping all around, remembering the day Katherine and I brought her home from the hospital after she was born.

"Lil!"

She too is gone.

Tears fall. I must be dying. Maybe it was the headache in my office the day Stevie got sick. It was so bad; I had never slept at my desk that long. Looking at Stevie now, I see him as he always was—in a uniform. If not soccer, then baseball. He looks at me with a half-smile. "It's all right, Dad."

I cry because I know it isn't.

Katherine tries to stop Stevie from leaving, but it's too late. He is gone. It is only Katherine smiling back at me now. I have no words. Is this how the process of dying works—our most beautiful important moments flickering in our hearts and minds like old movies? My beautiful Katherine, who could fix anything and make any place feel like home just as long as she was there. Oh, God. I'm still a young man; we have so much life to live. I struggle and fight to stay with her.

Something profound and overpowering pulls at me. Stop fighting; let go. Did the shadows take me from the room? Take my soul? I begin to feel in images. Falling. Sliding backward, a salmon swimming upstream, turning around. The hell with the struggle. Just let go. It feels good. I'm dead. This must be what it's like to cross over. Water is all around me. Back in the amniotic fluid of my mother's womb. Now I'm in a stream. A pool. No, an ocean. Vacation. Katherine, the kids, and I in Costa Rica, snorkeling. Fun. Underwater, looking, swimming to the surface, light—sunlight. There is no pain, no fear.

Now I need to breathe. I swim faster and faster toward the sunlight. Air… I need air! Breaking the surface, the sunlight hurts my eyes. I need to adjust to the blinding brightness.

Someone is holding my hand. Is it my father? Holding my hand so tight, secure. "Dad? Daddy? Am I dead?"

"No. God, no, but you had me scared there for a while, Jack."

"I'm not dead?" He shakes his head. A nurse comes over—the nurse from Stevie's hospital room. The one that only I saw?

"Where's Katherine? The kids?" I ask.

"Who?" my father asks.

"My family. Katherine—Your grandkids—Stevie, Lilly, Mike?"

The nurse and my father exchange glances. Yes, I'm sure she is the nurse from Stevie's room. I realize I am in a hospital room. There are crosses and rosaries everywhere.

"Dad?" I can't get my head straight; I'm so confused. He looks so young. "Dad?"

"You had an accident, Jack; you fell through the floor of that abandoned building."

What? What did he just say?

"No. No." I struggle with my speech. "That was Brick…that was my brother, Brick. That was a long time ago when we were kids."

Again, the nurse and my dad look at each other.

"Jack, you don't have a brother; you don't have any siblings." He speaks very carefully. "It's just you and me. Brick is your friend. He's the one who ran for help. You fell, Jack."

The nurse leaves the room to fetch a doctor. I begin to cry.

24

"I have a wife and kids. Katherine, Stevie, Lilly—don't you remember your own grandchildren?"

My father starts to cry. "Jaaack. Baby, you're thirteen years old. You had a terrible fall. We've got to get you better. Someday you will have a wife and kids."

Dad is talking to me, but I don't hear him. It is Katherine's voice I hear, along with Mikey's squeal. I close my eyes and feel the tears slide down my cheeks. For the first time, I feel the intense pain in my head, back, and legs. Fuck, what a wicked headache!

The nurse returns with Dr. Klein. He is serious but happy to see me alert and awake. They whisper their worries that I may never walk again. The doctor then goes into action, pulls my covers down, and begins to examine me. He touches my toes, my legs. "Can you feel this?"

"Yes."

"How about this?"

"Yes."

They are ecstatic; the nurse actually claps. My father puts his head in his hands. Is he crying? Everyone is so pleased.

"Why is everyone so happy I can feel you poke me?" I ask.

"When you were unconscious, you didn't respond to any of my touches, all the times I pricked your legs," Dr. Klein says.

I just want to go home. To California, my wife, my kids.

Dad sits down like the weight of the world has been lifted off his back.

"Pain?" Dr. Klein asks me.

"Everywhere, including my fucking ass."

Dad looks up as Dr. Klein laughs. I don't curse, especially in front of my father, or my kids. Dad would never allow it. He gets mad when I yell Goddamn, but right now I want to curse. I want to scream and rant. Nothing makes sense. Me? Thirteen? Bullshit. I'm forty-seven. None of this is right. None of it!

- - -

It takes me a couple of days to realize it, but Dad appears to be correct—

25

I really don't have a brother. Brick is a friend; he did not get hurt. Apparently, I was the one who fell through the floor of an abandoned boarding house and fractured my skull, my back, and both my legs. They were afraid I would die. Now they are afraid I will never walk again. I cry a lot, with persistent headaches that worsen if I don't take some strong medication. There's nausea. Sometimes, I vomit. One day, I thought my nose was bleeding. It turned out to be drainage. My ears also leak. I'm a real fucking catch! Oh, and I can't stop cursing; it's like I have Tourette's.

They want me up to do physical therapy. I have no interest in trying to use the balance bars, squeezing balls, or strengthening my upper body. My legs won't stand. Lots of work—and pain!

My physical therapist, Theo, is working my ass off. "I'm fucking tired!"

No response.

"Where's my wife? Where is Katherine? Does she know you guys are overworking me?"

Theo looks at me strangely. "Maybe we should stop," he says, coming over to check my vitals. Everything is fine with my numbers. "You messing with me, kid?"

Seeing myself in the mirror is a shock. I'm a kid, not the man I really am. I feel paranoia, anxiety, fear, and doubt. Along with mental and physical pain.

"Can you help me?" I ask. "What did they do with my body?"

He looks at me questioningly. He thinks that I am either fucking with him or insane. Theo doesn't answer. Well trained, I think.

"What did they do with my fucking body? With my family!"

Other patients and staff in the room look at me.

"This is fucking bullshit. Why are they using me as an experiment?" I am in a full meltdown. I cannot stop and will not stop. "What is this place? Why are you fucking doing this to me!"

Theo is drowning in my questions. "This is a hospital." He picks up my folder. "You had a fall."

"That's fucking bullshit. That was my brother, Brick." Theo gets my wheelchair. "Fuck you! Fuck you all! I know what you are doing!" I add.

- - -

The therapist comes to work with me twice a day. My afternoon session doesn't go any better. I become enraged, asking for Katherine. "Get my wife!" This time, the therapist laughs. "Wife? What are you, twelve?"

I become belligerent. "Fuck you! You are a fucking dork. You ugly motherfucker! How did they do this? How? Where are my kids?"

I stop doing therapy. I have completely lost my mind.

- - -

Dad has gone back to work. He visits as soon as he gets off each day. He comes in with a piece of pie as a treat, like I am a kid. This guy is not my dad. How could he be? I was with my dad when he passed away. He was an older man. This guy is a pod. A fucking alien!

"Jack, they tell me you had some difficulty in physical therapy today," he says.

I do not answer him. I'm not going to. He starts organizing things in the room, takes the pie out of the box, places it on my tray. "Jack, these people are trying to help you."

"Where is Katherine?"

He shakes his head. "Not this again."

"Yes, this again. Where is my family?"

"You are thirteen," Dad yells. "You fell through the floor in an abandoned boarding house; which, by the way, I told you to stay out of. And fractured your skull."

"That was Brick!"

My father, this pod, is clearly upset. "No, Jack, I'm afraid not. It was you! And you know how I know that? Because I sat here day after day, night after night, praying you wouldn't die."

His voice breaks. Nurses gather in the room to see what all the commotion is about. "Mind your fucking business!" I yell at them.

Dad turns and glares at me. "Watch your mouth."

I pick up the pie and drop it to the floor like a two-year-old. Even I am not me.

- - -

Dr. Klein and the therapist discourage me from talking about Katherine and my kids, which I do incessantly. They don't know what to do with me. I am making everything difficult and everyone uncomfortable. I'm insane! I fell through the floor, fracturing my skull. Then I was unconscious for almost a month. Now that I am awake, I've gone off the deep end thinking I have a wife and kids. Dr. Klein brings in other doctors; one of those doctors tells my dad that profound confusion is not unusual. They talk like I'm not in the room while holding a medicine ball between my legs.

"I'm not deaf, jerk off!" I yell. "I'm just profoundly confused."

The physical therapist fights a laugh. My dad, this pod—whatever the fuck he is—is mortified. He has been telling stories to the staff about what a good little Catholic boy I am. Now that I am awake, all those stories seem like balls-ass lies. I am contradicting them with my fucking mouth. I'm more like a drunk sailor on a Saturday night.

Before my dad has a chance to reprimand me, Dr. Klein shakes his head in a "let it go" manner. "Mr. Kelly, you will see a lot of agitation, combativeness, and other unusual behavior—like the talk about the wife and kids—but it will go away, or lessen at the very least." They think I'm angry because of all the therapy. It's because I'm so sad.

He wants me to see a psychiatrist. He says it will help clear the cobwebs. I know it's because I won't let go of my family. Some days, I can't get out of bed. Dad and I fight a lot. It is like I was in some horrible car accident and survived, but my wife and kids were killed. I have survivor's guilt.

When I am alone, I cry a lot. Memories of Katherine, my kids. Playing games, teaching them tic-tac-toe. Taking the kids to Disneyland. It just can't be. It makes me ache. I cry so hard I vomit.

A psychiatrist has been brought in to work on my head. Dr. Melvin is a nice man. He sits with me and my dad a couple of days a week. They think the fall has altered my personality, with all my cursing and this "family" I've lost. They are afraid I am in full depression, worried it will affect my recovery. Dr. Melvin asks me how a thirteen-year-old boy can have children.

"Don't be so condescending," I say to him, which my father doesn't like.

He starts giving me shit about it, but Dr. Melvin tells him it's all right. That it's very important for me to express myself. I like that. He listens to me give their birthdays, their hobbies. He occasionally writes things down. We aren't getting anywhere with my head.

Physical therapy is a must; they have convinced me of that. It is very difficult and painful. Swearing is the only way I get through it. I mean, I fucking swear! Sounds ridiculous. But I can't—won't—forget that life.

Finally, I begin making big progress with physical therapy. They have me swimming twice a week in a private gym. Physically I am getting stronger.

Aunt Paula and Uncle Willy visit me in the hospital and bring me candy and a comic book to read. Aunt Paula is the only one who seems interested in my "wife and kids." Dad makes sure she knows it is a taboo subject.

- - -

We go home to our railroad flat, located in a pre-war five-story walk-up. When I say pre-war, I'm talking about World War I. I'm glad we are on the second floor because dad will not carry me, even though he could. One day, I crawl up the stairs crying, just to show him how difficult it is, and he lets me. Our apartment is so much smaller than my home in California. Dad has set the apartment up so I'm always working. He has a long rope, the kind you use to tie a boat to a dock. It goes straight down the apartment from the kitchen radiator to the living room radiator. My father wants me to use the rope to get around the apartment instead of relying on crutches or a walker.

They told us immediately after the incident that I would never walk again, that I would be wheelchair-bound. Dad said 'no' and then made me say 'no.' He has signs all over our apartment: "I will walk on my own." "Anything is possible with God." Now he is giving me dates—goals—as to when I should be able to reach each step. I keep on cursing! Fuck, I went from the nice kid who would barely say dammit to motherfucker this, fuck that. Dad said you can say whatever you want as long as you complete the task. He always sings this stupid song, "High Hopes." I hate it. I'd like to stomp all over that motherfucking ant!

Getting up in the middle of the night to pee is daunting. "Help me! Help me, Dad!" I yell.

29

I don't want to get out of bed, but he won't come. I hang onto the rope, trying not to fall or piss myself, and I keep yelling for help. His idea of helping is to coach me.

"You got this, Jack! Don't give in! Call on the Holy Spirit! Find your power!"

One night I have the rope under my arms swinging back and forth. I began to cry and piss myself at the same time.

"I hate you! I hate you! This is child abuse!" I yell.

He returns with a change of underwear and pajamas. "I'll leave them in the bathroom for you."

I drop to the floor and lay there crying. Feeling as sorry for myself as anyone could ever be. "I should have died when I fell. I wish I would have."

"Yeah, well, God had other plans for you," he says as he goes back to bed.

I lay in my urine-stained clothes all night. In the morning he picks me up off the floor and helps me shower. "Is this what you want—someone to help you shower the rest of your life?" he asks later, as I eat my breakfast. He starts taking down the rope and signs. He carries me downstairs under my protest. That night, I ask him to put the rope and signs back up.

I fight to make it into the bathroom every day like I am slaying a dragon. Nothing will stop me from getting on my feet again.

MY NEXT CHAPTER

My dad and I continue to see the psychiatrist. He asks me if I would like to see him alone. "No. I like my dad being here."

Dr. Melvin wants to try hypnosis. He also wants to bring in a woman who specializes in past life regression. This does not sit well with my father. He tells Dr. Melvin very firmly we are Catholic, and there is but one life on this earth. Dr. Melvin is very respectful. He says it's just a tool to try and help me with my obsession over this supposed family of mine. Dad wants to talk with his parish priest first. What about talking to me first—don't I get a say here?

Father MacDonald, who apparently came to visit me after my fall, is not at all enthusiastic about past life regression or hypnotherapy. "You might be going down a slippery slope here," he says. Finally, my father asks me what I think. "Nothing to lose," I say, curious about the idea of a past life. My father agrees.

We leave for Dr. Melvin's office Saturday morning. My father is silent as we make our way to the subway station. He wants to help me with the stairs but fights the impulse. He is unusually silent. When we get to Dr. Melvin's office, there is a woman there. She has an English accent and is very well dressed. Smells like lavender. Her name is Margaret. Margaret asks me to sit on the floor on pillows, with my back up against the couch. She fusses over me and that makes my dad comfortable. We talk about meditation.

"Do you know what it is?" Margaret asks in a smooth, silky voice.

"Not really," I lie. My dad made me look it up before we came, but to me, they are just words in a book. I see dad looking at me, so I clarify. "I know the definition, but not really the purpose."

Margaret tells me what it is and why she wants to use it today. She and her voice are both very calming. "The purpose of meditation is to train the mind or induce a mode of consciousness, either to realize some benefit, or for the mind to simply acknowledge its content without becoming identified with that content."

I stare at her. She is pretty and my age. Mid-forties, not thirteen. Margaret turns on soothing music. "Concentrate on one thing, one word." she says.

"Like what?"

"Any word."

"Hmmm." I can't think.

"There is no right answer. A word or an image that you like."

Hockey? No, too active. Oxygen? No, water. I'm about to say it aloud to see if it's a good word, but before "water" goes from my brain to my lips, she stops me.

"It's for you; we don't need to know it." I nod. Water. "Imagine you are with your word, if it's an object you are close to it, near it, in it. If it is a person you are with them."

I envision myself in the ocean in Costa Rica with my kids. Katherine is watching us from the shore. I am tossing them around. The water is warm, and I float. Margaret has relaxed me to the point where I'm floating—not physically, but mentally. Feeling as light as a feather. I'm fighting to stay upright and keep tilting to the left. It is a funny sensation. Just me and water, doing laps in a pool, water skiing on Castaic Lake in the foothills north of L.A.

"Okay, Jack, you can come back to this room," I hear her voice say.

Apparently, a good amount of time has passed. It feels like minutes to me, but it's been more like a half-hour. Margaret gets up off the floor and sits on the chair. "How do you feel?" she asks.

"Good. Like I just woke up from a nap."

"Tell me what you felt and saw."

I get uncomfortable, because I know the answer is wrong; it's not what they want to hear. "Hmmm." I'm being careful.

Dr. Melvin smiles at me, and I smile back. "Were you by water?" Margaret asks.

"Yes." She looks at me, wanting more.

"Don't overthink it, Jack."

I look at my dad, who smiles and nods. "Well, I was in the ocean in Costa Rica with my kids." I wait for judgment; there is none. "Doing laps in my pool, mainly water, my family, by water and in water."

No past life for me, apparently. I am a new soul.

My father keeps quiet in the office, but later we stop for a slice of pizza. "Jack, there is only one life on this planet—this one. That's why I want you at your full potential, so you can live it to the best of your ability." He sips his drink. "You want another slice?"

"No."

"Look, I'm not one of those people—I'm not saying past lives are wrong for Hindus or Buddhists. But you and I—well that's not where we live or what we believe."

- - -

We keep meeting with Dr. Melvin. He wants me to believe it was a dream. Katherine and the kids are a dream, well-imagined, but still a dream. No matter how happy I think I am with just my dad, we are incomplete. Not a full family. I've grown up without a mother, which I have felt very sad about at times. I've also grown up without a brother or a sister, and this is a need I have suppressed. When I go to the birthday parties of peers, or someone has a conversation about their moms or siblings, poor little Jack is just empty and alone.

Bullshit!

Dr. Melvin is very careful as he speaks. "The trauma from the fall, the insult to the brain, has released what you have always been feeling: this need—this want—in you to have a full family, like your friends." He pauses a beat before he continues. "So, Jack, you created the perfect family for yourself. A

33

beautiful wife, three wonderful children—all very unique in their habits."

The room is silent. I want to understand. There is something in what he is saying that has an element of truth. Of course, I always wanted a mother. What kid doesn't? I used to ask my father if he could get me one. Also, I always wanted some brothers and sisters; geez, there are kids in my school that come from families of eight or ten.

Growing up, my dad always had these little sayings. "Actions speak louder than words, Jack." "You can lie to me, Jack, but don't lie to yourself. It's detrimental and destructive; you only hurt yourself when you lie to yourself."

I should have welcomed the truth, but actually it pissed me off. What? Dad and I are not a good enough family?

"That's bullshit," I say, looking at Dr. Melvin.

"Okay, Jack." He gets up and opens his closet door. On the inside of the door is a full-length mirror. "Look in the mirror, Jack."

I vacillate. Finally, I get up and walk to the mirror and look. He waves his hand at the image in the mirror. "Is this person—this boy of thirteen—capable of having a forty-five-year-old wife and three kids, one that is almost the age of this boy in the mirror?"

I look at myself for a long time. The reflection is of a kid, so, yes, I am a kid. Only, it doesn't matter to me because if the dream was caused by my fall, I can never be—will never be—as happy as I was in that dream. So now what? Someone explain that to me. Explain how I can be that happy again! All I want to do is scream, but I don't.

"Tell me, Jack?" he says again.

Breathe deep, Jack. "You don't see a forty-seven-year-old man in that mirror, doctor?" I whisper.

"Sorry?" he says, looking puzzled.

Stepping closer to the mirror, I reach out and touch my image. "Please tell me you and I are seeing the same image, Doctor. I'm staring at a forty-seven-year-old man, and he is staring back at me."

My father sits straight up, fear in his eyes. Margaret does not speak or move. Dr. Melvin looks at me and then at the image in the mirror.

"What?" he says, and looks at me like one of us has gone stark-raving mad. "Jack, are you feeling okay?" he asks softly.

"Yes, doctor, I feel fine. It's just…" I stand still, looking at my image in the mirror like I'm staring at a ghost.

After a couple of beats, I bust out laughing. "Of course, I see a boy in the mirror. What the fuck do you think I am? Crazy?"

- - -

On the way back to our apartment, Dad lets me know he is not amused by my antics. That I can handle. It's the apology afterward that makes me feel bad.

While walking up Second Avenue—well, limping up 2nd avenue with my dumb fucking walker—he spills. "You know, Jack, I should have married again. A child needs a mother, but the two options I had were… well, Helen, who I had a lot of fun with, but she drank too much and was not the motherly type. Alice, on the other hand, would have been fine as a mother, but the idea of waking up to her for the next thirty years? Well, I just couldn't do it, Jack."

I laugh. "Don't be ridiculous; it's your life, too. Besides, you can make it up to me by getting tickets for the Yankees this summer." I say it with a smile.

When I get home, I take a small black notebook and write the names Katherine Kelly, Stevie Kelly, Lilly Kelly, Mike Kelly in it. If they are not real in this dream, in this life, they are the souls that kept me alive when I was in the hospital fighting for my life. I refuse to believe those beautiful people could have simply been imagined. They loved me and walked with me. I held them in my arms. Will I ever know such happiness again? Dr. Melvin, my father, and the medical staff sit me down. They want me to stop thinking of them, obsessing on a life that doesn't exist.

"It's not healthy for your long-term recovery," Dr. Melvin says firmly to me.

I know it to be true even though the evidence tells me it's not. But how do I argue with them—without coming across as crazy? I decide to take their advice, but not to believe it…

Yes, I will try to move on—to forget—but I write their names down in my black book through tears. These are the souls that saved me and without them I surely would never have recovered from my fall. Tucking the book under my mattress, it becomes my book of souls. As an afterthought, I take it back out and add my father's name, along with Aunt Paula and Uncle Willy.

These are the souls I need to take care of now. Maybe that's why I came back.

BACK TO SCHOOL

Everyone says it's a miracle that I've recovered so completely and that I am getting on with my life. Excelling, even. My dad makes arrangements with the nuns—the principal, Sister Thaddeus, as well as my eighth-grade teacher-to-be, Sister Elizabeth—to allow me special privileges. When my migraines come, I am allowed to lay my head down at my desk or raise my hand to excuse myself and go into the empty classroom across the hall. Everyone makes a fuss over me, including teachers of years past, office staff, and parents. It is embarrassing, to say the least. All the attention makes me uncomfortable. Also, being back in eighth grade with my old classmates when I am really a married man with children is beyond weird.

One day in school I forget myself and begin talking about Katherine and my kids. I get more than a few strange looks. Can't say that I blame them, but it puts me on guard. Fortunately, Sister Elizabeth has seated me by the window in the middle of the row. From time to time my mind drifts out that window, admiring the apartment building across the street, occasionally looking at Apartment 3C. There is a man who seems to be home during the day, which I find odd, because he's not old. He smokes a lot. Some days he sits in the living room with his easel, painting.

We have a new thing in eighth grade this year: studying or reading time at the end of the day. Typically, I put my head down and spend the majority of that time thinking of Katherine and the kids. It is not permitted by Dr. Melvin to entertain this idea. After all, it's a "brain insult" that created them or so he keeps telling me. Dr. Melvin and Dr. Klein sat my father and I down more than once and told me—us—"Jack, the fall created a false memory. It created trauma to your brain. In order to move your story—your life—forward, you have to give this up."

Sounds nuts, but I know my family and that life to be true, although the evidence tells me it's not.

Today I use the migraines as an excuse to rest my head so I can look again in the apartment. It is a beautiful building with floor-to-ceiling windows, giving it a fishbowl effect. The shades, if they have any, are never down. The building also has a charming little park you need a key to visit. Apartment 3C has become my viewing target. There is something about the apartment and the man who inhabits it that really intrigue me. He appears to float through his day with no real purpose. Still, I feel like something is not right in Apartment 3C.

A cleaning woman comes into the apartment with a basket of laundry. She has no real interaction with the man, which I find queer. He stands at the window smoking a cigarette, seemingly a prisoner of his beautiful apartment. His hair is long, over the ears, but not quite shoulder length; he has a mustache—mid-thirties? I'm guessing, of course. The man looks out the window and appears to be peering into my classroom. It is as if he is watching me watch him. The cleaning woman puts the laundry on the couch and leaves the apartment briefly. The man tosses it onto the floor. Sister Elizabeth stands, distracting me, and I turn my focus to her. I wonder what she looks like without her habit.

The pulse in my head starts, makes me feel like my head is going to explode. Fortunately, it does not turn into a migraine. However, it brings clarity; I can see things I couldn't previously see. A yellow cloud surrounds her. I get the strongest feeling that she has an abnormal breast. Looking at her chest I sense that there are three nipples—no, three breasts.

Geez, Jack, I think, embarrassed, what a perv—she is a nun for God's sake. If I ever told anyone this, I would never live it down. Purgatory for me. But, seriously, I'm sure the breast is abnormal; it is also a trouble to her. I know this; don't ask me how, but I know it.

38

I've stopped seeing Dr. Melvin. Not because he insists that I stop thinking of or speaking of my family. Besides, I would never tell him any of this anyway. It's too weird. However, it dawns on me this also could be related to my fall. What about my keen sense of smell? I can pretty much smell what everybody in my apartment building is cooking for dinner. Never could before. I think I can smell people's apartments, their fears. How weird. I close my eyes and drift off into an afternoon nap.

I awaken with a jolt, realizing the other school kids are gone. There are shadows and spirits sitting on desks, in chairs, in place of my classmates. Their smells range from bad, like farts, to good, like herbs or exotic lotions— amber or musk. Sister Elizabeth is in the front of the room at her desk. She has replaced her habit with a judge's robe, and the classroom is set up like an old-fashioned trial. Several of the shadows—are they spirits? demons?—are serving as jurors.

Sister speaks, and quite frankly it scares the shit out of me. She has a man's voice. "You have been accused of seeing the devil's book of witchcraft. How do you plead?"

I look around the room to see who is on trial. All heads turn to me. Clearly, I am dreaming. They begin to yell out, "Make him pray! Make him pray! Make the witch confess."

Not all the spirits are yelling. Some appear to be praying. They stare me down and circle my desk. Some point at me and continue to yell: "Make him say The Lord's Prayer!" I say it quickly, but mainly to myself. They continue to chant and yell at me, but now I yell back.

"Now you! You say it! You fucking say it! Motherfuckers!" I scream.

Sister stands up from behind the desk, startled. The spirits disappear. She stares at me with a look between incomprehension and fear. "Are you okay, Mr. Kelly?"

She speaks very softly. Now out of my haze, I realize I am sitting cross-legged on my desk. And although dreaming, I have yelled out those words.

"Oh, Sister," I stammer. "I was asleep—dreaming."

She regains her composure. "Do you use those words in your dreams, Mr. Kelly?"

I play dumb. "What words? What did I say?"

"Never mind. Get your school bag; everyone has gone."

As I step out of the school building, I look at Apartment 3C. The man watches me from the window. What does he want? I cross the street and check the name on the mailbox. "Kasper Greenstreet." I must figure out a way to meet him. I peer at my classroom window. Sister Elizabeth is watching me.

THE NEW WORLD

Aunt Paula puts on her makeup like a surgeon. I sit at the table eating a stale bagel. I am spending a lot more time with her. She is my dead mother's sister. She and my Uncle Willy are the only relatives from our immediate family who did not leave New York for Long Island. So I know them best. Aunt Paula and Uncle Willy have some problems; they like to drink. Unlike my dad who has a couple here and there, they are big time boozers. Middle-of-the-day drinkers. Uncle Willy has lost quite a few jobs over the years due to the drink. Typically, we see them over the holidays, or for big events, like me falling through the floor in an abandoned boarding house. Aunt Paula has stepped up her involvement with me. She takes it upon herself to meet me after school for a milkshake, or to talk. She is obsessed with my fall. Not the fall exactly, but more its aftermath. By everyone's account, I had a near-death experience. That's the stuff that is most interesting to her.

"Do you remember anything, Jack?" Aunt Paula asks, widening her eyes to pencil around them.

"Not really."

"Did you see a bright light?"

She is on to the lipstick but first she puts a little Vaseline on her lips. Aunt Paula wears a lot of makeup; she is still pretty, in an older woman way. The apartment is a mess, but she is meticulous with her appearance. She picks up perfume and sprays way too much on herself. Aunt Paula and I have always gotten on well—same with Uncle Willy. My dad says they are harmless, except to themselves.

"Did you see your mother?"

"What?" I am not sure what she is talking about. "Aunt Paula, where would I see my mother?"

"Jack, you're a smart kid. Don't tell me you have never heard of seeing a bright light or of spirits, people from the other side coming to meet a loved one when they have come close to…" She stops, afraid she has gone too far.

"Close to what?" I am being a shit. because no one will come right out and say, "You were clinically dead. So, tell us, what was it like?"

"Are you ready?" she asks. I want to be a wise ass and say I was ready an hour and a half ago when I got here, but that would be childish—mean.

"Yes. You?"

"How do I look?"

"Great."

We walk down 3rd Avenue and turn onto 22nd Street, walking past Epiphany and the Gramercy Terrace. We're in a rush because of my aunt's inability to be anywhere on time. The man, Kasper Greenstreet from Apartment 3C, is standing outside the building smoking a cigarette. Another man walking his dog stands next to him on the curb. They are not together. This is exciting because he never leaves the apartment. He turns and stares through me, making the hair on the back of my neck stand at attention. Being this close to him gives me a chill. My aunt feels it too and grabs my arm. We walk past, and he turns to watch us.

"Do you know him, Jack?"

"Not really."

"Not really? What does that mean?"

"It means I've seen him before."

"Well, stay away from him and his little dog."

I look back over my shoulder, but he's disappeared into the building. I don't explain that he is the other guy—not the man with the dog.

When we reach 2nd Avenue, she hails a cab. It's not that far of a walk, but time is now an issue. The cab pulls up in front of two high-rise white apartment buildings.

"Here." She points as we walk into one of the Towers on Riverside Drive. "Jack," Aunt Paula says, covering her face with her hands. "I have always been upfront with you, right?" I nod my head because she has. "I would never want to undermine your father."

Here comes the "but" or "only." "Only, this guy is the real thing. He is so expensive, but Vivian told him about you, and he is willing to see—read you—for free."

"Vivian?" We are going to take advice from Vivian? Aunt Paula rolls her eyes.

"I know but I met him at a function—saw him in action. He is scary good." She catches herself. The word scary may not be the ideal word in this case. "Not scary…" Aunt Paula says with a forced laugh.

"Come on," I say. "I was dead, remember? Not much scares me anymore."

Tap, tap, tap, her high heels click along as we cross the marble tile lobby. Aunt Paula and I step on the elevator. She is visibly nervous, wiping her palms on her flowery dress.

"What number?" I ask. She pauses. "Don't tell me thirteen," I say, half kidding. Aunt Paula presses thirteen, and we both laugh. She then presses nine.

An older Asian woman opens the door and walks us through a long, mirrored foyer into a small den, decorated in white wallpaper with symbols of Greek gods. She waits for the woman to leave before asking, "Are you nervous?" I shake my head because I am more curious than nervous. I've always been the boy a little above average in my studies and in sports but not really great at anything. However, since I made a full recovery in the face of great odds, now I am the most interesting kid in the neighborhood. So nervous? No.

We expect the woman to come back in and get us when Mr. David is ready. To our surprise, a thin man looking like a Wall Street broker, or a lawyer, comes gliding in. No one would cast him as a psychic on television. Hmm, he is smart enough to be a great fake.

"Jack and Paula?"

"Yessss!" an enthusiastic Aunt Paula sings as she jumps to her feet. He shakes our hands and is very cordial.

"Come with me. The other room is where I work."

He leads us down a hall and stops in front of what looks like a sliding door in one of those fancy Japanese restaurants. A painting of a Japanese landscape spreads across the red lacquer door. Mr. David slides the door open. There are no chairs or tables, just very large pillows and yoga mats on the floor.

Mr. David looks at Aunt Paula. "Do you need a chair?" I can tell she wants one, but she says no.

He motions for her to sit. She looks around like she is about to climb a mountain in high heels. Holding the bottom of her dress down, she leans against the wall and slides down to the floor.

"Why no furniture?" I ask.

"I like things simple," Mr. David says.

Aunt Paula is on all fours, fighting to get into a sitting position. Her dress is much too tight for this exercise.

"It's not religious?" I ask.

"Well, I am a Buddhist, but no."

"Can you be a Buddhist and a psychic?"

He laughs. "Well, yes. Do you think you can only be one thing?"

"I don't think there are many Catholic psychics," I say.

"Trust me, there are plenty of psychics who are Catholic. They call them mystics."

In a moment, Mr. David and I are seated comfortably on the floor. He has a box by his pillow. Aunt Paula swings her legs behind her. I'm sure she did this move as a girl, only now it is a struggle. She is like a fish out of water.

Taking Tarot cards out of the box, he shuffles and puts them down in front of himself and begins to flip them over. "You have any questions for me?" Mr. David asks, without looking up. I shake my head.

He looks in my eyes. "Who's Katherine?"

Wow. I pause for a moment. "Katherine?" I shake my head, feigning confusion. "I don't know…" I look at Aunt Paula. "Do you know a Katherine?" I'm not sure why I'm playing this game—of course I know Katherine. She's my wife!

"Doesn't matter," he says, spreading the cards. Mr. David reaches into the box and takes out a small bottle. "Do you mind if I spray the air?" Aunt Paula and I both answer "no. It's nice." Maybe eucalyptus—with something else.

"What's it for?" I ask.

"For? Nothing really, just a scent to relax."

"So, then it's meant to relax?"

"Yes. It's to relax," Mr. David says.

Mr. David is not at all what I or Aunt Paula expect. He talks to me about dreams, premonitions, intuition. He asks if I know their meanings.

"I think so..."

He gives me the definitions anyway. "Intuition is the faculty of knowing or understanding something without reasoning or proof. Some philosophers believe it is greater knowledge—not just instinct. Have you ever felt that way?"

"I'm not sure." I think of Sister Elizabeth and the abnormality in the breast area, picking up people's smells, but I'm not going to say anything. Especially with Aunt Paula in the room. He presses a button and the woman comes back into the room. Mr. David asks her to take Aunt Paula to the kitchen and get her some tea. I help her up.

Once she is gone, he asks if I know Ella, Liz, or Elizabeth. I just about shit myself but I play dumb. "It will come to you. The key to tapping in to your intuition is to be still—listen. Trust your gut. If the hair on your neck stands up, pay attention. Don't let people drain you. Try and remember your dreams." He has lots of advice and doesn't seem to want anything in return. Too good to be true?

Then he asks, "I would like to teach you to meditate. Is that okay?"

We spend the next thirty minutes doing meditations. He teaches me breathing techniques and gives me two cassette tapes with Zen music, Gregorian chants, some Om chants to help me center myself. "Tap in," as he calls it. I love it.

"What's a normal day at school like?" he asks. I give him a rundown, leaving out my fixation on the apartment and the man across the street. "Are you done with your physical therapy?" Here and there, he will drop a little nugget on me. "Did you get your limp to the point where you are satisfied?"

"Why? Do I still have it?"

He shakes his head. "But are you satisfied? You know, sometimes we walk around with minor afflictions that become the Titanic. Some are self-created."

I nod.

"Are you tired? Would you like some tea?" he asks.

"I'm not tired, but tea sounds good."

He gets up. "Mr. David, how did you know you could do this?" I ask. "This?"

"You know…read people, their emotions, their thoughts."

"Can you read people, Jack?" he asks.

I shrug. "I'm not sure what it is. I…I just know that after the fall the world looks and feels different."

"Do you doubt what you are feeling? Your ability?"

"How do you know I have abilities?" I ask.

"Do you?"

"Can you just answer me?" I say, a little too testily. He waits me out. "I don't know. I sense things, I feel things, I see things. I smell things. But am I crazy? Dr. Melvin said I had an insult to my brain."

Mr. David puts his hand on my shoulder. "No, you're not crazy, Jack. When you walked in, I thought, wow, this is a bright light. All the fall did was turn up the volume to a gift that was already there." He opens the door. "Embrace it because it's not going away."

APARTMENT 3C

Mr. Greenstreet waits for me. He stands by his window smoking a cigarette and looking into my classroom, waiting for my company. I oblige while being very careful of Sister Elizabeth. She seems suspicious since my verbal outburst as good Catholic boys don't use those words. But I like the new me. The old me was always so worried about being good, pleasing everyone. This new kid with the vulgar mouth is really liberating.

Don't get me wrong, I am not happy about the fall. I miss Katherine and the kids. I can't or try not to speak or even think of them anymore. The pain of losing them is too great. Not to mention getting over my broken body. As Dad says, "That is all behind us now, Jack. You move physically like nothing ever happened. Now you have to keep your head on straight."

I never tell him about the emotional pain—only the headaches. From time to time, I need a pill because my head hurts so badly. The meditation Mr. David taught me really helps with the physical and mental anguish. He is teaching me yoga and has told me to reach out whenever I feel the need.

Mr. Greenstreet is waiting. In ten minutes, it will be study time, and I want to go into the other room and communicate with him. I walk up to Sister's desk, and she looks up and smiles.

"Can I go next door?" I ask.

She nods. "Are you okay, Mr. Kelly?"

"I will be if I can just rest."

It is easier to watch him from here. Not so obvious. I sit on the window sill and lock onto Mr. Greenstreet. He is painting on a canvas. I use the tools that Mr. David has taught me and I go into a deep meditation.

KASPER GREENSTREET

Kasper Greenstreet runs across 23rd Street carrying his tripod, along with a large bag of paints. He is late as he rushes into Madison Square Park but he is always late. He dresses the part of an unconventional man, an artist. Kasper looks around for someone. He finds him: businessman Mitch Michaels, who is sitting on a bench reading the newspaper. Mitch is dressed in a sport jacket, tie, and wearing Florsheim shoes.

"Sorry, sorry, I know I'm late," Kasper says.

"It's okay. Your coffee is probably cold." Mitch hands him a container of coffee. He appears to be used to or unfazed by Kasper's lateness. Kasper sets up his tripod. "Here's a bagel. I figured you didn't eat breakfast."

"Oh. Okay. Thank you," Kasper says, sitting down to sip his coffee. "What are we doing?"

Mitch looks at him. "We were supposed to have a little breakfast. You were going to draw; I was going to read."

Kasper nods. He is not really interested in the bagel. "I'm assuming you ate yours?"

Mitch crumbles the bag. "Sorry, my tardiness is a pain in the ass," Kasper says.

Mitch nods. "It can be, but it's a beautiful day. So, let's just relax."

Kasper takes out a sketchpad and a drawing pencil. He begins sketching the park with the Flatiron building in the distance. They are silent. Mitch reads his paper, and Kasper sketches. A couple of young boys are shooting paper clips at the pigeons with rubber bands. Neither man is bothered by it. Kasper puts his sketchpad down and leans back. "So, what are we doing?"

Mitch smiles at him and laughs.

"No, no I mean what is this? This is, what, the fifth time we've met for breakfast or lunch here."

"Well, I love this park…" Mitch says.

Kasper shakes his head. "I mean… what are we?" He speaks with dramatic flair, motioning at both of them with his hand.

Mitch looks at him. "What is bringing this on? If we continue to gravitate to each other at dinner parties, art openings, but can't have lunch…"

"No. You have been married for twenty-one years; you don't stray. This is not a pick-up because God knows I have had many of those; if it were, it would have happened by now. We would have done it and moved on—kept a working relationship."

Mitch searches for the right words. "Must I define it?"

"Yes."

Mitch folds up the paper. "I love you."

Kasper smiles. He jumps up from the bench. "I love you, too. Why are we here? Let's go back to my place."

Mitch tries to back up. "I love you but I don't want to have sex with you." Kasper sits back down tilting his head.

"You mean you love me like a friend?"

"No."

"Like a brother?"

"No."

Kasper jumps back to his feet and raises his hands in confusion. He walks away from the bench, comes back, sits down again. They sit in silence, then Kasper says, "Like a cousin? Like a pet? Like a child? Like someone you know at church, someone you met on the subway? I mean, give me a fucking clue here. What are we?"

"I love you. I love you," Mitch says softly.

"Like Susan, your wife?"

Mitch laughs. "Why must it be like someone else? I...I love YOU, Kasper Greenstreet. Not like Susan—I love Susan because she is Susan."

Kasper is determined. "If you love someone you want to have sex with them."

"Not always."

"So, you don't have sex with your wife?"

Mitch stops and stares at him. "Of course, I have sex with Susan."

"Then you love me like a brother."

Mitch shakes his head. "I wake up in the morning, pour a cup of coffee, and I think of you. When Susan tells me someone is interested in one of your paintings, it pleases me. I always include you in any of our marketing for the gallery." They sit a moment in silence. "Quite frankly, for a straight, married man, I think of you way too often."

Kasper shakes his head and smiles.

"I've never had homosexual impulses—I mean, I'm forty-six, and this is uncharted territory for me," Mitch continues. "The thing is: I don't lust for you; I...I just have love for you." They sit for a moment in silence. "Now can we just sit here with each other? I'll read; you can sketch."

Kasper picks up his sketchbook and begins to draw a small boy. The boy is Jack Kelly, playing with marbles, looking up at something only he can see. Kasper becomes fascinated with Jack's ethereal presence. He spends the rest of his time in the park, drawing Jack from several different angles, no longer interested in his conversation with Mitch.

SISTER ELIZABETH

The bell rings. I jump down from the window sill in the empty classroom across the hall. Everyone is rifling through their desks and packing their books up for the day. Me? I am in no hurry. I must find a reason to knock on the door of 3C.

"Mr. Kelly, don't forget to get your book of raffle tickets for the bazaar."

"Of course, Sister."

I take the raffle tickets from her desk. Normally, this is a pain in the ass. Usually, I just hand them off to my dad to sell at work, or my Aunt Paula to sell at the corner bar. Not this year.

"Mr. Kelly, can you wait a few minutes? I'd like to have a word with you."

It sounds like a request but it's a directive. "Of course, Sister."

I remind myself to keep my eyes on her forehead, not on her breasts. Looking her directly in the eye can also seem disrespectful, so I mustn't do that; I must stay on her forehead.

"How is the pain, Mr. Kelly?"

I don't want to lie because that is not the kind of kid I am, but the highlight of my day is to watch Kasper Greenstreet and I don't want to give that up. I do have pain—lots of it. The headaches can turn into migraines. Sometimes my back and neck are so sore it makes me irritable. However, the pain rarely comes when I say it does at school—so that makes me a liar, right?

You're staring at her chest, stupid, stop, stop. Looking above her, I see the cross on the wall; oh, how can I lie now?

We both start to speak. I immediately stop. "Mr. Kelly, sometimes it is difficult to understand why we have been given the cross we must bear."

"Sister?"

"In life, some have great difficulty. I'm sure you see the children on 23rd Street going to the school for the deaf?" I nod. "When you get your headaches—remember the Lord suffered."

"Yes, Sister."

"What I'm trying to say is our—your—suffering can bring you closer to God. Give us—you—grace."

My eyes are locked onto her breasts. Awkward. However, now I understand that the abnormality is causing her great mental and physical anguish. I pick up images from her past.

Elizabeth Conner never wanted to be a nun when she grew up in a small town in Pennsylvania. Her mother was not married when she got pregnant with Elizabeth. The "shame" her mother brought to her grandparents hung in the house like the curtains they made by hand.

Harold Conner, Lizzy's grandfather, owned a small business and was not about to leave town. Her grandmother, on the other hand, took this action on her daughter's part as an affront to her mothering skills, her religion, and her person.

Lizzy matured slowly, both a blessing and a curse, because as puberty began to come, Lizzy discovered a troubling sign. As her breasts developed, her right nipple separated, creating a third breast.

PETER CAIRO

Butterflies fill my stomach as I wait outside Gramercy Terrace for an opportunity to slide inside with my raffle tickets. Not a great way to spend a Saturday afternoon, but I'm on a mission. The Sloan's grocery delivery boy peddles up on a bike. He takes out a box of groceries and rings a bell.

"Yes?" comes a woman's voice from the intercom.

"Sloan's, ma'am."

The door buzzes, startling him. He fumbles with the box. I grab the door like I live here and open it wide.

"Let me help you."

"Oh, thanks," he says.

I realize he's not much older than I am. His clumsiness makes it clear he is new to the job.

He walks to the elevator. I hit the stairs and head up to 3C. Ringing the bell, I hear the sound of footsteps and wonder how Mr. Greenstreet will react; he seems as obsessed with me as I am with him. The door opens.

"Yes?" A fairly tall, dark-haired man in his mid-thirties stands looking at me.

"Mr. Greenstreet?"

Who is this guy? This is not the man I watch five days a week living in this apartment.

"I'm afraid I don't know who that is…" he says.

I stand there with my raffle book in hand. "Oh. Well. I must have the name wrong. I'm selling raffle tickets for the Epiphany bazaar."

He opens the door wide and says, "Come in."

The apartment is beautiful, carefully put together like something you see in a magazine. No clutter. A desk with little on it, all perfectly organized. A couch to enjoy the open view. A table here, a stand-alone lamp there. Windows and shades are open, filling the room with natural light. I'm looking outside instead of inside, for a change.

"You know, I graduated from Epiphany."

That surprises me. "You did?"

"Isn't that how you found me?" "He looks at the raffle tickets. "Although, you were looking for a Mr. Greenstreet?"

I don't answer. "Did you just move in?" I ask, changing the subject.

"No." He looks around the apartment, smiling. "Less is more. If we are going to do business, I should know your name."

"Jack. Jack Kelly."

Do business—I like the sound of that.

"How much, Jack Kelly?"

"It really is a great apartment," I say, adding, "Fifty cents."

"That's ten dollars for the book." He flips through it. "Listen, I was just getting ready to fix a sandwich. You want one?"

"No, thanks."

"How about a Coke?" He hands the raffle tickets back to me.

"Sure, I'll have a Coke."

I thought he might buy the book, but he's handed it back to me.

My dad would kill me if he knew I was in some stranger's apartment selling raffle tickets. But I need to know who's in this apartment during the week. Who is Mr. Greenstreet? Is that really his name? Why am I so drawn to him? In the meantime, I want to know who this guy is.

"Do you have kids?"

"No," he says, handing me a Coke and a coaster.

"Are you married?"

He laughs at my forwardness. "Not anymore. I'll take the book," he says, heading back into the kitchen.

Jack, this guy could be a murderer for all you know. Maybe he killed his wife.

"Can you write my information on the tickets, so I don't have to?" he asks. "There is a pen on the desk."

Mr. David tells me to trust my intuition. My intuition tells me he's a good guy—no murderer here. "Umm, what is your full name? I need it for the tickets," I ask as nonchalantly as possible.

"Peter Cairo." He sits down at the dining table. "You sure you don't want a sandwich?"

"No, I'm good."

I smell cigarette smoke in the apartment but I don't see any ashtrays or cigarettes around. I also notice several walking sticks in the holder at the front door. I thought I noticed him walking with a slight limp.

"Thank you, Mr. Cairo, for buying the book—that's very generous of you." I continue writing.

"You know, I used to have a limp," I say. "Still do when I get tired."

"You did?" he asks. "How did that happen?"

"Oh, I fell through the floor at a condemned boarding house about a year ago. They said I'd never walk again."

He stops eating his sandwich and looks up at me. "I've heard your story. You had a lot of people praying for you."

"Really? I mean my dad and Aunt Paula kept telling me that but I wasn't sure if they were just trying to motivate me."

"I got clipped by a taxi cab on 5th Avenue. Someone accidentally banged into me while I was waiting for the light to turn green. It knocked me into a moving cab. As you can see, I still have a bit of a limp."

"I didn't really notice your limp," I lie. "I just saw all of your walking sticks."

Mr. Cairo goes back to his sandwich; I go back to writing. I don't know why but I get the feeling that it wasn't an accident—more like someone deliberately pushed him off the curb.

"Are you a smoker?" I ask.

"No."

"Do you smell cigarette smoke?" he asks.

"Yes, I do. It smells as if someone is in the room with us smoking."

He stands up to clear his plate.

"Exactly." Mr. Cairo returns quickly from the kitchen. "I smell it all the time. I had the place painted and the carpets pulled up, but nothing works. Thought it might be coming from the neighbors, but neither one of them smokes. Guess it could be coming from downstairs in the street."

"Do you live with someone who smokes?"

"No. I live alone."

"What about a brother or friend who comes by when you're not home?"

"What? No? I don't have a brother."

I'm getting close to finishing the tickets. I'm also puzzled about Mr. Greenstreet. Clearly, I've been seeing him or someone else in this apartment for weeks. Maybe he's just some guy who lives in the building, or a worker who uses Mr. Cairo's apartment. To what? Paint? Stand by the window and smoke? That's ridiculous.

Mr. Cairo takes out a ten-dollar bill and gives it to me. I hand him the book.

"Thank you, again," I say, and leave still frustrated about Kasper Greenstreet. But I am fond of Mr. Cairo and I think there is more to his accident. Outside the building, I check the name for 3C. "Peter Cairo," it reads.

MYSTIC COFFEE

Two women, an older man, and I are taking yoga classes with Mr. David. He brings in someone to guide us. We do a half-hour of yoga and a half-hour of meditation. Afterward, we go for coffee and a chat. It's quite a group. All very grown-up. I wish I could tell my dad about this little meet-up of ours, but he would not understand. We all have some type of "ability," although I am still trying to figure out and harness mine. One of the women conducts seances, which I am never invited to attend. The older man and the other woman love their Tarot cards; they read for each other on occasion. Everyone gets a reading, except Mr. David and me. It's just the way it is. I have not developed the courage to ask why.

Yoga and meditation have really been a gift. Yoga has not only helped with my pain issues but also opened my mind to pray in a very different way than I have been taught. The yoga positions really help with my neck and back. If I start to get a headache, I find that downward facing dog can stop it before it turns into a migraine. I've begun to incorporate yoga at home when I am alone, to start or end my day. I also find that I pray better while doing yoga and meditating.

The yoga and meditation teacher rotates between several people. Today, we have a bald man who has us work on our Ujjayi breath. Ujjayi means victorious, which at first I didn't understand. Now it's the center of everything for me. It helps me sleep and helps with stress. He calls it the "oceanic breath" because it sounds like waves crashing to the shore.

"Yoga is just poses if you are not breathing."

True. When I am in a twisting or balance pose, everything seems to be less of a struggle if my breathing is good; it's the same in life.

The class always starts with an intention; today, mine is Sister Elizabeth. She keeps coming to mind; I feel pulled in her direction. From there, my mind drifts in and out because he has us doing Warrior I, II, and III—staying in each pose longer than I'm used to. I chuckle about being in this room— I mean, yoga? No one we know does yoga. It's for people from India and hippies, right? Geez, psychics, Tarot card readers, yogis?

The yoga teacher interrupts my thoughts. "Let's get ready for Savasana."

Savasana is the corpse pose. A little creepy, right? This pose gets its name from the recumbent posture of a dead body. It is a position of rest and relaxation and is usually practiced toward the end of a yoga session. A yoga session typically begins with activity and ends in rest, a space where deep healing can take place. Ah, but here is the key: when you come out of it, it feels like a rebirth, a personal rebirth. At least that is how one of the yoga teachers describes it. I like that. You can just spiritually start again at that moment. Reboot. That is how I have begun to think of my fall—a rebirth!

It's easier for me to meditate after yoga. I think of Sister, picking up things about her as a girl.

Lizzie Conner is smart but not clever. Her fears have begun to rule her life. She is distracted when she is out with friends. She has pushed away a boy with whom she was friends since grade school. Marriage is not for her. Not unless God or the Saints heal her. She spends her time and energy praying… for what? Two normal breasts? First, she was the girl without a father, a bastard. Now she's a freak—a witch?

Mr. David leads us out of our meditation. It takes me a moment to let the thoughts of Sister go. Everyone wants his attention: "I saw this…" "I felt that…"

I wait until I have him alone. "How do I know if I'm making something up in my head, or if it's my intuition that is actually picking it up?" I ask.

"Sometimes we get it wrong, Jack, but it's usually coming from somewhere.

Trust yourself." He smiles. "You'll know, you can tell the difference."

Afterward, we sit around with coffee or tea at this cool little lunch place, very "Bohemian." They are all very nice and helpful. I'm a tea drinker; I just don't get the appeal of the coffee taste.

"How's it going, Jack?" the older man asks. "Raphael," because he reminds me of the "Lovers" card in Tarot. He always seems to draw this card when someone does a reading for him. I think, well, I feel it's because he is very much like the archangel Raphael—someone who heals. A powerful presence with a booming actor's voice. The two women always kid him that he is going to meet someone and fall madly in love, but he says he has already done that. Raphael was married for forty years until his wife died.

One of the women I like to call "Star." Let me be the first to admit that I am a baby when it comes to the Tarot cards. I don't have a deck and I don't truly get or understand them. However, she reminds me of the "Star" card. The "Star" card depicts a naked woman who represents freedom and natural expression. That is completely different from the way she looks. Star is overdressed, overly made up, with lots of bangles and flair. She wears multiple layers of clothing and always carries a large bag with two smaller bags inside. I don't know why exactly, but this is her way of being naked.

The second woman reminds me of Susie Homemaker. She is a short, plump lady with short red hair who smells like Camay soap and speaks with a Vassar accent. "Susie" usually brings some type of homemade scones or granola. They all kid her about what ingredients she laces the food with. Marijuana, I'm guessing. All she does is giggle and say "I would never, never..." then quickly adds, "Offer it to Jack if I had put something illegal in it." They all laugh. None are TV or movie cutouts of mediums or psychics. Just run-of-the-mill people you sit next to on a bus.

Mr. David acts like one of us when he is with us, except he is not. He is above us, not in any pompous way, but he is just more ethereal. People pay a lot of money for a reading with Mr. David. His gift is "pure." At least that is what I've heard the others say.

We sip our coffee and tea. Star takes out her Tarot cards and begins placing them on the table. She is jingling away with all her bracelets when Mrs. Dowd, the fourth-grade teacher at school, spots me. Mrs. Dowd has her coffee-to-go in hand and stops at our table to look at us with a discerning eye.

She spots the Tarot cards just as Mr. David comes back to the table and sits. Her demeanor tells me she knows him, or of him.

She turns to me like an explanation is in order. "Hi. Mrs. Dowd," is all I have.

Mrs. Dowd smiles. "Mr. Kelly," she says, then turns and leaves.

Yikes, I hope this doesn't get back to my father.

"Jack?" Rafael's theater voice breaks into my silent monologue.

"She is a teacher at my school."

They all nod. None of them knows that only Aunt Paula is aware of my meet-ups with them.

PETER CAIRO

Before the fall, I never kept any secrets from my dad, but since then, there are many things he does not know about me. That does not make me happy or proud, because I want to be a good son. Now, Dad is sitting with Uncle Willy at the bar having a beer. Aunt Paula and I are sitting in a booth, me drinking a Coke, she a white wine spritzer. She wants to know everything I've been doing, thinking, and feeling. "Are you experiencing anything—like visions, or dreams?" she asks.

I won't tell her about Sister Elizabeth; it would be too weird. Instead, I tell her about going to yoga and the meditation class with Mr. David.

She loves that. "He's really something, that one," she says. "Does he ask about me?"

I look at her like she has lost her mind, but she cracks up. "I'm kidding, Jack—geez—don't ever lose your sense of humor." We both laugh.

She asks me how I feel about being a thirteen-year-old with a group of older psychics. "Truthfully, I don't feel thirteen. They are all nice, supportive people."

She sips. "Well don't stop being a kid, Jack. You are only a teenager once—have fun." This is fun for me now.

Uncle Willy is trying to talk my father into another beer. Dad does not appear to be weakening and gets up from the bar. Aunt Paula is disappointed. "Jack, do you know if Uncle Willy is going to hold on to this job?"

I tilt my head and smile. "You don't need to be a psychic to know Uncle Willy has a hard time holding on to work."

"Wise ass." She gets up and gives me a bear hug, then takes my dad's seat at the bar.

The night air greets us as we leave the corner bar, heading east on 23rd Street. "What do you want to eat?" Dad asks.

"There's a new McDonald's on First Avenue."

No response. That usually means no. We walk past Cosmo's diner. Peter Cairo looks up from the menu and spots me at the same time I spot him. He smiles and waves us in.

Dad is a little puzzled. "Who's that?" he asks.

"Mr. Cairo. I told you about him. He's an Epiphany alum; he bought a book of raffle tickets from me."

"I don't remember you telling me that, Jack," my father says with a slightly irritated tone. Before we have a chance to debate it, Peter introduces himself and asks us to have dinner with him.

Peter has a nice way about him, and Dad is hungry, so he agrees. By the time we all sit in the booth, Dad and Peter are discussing people they both know. Dad went to school with the oldest Cavanagh brother, and Peter with the youngest Cavanagh girl. There are eight kids in the family, so clearly Dad is older than Peter. When Dad was a kid, he also was part of P.A.L.—the Police Athletic League. Peter's dad is a retired detective who was a volunteer; dad thinks he remembers the last name.

We never get into exactly how Peter and I met, which pleases me. After we order, the two begin talking about me. Peter never leaves me out of the conversation, which I like. "What high school are you guys looking at?" Peter asks.

"Depends on my scores," I say.

"I like La Salle. Xavier is a great school, but very expensive," Dad says.

"I went to Xavier," Peter says.

"I was thinking Immaculata."

"It's a good school." It's clear neither of them thinks it rates with Xavier or La Salle Academy.

"Why not Xavier?" Peter adds.

"Well, like Dad says, it's expensive. Besides, I'm not sure I'm smart enough."

"Most of the Catholic high schools are expensive," he says. "You can get scholarships—partial scholarships. I know someone on the board."

The food comes. I ordered a cheeseburger and fries. Dad and Peter both ordered the pot roast. I notice Peter doesn't eat much. He pushes the food around. Dad, on the other hand, eats like it's his last meal.

Peter points out Xavier High School's good and bad points. "It's top-rated. No girls."

His entire face changes when he talks about going to college at UCLA. Like someone turned on an inner light. "It was wonderful! That campus was beautiful! Great education. Some wonderful years out there in Los Angeles."

"What was your major, Peter?" I ask. Dad looks at me—he thinks I should call everyone older than me Mister or Miss.

"I majored in business, then went on to get a law degree."

"So, you're a lawyer?" Dad asks.

"I represent producers and directors for stage and television—contracts…"

"Why did you come back to New York if you loved L.A.?" I ask, thinking I'm too forward for Dad.

"Well…" Peter starts, before Dad interrupts. "You don't have to answer that—if it's personal."

Peter smiles. "Not at all. My marriage ended, then my father had a stroke. Mother needs some help, some guidance. An opening came up in New York at the same agency, and I jumped at it."

My dad and I speak at the same time. "How is your Dad doing?" my father asks.

"You're divorced?" I blurt out.

"Jack, for God's sake, where are your manners?"

The table goes quiet. I look at Peter, waiting for an answer. He smiles, trying hard to be respectful to my dad. Speaking directly to Dad, he says, "I'm fine with it, but if you think he's too young…"

"That's not it. He just needs to understand that some people might want to keep certain things private."

Peter nods. "I'm sorry," I say. "I understand if it's private."

"It's nothing sordid," Peter says with a grin. "Sheila was originally from Minnesota and went to Los Angeles to become an actress. It didn't work out. She really hated the business and the city—and wanted to move back to Minnesota."

"Too cold in Minnesota for you?" I ask.

"Quite frankly, she didn't want me to come—which was fine with me. Raised Catholic, I didn't want a divorce. But I didn't want to be married, either."

"No chance of reconciliation?" Dad asks.

"Honestly, Mr. Kelly, there is nothing to reconcile. In the end, we realized we are very different people with very little in common. What should have been a nice little romance turned into a wedding—then into a divorce. The few times she came to New York, she didn't like it. No, I think we're better off starting something new."

Dad looks at me, then back at Peter. "How is your Dad recovering from the stroke?"

"He's home but wheelchair-bound. He can't use the right side of his body—can't really speak. Lots of grunting. The doctor says he's plateaued. It's been hard on both of them."

"They must be grateful to have you back in New York." Dad's so serious.

"Yes, but I was in an accident, so I was useless for a few months. You must think I'm bad luck. Divorced, father has a stroke, hit by a cab..." Peter says, trying to be funny.

"You have brothers and sisters?" I look at Dad after he asks the question.

"No. I'm an only child."

"Me, too," I say.

"Yes, we have that in common," Peter says, "as well as both of us being in accidents."

Peter takes the check and won't let Dad pay. "I have a proposition for you," Peter says to me. "If, of course, we can get your dad's approval. I need somebody a few hours a week to run errands—mostly for my parents. I also need someone to sit with my dad for a couple of hours on Tuesdays between three and five so my mother can get back to her Canasta card game."

He looks at both of us. "Yes!" I say.

"Hold on." Peter says."I'll pay minimum wage, but we need your dad's

66

approval."

"Dad, you always tell me to get a job when I ask for money."

Dad shakes his head. "That's a joke, Jack. But sure, as long as it doesn't get in the way of homework."

Peter takes down my number. He will type up a schedule for everyone's approval. This is great. I like Peter and I can find out more about his "accident." As well as the man I see in his apartment. Mr. Greenstreet. Is this who he is talking about when he refers to starting over?

KASPER GREENSTREET

Kasper Greenstreet sips his wine and watches the party with complete detachment. Wealthy hostesses love to get artists, writers, and actors in the same room with their friends. It's supposed to be a cultural evening for the upper class. Kasper looked at it more as getting them laid with an "up and coming" someone. Especially this one, "Mrs. Hudson Valley Lockjaw," with her capped teeth and five ex-husbands. He rolls his eyes and grabs a couple of shrimps from a passing tray. In between bites of the shrimp, Kasper remembers someone correcting him once: "It's Larchmont or Locust Valley lockjaw—not Hudson Valley."

Seriously? he thought. Which one sounds better? Hudson Valley— right? Kasper's understanding of "Hudson Valley, Locust Valley, whatever the fucking valley lockjaw" was the manner in which someone spoke—by opening their mouth as little as possible and moving the jaw and lips ever so slightly. As if they were two rich or too smart to be bothered to open their mouths all the way. Think Franklin Roosevelt or Katherine Hepburn. It's also about the delivery of the speech. They might say something like, "I'm terribly glad to have met you," while implying that they are not terribly glad to have met you at all and wish you would go away.

Oh, no, here she comes. "Kasper, darling, so nice of you to come."

Meaning "and suck down all my booze." Yup, she'd be a great ventriloquist. "More wine, darling?" She motions for the waiter. "It's a California cabernet; California wine is undiscovered." Meaning "sort of like your art." She waves to a woman across the room. "I want to introduce you to Peggy; I think she will love your work." Love? As in buy? Because he is not sleeping with her and he will pretty much sleep with anybody.

As the waiter comes to pour him wine, she flitters off. Kasper motions for him to fill the glass. He's a regular explorer, hoping to discover how drunk he can get on California Cabernet. The waiter is kind of cute, so Kasper holds him hostage for a moment with small talk. He always has a hard time talking to the grown-ups at these things. Always feel like he's whoring, trying to peddle his art. Blah, Blah. He can get kind of prickly, especially after some libations.

Uh oh. Susan and Mitch are here—what a handsome couple. Susan will drag around everyone who shows at the art gallery to meet the folks. Commerce first! Should I feel a little weird after my conversation and flirtation with Mitch? He loves Susan, besides, Mitch never slept around.

She calls Kasper over. "Slow. Drink slowly. Have fun, but drink slow," she says. Too late for that!

Mitch and Kasper make fleeting eye contact. She looks at him. "Let's go say hello to our host."

She looks at Kasper. "Mingle."

The evening gets lively. Their hostess plays this dance game where she partners you up with someone. Not your spouse or the person you came to the party with. She loves to mix it up—women with women, men with men, men with other people's wives, women with other people's husbands. It's supposed to be risqué, adding a little naughtiness to the night. Rumor has it she found her latest husband playing this game. When the music stops, you are supposed to change partners, switch to a new person. It can go from the Hustle or the Jitterbug to a slow dance. Kasper likes that.

Their hostess loves the power of choosing for you. She starts Kasper off with Peggy from across the room. Disco starts playing. Donna Summer. Peggy is not a good dancer and flops about like a turkey flapping her wings, unable to fly. Kasper gets his sexy on. Peggy looks at him like he farted. Fine. Mrs. Hudson Lockjaw stops and starts the music at her own discretion. Susan and Kasper partner next; it's "The Hustle," which they both speak. She is very light on her feet. They have danced many times together, so she follows easily.

The music stops and Kasper spins Susan to her next partner. There is a lot of laughing and stepping on feet. Some of the older guests drop out as the music finally slows. Kasper looks up. His partner is Mitch. Typically, when a heterosexual man gets another man it turns comical, especially if the music is slower. Kasper grabs him and pulls Mitch into him. They do the foxtrot. Left hand in his right hand, Kasper's right hand on his lower back. Mitch smiles and switches their hand positions. "I lead," he says firmly.

They dance. He's not as good as Susan, but then again, he is not leading. There is electricity between them—no doubt. He is very "male." His body is fit. Their gaze is locked on one another. He does not look away.

"You haven't called," Kasper says, embarrassed the moment the words leave his lips. He should have listened to Susan's warning: "Drink slow."

"I knew I'd see you tonight," Mitch says.

The music stops. Kasper looks around to see who our next partners will be. Mitch and he are "star crossed lovers," at least in his mind. Lines from the song "When Will I See You Again" come to him: "Are we in love or just friends? Is this the beginning? Or is this the end?"

Quite frankly, Kasper has never felt "gayer" than he does right now thinking of that song. Kasper would love to give him a jump, but at the cost of risking his friendship with Susan, who also represents his art? There are still laws about these things—sodomy laws. Happily married successful men might leave wives for their secretary, but they never leave them for a man. Besides, Kasper married to his work—to his art.

The music starts again. They are in the ballroom stage of the dancing. Mitch does not move. Instead, he reaches out and takes Kasper's hand. Surely, they are turning heads, but he can't be bothered to look. "You make me feel like a schoolboy," he says with the right amount of mischief in his eyes.

Kasper? He is drunk on California Cabernet. And him. "But still no desire to see me naked," Kasper says, looking for what? A fight? An announcement of some kind?

His mouth is very close to Kasper's ear. He thinks Mitch is going to say something very profound, but he says nothing. Kasper likes Mitch's breath in his ear. He has Kasper turned on. Catching himself, he immediately

71

backtracks. What is going on here? Is this some game? Midlife crisis? He handles Kasper like he's a woman, which bothers Kasper. He thinks, Fuck, I'm a man!

Kasper pushes himself free. Mitch is startled by his sudden abruptness. "Go to your wife." The two of them stand there as the music stops. "I'm done dancing."

Outside the building, the waiter and Kasper smoke a joint. They are making plans to hit another party. Susan, Mitch, and another couple come out of the building, laughing, leaving for the night. Susan waves. Kasper smiles, glad Mitch sees how easy it is for him to pick up a date. He smiles and nods back in that superior manner of his, which pisses Kasper off. Before he can react, they turn and are gone.

- - -

I watch Kasper Greenstreet stand and smoke in Peter Cairo's apartment, baffled. How's he getting in? I decide to take the last few minutes of my time alone in the classroom to get in "child's pose," and do some "Om" chanting, in order to relax and clear my head. I'm meeting Peter Cairo's mother and father after school today.

I don't hear the door open. Sister Elizabeth sticks her head in to check on me. Not what she expected to find. "Mr. Kelly?" Oh shit. "What are you doing, Mr. Kelly?"

"Oh, just stretching my back and neck, Sister."

She stands there with her arms crossed as I get up from the floor. "What's that sound you're making?"

"Sound?"

"Yes, Mr. Kelly, the sound?"

"Sorry, Sister, I didn't realize I was making a sound."

"Hmm..." She does not believe me.

I walk with a couple of school friends to Stuyvesant Town, which is where Peter Cairo's parents live. Stuyvesant Town is a massive group of residential buildings built after WWII, eighty-nine or ninety buildings in all. It runs from 14th Street to 20th Street. Rents are pretty expensive.

Peter is waiting outside his parents' building when I get there. "Jack, thanks for coming."

On the way up in the elevator, he gives me a little background on his dad. He was NYPD. Worked his way to detective, retired, and had his stroke about six months ago. His mom did some modeling when she was young. Got married and did what most women did in the 1950s and 1960s: take care of their husbands and children.

Mrs. Cairo is still beautiful, tall, slender, timeless. "Excuse the house" are her first words to us.

Peter introduces us. "This is Jack, Mom—Mom, Jack."

She shakes my hand. "Julia. Call me Julia."

Mrs. Cairo—Julia—gives Peter a big hug. You can tell she adores him, that they are very close.

"Hi, Mom."

"Are you hungry?" Julia asks him.

"Mom, we're here to help you. No, I'm not hungry."

Julia rubs her hands. "You got so skinny. I just worry."

The elder Mr. Cairo is sitting in a recliner in the living room, directly off the entry. The room is messy. Two card tables are up, both with teacups on them. A half-eaten bowl of broth sits there as well.

"Pop," Julia says loudly, talking to her husband. "Peter's here."

"Mom, Dad knows I'm here…" Peter says, whispering. "He can see fine."

Mr. Cairo follows them with his eyes; he seems to speak with his eyes. Am I making it up or picking it up? I think I am picking it up. He gives a grunt as a hello.

"Hey, Dad. This is Jack. He's going to help you and mom a couple of days a week."

"Hi, Mr. Cairo." I start to reach out to shake his hand. The right side of his body is tilted. He has no use of the right arm or leg, which affects his balance. Peter explains it as aphasia: "I think he understands you, but he cannot communicate words or meaning back to you."

Peter gives him a hug.

Julia reminds me of a woman who is used to being in control, having everything go right. She is overwhelmed in her present life, which creates fear and anxiety in her. I know this is going to sound weird, but I can smell it.

Peter makes small talk with his father about work. "You still watching *Undercover?*" His dad grunts. "I handle a couple of the directors on that show." The elder Mr. Cairo nods and smiles. "You waiting for the 4:30 movie to start?" Another grunt. "Listen, Pop, I need to talk to Mom for a minute. Jack is going to sit with you and get acquainted. Okay?"

Peter gets up to leave the room. His dad watches him closely. It appears to me? Feels to me? I am picking this up; I know I am. Mr. Cairo is not thinking of Peter by name but rather as a blue blanket that moves. Interesting. He turns his gaze on me. I let out a small chuckle. I am a big question mark over his head.

I pick up a TV Guide on his tray and look to see what the movie will be at 4:30. He is watching me, the question mark over his head. I like that. It means he is in there, thinking, "who the hell is this kid?"

"Have you ever seen *The Maltese Falcon*, Mr. Cairo?" No answer, but a big gun appears over his head. "So, you did see it…" I speak. The question mark that represents me sits over his head and is now pulsating.

I continue as if we are having a normal conversation. "I'm a big fan of Humphrey Bogart." A 1940s Fedora detective-style hat floats over his head. Perfect. Finally, I feel I can be of service. "My dad has one of those hats. He never wears it."

The question mark is very big now and very red, it continues to pulse.

"Jack." Peter calls me from the kitchen.

I walk to Mr. Cairo before I go into the kitchen. "I am a friend, Mr. Cairo; you'll see." The question mark returns to its normal size, with no color, no pulsating movement.

Meanwhile, Julia is losing the debate with her son. Peter is firm in a loving way. "Jack will be here on Thursday afternoon; you will return to the canasta group."

"I just thought he was going to do errands," she says.

"Mom, Jack is a very smart, very mature young man. You have to trust me on this…"

Poor Julia, so afraid. Smells like really bad body odor, although she is wearing perfume and doesn't really smell. It is the smell of her emotions, and only I can smell that.

"Mom, it's a tough situation, but we'll get through it."

Julia writes down my number. I already have hers. "Monday and Thursday, and if you need more, we'll go from there. You know, Jack is running errands for me on Wednesday," Peter reminds her.

Julia likes that. "Good, now you'll have food in the fridge."

Peter and I are set to leave. "Can't you stay for dinner?" Julia asks Peter.

"No, I have to go back to the office for a little while. I'll come on Sunday."

We walk into the living room, where Mr. Cairo is watching the start of the movie. He looks up and sees his wife; I notice a big red heart over his head, followed by a bright blue blanket for Peter and a black question mark for me.

NOT MY DAD'S RELIGION

It's late Saturday morning, Dad and I are heading out to a party in Queens. One of his cousins is throwing a big engagement party for their daughter. We don't usually go to these things, but Dad wants to get out of the city, do something different. Honestly, I'm looking forward to the two of us spending some time together, catching up. He has wanted to know where I am every minute since my fall, which is suffocating me. When I rebel, his answer is always the same: "I never thought I had to worry about you playing in an abandoned building." Can't argue with that. However, it can be a little manipulative; it makes me feel guilty. Letting me work for Peter Cairo and his parents is a huge thing. I want my freedom back!

We are in no hurry. My father has the subway schedule. He says we have plenty of time. Dad always likes to be ten minutes early. On our way down the stairs at the 23rd Street station, a man coming up the stairs says something to me.

"What?" I ask.

The man looks over his shoulder without saying a word and continues on his way. Dad looks at me. "Thought that guy was talking to me," I say.

"He didn't say a word, Jack."

In the station, my sense of smell heightens. The smell of the tunnel mixed with perfume, newspaper, and urine fills my nostrils. On the platform, I hear a low murmur of voices, kind of like someone changing a radio station very slowly. Two or three conversations come to me at once. A man is standing against the wall, his yellow shirt as bright as the daylight we just came from. It hurts my eyes, makes me look away. Two women whisper to each other; it sounds like they're yelling, "He's so cute!" I look at a man sitting on a bench reading the newspaper. The sound of him turning the newspaper is in surround sound.

In the distance, the humming of the train wheels is loud and coming closer. "Train's coming," I offer to distract myself from the noise.

Dad shakes his head, looking at his watch. "We have a good thirteen minutes."

More people come down from the street and find spots along the platform. Voices get louder, more voices in my head; deciphering them is a problem. Looking around, I find it hard to know or feel exactly where the voices are coming from. They seem to be bouncing off the station's walls, increasing in volume and frequency. Most people are standing alone, one or two conversations going on. The noise level is that of a crowd at a sporting event.

Voices are crowding me! "I should just jump in front of this train…" "No more, I can't take any more…" "If he loved me at all…" "Where am I…?" "Just one more fix…" "Pregnant! Pregnant!" The wheels of the train get louder.

Within a few minutes, the platform is crowded, and the voices become a chorus of "Carmina Burana" in both Latin and English. "O Fortuna, Velut luna statu variabilis, semper crescis aut decrescis; vita detestabilis nunc obdurat et tunc curat ludo mentis aciem egestatem…" "O Fortune, like the moon you are changeable, ever waxing and waning hateful life first oppresses and then soothes as fancy takes it poverty and power it melts them like ice. Fate—monstrous…"

Stepping away from my dad, I do a 180-degree turn to get a better look at everyone. I peer down the tunnel for the lights of the train. The wheels screech, getting louder and louder, as are the voices. I'm dizzy.

Different voices speak simultaneously. "If you had the balls…" "He's going to die…" "Lunch at…" "She is beautiful…"

These are not conversations I am hearing; these are the voices in their heads! They get louder and frantic; it's as if someone is turning a radio station too quickly for me to hear anything clearly. Maybe a word—a noise. "Jump! Jump!" The humming of distant trains. Squealing wheels!

I look for a person preparing to jump. The platform is crowded, with both the living and the dead. Shadow people have also filled the station in all their masquerades. They are on the tracks, platform, and benches. They overwhelm me with their foul odor and deceptions. Several creatures come out of the tunnels. They have freakishly long bodies with horse-like skeleton heads and melted flesh hanging from their faces, so it appears. These things walk on two hind legs and long arms and hands dangling with animal nails. Serpent's tongues move in and out of their mouths. They have green teeth.

Come on Jack, come on! I try hard to clear my head. The sound is too much for me to handle. I can't think or concentrate. I am scared, as scared as the moment I felt the floor cave beneath me. Voices yell, "Jump!" "Get some balls!" "She's…" "Dead…" "What is death?"

All of the shadows are staring at me. I know them! "You have no power here, Jack!" they screech, matching the tires on the train as it comes closer to our station.

Everything is flashing before me, the roar of the floor, the freezing hospital room, the moment I wake up. "You'll never walk!" "Never!" All that therapy, all that pain. The rope in the apartment. Wetting myself.

I begin to hyperventilate. "Dad," I say, too softly for him to hear.

"Jump!" "Hate her…" "Witch…" "Fake family!"

Shadows bounce around the tunnel—they are on the walls; they are next to me. Smelling me. "You should be dead!" "Dead!" The creatures trot up the tracks, some running on all fours. They leap around. One is on the wall behind me.

The music from "Carmina Burana" gets louder, the voices screaming to match its chorus. Shadows taunting me… "You have no power!" "No power!" "Jump!" "Jump, Jack!" "Jump!" I can hardly stand up. The weight of the words, the sounds are drowning me. "Your father will be better off without you!" "You!" "You and your fake family!" "Disrespectful boy!" "Sooo disrespectful!" "JUMP!" "Go ahead, Jack, jump!"

It is too loud. My head is exploding. I am going to burst!

Dad looks at me. His mouth moves, but the multitude of choirs in my head and on the platform drowns out his voice. Reading his lips, I know he is saying my name but I can't hear him—I am floating away. The train hits the station as I lose my breakfast in a projectile vomit.

Everything is suddenly far away. Dad looks shocked, grabs me, walks me to the bench. A man throws his newspaper down over my mess. Dad makes me put my head between my legs. There is quiet, sweet beautiful silence.

"Jack? Jack?"

I hear my father's voice clearly again. The man with the newspaper comes over to see if I am okay. He then runs to catch the train before the doors close.

The train leaves the station without us. No one has thrown themselves in front of it. Everything is normal again, but me—I am exhausted. There will be no party in Queens for us.

- - -

I climb into bed. All I want is sleep. "Dad you should go…"

"No."

"Dad, it's just a migraine. It will pass." He looks at me. "I just need a nap," I whisper, but I need more than a nap.

It is dark outside when I wake. No lights are on in the apartment. What was all that shit today? I crawl out of bed feeling like myself again, no headache, no anxiety. There is a note on the kitchen table. "Meeting Aunt Paula and Uncle Willy for a bite and a beer."

Perfect. I leave for Mr. David's.

When I'm in the elevator, it dawns on me that I should have called first. I ring the bell. It's quiet. Maybe he's not home, but I hear voices. I'm thinking about ringing the bell again when the door opens.

It's Mr. David. "Jack!"

We're both surprised. I never show up unannounced; he never answers the door. "I'm sorry; I should have called" I say.

"No, no, it's fine," he says, opening the door. "I'm in the midst of doing some readings. Go into the den."

After a few minutes, Mr. David comes into the room. "Are you okay, Jack?"

I start to explain my day, the heightened sense of smell, the crippling loud sounds, the voices. "There were dead people all over the subway, mixing with the living, and then there were these other things—these spirits… demons… shadow people…"

"Do you know what they wanted?"

"Well, I think they wanted me to throw myself in front of the train."

He pulls back. "What?"

I tell him about the aborted trip to Queens, how I was picking up the inner voices in peoples' minds.

"Tell me about—what did you call them? Shadow people?"

"I know them from my fall. They were either in my hospital room or in my dreams."

"You can't remember?"

I shake my head. "It's not that I don't remember. They were in Stevie's room, which would make it a dream."

Mr. David is lost. I realize he doesn't know about my family. About the family I created.

I try to get him up to speed. "Okay, after the fall, while I was out of it, apparently I was dreaming that I was a man with a wife and three kids. It was very vivid. One of my children—Stevie…" It's been a long time since I allowed myself to open that door again.

Now, I feel crazy. I'm in a "medium's" apartment talking about a family that doesn't exist.

Mr. David is very patient with me. "It's okay, Jack. Tell me."

"My oldest child—Stevie—got very sick. These creatures, these shadow people kept coming and trying to take him from me."

"These are the things that showed up in the subway today?" he asks.

"Yes."

"You said there were dead people, too, or are these the dead people?"

"No. No."

"First, there are living people like you and me? Correct?"

"Yes."

"Then the dead—they were different from the living, how?"

"More transparent, like a hologram."

He nods. "Do the shadows look the same?"

"No, the shadow people are all different—some are…well, scary, smelly, demonic-looking eyes. Others are just shadows, not fully defined. It was overpowering, disorienting; I got physically sick."

"I understand, Jack. Tell me this. Who or what was the threat?"

"The shadow creatures."

"Okay. You said you heard people's thoughts; they weren't talking?"

"No."

"Were they coming from the living, the dead, the shadows?"

"All of them at the same time."

Mr. David nods. "Could you separate what each entity was saying?"

"The ones that I heard most clearly were the voices coming from the shadow people—they were taunting me, yelling at me, telling me it would be better for me to jump in front of the train. The other voices were mixed—I wasn't clear if they were coming from the living or the souls of the dead."

"Were they angry?"

"Some were."

"At you?"

"No."

"Were they in pain?"

I nod. "Some were."

Mr. David and I continue to flush out what happened in the subway. We go through the sounds and the smells, taking a walk through the spirit world.

"Now I wasn't there, but here's what I think," he said. "You are dealing with multiple entities; some are living, some are dead, some can move between the two worlds, some are stuck—trying to move on or afraid to move on. The vicious shadows are creatures that feed off the fear of the living and the dead. You have to be careful there."

We talk for hours, losing all sense of time.

"Question, Jack, when they were in your dream the first time trying to get your son. What did they want with him?"

"Dead—they wanted him dead."

"But you stopped them?"

Stopped them? "I woke up," I say. "It was a dream."

- - -

Mr. David insists on walking me home, for which I'm thankful but not happy. I really don't want my dad to meet him. I got away with Peter Cairo—might not be so lucky this time. "It's late," is all that he says.

We walk down 1st Avenue. "Listen, Jack," he says. "The next time this happens…"

It happening again makes me nervous, makes my voice go high when I speak. "Do you think it will happen again?" I ask.

Mr. David takes a deep breath. He doesn't want to lie to me, but he can sense my fears. "Probably. Try concentrating on what the living and the dead are saying—that's who we try to help."

"I told you, Mr. David, I was under attack. It was a lot to handle."

He nods, not sure how to help me. "If it gets too intense, shut the portal down."

I'm not sure what a portal is exactly.

"Can you?"

"Can I what?"

"Shut the portal down or tell me how?" I ask.

We stop and wait at the red light. "I've never had to deal with entities as intense as you did today." He speaks cautiously. "I've heard stories but, frankly, I just pass messages on from dead loved ones to the living who mourn them."

That's not the answer I want to hear. The light turns green as I sigh. "You opened the portal, Jack, which means you can close it. Understand?" he says.

I say yes, but "not really" is the truth. I don't understand any of this. "One thing I know for sure, Mr. David."

"What's that, Jack?"

"I definitely was picking it up today, not making it up."

He laughs. We are in front of my apartment building.

"Thanks for listening." I can't bring myself to say "walking me home." Shit, I'm thirteen; New York is my town!

I put my key in the lock and turn it very quietly, not wanting to wake Dad. As I open the door, I see a figure by the apartment at the end of the hall. Quickly stepping inside, I lock the door.

- - -

Nothing has changed since Saturday, yet everything has changed. No signs of shadows, no voices, no dead people getting my attention. A normal Sunday follows. On Monday morning, I'm back at school fighting to keep my eyes from rolling in the back of my head as we study algebra. No plans here on being an engineer. I'll probably become a cop or get into my dad's union, work down on the docks. Dad always says, "No way, Jack. You're going to college." Shit, maybe I'll head to California and take up surfing, or work at the beach reading fortunes. Jack the psychic!

But I do like history, American history—the good, the bad, and the ugly. Sister Elizabeth is having us read out loud from the textbook. I watch her at her desk. She is not following the text; maybe she already knows it.

I picked up snapshots of her when she was younger. There is a boy. She loved him. Name begins with an M... Matteo, Milton, Martin?

"Pick up, Mr. Kelly," Sister Elizabeth says, interrupting my daydream.

"What?" I have no idea where we are in the text. "Um."

Bobby whispers a couple of words. I'm lost. I flip the pages back and forth. I look over at Bobby's book, then up at Sister. "Sorry, Sister. I..."

"You're sorry? Why Mr. Kelly?" she says, walking down the aisle to my desk.

"I lost my place."

"You're not on the correct page." Sister turns her back to me. "Class, tell Mr. Kelly the page and the paragraph we are on."

A few classmates respond to her request. Bobby holds his book up, pointing to the page and the section. I read while seeing an image of Elizabeth as a teenager, running into her room, slamming the bedroom door. Thoughts of killing herself come to her for the first time... but not the last.

None of the dead come back, but some stay.

- - -

Peter asked me to meet him at Cosmo's Diner at 7 p.m. He wants to give me money for errands and a key to his apartment so I can drop off his dry-cleaning, groceries, and other items. It's 5 p.m. when I leave the apartment, much too early for Cosmo's.

Leftover dust from before my fall blankets me as I walk along 23rd street. A major theme in my life at that time was fear; although, I don't think I could name it. When I think about it now, I realize I was always afraid. As a motherless child, the thought of losing my Dad overwhelmed me. I'd sit at the window, waiting for him to come home from a date or having a drink with friends, scared shitless. Sometimes it would be very late; I would sit and wait.

My fears carried varying degrees of weight. I was terrified of becoming an orphan. I was afraid of not being smart enough at school. Who would help me with homework, how would I score on the Regents exam? Did God think I was worthy to make it to purgatory? Stupid things, like was my uniform clean enough, my shirt pressed properly? Dad and I became very good at ironing.

Whenever I was invited to a birthday party, I'd panic. What about a present? More than once, I went to a party without wrapping a last-minute gift. Oh, the woes of a motherless child whose father works and doesn't make enough money to hire someone to help with the kid. No one to make sure you have breakfast or finish a school project. I remember the fear.

Typical night noise fills the air, horns honking, bus brakes screeching, trucks passing, pedestrians everywhere. I try the library door. It's locked. I continue to walk.

The memories of that night come back to me in a rush. The cracking floor, sounding like ice breaking. First softly—then louder—then boom! A roar while the building swallows me. Disappearing from the light. Then nothing.

I drift down 23rd Street with no particular destination. Dad comes to mind, how scared he must have been when my mother was diagnosed with ovarian cancer. Then watching his young wife perish before his eyes, helpless. Trying to be both mother and father since. Then my stupidity of playing in an abandoned building. How much he aged while sitting by my bed.

What led me in there that night was fear. Brick and a few kids went in several times previously. I always "punked" out, either too cautious or too afraid. I made my excuses; in those days, I made excuses for everything. That night was different. I'm not sure why. Maybe I was tired of being scared.

- - -

I reach the Corner Bar, which is not on the corner of the street. I love that. Peering through the doorway, I look for Aunt Paula or Uncle Willy. I don't see them or anyone I know, so I move on.

Fear is an unpleasant emotion. Aunt Paula is always afraid of Uncle Willy losing his job. Uncle Willy seems unafraid of anything but is really afraid of everything. Sister Elizabeth is afraid of her body; Julia afraid of her husband's stroke. Being afraid is not being alive. You are hostage to it. Fear. Fear. Fear!

The 23rd Street subway station looms in front of me. Commuters, students, pedestrians in all shapes, sizes, colors rush up and down the stairs. They take no notice of me. Are you afraid, Jack? Is this the same stupidity that sent you into an abandoned building, or is this the hill you are willing to die on? A man brushes past me, pushing me away from the stairs.

I think the scariest places are the ones in our heads. Those are the real haunted houses.

Down the stairs I go, sweaty palms and all. People come and go, rush hour in full swing. No voices, no heightened smells, no accentuated colors. Just everyday life. As I walk the platform, I listen. I wait. The voices begin subtly. "Where will I get the money?" It is a college kid, very much alive, but I pick up his thoughts. "Just need a drink. One drink." An older woman. Then an attractive woman dressed in clothes from the early part of the century walks onto the platform. She is not of the living, more like an apparition. Did I see or hear her the last time?

"What am I to do? He won't even see me now. Pregnant. Pregnant, and he's married!" The color of her clothes pops brightly in comparison to everyone else's in the station.

A train screeches loudly from the tunnel, lights leading the way. I realize it is from another era. The woman walks toward the end of the platform and throws herself into the oncoming train. The brakes screech. Her body makes a massive thud as it hits the train. No one but me gasps.

"Carmina Burana" starts but quickly stops. I walk slowly to the edge of the platform and peer over to see where she jumped. In the tunnel, I see and hear several shadows climbing on the walls, sounding like cicadas.

Sounds of the floor cracking under my feet alarm me. I look down at the ground: it is firm. I stomp my feet. It is my mind, the shadows playing tricks on me.

Shocked, I watch as the woman crawls up from the tracks, a mangled mess. Her head is crushed. One eye focuses on me as she wiggles onto the platform. One arm is missing, and her legs face opposite directions from her body. She is in shock. But she was dead when I first saw her—right? "I killed my baby!" The voice sounds strange, her vocal cords smashed by the impact of the train.

I'm frozen. I want to fucking run but I don't.

Shadows in the tunnel walk on the platform in a menacing posture. She comes closer; her one eye locked on me. "I killed my baby!" she says again. I don't speak or move or breathe. "What do you want?" she hisses.

"I want to help you," I say.

She shakes her disfigured head. "You can't help me!" she cries. "I killed my baby."

I nod, too afraid to touch her.

Other voices rise behind me. "Jump!" "No power." "Money for sex." I block them out. Shadows get closer, as do these horse-head creatures. I hear and smell them. Focus on the woman, Jack! Focus on her.

"I can help you," I say. She stares at me; she is a bloody mess. "Do you want my help?"

The woman nods her head.

"You're dead," I say, as peacefully as possible. She doesn't understand me. "You're dead, Miss, not just the baby, but you."

She shakes her head frantically. Her movements are so fierce I'm afraid that either her head will detach from the body or she will combust.

"You keep doing this over and over again," I say. "It's not going to change."

I wait. She stops moving.

"Dead!" she screams, startling me. I look around the platform and realize no one else can hear us. Except the shadows. There is a long silence. Me shaking like a leaf, her mangled body twitching.

"It's time," I finally say. "You need to move on. Your baby is already gone. It has already moved on."

"Dead," she says softly.

Shadows disappear into the darkness of the tunnel. Their smell lingers.

The woman turns from me, dragging her mangled body slowly. "Dead." I hear her say again. Briefly, she appears as she was when I first saw her. Beautiful. Only, now there is no fear, no frantic thoughts. She is translucent. She walks through a concrete post and disappears into a light. A star? A portal? I'm not sure.

The station returns to its earthly setting for a splendid moment. No voices. No distress coming at me. Just us mortals waiting for our next stop.

The voices return, exploding all around me. I am back in the eye of the storm. The most hideous shadows climb the walls, the living and dead creating chaos with their chatter. "You must be punished!" "Jump!"

I need to get above ground. I am too tired to deal with all the noise. It is crushing.

I climb up the stairs and run into the night air. Sweat drips from my face; my clothes stick to my skin. It takes me a moment to catch my breath. My adrenaline carries me down 23rd Street. I decide fear will not be allowed in my vocabulary. Caution, mindfulness, vigilance, and prudence? Yes. But not fear. I will not hide or roll over. My fall was a new birth for me. It was as if God or the universe said, "Jack Kelly, you need to start again."

Aunt Paula says that having this intuition or communicating with the dead is a gift. Maybe an ability, but a gift? No. Whatever happened while I was "under, whatever" I see or hear, or don't see. It is not the same world, and I am not the same kid as before the fall.

- - -

It is past 7:30 p.m., and I am late for my meeting with Peter. He sits in the same booth as the night Dad and I had dinner with him. Peter is pushing his food around the plate when I press my face against the window, startling him. Peter smiles when he realizes it's me being a clown.

Cosmos is busy with the dinner crowd as I slide into the booth. "Sorry, I'm late."

Peter looks at me with concern. "Are you feeling okay, Jack?"

"I feel fine. Why?"

"You're very pale," he says and then repeats it. "Very pale. You are dripping with sweat."

"Oh, I ran here." Stop lying, Jack! Just say nothing.

Peter nods. "You hungry?"

"Maybe for dessert."

Peter signals the waiter, who gives me a long list of pies, cakes, and ice cream. I go with the chocolate cream pie and a glass of milk.

"I'll be right back—bathroom run," I say when the waiter leaves the table.

When I see my reflection in the mirror, it stops me in my tracks. I am a white face, with deep, dark sinus shiners under my eyes. Halloween ready! All I need is a little fake blood and a cape and I can trick-or-treat as Dracula. I hunch over the sink and scrub my face. No wonder Peter looked at me in alarm—I look like the walking dead. Wait, I saw the dead tonight; they look better. I splash water on my face and see the image of a man standing behind me in the mirror. When I turn around, there is no one there.

- - -

My chocolate cream pie is waiting for me upon my return. I annihilate it. Peter is amused at my unabashed attack. "Would you like another slice?"

"Hmm." Do I?

He has left the majority of his meal on the plate. "You don't really seem to like the pot roast. Why do you order it?" I ask.

Peter looks down at his plate like he's just discovered he hasn't eaten much. "Actually, I do like it; I guess I just wasn't hungry tonight."

You didn't eat it the last time either, I want to say, but don't. "Not big on eating at home?" I ask.

He takes a moment, as if he has to think about it. "It's hard to plan. Sometimes I have a dinner meeting after work. Cooking for one doesn't seem worth it."

Peter opens the white envelope lying next to him. He has several clipped notes with either a check or money attached. He goes through each one. The first one is a check for $13.09 made out to Savoy Dry Cleaners. I'm picking up a suit and several shirts. Then there's a check for Halpern Pharmacy. He needs a prescription picked up but doesn't tell me what it is. The next list is a couple of things at the A&P for his mother to be paid with cash.

"Also stop at the ice cream parlor," he says, handing me the last note with $10 attached. "Get my dad a pint of the Neapolitan." I nod. "My mom may object, so don't advertise it. Once it's in the house, she won't deny him the pleasure."

"Your mom doesn't want him to eat ice cream?"

"She says he can't exercise, so no, I guess not. Julia worries about his weight."

"Is Julia a worrier?"

"She never used to be—at least I never saw it. Mom always seemed like she could handle anything."

Peter hands me keys to his apartment and mailbox. They are on a UCLA keychain. I hold it up, smiling. "Thought you might like that," he says with a smile.

Outside, the night air feels good on my face. I wonder if I'm still freakishly pale but can't bring myself to ask Peter. He looks at his watch. "I should walk with you to your building—it's 9:30."

Geez, what is this? I grew up in this city. This is my town! Why does everyone want to walk me home all of a sudden? I'm fucking thirteen. I fight demons for fuck's sake!

"This is not late. My dad lets me stay out to 11." I say.

"On a school night?"

"Peter, I'm thirteen. Besides, you live around the block; I'm three blocks the other way."

My intuition tells me Peter doesn't want to go back to his apartment. "What about your leg?" I ask.

"What about it?"

"Does it bother you?"

"You mean because of my limp?" I stare at his cane. "A little, but I need to walk."

I stop fighting, and he walks with me toward 2nd Avenue. "Did you ever think that someone pushed you into the cab?" I ask.

He stops and looks at me, like, "how the fuck did you know?" But his answer does not agree with his expression. "Why would someone want to push me, Jack?"

90

"I don't know. Lots of crazy people out there…"

Peter gives detailed instructions on where to hang the clothes when I pick them up from the dry cleaner and where to put his mail. He asks about school, about how I like Sister Elizabeth as a teacher. My strong subjects and other things.

Twenty-fourth Street is dimly lit between 2nd and 1st Avenues. Saint Sebastian church is boarded up, ready to be torn down and replaced with apartment buildings. Urban renewal or something like that. "I bet the church made a good penny on that sale," I say, not meaning to be as snide as I sound.

"Do I detect a little cynicism, Jack?"

Before I answer, we both hear the sound of someone walking behind us. When we turn, no one is there. We exchange glances. A rustling noise comes from inside the boarded-up church, the sound of a lid from a garbage can hitting cement in the distance.

"Is that someone standing on the side of the church?" I ask.

Peter looks. "I don't think so…" He encourages me to pick up the pace.

Night noises. Sirens in the distance. Footsteps. Windows shutting. Peter turns back again. Nothing.

"Peter, do you smell cigarette smoke?"

"Yes. I can't seem to get away from it."

We get to the corner of my apartment building on 1st Avenue. A man and woman come out of a small ethnic grocery store. Several people are walking. One of the people is Kasper Greenstreet. He is smoking a cigarette and staring at us from across the street. I should do something, but I don't. A bus drives past. Kasper Greenstreet vanishes.

When I get upstairs, I take out my notebook and add the pregnant woman who kept jumping in front of the subway train to my list of souls. On instinct, I add Peter Cairo's name. He is another soul I must look after.

KASPER GREENSTREET

It is a large studio apartment by New York standards but still small and cramped. The room is an artist's, filled with canvas boards, paint, and easels. Supplies fill every space in the room. Drop cloths are thrown all over an unmade bed; the small kitchenette is covered with paint brushes and bottles of finished and unfinished wine. Kasper Greenstreet, "king of the painted portrait, "smokes a cigarette" while working on the portrait of a woman. Several people he met at Mrs. Hudson Valley Lockjaw's party have commissioned him to do theirs or a loved one's portrait. It is beneath him, except when he cashes their checks.

Kasper laughs at himself. He knows he is full of shit but he loves his artistic temperament, displaying it whenever he can—even when he is alone. The portraits promise good money. They have also inspired him to create a very different kind of project. He begins by painting the most flattering portrait for the client as he can. Then he paints a second portrait that is abhorrent. Is it who he thinks they are inside? Maybe not fully, but he loathes most of them for their self-aggrandizing. He is in the midst of the second portrait of Mrs. Hudson Valley Lockjaw. Kasper is inspired; he hasn't had an original thought in years. The landscapes that Susan could sell were boring to paint. Now, he has finished with two people. The four portraits are covered in the corner.

He picks up his hunting knife and cuts the tip of his finger. Holding his finger over the paint, he drips his blood into the red and the blue pigment. Unhappy with the small amount of blood, he cuts another finger. Kasper is inspired by working on her eyes, lips, and jaw. The mix of blood in the paint is still not good enough after his third finger, so he cuts his wrist. Perfect; it provides a greater amount of blood in the paint. He mixes it, achieving the color he wants for the eyes, the lips.

Kasper is not a joyful person. He's fun, great to party with. But joyful? Never. "Happy" means nailing someone—preferably a dude. Love, joy, blah. But sex or drama? He is in! Love is what he feels for his work. He doesn't give a shit if anyone else likes it. He smokes another cigarette—a joint. Smoking a bone, music blasting, painting. Ah, bliss.

He studies the painting, especially the face, looking for the perfect amount of repulsion. However, he is still not content with the colors. Kasper grabs the knife and messes with the small cut on his wrist. He drips a small amount of blood directly on her lips. Not enough. Taking the point of the knife, he goes back for more and drips the blood into the paints in front of him. Mixes. Tries the lips again. Almost there. He takes the knife to his wrist again—and cuts too deep. The blood squirts. Kasper tries to get the blood into the paints. Shit, that hurt! Shit! Don't waste any.

He grabs a drop cloth and ties it around his wrist to control the bleeding. He picks up his paintbrush and goes back to work. Perfect. That's the color he wants.

Kasper works non-stop. Mrs. Hudson Valley Lockjaw looks amazing in a disturbing, psychological way. She captures all of his impressions of her. Happy with the results, he stops and pours himself a glass of wine. The drop cloth around his wrist is red with his blood. Fuck. He takes it off and tries to squeeze it into the paint. The wrist continues to bleed. Time for stitches? Kasper grabs another drop cloth and wraps it around the wrist. Same story. He might need to head to emergency but hates to stop working when he's on a roll. Another joint, another glass of wine, another hour.

Mrs. Hudson Valley Lockjaw is finished. Maybe he'll revisit her hands.

- - -

Bellevue Hospital's emergency room is a shit show. They stitch him up; however, there is a little snag. They think he cut his wrist on purpose, which of course he did, but not for the reason they think.

Dr. Bowler is the fourth person to ask the question "Tell me again, Mr. Greenstreet, what happened?" He asks it in that "caring doctor" way.

"I'm a painter, Doc, on canvas—not walls," Kasper says, thinking he should have avoided that last shot. His words slur. "Well, Doc—doctor—I sliced my paint tube, well, tried to slice my paint tube with a hunting knife. Missed and got my wrist."

The doctor doesn't believe him. Kasper's mind begins to race; I should get up, leave—I don't want them sending me to the psych ward. Shit, I didn't realize how buzzed I am, or how good-looking Dr. Bowler is...I'd like to get me some of that.

"Is there a problem, Doctor?" Kasper asks.

"I'll be honest with you...it looks deliberate."

"It was an accident! Why would I come here if I wanted to kill myself?" Kasper says, raising his voice.

Dr. Bowler stares at him.

"I have way too many good things going on right now but maybe a couple of years ago," Kasper says, trying to be funny. As an afterthought, he thinks he should just shut the fuck up. "I'm kidding, Doctor. Call my agent; she'll tell you."

Dr. Bowler takes Susan's number. "Someone should pick you up," he says. "You might not want to use sharp knives when you're drinking."

"You know, Doc, I'd love to paint you..." Kasper says, trying to be charming.

Dr. Bowler smiles. "I'm very busy."

- - -

About thirty-five minutes later, Mitch, not Susan, shows up. Dr. Bowler and Mitch hit it off, which annoys the shit out of Kasper. Mitch tells the doctor what a talented artist Kasper is. Flattery will get you everywhere, so Kasper's annoyance disappears.

Leaving the hospital, Mitch asks how it happened. Kasper vacillates between the story he told the hospital and the real one. "It's a long story, but it was an accident."

"Can you walk or do we need to get you a cab?" Mitch asks.

"Do you have time to come to my apartment?" Mitch looks at him. "I want to show you something."

"What do you want to show me?"

Kasper pretends he's insulted but isn't really; it's just the momentary role he plays. "You always think I'm on the make."

The apartment is just how he left it, music blasting, shit everywhere. The two portraits of Mrs. Hudson Valley Lockjaw lay side by side. Mitch is stunned. Kasper's not sure if it's the mess in the apartment he objects to or the paintings themselves. He uncovers the other two people that he's finished painting. "The Duke," in his fake uniform. One of the portraits reflects the outwardly dashing, handsome man he is; the other, the phony prick inside. Then there is "Peggy, Patron of the Arts" in all her jewels that radiate her social standing. The second portrait depicts a naked frightened woman trying to cover her private parts.

Mitch walks about the small apartment, unable to take his eyes off the paintings. He appears moved but taken aback at the same time. Kasper wants to grab him, shake him, and say, "well, what do you think?" But waits impatiently instead.

Finally, Mitch asks, "Have you shown these to anyone?"

"Just you."

"Is this why you cut your wrist?" Mitch says sarcastically making Kasper want to cut his. After a long-ass pause, Mitch says, "They're amazing."

Kasper walks over to him. "Don't fuck with me."

"I'm serious—I think they're amazing!"

Before he has a chance to continue, Kasper grabs his face, kissing him hard and long on the mouth.

"Hold that thought," Mitch says, before adding. "You need to show these to Susan. You need a few more for an exhibit."

Is he fucking kidding me? I just kissed him. This is that moment when it finally happens. We have been circling each other for months.

"Seriously. These are special," Mitch says, pointing to the portraits. His voice intrudes on Kasper's inner rant.

"Yes, I thought so, too." Kasper thinks: Ah, fuck it—a kiss is just a kiss, right? This is my artistic breakthrough! Fuck, I am so happy! Kasper grabs a half bottle of wine. "You want a glass?"

Mitch looks at his watch. "No. I'm already late."

Kasper pours himself some wine in a dirty glass.

Mitch walks to the door. Stops. Turns back to Kasper. "They're really wonderful!" He stands there, nodding his head. "They're amazing."

For a brief moment, Kasper thinks he's going to come back in. But Mitch turns and disappears into the hallway.

THE CAIROS

I walk into Woolworth's to look for a coloring book and crayons for Mr. Cairo. I'm not quite sure why, but it feels right. Today is the first time Julia is returning to her weekly canasta game, which will give me some time alone with Mr. Cairo. I've been thinking about the pictures appearing over his head. I want to work on that, maybe use the coloring to help with his inability to verbally communicate. I decided on a *Sword in the Stone* coloring book. Never read the novel but I did see the animated movie. Plus, I love metaphors. After getting the crayons, I grab myself a notebook to keep a few notes about Mr. Cairo.

Walking through Stuyvesant Town relaxes me. Fall is here—my favorite season. The leaves on the trees have the perfect amount of autumn color, the cool breeze on my face creates that perfect sway in the branches. It feels like God is in the trees all around me. Red and gold leaves float to the ground around my feet. I feel like I'm going to live forever. Of course, I know I won't, at least not in this form. My memories drift to Katherine and the kids. How much fun we used to have getting ready for the fall season and Halloween. Pumpkin patches, hayrides, putting scarecrows out on our front porch, carving pumpkins. It makes me sad, realizing Katherine will never be in my arms again.

The scream of a police siren shakes me out of my self-defeating thinking. "They're not real, Jack! You had an insult to the brain."

Shit, maybe none of this is real. Maybe it's all an illusion.

I ring the doorbell and knock twice before Julia answers the door. She is smartly dressed in black slacks, a white shirt, dangling earrings. She is beautiful. However, I am immediately hit with the smell of vinegar. It flows off of her body in waves. "Come in, Jack; I like a man who is on time."

Julia is always polite, naturally charming. Well, she once was. Now she is a bag of nerves. "I don't know why my son is insisting I get back to my normal activities. Nothing is normal," she says, fluttering around the apartment, looking for her purse.

Mr. Cairo is sitting in the living room in his wheelchair. He greets me with a waving "?" It appears like a flag blowing in a soft breeze.

"Hi, Mr. Cairo. I brought you a coloring book." I hold it up. "*The Sword in the Stone*. Maybe we can work on it later."

The smell of sauerkraut fills the room before I realize Julia is behind me. Gone is the vinegar smell. "I don't know if that is a good idea," she says. "He has no use of his right hand; Pop is a righty. I don't want to frustrate him."

Julia takes the coloring book but not the crayons. She places it on top of the refrigerator. I wonder if that was where she placed things when Peter was little and she didn't want him to have something. The ice cream sits on the counter; she doesn't see it.

"Here is Helen's number," Julia says, pointing to a pad by the phone. "Call me if you need something." She stops. The smell of vinegar returns. "This is stupid; I don't even care about canasta. I'm not going."

Mr. Cairo looks at her, a "noose" hanging over his head. I'm not sure what that means.

"Oh, Julia, please go!" I say. "I brought the coloring book because when I was in therapy, they would have me color—it helped me with coordination. It can be soothing," I lie.

I Really have to stop that. The vinegar smell is overwhelming. Does Mr. Cairo smell it, I wonder? "Besides, Mr. Cairo wants you to go…don't you, Mr. Cairo?"

Julia is looking at me; I can't read her face. She would make a fine poker player. I'm looking at Mr. Cairo when a bobblehead appears over his head. I can't make out the team—maybe the Mets —nodding yes. She walks over to Mr. Cairo. He has a broken, crooked smile, which kind of makes him look weird, but it's a smile nonetheless. A big red heart hovers over his head. Then the bobblehead returns—his head rocking in a forward motion—clearly it means yes. Mr. Cairo reaches out to her with his left hand. The vinegar smell dissipates.

Julia holds his hand in both of hers. After a moment, she gently places it back on the chair. She turns, picks up her purse, and places a sweater over her shoulders. "I'm over by playground five, so call me if you need anything. I can be back in ten minutes. Okay?"

"Don't worry about us, Julia; we will be fine." I can smell her perfume now. The smells clearly accompany her emotions.

The minute Julia is out the door, I show Mr. Cairo the ice cream. "From Peter," I say. A big block of ice cream appears over his head, followed by the blue blanket that represents Peter. "You want some now?"

A door shuts. I want to be sure so I ask again. The door shuts again. "That means no, correct?" I say, confirming what I already know. The bobblehead nods yes.

I put the ice cream in the freezer and take the coloring book off the refrigerator. I bring out my little notebook and write down some of the symbols that Mr. Cairo has shared with me, as well as their meanings. I say them out loud to confirm, and to let him know I understand him.

"Heart equals Julia, blue blanket equals Peter, bobblehead equals yes, closing door equals no, question mark equals me, and gun equals detective."

"Coloring book?" Nothing. "Coloring book?"

After a minute, a rainbow appears. "So, a rainbow means a coloring book?" I ask. Nothing. We stare at one another. "Coloring book?" Rainbow. "Rainbow is for the coloring book?" Blank stare. "Bobblehead means yes. Correct?" Nothing. "Mr. Cairo? Bobblehead is yes?" Silence. "Yes?" I get the bobblehead. "No." I get the door shutting. It's confusing—is it because he thinks he's saying or thinking yes, or no? When I give the image or symbol first, that becomes a completely new word.

I pick up the TV Guide. "Television?"

Rabbit ears appear immediately. Not the antenna rabbit ears that sit on top of the TV but actual rabbit ears. Flipping through the listings, I find the

4:30 movie. "It's *To Kill a Mockingbird*," I say, looking up at him. "Do you know it? The movie *To Kill a Mockingbird*?"

Woody Woodpecker. No shit, it's Woody Woodpecker over his head. I bust out laughing but quickly contain myself. "No. Not Woody Woodpecker—a mockingbird."

The door shuts. I smile at him.

In the living room, Julia has a bookshelf with the *Encyclopedia Britannica* prominently displayed. I imagine Peter spending a lot of time with these books when he was in school.

Hoping that I can find a picture of a mockingbird, I rifle through them and come upon a picture of northern mockingbirds. The story is based in the south, but this will serve its purpose. Mr. Cairo looks at the picture, then back at me, a little confused.

"Mockingbird," I say. "This is a mockingbird."

He nods. "Have you seen the movie?" Bobblehead. "Do you like Gregory Peck?" Nothing. "Do you know who Gregory Peck is?" Bobblehead. "Good, so you know Gregory Peck." Door shutting. Now I'm confused. "It doesn't matter."

An image of a wind storm blows papers all over the street, the whole scene above his head. His face is red, like he's constipated. "Do you have to go to the bathroom, Mr. Cairo?" Door shutting. "Are you upset?" Door shutting. "Angry?" Door shutting. "So, you don't remember who Gregory Peck is—it's no big deal." The wind storm blows papers around in a whirlpool. It gets bigger! Shit! Now what, Jack?

"Are you frustrated?" The wind settles down. Bobblehead. "Ohhh. I'm sorry. You're frustrated because you know who Gregory Peck is, but you can't picture him?" Bobblehead. "It's okay Mr. Cairo you'll get there." Bobblehead.

Then boom! A big whale! "Gregory Peck?" A big whale?

Now I'm confused again. I remember watching a little bit of *Moby Dick* with my dad, thus the whale. Bogart was the Fedora because he made a great detective in the movies. Gregory Peck was Ahab in the movie, but the whale was what his brain could identify.

"How about some ice cream, Mr. Cairo?"

Bobblehead.

Afterwards, Mr. Cairo takes a nap in his wheelchair while I explore the apartment. It really is a nice three-bedroom, far superior to our railroad flat. Peter's room still holds all his awards and school pennants from Xavier and UCLA. The bed is more grown up. One of the bedrooms is set up like a den with a convertible couch, paneled walls, lots of books—very nice. The bathroom is super nice, although a chair sits in the tub to help with Mr. Cairo's disability. The medicine cabinet is overflowing with prescriptions—mainly for Mr. Cairo, but Julia has one or two as well. Valium. The master bedroom looks like it must have been very nice; however, now it's accommodating a sick person. There is a bedside commode, towels on chairs, a bedpan, adult diapers. I feel bad for prying and quickly leave the room.

Mr. Cairo stirs. I put the TV on, but he doesn't seem interested in watching the movie or anything else. "How about we color?" Door shuts. "Honestly, Mr. Cairo, I think it will be helpful for you. Until you get the use of your right hand back, you need the left hand to work better."

Nothing. But nothing is not a no. I go into my story about how the doctors didn't think I'd walk again. Blah, blah, blah. It's kind of boring talking about yourself, especially when you've told the story a few times before. Right now, I'm fascinated with people—well, certain people. Mr. Cairo, Julia, and Peter are part of that group. Mental note: I must add Mr. Cairo to my book of souls.

I wave the *Sword in the Stone* coloring book in the air, and he acquiesces. I push the wheelchair to the dining table, get the crayons, and open the book to page one. He has no control and scribbles all over the page. The wind storm blows papers up in the air above his head. Mr. Cairo tries again, scribbles more; the wind storm gets bigger. He flips the page. More of the same—it's bad, no control. Wind blows papers above his head.

"Okay, you're frustrated." Bobblehead. "Why? You just started."

He's clumsy turning the page. Tries again. The wind storm continues to blow papers.

"I couldn't stay on the page, never mind in the lines," I lied. The image changes to a field goal post with a football going through the middle. "I understand, Mr. Cairo—you want to stay in between the lines. That will be the goal. Practice. You'll get there, I promise." Will he? I hope so...

Julia seems happy that she went to play canasta. She smells like peppermint. She asks me if I want to stay for dinner. I'm too tired. I just want to go home.

Stuyvesant Town looks different in the dark. For some reason, it is deserted as I walk home. I've only seen one person. It is a cold autumn night, the only comfort for me is the birds singing in the trees. Guess they are the last that haven't flown south for the winter, or perhaps they're just the cold-weather kind.

Birds explode from the trees, startling the shit out of me. The blast makes me stop, regroup. I pick up the pace—then I'm stopped again by the mischief of rats and a nest of mice scurrying across the walkways, spooked for some unnatural reason by some unnatural being. It skeeves me out, watching their convulsive movements, along with their hissing, squealing sound. I jump onto a bench to get away from them. I know the reason for their fear.

They're out... I feel them... smell them.

It is me they want. These creatures are stalking me, but I am too tired to fight right now. Noises become amplified; lights are exaggerated. I know the drill; confusion is their weapon. The rats and mice scurry off to their hiding spots. Hopping off the bench, I run to 1st Avenue. I just want to get home. First Avenue is a welcome sight, even with the magnified noise and lights that give birth to a headache.

- - -

I am safe—home! Though our apartment will never be as nice as the Cairos' aesthetically. My headache increases, but I try to keep up my end of the conversation during dinner.

"You look tired, Jack. I hope you're not over doing it."

"I'm not, Dad."

"I know you like the Cairos, but wouldn't you rather join a team at the boys club?"

"No," I answer, wishing I could tell him all the things I'm feeling, doing, seeing. If he really knew what happened that day in the subway, I'm not sure he could handle it. Never mind the mediums, Tarot readers, yoga, and meditating in which I've immersed myself. Dad's been through enough with me; I don't want to put this supernatural shit in his lap.

I turn in early and make a pitiful attempt at reading my history book. A long blink turns into sleep.

Drifting in and out of a dream, I hear the sounds of an animal scurrying on the wall. Are they in the wall? It wakes me up. I'm sure that I'm not dreaming, only that I am in a bed that is not mine. The room is dark, with just a hint of light under a door. The noise increases; it takes me a minute to spot something crawling on the wall. It is much too large to be a rat or a mouse. I watch it crawl up the wall onto the ceiling but I can't move. My voice doesn't come. More scurry up the walls, across the ceiling. I freeze with fear. The room is very cold—cold enough to see my breath. Something's gotten ahold of my blanket and is pulling it slowly down. Sounds of the Cicadoidea bugs fill the room. They join the shadows on the ceiling and continue hissing. It smells. Why can't I move? Where is my dad?

The room is freezing. I am unable to cover myself. Unfamiliar noise pulsates all around, confusing me. Something's on the bed! It is a monumental task to separate my lips. There's no sound from me, but I am drowning in noise.

Shadows and bugs crawl up the walls to the ceiling as birds fly around the room. It is complete chaos. Shadows cling to the walls, which spin faster and faster like an out-of-control merry-go-round. Faster! Faster! They jump and fall from the ceiling onto my bed; there is nothing I can do. I'm trying to scream and kick but I am paralyzed. They are on me. Creatures crawl up my legs, grabbing my arms, holding me down. One changes form and wraps itself around my neck like a snake, choking me. In my ears, my nose, my mouth, they crawl. Close your mouth, Jack! It's too late to scream. Close your ears. Stop breathing so they can't get in your nose! It is too late. They are on me, sliding in me. My ears are filled with them. However, it does not lessen the noise—instead, it makes it unbearably loud. My nose—I can feel them entering—they stink! I clench my teeth in a last-ditch effort to keep them from crawling down my throat. It's too late—they are choking me. I fight to stay conscious.

Someone turns on the lights. It's incredibly bright. My lids are closed, but the light hurts my eyes. People and creatures circle me. Some are trying to help me. The ones helping me are dressed in white. They are yelling at me, but I can't understand; their language is foreign. I fight to get the creatures off me—out of me. But they are halfway down my throat; I'm choking on them.

It is bedlam all around me, but I just want to sleep. Let me sleep! Several people have my mouth open; they are trying to pull those things out!

"Jack! Stay with us! Jack!" My ears are clearing. They must have gotten them from inside my ears—my head. "Code blue! Code blue!"

What are they saying? They are trying to crack a code, to get those things out of me before they nest. Why are they in my body? I need to push them out. Exhale! Exhale! Blow them out! The man in white is pulling him by the tail, from inside my jaws. He is sweating. The woman in white is clearing them from my nose. What are these things? Why do they smell so bad? Don't let them nest, Jack. Don't let them feed on you. Must fight!

- - -

"Jack? Jack, wake up!"

It's Dad. I'm fully dressed, drenched in my own sweat, in my bed. I stare at him blankly, trying to clear the cobwebs from my head.

"You were having a nightmare. Flopping around like you were fighting with someone."

My history book is sticking in my side. "Sorry," I say.

Dad stands there for a moment. "Don't be ridiculous. You okay?"

Nodding my head, I lie. "Just having a bad dream, I guess."

- - -

I'm remembering all the things I want to forget. Forgetting all the things I want to remember. My son Stevie is on my mind, but I can't indulge that. I roll over, praying for sleep.

SISTER ELIZABETH

Sister Elizabeth is a puzzle to me; one-minute she is loving and kind, the next minute harsh. I watch her from a safe distance as she pushes her shopping cart around the A&P like anyone else buying groceries. Sister Elizabeth is with one of the retired nuns who taught at Epiphany several years back. She had quite a reputation at the end of her tenure. Personally, I never had her as a teacher; she left while I was still in the lower grades. So, my impression of her comes from the tales that filtered down through the years from kids who experienced her in the classroom. "Boy, did she have a right hook." "Don't want to get her mad!" "They made her retire…" The older nun looks perfectly harmless to me now.

While pushing a shopping cart, I keep my distance, working off a list Peter gave me. He is very specific; he never wants the cheap brand. Dad and I always look for the bargains.

I receive an image of Sister Elizabeth as a teenager carrying a pocketbook into church. There are just a few parishioners in the pews, which is what she counts on. She dips her hand into the holy water font and blesses herself. She looks around and takes a small Tupperware container out of her purse and quickly fills it with holy water.

"Following us, Mr. Kelly?" Sister Elizabeth asks as I read the label. Peter wants Dijon mustard for sandwiches, not just any mustard. As well as Earl Grey tea; none of that Lipton stuff. "Jack, would you mind grinding the coffee for me at the machine instead of buying one of those mass coffees like Yuban?" he writes on the list. Why would I mind?

"No, Sister," I say, looking up from my Earl Grey tea hunt. "Just doing a little shopping." Geez, nuns really like you to think they have eyes in the back of their heads. However, I've learned through the years that they use gimmicks, like using pictures on a wall that can give off reflections, to see what's going on behind them.

"Do you do the shopping at home?" the nun with the right hook asks.

"Not really." Stop talking, Jack. "It's a long, boring story."

"I'll be the judge of that," the older sister says.

I look to Sister Elizabeth for help, but she doesn't give me any. We stand there in awkward silence as I hold the Earl Grey tea in my hand.

"Well…" I feel pressured to talk, to tell a story that isn't their business. "I have a job." The old nun stands with her arms crossed, clearly wanting more information. "I pick up a few things at the store for Peter, so while I'm here I get what dad and I need."

"Who's Peter?" the older nun demands.

None of your business ladies, I think. "You don't know him."

"How do you know I don't know him?" she says tartly. I move to her left in case she wants to throw a punch.

Shit. Really? "Peter Cairo," I say in spite of myself.

"Cairo? Peter Cairo?" The old nun repeats. "Yes, I taught him in seventh grade," she says. "Cairo, it's an odd name. That's how I remember it."

I'm done with this one. I turn my cart to escape down the bread aisle. While I try to casually move away, the older nun says, "I heard he had an accident after his divorce. Fell in front of a cab." There's a long pause, and then, I'm not sure if she actually says the words or if I'm picking it up, but she adds, "probably jumped."

Sister Elizabeth puts her hand on the older nun's shoulder to gracefully lead her away. "Let Mr. Kelly finish his work," she says, looking at me compassionately. "Getting a job at your age to help at home shows good character, Jack. Don't forget to do your homework."

Off they go. As they walk away, I think of Peter—he jumped in front of a cab? No... pushed! I watch the two nuns from behind, their habits mixing with the fashion of the late '70s creating a dream-like visual for me. They seem so out of place. It is as if I'm watching two dinosaurs at the zoo.

The minute I walk into Peter's apartment, I'm hit with the strong smell of cigarettes and the overpowering sense that I am not alone. Standing in the foyer with the box of groceries in my hands, my initial reaction is to run. But I don't. Instead, I put the box of groceries on the kitchen counter and find a big butcher's knife for protection. Keeping my back against the wall, I move into the dining room. From this area of the apartment, the living room is exposed to me. I see nothing and no one. Just smell a strong cigarette and paint smell. The window blinds are up, and my classroom sits empty across the street.

Sweat forms on my upper lip as I stop in front of the bathroom. It too is empty. Peter's bedroom door is slightly open. I shuffle in front of it and think I should have called someone. What if Mr. Greenstreet is here? Carefully I push the door open with my foot.

KASPER GREENSTREET

Kasper Greenstreet sits in front of his easel, a half glass of Cognac in a brandy snifter, a partially smoked joint in an ashtray. An empty blood vial lies next to the paint.

No more cutting his wrist to get blood. He has a dear friend, well, a good friend, a friend with whom he shares pot and Quaaludes and who happens to be a nurse. She draws several tubes of blood for him every week, which he keeps in the refrigerator until he needs them for his paintings. He's not sure if the blood enhances the colors or gives him inspiration. Quite frankly he doesn't care. Kasper is doing the best work of his life. When Susan and Mitch came by to see the work, she flipped. She's organizing a huge showing.

Susan is also trying to get several prominent people, famous and infamous alike, to participate in the double portrait.

The first is Ricardo Hillibrand. Someone Kasper had a ball working with. Ricardo Hillibrand is a famous, older New York architect. He built many of the iconic buildings in and around New York City. Mr. Hillibrand was a young genius of a man when he built the spectacular Clymer Art Deco building for a Wall Street tycoon with the same name. He became famous as the "boy genius," enjoying celebrity more than he enjoyed work, and he loved his work. Mr. Hillibrand is as vain as he is famous. He has been married to an heiress, a movie star, and a hat check girl—just a few of his many lovers. He made a fortune, spent a fortune. To say he's had a colorful life would be an understatement.

At the meeting, Susan told him about the project with great enthusiasm; he was only half interested.

Susan excused herself, and Kasper began his sales pitch. He told Mr. Hillibrand he worshipped his work, that it was equal to the great cathedrals and palaces of Europe and that his buildings would outlast them all. "People tour New York just to see them." Closing the deal, with a whisper, "I want to paint you in the nude, make you as iconic in oil as your buildings are in steel." Mr. Hillibrand stared at him for a moment before the smile came to his face. The man is very vain. His ego is the size of New York. He works out every day, has had several facelifts, loves the press.

When Kasper begins work on a portrait, he starts by taking photos of the person in different poses, then sketches them in the three poses he likes best. The actual painting, he does alone. While in the studio with his subject, Kasper spends his time flattering them so they are at ease. He needs them to be all in on what he's trying to accomplish. He pretends to worship him. He is everything that's been written—and more. Kasper even has the pleasure of nailing him on multiple occasions. Guess those "switch hitter" stories about him are true. Mr. Hillibrand loved being nude, not an ounce of modesty.

In the first portrait, Kasper paints various parts of his most iconic buildings as body parts. The massive stained-glass windows on the landmark train station he designed can be seen in his eyes. The famous murals in the lobby of his most prestigious buildings become his brain. The iconic 100-foot spire and gargoyles from his Clymer Art Deco building become his private parts. The black apartment towers on Riverside Drive merge with his legs.

For the second portrait, Kasper contrasts the power of his work with that of an aging man with a crumbling body that hasn't built something new in twenty-five years. His legs are bent from the weight of his age, arthritis, excessive living. Hungry eyes reveal his hedonistic tendencies. His lustful tongue protrudes from his lips. An upturned nose and chin reflect his pride and vanity.

No one but Mitch and Susan have seen any of the finished work. On one of the days, Kasper is working with Mr. Hillibrand, Mitch comes to see him. He wants to talk about business, but Kasper is in the beginning stages of photographing Mr. Hillibrand. They have been drinking wine; it is clear to anyone there has been sex. Anyone but Mitch. Mr. Hillibrand is naked; Kasper in boxer shorts, no shirt. Mitch stands awkwardly in his sports jacket and tie. They make quite a threesome.

Mitch is clearly uncomfortable and doesn't stay long. "This can wait," Mitch says, shuffling around the room. "Work first—tried to call, but you're not answering your phone."

"I never answer my phone when I work. You know that…" Kasper says.

Mitch never mentions anything about that afternoon. Was he jealous? Did he need a drink the minute he left? Not sure if it was the male nudity that made him uptight, or the fact that Kasper was clearly having sex with Mr. Hillibrand. Doesn't matter—all that matters to Kasper at the moment is the work.

Kasper drags his drunk ass through the shower; he's running late to meet Susan and Mitch. Susan has never been as excited to show anyone's work. She can hardly contain her exuberance. They all agree Kasper's work comes first, but he is chronically late, even when he's not working.

Susan is sitting alone in a booth when Kasper arrives. He slides in next to her. "I'm not used to seeing you so happy, Kasper," she says.

"Yeah?" he says, looking around for Mitch. Happy? Happiness… it's not sustainable. Kasper doesn't think in those terms. Inspiration is the only emotion he wants or desires.

"Where is Mitch?"

"Running late," Susan says, sipping her martini.

"Late? He's never late," Kasper says, calling the waiter. It's been an hour since he's sipped or smoked something.

Susan laughs. "I know," she says as Kasper orders a glass of red wine.

"I'm glad we're alone—I never get you alone," he says.

"Oh, that's not true…" She has this "Jackie O" thing about her.

"Can I paint you for the collection?"

Susan stiffens, and then looks up as Mitch comes in and walks toward the table. He picks up the wine that the waiter has just dropped off for Kasper and takes a taste.

"Same," he says before the waiter leaves.

Mitch and Susan share a glance. It speaks volumes. It's "hello, my love, how was your day, missed you," without a word.

"I've asked Susan if I could do her portrait for the show," Kasper says.

"Does she have to get naked?" Mitch says rather defensively.

"Only if she wants to."

Smiles all around. I'm guessing he did not brush that afternoon off... Kasper's ego likes that.

"As flattered as I am," Susan says. "I'm not sure as your agent I should be in the show."

They drink.

"What about Mitch here?" Susan offers. Before Kasper has a chance to contribute, Mitch says. "I won't be getting naked."

Raising his glass, Kasper says, a bit too harshly, "No one wants you naked."

Susan quickly brings out her notepad with dates and places for the show. "My gallery is too small," she adds dramatically. "This is going to be a happening—the event of the season."

"I've finished Mr. Hillibrand, and I've sketched Desiree Diamond."

"You did?" Mitch is impressed.

Desiree Diamond is a supermodel. She exploded onto the scene like a supernova about five years ago. Now a heroin addict, she hasn't been on a magazine cover in a year.

"Your call," Susan says. "Not sure how reliable..."

"I got some really good sketches—probably going to skip the photography part—don't want to scare her."

The three are great playmates, laughing like kids or close cousins. Mitch is the most uptight, which makes it easy for Susan and Kasper to tease him. He laughs at himself, which Kasper finds charming.

"I'll leave it up to you guys which one of you I should paint," Kasper says, being naughty.

"What about a self-portrait?" Mitch asks.

Susan quickly chimes in. "That's brilliant."

DUSTING OF SPIRITS

Holding the knife steady, I pull up the bedspread. Nothing, not even a pair of slippers. I walk to the closet quietly and put my hand on the door knob, turning it slowly before swinging the door open, my knife in hand. Nothing. Just the most organized closet I have ever seen. Peter has shoe racks, sweaters, suits organized by colors, tie holders, shirts with tags still on them. It amazes me—the meticulous level of detail.

A noise from the living room brings me back to fight mode. A trace of smoke floats in the air. It is smoke, right? I do another lap around the apartment and find nothing.

How can I tell Peter that I see a man in the apartment from my classroom? Kasper Greenstreet? How can I tell him that this guy may be some kind of lunatic? Why does he come to Peter's apartment in the middle of the day? What is it he wants?

Down in the lobby, I get Peter's mail. I look at the names on every mailbox. No Greenstreet. I know I saw that name on the buzzer. Who is Kasper Greenstreet?

A well-dressed, middle-aged woman comes into the mail area. She looks me over. "Good afternoon, ma'am," I say with my best Catholic schoolboy manners and a smile. "I work for Peter Cairo, 3C."

She nods. "Don't know him."

I pick something up from her, so I ask, "Do you know Kasper Greenstreet?"

Long pause. "Don't know him either," she says, closing her mailbox. She checks to make sure it's locked, looks at her mail, and says, "I did know the Michaels briefly." She sees the puzzled look on my face. "They lived in 3C when I first moved in the building—before the last two tenants—and your Peter Cairo."

There is something here; she is telling me something. Although, I'm not exactly sure what.

"The Michaels?" I ask.

"Yes. Mitch and Susan Michaels." She glides past me.

"How long ago?" I yell after her.

Turning back like someone is taking her photo, she assesses me before speaking.

"How long ago?" I repeat, nodding like an idiot. "Yes. How long ago did they live in 3C?"

She smiles. She is beautiful. "Time—I'm not very good with time. Could be four years, could be six." She turns to leave, then looks back at me. "Why do you want to know?"

I hunch my shoulders. "Because you mentioned them, didn't mention any of the other tenants."

I get the feeling from her that her thoughts are like pictures, photos. Her posture conveys a pose, an emotion. She is thinking now, touching her hair.

"No one has lasted in the apartment very long since the Michaels," she says.

"Do you know where they went?" I ask.

She raises an eyebrow, hand on her left hip. "No. I didn't really know them." She's lying. "All I know is they owned an art gallery."

INTUITION?

All twenty-six of us sit with our hands folded on our desks, watching the clock, waiting to go to the Natural History Museum on 79th Street. It is the first of three class trips we will take this year. Sister Elizabeth and three chaperones—my classmates' mothers—will break us into two groups of thirteen kids. We will walk to the 23rd Street subway and head uptown to West 79th Street. I haven't been back in the subway since the last adventure, and truth be told it had me up last night thinking about it. Sister gives each of us two subway tokens and cautions us to hang onto them.

"Otherwise, it's a long walk," she says, knowing she would never allow us to walk.

Sister Elizabeth has a formula for dividing the class, but it is a secret to us. Unfortunately, I am in her group. The goal is to keep all of us together. She also insists on a buddy system. Bobby Mac is mine. We have known one another since we were six, so it's an easy friendship. It is all regimented. The class breaks into pairs and walks to the subway station. Bobby and I spend a lot of time talking about sports. Bobby asks me what I've been up to lately. How can I explain?

It is the quintessential fall day. Red and gold leaves fall from trees, reminding me that winter is coming. The sky is sunny and blue as we descend down the stairs into the belly of the city.

My classmates are making way too much noise for me to pick anything up. I'm grateful for that. One of the mothers keeps saying, "Stay together, stay together." She is new to this and nervous. Everyone has their tokens. Sister makes us go through the turnstiles single file so she can take a head count. Embarrassing. Most of the early morning rush hour has quieted down, so it is not hectic. Sister Elizabeth leads the way to the platform where they corral us so no one runs off or jumps in front of a train. Just kidding.

Finally, the train pulls into the station. There are plenty of seats. A couple of the boys swing on the bars and immediately get yelled at. I grab a seat. Sister orders everyone to sit; she will not put up with any bullshit or kids getting hurt. At our second stop, a young man of approximately twenty-five steps on to our car. He is clearly on drugs. The nervous mother is horrified. "Stay together," she chirps anxiously. None of us has moved. Stumbling, he almost lands in Peggy's lap. She immediately jumps up and squeezes in with a few of the girls across from him. Giggles and drama all around.

The train moves in a swaying motion, which appears to rock the man to sleep. Actually, he has fallen into an "opioid nod." In his opioid dream, he finds himself walking along a stream on a mountain range. I close my eyes and "dream walk" into the man's vision. The serenity of the landscape is overshadowed by the thinness of the air, the eerie silence, the lack of natural sounds. The sounds of steel wheels interrupt my perception. His head rolls; his world is not this world. Lights flicker on and off for several seconds. Watching the man in his drugged-out state, I get a glimpse of his heroin desire, trading five minutes of catatonic wonderment for days or weeks of torture.

The lights go off. I lean back and wait with no anticipation for their return.

Stepping back into his dream, I prepare myself for the shallowness of the air, which affects my breathing. In the uncomfortable silence, it is clear to me that I am not alone. Fog rolls through, disturbing his idyllic landscape along the stream. Two shadows appear then disappear, creating a heightened level of fear in the man, who does not realize he is the master of his dream. He stumbles. I walk faster in an attempt to catch up to him and the shadows. Something wicked has followed me into this man's dream. Without warning, a force drags me out of this nightmare back into the train car. This creature with its horse head and burnt flesh locks me in a full nelson, pulling me out of my seat and smashing the glass in the window behind me. With its intense power, the dark force begins dragging me out of the window by my throat, my mouth. Its intent is to silence me. Prevent me from helping!

Lights flicker. Shadows, demons, and ghosts occupy our train car. Two spirits appear to be surrounding the drug addict—the shadows from his dream? Demons crawl along the ceiling with their horse heads and skeletal bodies. My upper torso is outside the subway car in the tunnel. The tunnel itself is dark, strangely silent. Swinging wildly, I fight to stay inside the car. I grab hold of the side of the window and bite down on its claw-like hand, which covers my mouth. It screeches, tightening its grip, its nails breaking my skin. Its fingers are between my teeth. I chomp down on them. The taste is awful. Spitting out its half finger, I grab at its demonic face, fighting with every bit of spirit I can muster. I pull myself back inside the train. The lights flash in schizophrenic fashion. I wrap my feet around the top pole for support, but the creature pulls the top half of my body back into the darkness, where the silence has been replaced by piercing sounds of animal screams.

As I hold onto the inside of the train, its nails tighten on my neck. I fight like an animal, biting anywhere I can on its body—its hand, arm, chest. My hand crawls up its scaly, hairy, nasty face until I find its eyes. Reaching up, I poke and pull at them. I use my index finger and thumb to push into the socket with all my might, grabbing hold of the eyeball until I have it firmly between my fingers. I yank it from the socket, and the creature's screech matches the sound of the train wheels. It loosens its grip; I meet its strength with mine. Working my way back into the train car, I turn to face the creature, grabbing at its other eye. It tries to defend itself. Only, it is too late—I have the other eyeball in my hand, blinding it. It lets go of me completely, digging its nails into the ceiling of the train car for stability.

The lights continue to flash as I take hold of the train strap. I am stuck between reason and delusion, lost in the "in-between," with only instinct as my guide.

I swing from the handles like a swashbuckling pirate and kick the creature out of the window into the dark tunnel of the subway. It bounces between the walls of the tunnel and train before disappearing into darkness.

I hear a loud gasp come from the addict and watch as his soul is ripped from his body by two shadows. Lights on the train go dark.

Sister Elizabeth, the nervous mother, and my classmates stare at me, standing on the seat in fight mode.

"Mr. Kelly," Sister says. It takes me a moment to understand that no one else has witnessed anything, but the window behind me is broken. "Mr. Kelly," she says, louder and firmer this time. "Are you all right?"

Before I can answer, I see the addict is dead. His eyelids are open, eyes rolled back, jaw gaping and slack. "He's dead," I say, pointing.

"Oh, my God!" the nervous mother cries out. Sister reaches up for the rosary beads around her neck. The kids closest to his body jump away as if there is danger in his stillness.

We pull into the station.

Two women step onto the train as the doors open. Immediately they understand the gravity of the situation. One of the women pulls the emergency cord to keep the train stopped. The other steps back onto the platform and calls for help.

We are in limbo, standing or sitting on the platform as the police get the body ready for removal. A transit officer and an NYPD officer are speaking to Sister. The nervous mother, as well as most of my classmates, watch me. Peggy stands next to me. "Are you okay?"

"Yeah. Are you?"

Peggy turns her back to the group and faces me. "You are white as a ghost." Shit, not again. I know the look she is talking about; not flattering! "You looked like you were having some kind of fit on the train. You broke the window," she adds.

"What?" She looks around as Bobby walks over. "What was I doing?"

"Shaking like you were being electrocuted," Peggy says. "Bouncing off the window, swinging wildly," Bobby adds. "Why are you so white?"

"Jack, you have scratches on your neck," Peggy says.

Sister Elizabeth walks toward me. "You two—over there." Peggy and Bobby walk away. "How are you feeling, Mr. Kelly? Where did you get those scratches?"

"Fine, Sister. I wasn't aware of the scratches."

"When was the last time you saw a doctor?" she asks, like a prosecuting attorney.

"A month ago, I think."

"I need to have a conversation with your father."

"Why?"

"Why what, Mr. Kelly?"

"Why do you need to talk to my father?" Then as an afterthought, I ask, "Why can't you talk to me?"

"Excuse me?" Her tone is not friendly.

"I'd like to know what you would say to my father about my health that you can't say to me."

Sister glares at me. "You want to know why I want to talk to your father?" I can see she's mad. Poor choice of words. "Where do I begin, Mr. Kelly? I am concerned..." She doesn't finish.

We stare at each other. How about just saying "it looked like you were having some kind of fit on the train?" Stop looking at me like I'm one of those haunted spirits that tortured the shit out of that young man who just died. The same ones that were attacking me during the train ride. Because quite frankly, Sister, I am not wicked. I'm just some kid overwhelmed with the spirit world since I woke up from a coma after a near-death experience.

Of course, I say none of those things. "Yes, you should talk to my dad if you'd like."

Sister walks away with the flair of a bullfighter who has just slayed the bull.

- - -

Sister Elizabeth makes the decision to abandon the museum. I couldn't agree more. What a fucking morning. I'm exhausted. Say a prayer for the dead man, Jack, and add him to your book of souls.

She decides we will walk back to school, since we did not get very far on the subway. "Let that be a lesson to all of you! Stay away from drugs!" she says to the class.

All of us mourn for the man, for ourselves, for the day we did not have.

"Are you okay?" Asks the nervous mom. She looks at me with empathy.

121

There is also something else in her eyes. Understanding? For my health? My dilemma with Sister? Or was she picking up something on the train as well? A question I wish I could ask.

We walk in a pack. Sister Elizabeth leads the group. As we head back to school, the trees are in full autumn glory, leaves falling quietly and decorating the concrete streets. Autumn makes me feel like I did when I fell in love with Katherine, like everything is possible. Today, I allow myself to swim in the memory of her...

Standing underneath a maple tree on campus, a California fall day. I lean in and kiss her lips, her mouth, her neck. That long, beautiful neck. Nibbling, I whisper, "I loved you before I met you." Katherine laughs, throwing her head back. I remember thinking—oh no, Jack, you're moving too fast with the "I love you." But she looks at me, all smiles. "Be careful, Jack Kelly, I may never let you go." That was one of the happiest days of my life.

Jack! There is not and never was a Katherine; an insult to the brain created her. How, how could it have done that? How can I ever let her go?

The honking horns of midtown traffic rouse me from my daydream. Several of us get caught at the red light on 34th Street, including the nervous mother. She is in full conversation with two of the girls in my class. She sees me, smiles, continues talking. Thank God for her, because getting caught at the light by myself would have caused Sister Elizabeth to see it as a slight to her authority.

I'm living in my head until the biggest woman I have ever seen stands next to me at the light. I'm not talking fat. I am talking physically large, tall, big arms, legs, ass. She is a black woman with a huge blonde wig, gold skirt, frilly coat, and dangling earrings.

"Look at this shit!" I hear her say.

"What?" I ask.

She gives me a side glance from under the longest fake eyelashes I've ever seen. "I'm just going to do it. I'm going to put on my skin-tight white rhinestone dress and eat a bottle of sleeping pills. Go to bed and never wake the fuck up!"

Okay. I'm "picking it up." She hasn't verbalized anything.

"No. Maybe I'll get in the tub, write a suicide note. Name names, slice my wrists."

Shit, I think, looking down at her mammoth-sized feet in stiletto heels. Say something to her, Jack; you've been handed another chance today.

"Don't do it. Nothing can be that bad," I say quickly.

She looks over and down at me, puzzled. This time she points with her jumbo hands and painted nails to herself. "You talking to me?" she says in a breathless voice that does not fit her body. Here we go. This woman can literally pick me up and throw me across the avenue. She is going to think I am bat shit crazy.

I point to my head and then my heart as I speak. "If you are having thoughts of ending your life, then, yes, I am talking to you."

The light turns green, and we both stand there. "We should go." I point to the green light. "I'm with the school group."

She looks around for the first time. I step into the street, and she follows. "How do you know what I'm thinking; you practice voodoo or some shit?"

"No," I say. "I'm Catholic. We're not supposed to mess with the occult."

"Then how do you know what I'm planning?"

"It's a long story, but don't do it." I then ask her why she wants to kill herself. At this moment, I realize she is a man dressed in woman's clothes.

"You have any idea what it's like to be a man in a woman's body? A Black man, no less?"

I shake my head. "No." I look her over.

"A big Black man," she adds.

"Maybe you should wear flats," I say, not meaning to be funny. But she finds it hilarious and breaks out laughing. Looking down at her shoes.

"You know how much these things cost? Plus, they look good, but they do kill my feet."

The nervous mother grows nervous again when she sees me talking to the transgender woman. She keeps looking over her shoulder as we cross the street.

"You're psychic, right?" the big woman asks me.

"Kind of, but I prefer to say I listen very carefully to the Holy Spirit."

"You got something. I'll tell you that. How else would you know what I was thinking?"

Sister Elizabeth has stopped up the street. She is waiting for us.

"You like being psychic?" the woman continues.

123

"If I feel like I helped someone. So, don't do anything rash. Okay? There is something better for you."

She smiles for the first time. "Do you know what that is? A man maybe?"

I slow down my pace and stare straight ahead. She sees the nervous mother looking at us, too afraid to intrude. There is also Sister Elizabeth looming, waiting for me. "They with you?" she asks.

"Mhhhm…"

"Well, I'm turning here, so don't worry about me," she says breathlessly.

"I'll take that as a metaphor. You will not harm yourself, right?"

Sister Elizabeth walks toward us.

"That's correct," she says, walking away from me. Then she turns back, shows her heels, and yells, "Might even start wearing flats."

I decide she will go in my book of souls as "beautiful big feet;" it seems fitting. The man who died on the train will go on my list as, I don't know, "lost soul?"

We get back to school. I do not get the cold shoulder. Instead, I get frostbite.

MYSTIC BRUNCH

It is my Mr. David, yoga and meditation day. Yoga is my prayer time. For forty-five minutes, I am able to turn everything off and dance with God. When I am done with class, I am ready for the world again, ready to understand what is happening to me. It never fails me.

I sit and sip tea with the crew in our Bohemian coffee house. There is a lot on my mind. I ask Mr. David if I can share first because I need advice. Starting with the subway, I give them the details of the OD, the transgender woman, my spiritual battle. Of course, I leave out the actual physical fight—don't want anyone to think I'm completely nuts. Even among people who believe deeply in the paranormal. In describing the fight, I present it as demonic voices that only I could hear. "Do you think it was keeping me from helping the man who died?" I ask.

Raphael is the first to answer. "Divide and conquer," he says. He quickly adds, "Let me be clear. I'm not saying you could have prevented it. I'm just saying that they can use distractions."

"Sister Elizabeth and my classmates thought I was having a fit."

"Why?" asks Susie Homemaker.

"Like an epileptic fit?" Star asks.

"My friends said I was shaking and swinging wildly. I was also white as a ghost."

"When was the last time you went to the doctor?" Mr. David asks, which surprises me.

"You think this is medical?"

"No. I'm not saying that. I just want to make sure that what is happening to you is not putting your body under stress."

"But you think what I'm seeing is real?"

A chorus of answers follows. "Of course, it's real!" Susie says. "Spirits can attack in many ways," Raphael adds.

"Did you say you felt or saw spirits around the man who died?" Star asks. "Both."

She looks at Mr. David. His facial expression suggests, "See?"

"You have a strong instrument, Jack. Just make sure you are taking care of yourself. I don't want you to get sick," Mr. David says.

Next, I tell them how upset Sister Elizabeth was with me for talking to the transgender woman, to which Raphael says, "Jesus helped the undesirables of his day, so don't let that bother you."

"Thanks. Actually, somehow I think she blamed me for the entire morning."

"That's ridiculous," Star says.

I nod, then add, "This happened before. I fell asleep in class due to a migraine and apparently at some point I sat on my desk and started to curse."

Susie Homemaker laughs and then quickly composes herself. "Jack, people like you—like us—are not always accepted."

Mr. David jumps in. "You helped that person, Jack. You went with your intuition. You'll get a lot of judgment, maybe even a little persecution. Stop if you want to stop, don't do it because someone else doesn't understand. We are all on our own spiritual journey. This is yours."

Finally, I mention Peter Cairo. They know I work for him and his parents doing chores but they don't know how I met him, so I explain how I went to his apartment the first time.

Mr. David interrupts me. "Jack, that was not smart. There are some scary people in this world. You have to be wiser."

"You're right, but I just felt this strong sense that I had to do it. The man who lived there was Peter Cairo, not the man I see in the window."

Susie Homemaker interrupts. "Could it be a friend of Peter's?"

"No. I asked Peter about him, if he was his brother, or a friend."

"Well you're young, Jack. Maybe it's a friend he's not comfortable talking about," Susie Homemaker says.

I look at her. "You mean like a lover?" I ask.

Their glances give them away. "Well, yes," she says.

"No. I would know if he was lying. He's had the carpets changed and the apartment painted to try and get rid of the smell of cigarettes."

I'm so immersed in my conversation with the group that I don't notice that Mrs. Dowd, the fourth-grade teacher, has come in. So much for my psychic abilities. This is the second time I've run into her here. She gets her drink and makes it a point to stop at our table.

"Mr. Kelly. Running into you here is starting to be habit forming. Aren't you a little too young to be drinking coffee?"

"Oh, I'm drinking tea."

Mrs. Dowd looks around the table at the eclectic group of characters, expecting an introduction. Awkward silence.

Finally, Mr. David speaks up. "Hi, I'm Michael David." He stands up to shake her hand. She pretends her hands are full with her drink and purse.

"Yes, I know who you are," Mrs. Dowd says sternly.

Mr. David is a class act; he doesn't miss a beat. "Oh, that's right. We met you the last time you ran into Jack here." It's clear to everyone at the table that is not what she meant, but it does end the conversation.

"Bye, Mrs. Dowd. I'll see you at school," I say. She heads out.

"Where were we?" Star asks after a beat.

"Trust me," I say. "It's not a lover. But I do get the feeling that something or someone is making Peter uncomfortable."

"Is it a ghost?" someone asks.

"No. I've seen the man in front of the building. I also saw him one night after Peter and I had dinner. Here is the thing: whenever I drop something off in his apartment, I smell cigarettes and paint. The other day I felt a strong intuition that someone was in the apartment. I went through every inch of the place. No one was there."

Mr. David sits straight up. "Okay, Jack, I don't want you to stay in that apartment if you think a grown man is sneaking in."

"I'm being careful, smart."

"Smart would have been leaving the apartment and calling Peter."

I nod but I know what I have to do. I'm not going to let fear rule me like it has before.

They continue to throw out ideas. "Has anyone died recently on his floor?" "What about in the building?"

"He is saying it's not a spirit," Mr. David says, taking control of the conversation. Then Susie Homemaker jumps in. "It can't hurt to smudge the apartment anyway."

"Smudge? Don't know what that means."

"It's a practice you can use to cleanse an area of negative energy, of spirits who might be trapped." Mr. David says. "Use white sage. I'll give you some. You can also set mirrors opposite one another, which can enhance the aura of his apartment."

"What about placing crystals in the corners of the apartment?" Star asks.

Mr. David nods. "Yes, and prayer helps. Are you sure it's not a spirit? Because I don't want you messing around with a sociopath, or someone with a vendetta."

Raphael jumps in. "See if you can find out if someone died on the floor—in the building recently—maybe even a worker? They may not have crossed over yet; they can still be wandering around a familiar place, afraid to leave."

Mr. David checks his watch. "Before you take matters into your own hands, Jack, make sure Peter is okay with whatever you plan to do."

I nod.

My dad picks me up early from school for an appointment with Dr. Klein, my neurologist. Dad has to take the afternoon off, which he is not happy about. Sister Elizabeth in particular put a lot of pressure on him to have an updated exam.

Dad doesn't scream at the nun or the school, but in the apartment, he does a lot of yelling—at me. "Why the hell are you standing on the seats in the subway? We just saw the neurologist!"

I am at an impasse. I can't tell the truth to Dr. Klein because—let's face it—if I did, they would have me committed. Only, I can't pretend I'm having a seizure or that I can't remember anything. So, it's a no-win situation.

In the exam room, Dad and I wait in silence. We are becoming strangers;

I take the blame for that. Dr. Klein comes in. He is cooler than any doctor on TV and looks like he should be a news anchor. What I like most about him is he talks directly to me when he asks a question.

"Jack," he says, shaking my hand. "Mr. Kelly." He greets my dad with a nod and a smile.

"I'm surprised to see you today, Jack. Is something wrong?" He looks at the file. "I saw you less than three months ago."

My dad jumps in immediately. "Quite frankly, Dr. Klein, Jack's school is insisting we see you."

He then looks at me. "Would you like to get him up to date or would you like me to?"

My anger rises. I want to scream at the top of my lungs. Fuck! Fuck all this bullshit! I want to get up and leave the room. Only that would be childish, and I have demons to slay. So, I bite my tongue and sit on my hands so I don't jump up and scream.

"No, Dad, Sister Elizabeth spoke to you; I think it best if you tell him," I say. "I'll jump in where I need to…"

"Well…" Dad goes into the versions of that morning given by the Sister, the school, the nervous mother, and probably half of my classmates. Doctor Klein is very respectful of my dad. When Dad is done speaking, Dr. Klein looks at me.

"Okay, let me examine you."

First, we test motor function and balance. He does what he has always done—pushes and pulls against my hands and legs. He checks my balance then has me sit on the exam table. Dr. Klein takes out the dull needles, tuning forks, alcohol swabs, and checks my ability to feel. He asks how I've been. "Fine." Shines light in my eyes. It is easy because I know what I know—no seizures here. Dr. Klein asks my dad if he can have a few minutes alone with me.

After my dad leaves, he looks at me. "What's going on, Jack? What happened on the train?"

How can you tell a story and leave out its soul? What is the most important thing that happened that day?

"A man died on the train, directly across from me."

"What? Your dad never mentioned that."

"Because they are all preoccupied with me shaking and standing on the seat."

"Tell me about the man."

"He was an addict. When he got on the train, he was super fucked up. Guess he OD'd…"

He calls my dad back in and hooks me up for an EEG. No seizures.

Afterward, Dad and I go back into the exam room to talk to Dr. Klein. "Mr. Kelly," Dr. Klein says to my dad "nothing has changed. I don't see anything different here to be concerned with. Is his school, his teacher, taking into consideration that a man died on the train?"

My father puts his head down. "Look, Dr. Klein, I agree. It's just the Nun is saying his behavior has changed. He was white as a ghost, talking to a hooker, standing on the seats."

"She wasn't a hooker; she was a transgender woman or cross-dresser," I interrupt.

"Transgender woman or cross-dresser, prostitute—what difference does it make? Why are you, a thirteen-year-old boy, walking with and talking to hookers—transgender woman or cross-dresser or whatever—on a school trip? Are you trying to be disruptive?" Dad pauses, then adds, "He's having nightmares again."

"I had one!"

"You had more than one; I stopped waking you up."

"Well, Jesus hung out with outcasts—think about that, Dad."

"Oh, now you're Jesus?"

"I'm not saying that!"

We start yelling, and our dirty laundry is hung out in front of the good doctor.

We go silent.

"Look, I know this was traumatic," Dr. Klein says. "He is a teenager, Mr. Kelly. His recovery—his health—is good."

Dad wants something more concrete to appease the school. Dr. Klein gives it to him. "I'm going to schedule a cerebral angiography and a CAT scan just to make sure I am not missing anything."

Sister Elizabeth is making us jump through hoops. Aunt Paula picks me up so I can have the other two tests done. Sister Elizabeth and I are civil, but that is about it. It takes all day with the waiting around, but I take the tests. Now we—I—wait for the results.

PETER CAIRO

Peter sits at his desk remembering the excitement when he first returned to New York. His hometown. He subleased an apartment even though Peter's parents, especially Julia, wanted him to live with them. He felt guilty about saying no, but moving back in with mommy and daddy in his late thirties was not an option. His father recently had a stroke. The idea of saying no made him feel like a "bad son." Guilt.

The apartment had always been a temporary fix while he looked around the city, putting in applications in buildings where he desired to live. Two of the places were Gramercy Terrace and the Dakota. Gramercy Terrace was directly across from his elementary school, Epiphany. He always loved its architectural style and cute little garden area belonging to the building. Peter had attended a party there as a kid with his parents. The apartments were open, filled with great light. The Dakota, on the other hand, was Gothic revival; a style he also loved. He knew the Dakota was too expensive for his budget but went after it anyway. No wife. No kids. No crazy expenses.

Peter liked the neighborhood where his sublet was, but the apartment was tiny, and he wanted to be geographically closer to his parents. Coming back to Manhattan, he was optimistic for the first time in years, even though his marriage had failed for a variety of reasons. Being an only child, Peter could easily keep himself busy with work, reading, riding his bike, and playing his guitar. His ex-wife, Sheila, was restless. She hated where they lived, so they moved twice, making Peter's commute longer and longer. She was disappointed in the business of acting, didn't read, and was always looking to be entertained. Their incompatibility should have been no surprise to either of them. However, once the conversation of divorce started, that overwhelming feeling of being a "failure" sent him into a bit of a spiral. She wanted to move back to Minnesota. For a brief moment, Peter entertained the idea, though he felt it was more a desperate attempt to avoid divorce rather than wanting to be with the woman he loved. In the end, she made it easy for the both of them.

"Peter," she said. "I just want to start over."

Very simple. They both took what was theirs, moved back to their hometowns, and began anew.

Once in New York, Peter reached out to old friends. He started dating Lee, a bright, beautiful, exciting woman with very similar interests and tastes. He was in love again with a delightful lady as well as Manhattan and his work. Life was good and became even better when he got the call that an apartment came up at Gramercy Terrace. Peter walked through Apartment 3C and leased it immediately. The only thing he wanted now—needed, really—was to get his mother more help. Julia seemed easy-breezy, but she could be difficult. Nobody they hired worked out. "They talk too much. They're nosy," she'd say. Or, "She doesn't know what she is doing." Or, "The only men I want in the house are you and Dad."

Peter wanted her happy and he wanted his father taken care of—everything else in his life was flowing beautifully.

With keys in hand, Peter and Lee walked through the apartment. The living room faced 22nd Street with floor-to-ceiling windows, creating walls of glass. It brought the outside in. The two bedroom windows looked out over the small garden on the west side of the building.

"Not many apartments like this one in New York," Lee said, offering to help him decorate.

The building's leasing agent noted that there was a small storage in the basement with a deadbolt and no key. With nothing to put in the storage, he overlooked what was, at the moment, a minor inconvenience. He was much too excited about landing the apartment to make a fuss. Besides, he could take care of it later. First, he and Lee had some shopping to do. Peter bought a king size bed, and they made use of it immediately. They couldn't keep their hands off one another. Every Saturday, they would have breakfast and go shopping. Her taste was exquisite. Each room was carefully thought out. The only room he could not settle on was the second bedroom. Would it be a den? Office? Guest bedroom? Lee mentioned it would be a great room for a nursery. That's the one room that didn't quite get finished. He settled for a pull-out couch and a dresser. Lee was wonderful, but Peter was not ready to marry again or have children.

The apartment itself was aesthetically perfect. However, Peter began finding it difficult to sleep. From the time he was a kid and through college, Peter insisted on sleeping with an open window. Now it seemed the cigarette smoke of one of his neighbors was coming in through the open bedroom window. Its effect disturbed him. Peter bought a fan in an attempt to neutralize the smell; it didn't work. Shutting the window also cut off the subtle city noise that was a lullaby to him as both a kid and an adult. He could not get settled. Lee began sleeping over less and less due to his restlessness in the middle of the night.

"I have an early morning," she would say whenever he asked her to stay.

With Lee no longer beside him in bed, something else began happening. Peter began waking up with the feeling that someone was in the apartment. Jumping out of bed, he'd grab his baseball bat and go from room to room in search of an intruder. All he found were shadows. The perception that someone was coming into the apartment while he slept was not rational, yet it would not leave him. Peter put a deadbolt and chain on the door. He bought night lights, placing them in every room. One night he woke up, startled by a dark shadowy figure standing at his feet. The hair on his body stood at attention; he froze. Pure, unadulterated fear. Finally, he crawled out of his bed to grab the bat. It appeared to be an illusion created by the street lamps. He repositioned the bedroom light and bought a blackout shade; none of it helped.

Peter was not easily frightened, but now he was terrified at the thought of going to bed. On one of his many sleepless nights walking around the apartment, he heard a noise in the small garden on the side of the building. Peter opened the bedroom window and saw a darkened figure sitting alone on a bench, the light from a cigarette glowing.

"Excuse me." No answer.

"Sir!" No answer.

"Madam!"

Nothing.

Peter rushed down the stairs into the garden, but no one was there. He looked around for the remains of a cigarette; there were none. He ran back into the building; the lobby was empty. The elevator was stopped on the third floor. His floor. He rang for the elevator then decided to run up the stairs two at a time. When he reached the hallway, the elevator door was closing. Peter looked up and down the hall. There was no sign of anyone. Shamefully, Peter walked the hall, putting his ear to his neighbors' doors. Silence.

Inside his apartment, Peter worried about having left his apartment unlocked. He began turning the lights on in every room. Peter picked up the bat and did a full search of the place, including the closets. The lack of sleep was making him crazy.

Peter did not smoke pot; he never did drugs recreationally. Not even in college or out in Los Angeles. But now he asked his doctor for a sleeping aid. He filled his first prescription for Valium and cautiously began reaching for them at night.

Checking his watch, he realized Jack was going to be late for lunch. Peter didn't really mind; it gave him a little more time for work.

WHISPERING LOUDLY

Instead of dinner with Peter this week, I'm meeting him for lunch. He asked me to come to his office on Madison Avenue between 58th and 59th Street. Peter told me to take a cab, that he would pay for it. I would rather take the bus. The bus is not crowded, just a sprinkle of people on this Saturday morning. A woman about twenty-nine sits near the front. An older woman sits in the middle of the bus across from a napping worker with his head buried; his age I can't determine. A couple of college kids are in the rear.

I take the seat across from the woman in the front. A man in his fifties gets on at the next stop. I immediately get a feeling that something is wrong. I feel like he is sick or going to have some kind of health problem in the near future. There is also a smell to him—a smell that only I can pick up on. Looking around the bus, I'm not getting the psychological feedback that I get in the subway station. It allows me to step into the energy—the thoughts— from others; it comes more easily.

The woman across from me keeps looking into a compact mirror, fussing over her makeup. All of her thoughts fall on a boyfriend. It is not a good relationship. She keeps alienating family and friends, bending over backward. It will never work. The older woman in the middle section has dead eyes, I mean nothing—barren land. The college couple in the rear share their joy; it bounces around them like a beach ball. They bring a warm light into the bus.

135

The noise level increases. I wish I could control the dial. Must learn how to do that so I don't get confused. Don't want any seizure-like activity lighting me up.

The worker continues to nap. I feel nothing from him, either. Is he too close to the older woman's energy, or is it the reverse? Maybe they hold quiet energy, or I'm just not tuning into them. Back to the man, there is something definitely going on with his body. His smell is that of an incinerator; something is burning.

I perceive the sounds of someone being smacked hard, which brings my attention back to the woman across from me. She is sitting very still. A voice is yelling at her, but I can't pick up the words. Momentarily the older woman distracts me, but nothing has changed. She is a desert.

Outside, the noise is elevating. I close my eyes, trying to neutralize its impact on me.

There is laughter from the couple in the rear of the bus, maybe an octave too high.

The woman across from me is back to her compact, checking her makeup again. She is not unhappy but she is not happy. Just very confused.

A mother and her three children board the bus. They are heading to the zoo in Central Park. The little girl asks her brother what animal he wants to see. That's how I know.

Who am I here for? It is clear that the man the woman across from me is on her way to see is bad for her. But before I figure that out, the man with the health issue pulls the cord to let the driver know he wants to get off at the next stop. I pick up a volcanic explosion—a heart attack? Stroke? Heart—yes, I think heart. We are somewhere in the mid-forties when the bus stops, long before my destination. Impulsively. I get off with him. I look at the woman across from me. It is too late to speak to her. I had to choose.

After following the man for a couple of blocks, I finally muster the nerve to do and say something. He is heading east. I need to go to the northwest.

"Mister! Hey Mister!" I yell.

He doesn't turn. Running up to him, I continue to call out.

"Mister!"

He doesn't recognize me from the bus but still answers. "Yes?"

Catching my breath, I pray: Holy Spirit enlighten me. "Sir, can I tell you something?"

He looks around to see if it is some kind of gag. After a moment, he says, "Sure."

"I was on your bus just now and I have a strong need to tell you that you should have your heart checked."

"What?"

"It might be nothing but it is a pretty strong feeling I'm getting."

He stares at me. "Is this a joke? Some kind of prank for some group you want to join?" he asks suspiciously.

"No. No. Nothing like that. I know it seems a little crazy but I feel strongly about it. I don't want to scare you."

The man nods his head and looks around unsure. Finally, he says, "Thank you. I'll take you up on that and call my doctor."

I watch him leave, feeling accomplished and crazy at the same time. Mr. David had said, "Be of service but don't be attached to the results." I must remember that.

- - -

Peter's office is what I expected it to be—organized. He is happy to see me even though I am tardy. "I took the bus," I say.

I do not mention getting off the bus or any of my metaphysical moments along the way. Peter shows me around the office. A small group of people are working. He introduces me to a couple of his colleagues. "This is Jack Kelly, the kid I was telling you about. He works for us." Niceties all around.

We walk to a very nice bistro on Madison Avenue. I ordered a burger with frites—fries in French. Peter suggests I get the steak, but I really want a burger. He gets a Niçoise salad. I eat like I haven't seen food in days; Peter pushes the salad around the plate. This guy is not a good eater. I have yet to watch him finish a meal.

"Aren't you hungry?" I ask.

"Who are you, my mother?" he says.

"Yeah, I guess that sounds annoying," I apologize. "How is the cigarette smell?"

"Funny you should ask. A woman at work told me to clean the apartment with vinegar, which I did."

"Vinegar? Think I'd rather have the cigarette smell," I say, trying to be funny.

"Well, it worked for two days before the smell was back. Now I have a lovely mix of cigarettes with a hint of vinegar greeting me when I come home." We laugh.

Our lunch arrives, and Peter tells the waiter we would like the chocolate soufflé. Looking at me, he says, "It takes a while."

"How have you been?" Peter asks. He takes out two white envelopes. One is my pay; the other is the list of things he and Julia need me to do, along with the money to do them. "Don't want to forget," he says, like that is even possible.

Waiting a beat, I go into a diatribe about my week, how I got into trouble for talking to a transgender woman: "Sister thought she was a hooker."

Peter looks flabbergasted. "Wait. What? Where was this?" he asks.

"On a class trip—oh, and this man died right in front of us while we were on the subway." Peter stares at me. "Not to mention that they think I was having a seizure."

He slows me down. "Wait a minute, Jack. This all happened on the same day?"

I nod while shoveling fries into my mouth. I can feel the lawyer surfacing in him.

"How did the guy on the train die?"

"Looked like it was a drug overdose, but I don't know what the autopsy showed."

"Why do they think you had a seizure?" he asks.

I shrug my shoulders and decide not to tell the full story, no standing on seats, no swinging. "I don't know."

The waiter clears our plates and asks if we would like coffee or tea. Peter wants an espresso; I ask for tea. "Something must have happened, Jack, if someone thought you were having a seizure," he says.

"Well, I was shivering—pale. It was a shock," I lie. Gee, I have to stop that! I really do.

The waiter places the chocolate soufflé in the middle of the table. Peter puts a hole in the center and spoons some whipped cream into the hole. "I've never had a chocolate soufflé before; hell, I've never even seen one," I say.

"You're in for a treat."

"So, the vinegar didn't work?"

"Not so fast. Where did you meet the transgender woman?"

The soufflé is off-the-charts good. "Just walking along the street. We basically said hello. Sister Elizabeth made it seem like I was trying to pick her up. Like I sinned."

Peter raises his eyebrows. "Society judges what they don't understand," he says.

Did he just give me an opening? "Do you believe in the supernatural?" I ask.

"What? How did we go from a transgender woman to the supernatural?" Peter puts his spoon down. This guy eats nothing; I'm knocking off the entire soufflé by myself, after eating a big burger. He pushed the salad around the plate and barely ate.

"You said society judges what it doesn't understand, so I'm asking about the supernatural, things we don't understand."

"Hmm." He calls the waiter for the check. "Well, I kind of believe in God. God is a supernatural force, right? So, I'd have to say yes."

What a lawyer. He pulls a credit card from his wallet and puts it down. Peter also looks briefly at a newspaper article folded inside his wallet. Doesn't mention it. Everyone I know pays with cash.

"I'm guessing you do or you would not have asked the question," Peter says, folding the article back up.

"Not sure."

"You believe in God, Jack?"

Taking a deep breath, I say, "Yes, but maybe not the way I've been taught."

Peter studies me. "Let's get out of here," he says, standing.

We walk for a bit. "You going back to work?" I ask.

It takes him a moment to answer. "You in a rush?"

"No.

"You feel like walking a bit?"

"Sure. Any place in particular?" I ask.

"No."

We walk a few blocks without talking, which is always difficult for me. Since I was a little kid, long silences have made me nervous, like I'm boring, like it's my job to fill the quiet. I've been known to have the "gift of gab." But I feel Peter is just looking for company, not necessarily conversation. Still, I decide to fill the quiet. What can I say—I have a bit of an agenda.

"Would you let me burn white sage in your apartment?" I finally ask.

He looks sideways at me.

"A friend of mine told me it's great for clearing energy—odors." Not sure what I expected, but his simple "sure" was not it. "What time do you need to be back at work?"

"I've no time constraints," Peter says with a smile.

- - -

It is my first time in The Third Eye psychic bookstore. I'm not sure what to expect. I look at Peter, and he is unreadable. The store is a menagerie of books, smells, and artifacts of every deity known to man. There are crystals and stones in every shape and color, with crosses, Buddha statues, Tarot cards, candles, and herbs for spells—casting out everything from old lovers to evil spirits. Peter gravitates to the book section. I pick up white sage, while also going through canisters of incense and herbs.

Did you know that sandalwood helps with healing, raising spiritual vibrations, protection and exorcisms? Exorcisms? That's correct—exorcisms. \ Geez, Jack, you need to go to confession.

Black salt absorbs negative energy; I grab some of that. Dream catchers can remove negative dreams and bad energy. Can I hang it under my desk at school? Experiencing this shop is captivating; there are potions and lotions for all kinds of problems, real or imagined. I go to the counter with my items. Peter is still looking at a book on past lives.

"Peter!" I yell a little too loudly.

He looks embarrassed, puts the book down, and walks over to me. "Let me pay for that…"

"No, some of this is for me," I counter.

They ring up my items, and Peter immediately throws down cash, which covers everything. "Your money's no good when you're with me, Jack."

We walk outside the store. "How do you know a place like this, Jack?"

"I'm not a kid…I know things…" I say, way too defensively.

"I never used any of those words, Jack. I asked you how you knew a store like The Third Eye. It wasn't meant as an insult or an indictment."

"I'm sorry; that was defensive of me. I'm just interested in the sixth sense. A friend of mine told me about it, and I thought it would be worth a look."

"Well, it was very interesting. Was it the same friend who suggested burning the white sage in my apartment?"

"Yes."

Peter nods and says, "I was in a new age store in Los Angeles years ago."

Hmmm, I think—new age. Not occult or sorcery or any phrase some other people might use. Must not let labels create negative thoughts in me or stop me from having new experiences.

PETER CAIRO

Peter was losing Lee. He rarely enjoyed the pleasure of her company anymore but was trying hard to keep her in his life. They shared a lovely dinner at the Four Seasons, followed by a night at his apartment reminiscent of their earlier time together. His sleeping had slightly improved with the help of Valium. However, it sometimes left him with lasting fatigue. When Lee asked him about it, he blamed it on work. They decided that Sunday would be their day—go to the movies, brunch, a museum, anything to be together, which left Peter optimistic. There were moments of great clarity for him, but he could not quite shake the feeling of being watched in his apartment at night. Now it was spilling over into other areas of his life. One night, he was given orchestra tickets by one of the firm's clients for "A Chorus Line." Lee joined him, and they had a wonderful time. Afterward, he saw her back to her apartment, had a nightcap, and decided to walk home.

It wasn't very late, but the walk grew creepy. Somebody was messing with him, walking when he walked, stopping when he stopped. Growing up in the city he was used to certain things, but this was different. He was being followed. Peter decided to hail a cab.

Everything made him jumpy. Never had he been such a worrisome person. At home, Peter found himself unable to sleep. Tried reading. Couldn't get into the book so he looked at a contract. No luck. He decided to watch

The Tonight Show instead.

The intercom for his apartment rang. He checked his watch and was initially irritated, but remembered Lee had surprised him once before by showing up late. His mood turned from irritation to hope. He picked up the phone. "Yes?"

Static. "Lee?" Nothing.

Peter made a cup of chamomile tea and went back to watching *The Tonight Show*, hoping to get drowsy. Just as he grew comfortable, the intercom rang again. Peter thought about ignoring it, but the ring was persistent.

"Who is this?" he barked into the phone.

Static.

Peter shut the television off and got the apartment ready for what he dreaded—another long night. Inside the bedroom, the intercom rang again. Annoyed, Peter put his pants on, grabbed his baseball bat, and headed out the apartment door. Before closing the door, he took his keys from the hook and locked it.

Outside, Peter stood like he was at home plate, ready to swing. But he could not see a single person on the street in either direction. He waited. Maybe some obnoxious teenagers rang his buzzer and then hid behind cars. He looked again. Silence. Not a soul anywhere. Leaning up against the building, he looked at Epiphany, his old school sitting quietly across the street. Peter crossed the street and stood in the entrance of Epiphany, where no one could see him. He'd be waiting when the person rang his buzzer again. Peter stood there for fifteen minutes before giving up. He checked the garden area to see if the smoker was back; it was empty. Then he decided to sit on the bench inside the garden area with the bat in his lap. The garden really was a beautiful oasis in the middle of a hectic city.

He took a long blink and fell asleep, landing in a dream…

On his way to work, the city was deserted. No cars, no trucks, no people. It took him a moment to realize he was alone. Peter started to knock on the doors of businesses that lined the streets. Locked. Nobody inside. Sounds of footsteps behind made him hopeful, but when he turned, it was the same empty streets that were in front of him. Turning around, he decided to go back home, saw a church, and ran up its stairs. Doors were locked. He began banging on the church door. No answer. Sounds of footsteps coming up the church stairs turned him around. Emptiness everywhere. He ran down 1st Avenue but could see no sign of life. In Stuyvesant Town, the playgrounds and walkways were likewise devoid of people. Taking the stairs two at a time, he made it to his parents' apartment. Rang the bell. No answer. Banged on the door. No one.

"Mommy! Pop!" he yelled.

Peter awoke when the bat fell to his feet. Startled, he hurried back to his apartment. Inside the apartment the TV blasted, the shades up, and nightlights off. "What the fuck!" His fear turned to anger. Peter left no closet unopened, no space uninspected. The common thread to every other night was there was no one in the apartment. The disturbance made him reach for a Valium. It didn't help, so he took another one.

Morning came. Shutting the alarm clock off, he stumbled to the shower. The mirror told him all he needed to know. He was coming undone. Peter felt irrational from another poor night of sleep. He knew something needed to change. Maybe it all stemmed from being an overachiever with a beautiful, but controlling mother and a father who was a cop. Maybe it was the divorce, losing Lee. No, this all started with this fucking apartment! Regardless, he needed to act; he was drowning.

Torrential rain greeted him as he left the building. Looking for a cab was futile. So Peter headed for the subway. On the way down, he slipped on the wet stairs, bouncing off the wall before grabbing the railing. Peter found an open seat on the crowded train and closed his eyes. The gentle rocking put him to sleep where he felt nothing, thought nothing.

When he awoke, he was several stops past his planned destination. He got to his feet, frustration seeping from every pore in his body. Peter left the train and rushed up the stairs into the pouring rain. An empty Yellow Cab was coming up the street. Knowing their would-be competition for it, he rushed to the corner. For a brief moment, he felt like someone was following, or possibly trying to catch up, maybe beat him to the cab. Looking over his shoulder, he saw a man he knew—someone he represented at one time? No time to stop.

The corner was crowded with umbrellas, people vying for position to cross the street or hail his taxi. At the corner, he felt a hand on his back. Peter started to turn. The force of the ensuing push sent him flying into an oncoming taxi speeding up the street. It flipped him in the air and bounced his body onto the concrete sidewalk. He immediately knew that his hip was broken.

Lying in the hospital room, Peter tried hard to place the man's face. Why would anyone want to push him? Because clearly, he had been shoved into the oncoming car. It didn't make sense. He had no disgruntled clients, no bitter relationships. A lunatic? Mistaken identity?

The first few days were rough. The doctor switched him from I.V. to oral medication on the second day because he was eating so well. Julia came to the hospital, trying hard to keep it together, but failing. "Where is Lee?" she wanted to know.

"I didn't tell her yet." Julia was surprised.

She wanted a wife for Peter, someone to take care of him. Peter assured her he would let Lee know what happened but that he was quite capable of taking care of himself.

"How's Dad?" he asked.

"His sister is sitting with him while I've come to see you," she said, rolling her eyes.

Peter avoids the invitation to that sandbox and is glad when the physical therapist comes in to get him out of bed.

"Go, Mom. I'm okay."

Poor Julia—both her men down for the count.

When he's not at physical or occupational therapy, Peter is on the phone with his secretary searching for care facilities, making arrangements. Julia suggests he come to stay with her so she can supervise his recovery, but he will not. On day four, they ask him if he wants to go home or to a rehab facility. Peter decides on rehab for a week or two. He tells himself it's to get consistent therapy. But he's sleeping better in the hospital than he does at home; maybe it's the drugs.

Lee comes to the rehabilitation center to see him. She is miffed that he didn't call her immediately. If the relationship was struggling previously, it needs resuscitation now. Although Lee, being of good character, does not break it off while he's in recovery. Spending a week in rehab helps him get a good start with the physical recovery, and it's been months since he's slept this well.

While in rehab, Peter hires a woman for the day shift and a man to come late at night. It allows plenty of room for some private time. Maybe Lee will spend time with him.

Back in the apartment, Peter walks around without crutches or a walker. The woman, Alice, helps in the morning. She usually makes breakfast and does laundry in the building's basement among other housekeeping chores. The man, Tony, is a little Filipino guy in his fifties. He arrives at 9 p.m. They take short walks if Peter is up to it. Tony stays in the guest bedroom or living room when Peter sleeps. Physical and occupational therapy comes three times a week. A messenger drops off work or picks up completed work. The first week, everything is flowing. Lee arrives for dinner and brings Chinese food from a place they both enjoy.

But she is looking for an explanation. "What happened, Peter? You didn't even call me to tell me you had been hit by a cab."

What Peter knows is you can't go backward, but he doesn't say it.

"There was a time you couldn't wait to see me," Lee continues. "Couldn't keep your hands off of me."

"I still feel that way."

She raises her eyebrow.

"My sleep or lack of it was making me crazy. The only thing I seem to be doing well is work," he says apologetically.

The phone rings. It's a client who distracts him immediately, leaving Lee to entertain herself. Tony returns from the store with groceries. Peter supervises Tony's choices, showing him where everything goes. After multiple little distractions, Peter realizes Lee is standing in the living room with her jacket on.

"Don't go," he says.

But it's too late. "It's been a long day. I'm tired," she says, kissing Peter on the cheek. The moment she is gone, Peter knows she is really gone. Great, Peter, now it's you and the help, he thinks.

In the midst of a drug-assisted sleep, Peter hears someone in the doorway of his bedroom.

"Mr. Cairo? Mr. Cairo!" Tony whispers.

Peter sits up and sees Tony huddled by the door. "There is someone in the apartment, Mr. Cairo," he says, frightened.

Peter gets out of bed, grabs a crutch to lean on, and then the baseball bat. Tony starts talking very fast and low. "He was outside the bedroom where I was reading."

"Where is he now?"

Tony points to the living room. They are a team: Peter limping on one crutch holding his bat; Tony clinging to his side. They turn on the living room light; no one is there. Tony points to the kitchen. Nothing. All the lights are on in the apartment. They open closets in the hall, in the bedrooms, look in places no human can possibly fit. Peter does not explain to him that he has experienced this all before. That this is the reason he hired him—so he wasn't alone.

"Maybe it was the wind or mice," Peter says.

He stares at Peter, his eyes bulging from their sockets. "No, someone was here!"

Peter feels awful, knowing what he knows, but he goes through the drill to assure him. "Look, the chain is still on the door," he says.

This makes Tony more frightened, not less. They go through the apartment one more time; the result is the same. No one is there.

Peter spends the rest of the night trying to assure him it is just a noisy, creaky old apartment building. Somewhere in the wee hours of the morning, he goes back to bed, exhausted.

- - -

Peter is in a deep sleep when Alice knocks on the bedroom door to tell him the physical therapist has arrived. He tells her to send the therapist away. It doesn't take long before Alice joins in with the nuttiness of 3C. She comes up from the laundry room in the basement and tells him someone is hiding down there, or the place is haunted.

"Might be a rat or a varmint," he offers, sipping his coffee. He wonders how he can get out of his lease.

"Well, Mr. Cairo, it would have to be one gigantic rat that knows how to open and close doors," Alice says. "Could be maintenance."

After showering and shaving, he leaves for a walk. He can't stand this. Now he's avoiding the apartment during the day. Peter buys a couple of newspapers and stops at Cosmo's for a late breakfast.

In the living section of the paper a headline immediately catches his eye: "Nun Found Buried Face Down May Have Been A Witch." He reads on.

> "Archaeologists made a grisly discovery Tuesday after being called to a construction site by authorities, where they uncovered six skeletons, including a woman buried face down. She is believed to have been a Carmelite nun. Face-down burial was usually reserved for the wicked, and the thought is that the woman was either accused of witchcraft or practiced it. The construction site was once a Carmelite nun convent. The order lived there from 1875 until 1949, when it was turned into a boarding house and later condemned by the city. In addition to the nun's body, they discovered the bones of a stillborn baby; the skull showed evidence of blunt force trauma. Construction was halted on the high-rise co-op."

The sunny-side-up eggs stare back. Peter moves food around the plate, thinking about the nun. What comes to mind first is tongue in cheek: Was she a good witch or a bad witch? Or not a witch at all? Did the convent harbor sinister deeds? Was she murdered? Did she practice evil spells? Use voodoo dolls? Or was she just a woman accused of practicing witchcraft by people who were jealous of her or did not understand her methods?

The waitress slaps the check down on the table and asks, "Was anything wrong with the eggs?" Peter has no appetite. "I can have them make new ones," she offers.

"No. No. No," Peter replies. "I guess I'm not really that hungry." She moves on as Peter carefully tears the article out and places it in his wallet.

Alice is upset when he arrives at the apartment. She is pacing. "Where were you?" she demands.

"What?" Peter says, off guard.

"Have you been gone all this time?" Alice asks.

"Yes. I didn't realize I needed your permission."

She puts her face in her hands. "I'm sorry."

"What's wrong?"

"I thought you were angry with me. When I came up from putting another load in the laundry area, the clothes I folded were thrown all over the living room."

"You thought I did that? Why would I do that?"

Alice shakes her head. "I don't know."

"Maybe the laundry basket fell..." he begins to say, but Alice interrupts. "No, Mr. Cairo, the clothes were thrown all over the living room! All over! That's why I thought you must have come back and were angry about something I did."

Peter shakes his head; how can he explain? He doesn't have a clue about any of the shit happening in the apartment. He spends the rest of the day comforting Alice. They go down to the basement together to get the remaining clothes. The basement is what you would expect from an old New York building. It is in the bowels of the building with no windows, poor lighting. Alice is jumpy, but nothing out of the ordinary happens. It's been a tough week; he will be surprised if Alice or Tony comes back. They do not.

Then Jack showed up with some cockamamy story about selling raffle tickets.

Since returning to work, Peter is never home at this time of day—not even on Saturday—and is surprised when he hears a knock on his door. Some kid is standing in the hall as surprised to see Peter as Peter is to see him.

"Yes?"

"Mr. Greenstreet?" he asks.

"No. You must have the wrong apartment."

"3C, right?"

"Yes, but no Greenstreet here."

The kid goes into this story about selling raffle tickets, which opens up the conversation because Peter tells him that he, too, went to Epiphany. He jumps all over that bit of information. Only, Peter thinks he is full of shit, looking for someone or something. Peter's first reaction is to hit him with a couple of bucks and get rid of him. Only Jack Kelly is very persistent, very charming. Peter is also wondering if he was the kid ringing the intercom the other night. Maybe he is mad at this Mr. Greenstreet? There is so much shit happening in this apartment Peter can't explain; he lets him in.

The kid is curious. Checking out the apartment. He also asks about Peter's limp, which he has picked up on rather quickly. As inquisitive as Jack is about Peter, he is also very open about himself. He tells Peter he fell through the floor in a building that was being torn down. He's stunned because he remembers this story. It was pretty big news, especially in this neighborhood; it made the front page of The New York Times. It has been over a year, and he seems to have recovered completely. It's amazing, because Peter's recollection of the story was that he wasn't expected to live. Yet here he is. Looking at him, you would never know anything like that happened to him.

"If it's not too sensitive…" Peter begins. "Where did the accident happen?"

Jack smiles. "Why would it be too sensitive? It was a condemned boarding house."

"Was it originally the old Carmelite convent?"

He shrugs.

"On Seventeenth Street?" Peter asks.

"Yes. That's where it was — only I don't know anything about it being an old convent."

While he is filling out the raffle tickets, Peter pulls out the article — it is the same property. Jack's accident happened a year before these bodies were found. How strange.

Peter calls the school Monday to find out about the bazaar and the raffle tickets to make sure he actually attends Epiphany. That he is indeed Jack Kelly. It is all true.

Several days later, Peter had dinner with Jack and his father and hired Jack to help him and his parents. Jack smells the cigarettes in the apartment immediately, along with the other oddities that happen. Only he isn't spooked like Tony and Alice, it's as if he is looking for them. Peter's always been a believer that everything is random, only now… how can he?

SISTER ELIZABETH

Sister Elizabeth pours the holy water in her hand and washes her breasts in deep prayer. Looking in the mirror carefully, she examines her breasts for any signs of change. Nothing.

These thoughts do not belong in church. I feel like it is a complete invasion of her privacy; only they come at will—not my will. They must be for a greater good, only that is not revealed to me at this time.

The priest begins to read the gospel of Matthew 20 and 1-16. It is a welcome distraction.

> "For the kingdom of heaven is like a landowner who went out early in the morning to hire workers for his vineyard. He agrees to pay them a denarius for the day and sends them to the vineyard. About nine in the morning, he went out and saw others standing in the marketplace doing nothing."

I've heard this gospel before and quite frankly never liked it. The landowner pays the men who came late the same amount as the men who were working all day. It's not fair if you take it literally. However, the priest gives it a twist. "It seems blatantly unfair, yes? Although it is his vineyard, it is his money; none of us here can argue with that. Look at it like this: the landowner is God; we all are the workers. God is simply telling us that it doesn't matter when we come to him. In the morning—the beginning of our lifes at noon as adults, or late in the day—at the end of our lives. He will open his arms and love us equally. It doesn't matter when you come. Just come!"

Just come! I like this. I want to stand up and yell "I'm here, God! It's me, Jack Kelly!"

GREENSTREET

Desiree Diamond possesses the kind of beauty that men would kill to get next to. She exploded into America's consciousness on television commercials for shampoo, men's shaving cream, and a host of other products needing a beautiful woman to help endorse them. Within a couple of years, she became the girl everyone wanted to work with, from New York to Paris. She was sexy as hell, and there wasn't a magazine in the world whose cover she did not grace before Hollywood came calling. "Phenomenon." People used that word to describe her fame. She was everywhere.

So, Kasper has no idea what to expect as he waits for her, or even why she consented to sit for him, a no nothing painter. Before meeting her, Kasper did a lot of research—looked at tons of her magazine covers, even begging his way into a rough cut of the recent movie she made out in Hollywood. There had been consistent whispers about drug use, especially in the past year. All efforts towards trying to create two separate images of her for the dual portraits he was hoping to paint.

The movie doesn't change his image of her. Basically, it's about a detective investigating the disappearance of a beautiful woman who may have been murdered. The detective falls in love with the idea of her as told in flashback. Desiree speaks very little dialogue and doesn't do much in the movie except look wonderful. She jumps off the screen and steals every scene in which she appears.

Kasper sits and waits for her. It will come as no surprise if she never shows up. Besides a taste for drugs, she has a reputation for always being late.

The knock on his door at 3 p.m., the exact appointment time, catches him off guard. Like a schoolboy in over his head, Kasper slowly opens the door to find this gorgeous girl holding a cup of tea in one hand and a French cigarette in the other.

"Kasper Greenstreet?" she asks in that voice, that sultry, smoky, deep in a goddess kind of way voice. If anyone could ever live up to the name Desiree Diamond, it's this girl. She once did a big ad campaign for Tiffany's with the heading, "Desire Diamonds," in which she is not wearing anything but diamonds, necklaces, and bracelets—you get the point.

"Yes, come in."

My, he thinks, is she beautiful! Not perfect—just enough imperfections on her face to make Desiree more mysterious, more interesting.

Desiree turns out to be not at all what Kasper expected. First, she is not obviously high, although she may have had a taste of something on the way over.

"Thank you for meeting with me—I can't wait to paint you," he says a little too greedily.

"Oh? I hope our friend didn't tell you I said 'yes'. He's done that before without actually having gotten a 'yes' from me." Desiree lights a cigarette with the cigarette she hasn't quite finished. The friend she is referring to is Mr. Hillibrand, and he tends to think he has more power over people than he actually does. Kasper understands that. He also understands her drug use makes it all very fragile.

"I'd like to see what you're about—what you have in mind for me," she purrs.

He quickly throws what he had in mind out the window, because one more man flattering her is not going to whet her appetite. He needs to give her a feast. So, he talks about duality in life, in society, as he moves around the apartment pulling out art books.

"What I'm hoping to capture is who you are in your soul in one painting, and how the world perceives you in the other."

"Image?" Desiree asks as Kasper pours himself a Cognac. "I'll take one of those," she adds before he asks.

"No, not image, image can be a marketing tool. What I am talking about, for example, is that someone may see you as the most beautiful woman in the world." Flipping through the pages, he finds Botticelli's *Birth of Venus*. "Someone else may find you to be a contradiction." He locates Picasso's painting of Dora Maar. He piles them on his bed.

"What do you mean, contradiction?" Desiree asks.

He wants to say she's marketed as a perfect woman, yet there are the drugs and the disastrous love affairs. He keeps it to himself. Instead, he says, "People think you are beautiful, that you make a lot of money, that you have everything."

"What is everything?" she asks.

Placing all the books at her feet, he says, "Exactly."

Kasper opens each book to the paintings he wants to show her, announcing each one as he places it at her feet: "*Birth of Venus*—Botticelli, *Portrait of Dora*—Picasso, *Olympia*—Manet, *Mona Lisa*—DaVinci, *Girl with a Pearl Earring*—Vermeer, *Portrait of Adele*—Klimt, *Whistler's Mother*—Whistler, *The Sistine Madonna*—Raphael."

She slides down onto the floor next to him with the grace and poise of a yoga teacher. "Tell me what you are thinking," she says, looking at him with her steel-blue eyes, before turning back to the book.

"I'd like to draw you in a few of these poses, or maybe even a combination of several of them before deciding which or what to paint. Of course, it would be in contrast to the portrait of you."

Desiree studies the *Birth of Venus*. "Do you have a magnifying glass?" she asks without looking up. He gets two magnifying glasses, and they go through the painting in great detail. "There is duality in this painting, right?" Desiree asks.

"Yes, I guess she's meant to be an earthly figure who symbolizes physical love but also a goddess who inspired intellectual love."

Desiree looks at Kasper. He is a smitten schoolboy. "Did you make that up just now? Or did you read that somewhere?"

"Art history. I read it. I'm sure it's in the book."

She looks around at the other paintings. She picks up the book that shows *Olympia* by Manet.

"Olympia? Tell me about this one."

"It's obviously a nude. Why don't you read the note under the picture?" Kasper says.

"Okay, we can take turns." She says it like they are two friends in high school. "A nude depiction of a prostitute was an outrage among the people in Paris because it humanized prostitution. Hmmm… it also enraged the public since it was unusual for a woman, yet alone a prostitute, to stare at someone so bluntly as the main subject of the painting does."

They examine every inch of the picture.

"Picasso … don't you just love to say his name?" Desiree asks. "*Dora Maar.*' I just love this painting—although I don't understand Cubism."

They examine it with the magnifying glasses. "Love the hands," she says.

"His use of color," Kasper adds.

"Her eyes," Desiree says, tracing them with her finger.

"When someone referred to the background of a painting as 'the negative space,' Picasso supposedly said there was no 'negative space'…that is supposedly how Cubism was created."

Desiree looks up, waiting for more.

"Cubism is a style that has no clear lines between the subject and the background."

"Hmmm. You know I would love another Cognac," she says.

"Sorry, where are my manners?" Kasper gets up and pours both of them another glass.

They stayed on *Dora* and Picasso a long time.

Looking up at Desiree's face, Kasper lingers on her eyes, her mouth, her chin. He is a child at Christmas, hoping that the gift under the tree is that she will allow him to paint her.

Next, she chooses Johannes Vermeer's *The Girl with a Pearl Earring.* They lie on the floor without saying a word for the longest time.

"You want me to read?" he finally asks. "They say it's the Dutch Mona Lisa."

"I don't see that," Desiree says, followed by a long silence. Eventually, they discuss the painting's masterful portrayal of light and shadow. Duality. That interests her, but Kasper doesn't try to close the deal. He's afraid to blow it.

"Mona Lisa, Mona Lisa, they have named you. Did you ever see this painting in person?" Desiree asks.

"No. I've never been to Europe. Have you?"

"Yes. I've seen her twice." He waits for her to continue. "The first time I saw her was during Fashion Week about five years ago. A few of us went to the Louvre. We were all surprised at how physically small the painting was because the story of the painting is so large." Sipping her Cognac, she touches Mona Lisa's eyes, her smile. "I went back the next day by myself to really see her." Desiree turns the page, then flips it back to the portrait for one more long look.

Desiree turns to *Whistler's Mother*, an arrangement in gray and black by James McNeill Whistler. "So, 'Whistler's Mother' was originally a McNeill?" Desiree asks. She silently reads the synopsis next to the painting in the book. "Anna McNeill Whistler. Only she is known to us as 'Whistler's Mother.' I wonder if the painting would have had the same impact if it had been named Anna McNeill? Or just Mother. 'Whistler's Mother'—the apostrophe 's' makes it possessive, no?" Looking at her, Kasper hopes this painting doesn't turn her off in some way, prompting her to decide she would rather not have him paint her.

"You know, it became an icon in the States as a tribute to mothers during the Depression and ended up on a post office stamp." It's a throwaway line— he's trying not to lose her interest.

Desiree gets up on her knees. "You said you want to sketch me?"

"I would love to…"

"How about starting with this one?"

Whistler's Mother? he thinks to himself. This is where you want to start? Fuck…

He doesn't care. He's elated.

Kasper grabs his sketch pad, picks up a chair, and quickly tries to stage the sitting. Desiree studies the painting. She takes an old, dirty, square lace doily from an end table and turns it into the headdress of *Whistler's Mother*, then wraps Kasper's dark blue spread around her while looking around the apartment for other props. She settles on a napkin for the handkerchief and brings the book to the chair, leaving it open at her feet. Desiree takes a few minutes to get the posture and the hands right before going still.

Kasper wonders if he should be embarrassed because he has one of the most famous ladies of the past ten years sitting in his roach-infested apartment, letting him sketch her.

Kasper does several sketches of her as *Whistler's Mother*; she loves one. He hands her another Cognac and then lights a joint. She decides to have him sketch her as *The Birth of Venus*. With glee, Kasper watches her turn from Whistler's Mother to a goddess right before his eyes. Her body is very beautiful, the color of fresh snow. You cannot look at anything else; it would be like looking at the dark sky when a full white moon is out, just impossible. While moving her and some furniture around, Kasper notices the track marks on the back of Desiree's legs.

It's true: this beautiful lady is an addict. Kasper wants to care, and should, but what he wants more is to draw her. Then he can paint her.

Desiree Diamond as the birth of Venus will be coming out of a television set instead of the sea, how she was created. On one side, instead of a lady with a robe, he will paint a giant needle with dope shooting from it. Instead of a couple on the right side of her, Kasper will portray lustful men and a lecherous public gawking at her. But he doesn't whisper a hint of that to Desiree, who is as joyful in her nakedness as Kasper is in sketching her.

She seems to like all the sketches of her as Venus. Of course, she doesn't know it will be a TV set she will be coming out of, not a shell from the sea.

"We might as well do *Olympia*, since we're short on costumes," Desiree says, taking a shoelace out of one of his shoes and tying it around her neck to imitate the model in the painting. Even with a few Cognacs and a joint in her, she immediately gets her hands and expression to match the painting. It has been a long time since he's been with a woman; the thought of having sex with her is almost as captivating as drawing her nude. Only she is all business. There is no desire for him.

Desiree goes through the sketches of her with the same detached professionalism. She is a commodity, in the business of herself.

It is late. She finishes posing and dresses quickly. "If you would like, come with me to Fontaine's for a dress fitting tomorrow at four," she suggests.

"What? Yes, of course." He already has an appointment with Susan, with a possible chance of seeing Mitch, but work comes first. Star appeal. Desiree possesses it in mega-wattage.

The following afternoon, Kasper hides in the corner of clothes designer Fontaine's private studio and sneaks out a sketchpad. I've been invisible most of my life, he thinks, today more than ever I want to stay invisible. Don't want to piss off the "Great Fontaine." He has a famously bad reputation.

Kasper watches as the designer, as well as his employees, patiently wait for Desiree to come out of the dressing room in full hair and makeup. He says something in Italian to one of his assistants, and she immediately jumps up to see if Desiree is ready. Within minutes, Desiree glides gracefully into the room in a clinging, fire engine-red dress, her raven hair floating behind her. She is wearing red evening gloves with matching lips.

The designer's people let out a gasp at the sight of her—she is that electric.

A photo shoot is set up for the Christmas issue of *Vanity Fair*, the same time her movie is to be released. Two photographers snap photos of her from every angle, all in white. Disco music starts to play. Desiree raises her hand. "Can we get some Christmas music on instead?" she asks.

Fontaine's people begin running around. Fontaine yells upstairs to play Christmas music. He then kisses her gloved hand in a grand gesture and whispers to her. Within ten minutes, Christmas music begins to play, and the photographers begin shooting her, highlighting what will become known as the "Red Dress" when she hits the cover of *Vanity Fair*. Kasper sketches four very good images of her, which he will use to create the other painting.

He decides Desiree Diamond in the Vanity Fair dress, stuck in a Barbie doll box, to be one of her portraits. Originally, Kasper thought the first portrait would include her as the *Birth of Venus* coming out of a television set, but this is a better idea. Kasper decides to make the painting look "pentimento," an alteration in a painting evidenced by traces of previous work, showing that the artist has changed his or her mind about the composition during the process of painting. The word is Italian for repentance. His goal is to make it look in the portrait as if she has changed her mind about herself—repented from the image she has created—Desiree is Venus, Olympia, Whistler's Mother, The Girl with the Pearl Earring, Mona Lisa, Adele from the *Woman in Gold*, and maybe even the Madonna at different stages—moments of her life.

The shoot takes several hours from beginning to end. Once it is done, Fontaine breaks out champagne. Desiree takes a glass, kisses him, and heads back to her dressing room. As quiet as a mouse, Kasper makes his way back to the dressing room and knocks lightly on the door.

"It's me, Kasper."

"Come in."

That voice! Slipping into the room, he praises her. She is tired.

"Did anybody notice you sketching?" Desiree asks.

"No one but you."

"Let's see." He sheepishly shows them to her, only wanting to please her. He's afraid they won't but knows it's too late for her to object because he has enough material to paint her portraits. Desiree looks them over like an accountant. She smiles. "Very nice, Kasper. Can I call you? I'm very tired."

"Of course. Thanks for inviting me this evening. Watching you work was amazing."

She smiles.

- - -

Back in the apartment, Kasper takes two vials of blood out of the refrigerator to use for her red dress. Mixing his blood with the paint, he begins to paint her in a version of the Fontaine dress. This portrait flows easily for him; she is wonderful to paint on a big canvas. However, he struggles with the Barbie-like box. It keeps looking like a coffin, or is that just in his head? He adds more of his blood with the blue around the box to make it work. The background, or "negative space" behind her, is dark blue like the box she is in, making it appear she is floating in space with nothing to grab on to.

The telephone rings. Kasper looks up from the canvas. It is close to midnight. His first thought is to ignore the phone, but he doesn't.

"Hey."

"Desiree?"

"Yes. Meet me at Studio 54. I'll make sure the doorman lets you in." Click.

Paint and blood stain his clothes. He definitely needs a shower, but fuck it—it's late. He changes clothes and sprays on a little Fontaine's cologne, smokes a joint, and hits the streets.

It is a zoo. The line goes around the corner. Most of these people will never get in. Kasper has heard or read that the group Chic wrote their hit song "Le Freak" because they could not get into the club. How the hell was he going to get in? Walking sheepishly to the doorman, he says, "Kasper Greenstreet—I'm meeting Desiree Diamond."

Desiree is true to her word. Mentioning her name works like a witch's spell.

Inside, the bar is five deep with thirsty patrons, the dancers spilling off the floor. Thoughts that he is in a glossy version of limbo fill his mind. I must paint that image sometime. Reaching in his pocket, he caresses the weed he carries. He needs a taste. It takes one lap around the club before he spots her sitting in a private area on the edge of a couch. Mr. Movie Star has got her by the hand, whispering in her ear. Gay men surround the couch, wanting to touch her, have a word. All the straight men want to fuck her. All the women sitting with Desiree or standing nearby want to be her; it is an orgy of attention. In the midst of the most famous people in the world, she becomes Mona Lisa.

Kasper sits down and begins sketching her from a distance. She appears to look directly at him with Mona Lisa's eyes. Should I wave? No, she doesn't see me, or if she does, she does not acknowledge me. Has she forgotten that she invited me?

Desiree leans in and snorts a line of coke from the mirror Mr. Movie Star is holding. I miss her already, Kasper thinks.

It is the last night he will ever see or hear from her.

- - -

There are times when a painter struggles with artist's block, like a writer. Not his problem as of late. He paints all day. His first portrait of Desiree is done, and it is exactly what he wants. Working on the pentimento portrait is much more delicate and harder to pull off, but it proves great fun. Desiree looks marvelous coming out of the television screen as Venus. Kasper decides not to use a large needle on the side of her; however, he sticks with the lustful public and men. He hides the needles and the drugs in various other ways. Desiree as Whistler's Mother has a syringe in her hands rather than a handkerchief. Directly above Venus to the left is Desiree as Mona Lisa—still visible, but slightly faded. His version of Picasso's Dora is Desiree in all her contradictions, the golden girl with the tragic problem. The portrait of Adele in Gold shows Desiree with a mirror in her lap, a line of cocaine, and a rolled-up bill for snorting.

Not eating all day has made him crazy, not to mention the pot and the Cognac, but Kasper needs his blood on this portrait as well. Pouring a little more Cognac, he gets a vial from the fridge and mixes blood with the gold dress of Adele. Now feeling he is physically, emotionally, and spiritually a part of her, or at least her painting, Kasper sits back and reviews his work.

Kasper not sure how long he's been sitting looking at his pentimento portrait. He has a brush in one hand and Cognac in the other; he's either in deep meditation or he falls asleep. Time is an illusion—he doesn't know if it's been seconds or days. It takes an eternity for him to move the paint brush toward the canvas.

"It's perfect, as it is."

Kasper thinks he hears a knock on the door. Perhaps Mitch has come in? Is he in Kasper's mind, or standing behind him? Kasper drops the brush to the floor at the sound of Mitch's voice. "Why you sneaking up on me?" he slurs.

"Sneaking up on you? I knocked for ten minutes before opening the door. I stood behind you for another ten minutes trying not to disturb you. Wow!" Mitch says. "Kasper, it's wonderful."

He walks around the apartment, looking at all the empty Cognac bottles, all the leftover joints, and eyes Kasper from the side. "When was the last time you ate?"

"What time is it?" Kasper mumbles.

"Six p.m."

"Could be hours, could be days."

"It smells in here — you smell," Mitch adds.

Mitch clears off the bed, then comes back and takes Kasper under the arm and puts him to bed. Kasper falls asleep instantly and does not remember Mitch being there.

JULIA AND MR. CAIRO

I'm going through the list Peter gave me. The main item is to pick up Mr. Cairo's prescriptions on the way over to their apartment. It is Julia's canasta day, so Mr. Cairo and I will have time to communicate. As I walk to the drugstore on 23rd Street, I keep thinking about the people who lived in Peter's apartment before he did—the Michaels. If I find them, I may find the mysterious Kasper Greenstreet. Peter has given me complete access in my pursuit of Kasper; I have the name and number of the super of the building. I tried calling him a couple of times, but he never picks up. Can you imagine if you really needed help?

I've thought about it more than once, and people from the mystic group say it point-blank, "You may be dealing with a spirit." Honestly, a ghost would be the easiest explanation. However, the reason I do not believe that Kasper is a ghost is that Aunt Paula saw him on the street. I'm pretty sure that Peter also saw him on 2nd Avenue the night he walked me home.

What I've read—what I've been told—is that, typically, ghosts stay locked into one place. Kasper is wandering all over the city. Smoking in front of the building, following us around like he is part of the living. Not at all like the spirits in the subway.

I am ahead of schedule and decide to stop at Peter's apartment. Once inside, I decide this is the day. I will do my ritual. I light some white sage and walk through the apartment, trying to smudge and spread it everywhere. Next, I light some sandalwood. If it works in exorcisms, maybe it will keep this guy—spirit—out of the apartment. Standing in the center of his living room, I say a prayer that the apartment will be free of whatever is causing this turmoil. Finally, I hang two dream catchers, one in the living room by the window where I first spotted Kasper. I'm thinking I should hang the second in Peter's bedroom, so he can sleep better.

As I open his closet, the sound of the guest bedroom door slams. Turning, I hold the dream catcher up much the same way a vampire hunter in an old movie would hold up a cross. I walk slowly toward the doorway with Peter's bat. Just in case it's an actual living person.

The door to the guest bedroom is closed. I hang the dream catcher on the door knob—it is ice cold, which alarms me.

It brings me back to Stevie's hospital room. The night we had to change his room because it was unnaturally cold. That was when the shadows were at their worst, trying to get at him every night.

The chill outside the door snaps me back to the present. Now what? I push the door open, bat ready for action. It's even colder inside the room. No one is in the bedroom; I check the windows to see if they are open. They are closed. I light more white sage and wave it around the room. Does any of this shit really work? I hang the dream catcher inside the room. It only gets colder. Looking at the clock I realize I have to go. I don't want to be late for Julia.

I jog through Stuyvesant Town, worried I'm going to be late. Julia opens the door and is ready to go; only I can smell her apprehension. Onions, sour milk. I need to help her change that.

"You look beautiful, Julia," I say, meaning it. She really is a beautiful woman for any age. Julia tilts her head and looks at me like I said something in a foreign language.

"Oh, boy, are the girls going to be in trouble." Julia smiles and motions for me to come in. The onion and sour milk smell fades.

Walking into the living room, I greet Mr. Cairo. He looks up at me with his crooked smile. Julia begins like she does every Thursday. "I don't really feel like going today," she says.

"Do you want to get me in trouble with Peter?" I say.

"Peter… he's gotten very bossy," she says with a straight face. "Not sure where he gets that from. Mr. Cairo and I are very easygoing."

Wow. Now she smells citrusy. We do this same dance every week. "Here are the numbers, Jack. If you need me, I'm just a few buildings away."

"Don't worry, Julia—have fun—we will be fine."

The minute she is gone, I break out the coloring book and crayons and move Mr. Cairo to the dining room table. He is getting better at coloring inside the lines. I look around for their white and yellow pages. Mr. Cairo looks over at me.

"Phone book? The yellow pages?" I say.

A traffic light with the color yellow flashes over his head. He points to a broom closet, where I find the white and yellow pages. Flipping through the yellow pages, I search under "Art Galleries," looking for the name Michaels to be somewhere in the mix. No luck. There are, however, many galleries. Some with names of people, some with names like "5th Avenue Art" or "Night Gallery." I tear out the pages, which draws a look from Mr. Cairo. I start flicking through the white pages until I get to the name Greenstreet. I find roughly forty-nine people with the last name Greenstreet in Manhattan.

"Can I use your telephone?" I wait for either the bobbing bobblehead for yes or the slamming door for no. I get neither. Two pieces of thread hover above his head. One short, one long. I understand it immediately. "It's a local call, Mr. Cairo." He shows me the bobblehead.

"How's the coloring going?" Picking up the book with his left hand, he shows me he has colored in the lines. "Great."

As I dial people with the name Greenstreet, I have the following speech ready: "Hi, I am looking for Mr. Kasper Greenstreet, who lived on 22nd Street between 2nd and 3rd, or he may have known someone who lived in the Gramercy Terrace." Mostly, I get a lot of no's, as well as a lot of phones that no one picks up. I notice Mr. Cairo looking at me. The blue blanket for Peter is over his head. God, he doesn't miss a trick.

"I'm trying to find someone who may have lived or may have known someone who lived in Peter's building." Bobblehead and then three beach balls bouncing in the air. It takes me a moment. Mr. Cairo shows a bobblehead followed by three beach balls again. Which I take to mean he wants more, a better explanation.

"This guy is of no danger to Peter or me—more of a curiosity." That's true and a lie. Peter sleeps for shit, and I think it has everything to do with Kasper. I put a small 'x' by names where someone picked up and said "no" to the question, or a small check mark if I get no answer. I underline the last Greenstreet I call.

"Mr. Cairo, you were a detective—how can I find someone who may have lived in a building several years ago?" I ask.

Nothing appears over his head. He continues coloring. Carefully, I begin to tear some pages out of the phone book.

Is he ignoring me? Or did he not hear me? After a beat, Mr. Cairo looks up at me. Over his head is the actual commercial for the yellow pages. "Let your fingers do the walking." Followed by the picture of a man who looks like Moses.

"Oh," I say. "Old telephone books." Bobblehead nods. "Phone company?" Bobblehead. "Any other ideas?" Four eggs over his head, then a long pause. "Eggs?" Dropping his crayon. Four eggs. I start to speak. He raises his good hand to motion for me to wait. Mr. Cairo is struggling. Four eggs, two chickens. Papers blowing around.

"Frustration," I say. Bobblehead. Four eggs. "Four?" Bobblehead. One chicken. "One—oh 411." Bobblehead nodding.

"Can I use your phone?" Bobblehead. Mr. Cairo continues to color. I begin calling art galleries. My script is as follows: "Do Susan and Mitch Michaels own this gallery?" Mainly no's, though every once in a while they put me on hold and never come back. I'm striking out. I decided to give it a rest and concentrate on Mr. Cairo.

"Are you hungry?" Door shuts. "You want me to see what is on as the 4:30 movie?"

Mr. Cairo hands me a crayon. I look at it, only I don't immediately get what he is saying because I'm dense, frustrated, and in a hurry. "What do you want me to do with it?" He stares at me.

"Okay. It's a green crayon." He does that weird half smile, which is attributed to the stroke. Mr. Cairo starts flipping through the coloring book. Papers blowing in the wind. Great, now he is frustrated. He stops on a page that has a rock with Arthur standing on top of it looking down on men with horses.

I look at the picture in the coloring book and offer the crayon back to him. He takes the crayon and draws two lines for the horses. Hands the crayon back to me with his thumb pointing to the name of the color. "Yes, green." Bobblehead nodding. He points to the men on horses between the lines. Mr. Cairo then holds the green crayon up. "Greenstreet?" Bobblehead nodding. We stare at each other for a beat. "Greenstreet. What about him? I've called the numbers. I haven't gotten a match."

Again, he flips through the coloring book and finds a picture he has colored well. He points to the pages in the yellow pages that I have ripped out. Picking them up, I offer them to him. Bobblehead nods. "You think I should call the gallery and ask if they are owned by Michaels or Greenstreet?" Bobblehead nods again.

I get up and make us some tea. Mr. Cairo is tired, so I bring him back into the living room and turn on the 4:30 movie, to which he falls asleep. Immediately, I go back to making telephone calls to galleries to see if Susan, Mitch Michaels, or a Mr. Greenstreet own or work there. No luck.

The telephone rings. It might be Julia checking in, so I pick it up. "Cairo residence."

Nice. It's Peter. He wants me to stop at his apartment if I can on my way home tonight. "Not a problem."

Peter asks to speak to his dad. I tell him Mr. Cairo is sleeping. "Do you want me to wake him up?"

"No. No. Just wanted to say hi."

"Is there anything special you want to talk about?" I ask.

"Yes," he says. "Only it would be better if you were here in person."

I make one last quick phone call to Neue Gallery 21. "Hi, I am looking for a Susan or Mitch Michaels?"

The woman is kind of chatty. "Do they work for us?"

"They could be the owners of the gallery."

"No. This is corporate owned."

"Oh, well do you have a Greenstreet there or is he maybe in corporate?"

"Don't think so…"

"Okay." I get ready to hang up.

"Wait, you're not talking about the artist Kasper Greenstreet, are you?"

"Yes I am!"

"We do have a piece of his earlier work."

"Can I see it?"

"Sure. We open at 4 p.m. and close at 9. Do you know where we are located?" I read the address from the yellow pages. "Yes, that's us."

We hang up. My brain is not tricking me. I must trust myself, my intuition—stop doubting what I know to be true. I've seen him painting in the apartment.

- - -

I use my keys to let myself into Peter's building but knock on the apartment door. He opens it immediately. "What's up?" I ask as he looks around the hallway.

"Come in." I follow Peter into the apartment. Everything is normal. The smell of the white sage lingers in the air. But he doesn't seem right. "Peter?" He walks to the guest room and opens the door; it is freezing inside.

"When I came home from work, the room was like this. Were you here earlier?"

"Yes, remember? I asked you if I could light the sage."

"Did you notice anything weird?"

"The door to the bedroom was shut. When I opened it was cold in the room, but not this cold."

The heat is clearly working in the rest of the apartment. The living room is warm, hot really. Peter shows me the two dream catchers that I hung up.

"You, right?"

"Yes."

"One was on the floor in the living room, the other was on the floor outside the bedroom."

Outside the bedroom?

"Maintenance is going to check out the problem tomorrow. Can you come over after school and let them in?"

"Sure."

Peter looks at me. "It's weird, right?"

I nod. I've seen this movie before—that night in the hospital with Stevie. But I can't tell Peter about the shadows.

The minute I leave Peter's, I pull out the address to the Neue Gallery 21.

Neue Gallery 21 is larger and more extravagant than I expected. There are two levels. The first has a grand double staircase and a brightly lit room. There are several massive paintings on the wall. One looks like someone took cans of paint and tossed them onto the canvas. Inspecting it, my mouth drops at the price. Who the hell has a wall large enough, or a bank account big enough, for a painting that size? A tall, impeccably dressed man shows a couple around, giving information about the work and the artist. He glances my way; his look says "who are you and where are the adults with money?" Stopping along the way, I appreciate a sculpture, but sticker shock again keeps me moving.

I walk up the staircase to find a small, manicured woman at a square glass table with a telephone and a notepad. She is writing. "Yes?" she says without looking up.

"I called earlier. I'm here to see the Kasper Greenstreet painting."

She looks up at me, and a smile slides across her face as she gets up from the desk. "I'm Deli," she says, reaching out her hand.

"Jack. Jack Kelly."

"Are you here alone?"

"Yes."

"So, what makes you interested in Kasper Greenstreet?"

"Just exploring," I answer. The less you say, Jack, the better.

We walk over to a small painting that is dimly lit. It's beautiful, with lots of colors. A flower field. Very different from everything else in the gallery.

"This is his earlier work," I say, repeating what she told me earlier on the telephone, only she has forgotten and thinks I'm saying it like I'm aware of it.

"Yes, it is. Very different from his later work, as you know." The tall, impeccably dressed man is now upstairs without his clients.

"No. I've only seen his early work." That's not a lie. I've seen this painting, which is his older work, so technically that is the truth, right?

"Do you have any of his newer work?"

"No."

"Have you seen any of the newer work?"

Deli looks at me like I'm from Mars. "Kasper Greenstreet? Of course!"

"Where can I see those paintings?" I ask.

"Private collectors, but they might be in art books."

"How can I find him?" I ask, like the naive kid I am. Then I throw in, "Do you know the Michaels—they own an art gallery?"

The tall man stops what he is doing and stares at me with contempt. He walks over to the desk and writes something down on a piece of paper and hands it to me.

"You can find Kasper Greenstreet here."

I take the paper. "Thank you."

Deli stares at the man with a peculiar look on her face.

I smile. "Thank you, Deli; it's been an education."

- - -

I am ecstatic after getting Kasper Greenstreet's address. It makes taking the subway home less frightful. There are little movements, small whispers, but nothing serious. The subway car has plenty of open seats when I get on, so I take one in the corner, put my feet up, and relax. No hair-standing-on-end excitement tonight. I'm tired and drift into a light sleep.

Someone touches me, caresses my face, pushing the hair back away from my eyes. It startles me awake.

"Jack, why so jumpy?" Katherine slides next to me on the couch. She kisses my lips. "Boy, were you out. Snoring and everything." She giggles.

"I think I was dreaming."

"Yeah? About me?" she asks. Oh, how I love her voice.

"Always. Well actually I think I was in New York on a train and… I don't really know." Katherine puts her head on my chest and looks up at me. So sweet that look she gives me—the look of love. "Jack."

"Katherine."

"Jack."

I know it's a stupid little game, only we love to play it.

"Katherine…"

"Jack." She puts her finger to my lips. "We are going to have a baby."

The happiness that surges in me leaves me over the moon. We've been hoping—trying—a lot.

"Oh, my God, Katherine. A baby."

She kisses me with her lips, her tongue—oh, my delicious Katherine.

I open my eyes. Her beautiful face is gone; I am back on the subway train. My disappointment flies off the Richter scale.

Across from me is a shadow wearing a fedora. His head is down, as if looking at something. On the floor of the train, a human heart lies beating. I look at my chest and see blood dripping from where my heart should be. I bring my hands up and attempt to stop the bleeding. The shadow raises its head and looks directly at me. It's yellow eyes glow.

The train stops at the station, jolting me awake. Across from me, a man stares queerly. Have I been twitching again, making those convulsing motions? I stand up, look around to see a sprinkle of shadows watching me. It is 23rd Street—my stop. Stepping out of the car onto the platform, I am met by shadows and one of those creatures with the skeletal horse head. Hideous things with their long arms, legs, hands, and tail.

"The Lord is my shepherd; I shall not want," I say. "Though I walk through the valley of the shadow of death, I will fear no evil for the Lord is with me!"

They do nothing, try nothing. At the moment, I fear nothing! My chest and I are whole. Nothing is wrong except my broken heart. I miss my Katherine.

NONE OF THE DEAD
COME BACK, BUT SOME
NEVER LEAVE

School is long and boring. During study time, I map my route to Kasper's house, with the help of the subway map. Once the bell rings, I head straight to Peter's to handle the maintenance issue. The worker is on time. He turns the heat on; of course it works. Looking at me, he feels the heat coming from the radiator in the room and raises his eyebrows. Then checks a couple of things by the radiator just to humor me.

"It wasn't working yesterday; I was here," I say.

That changes nothing. The man does very little, yet the room warms up quickly. "Well, it's working now."

I feel the heat coming off the radiator.

The minute I leave Peter's apartment building, I'm hit with the sensation that someone is following me. This year has taught me a few things: what watches and follows does not necessarily need to be of this world. For a quick minute, I wonder if it is someone from my school. Stepping into a storefront, I indulge my paranoia. No obvious trail. I get myself settled on the train, only I can't shake the feeling that someone is with me. Would the

175

maintenance man follow? Maybe it's neurosis. Everything always comes back to the "insult" to my brain.

Once the train is in motion, I feel a chill come over me. I look around for all those things the subway seems to bring to me. Or brings out in me?

I decide to move to the next car and step into the "in between." Pausing for a moment, I stand in the middle of the two train cars. The "in between" is what I like to refer to as that place you are enroute to. Could be a physical destination, a state of mind, an emotion. However, you are detained long enough between the two places to get a sense of something else. Not of this world, not of the next. It can be the place where we learn the most. In my case, now standing between the cars, looking at the tunnel, I spot those creatures—skeletal horse heads, their tails dragging behind. Walking, hiding in tunnels like transients from another dimension.

A man looks at me from the window of the subway car I just left, which causes me to hurry into the safety of the next car. I turn back; he is no longer there. My heart races. I step further into the car and look for a seat. A man appears to be looking through the window from the in between place of the car in front. It's the same man.

Come on, Jack, they are fucking with you! You know the drill. Don't get jumpy.

I take a seat and prepare myself for the worst. Instead, the soft rocking of the train brings me back to the day the addict died. Maybe it's him following me, maybe he's trapped down here. Show yourself—I can help you.

I come out of the subway and walk through a neighborhood of storefronts. Following the address, the business district comes to an end. I find myself standing in front of a cemetery. Shit. I have to be in the wrong place. I look at the address and think either the man at the gallery is a complete asshole, or Kasper is dead. How else could this guy get in and out of Peter's apartment? That should have been easy. Everyone alluded to it...including Peter.

Walking through the cemetery is not scary but kind of peaceful. Very quiet. Inside the office, I get directions to Kasper Greenstreet's plot. I ask if they have a Susan or Mitch Michaels there as well. "Yes, they are here." Only they were cremated and in a community mausoleum with small individual crypts.

Outside the crypts, I see a man meandering around, causing me to hesitate. He looks my way. Do I know him? I feel like I do. Before I can get a good look, he leaves. I find the crypt of Susan and Mitch Michaels; they died on the same day. The date of death aligns with what the woman from Peter's building told me. I'm getting a migraine!

I look around at the other crypts and get a feeling, a dusting of energy, a scent, a chill that the man left behind. It makes me aware of how light my jacket is or maybe how thin my skin is beginning to feel. Kasper Greenstreet's plot is nothing special. Not for a famous artist. It's just an ordinary gravesite. He died within a year of the Michaels. Above me, a flock of crows appear, making ghastly noises. Not their usual sound. Crows are not typically referred to as a flock; they live in a group called "a murder." Did you know that? I read it somewhere. Crows don't scare me, but this cemetery just got really creepy. A murder is not the only name for a group of crows, of course. They are sometimes called a horde, or a muster. But a murder fits them better with the sounds they make, the darkness that is coming, the ominous feeling now blanketing me. The man I saw earlier at the Michaels' crypt suddenly stands a few feet from me. It is as if the crows have delivered him to me, or me to him.

My instinct is to run. I am dealing with myth, a hoax, a superstition, but what do you call it when you see it? Meet it? A spirit, a ghost, that is alive and dead at the same time. My body and soul are not pleased! It is like getting hit with the coldest and hottest day of the year within seconds of each other. Like the happiest emotion you may ever experience within a moment of your worst. I am frozen but in some bizarre way, I expect him to introduce himself.

You've been looking for me? Well, here I am.

Kasper Greenstreet is the man I've been watching from my classroom, but he looks much different up close. His complexion is ash, his wrists reveal his exit wounds, and blood appears to seep from them like a slow dripping faucet.

What I feel is not fear—it is greater than that! None of the dead come back, but some stay...

I fumble for my mantra, Psalm 23: "Though I walk through the valley of the shadow of death, I will fear no evil..."

My head spins with words, thoughts. None, however, that can make me disappear or get me back to my life. If you can keep your head, Jack, when all about you are losing theirs… Yours is the earth and everything that's in it… Light will always chase away darkness…

Kasper stares at me. All I hear is the sound of the blood dripping from his wrists.

Run, fool, run! Only, I don't. Looking down at the tombstone, I say his name, the date of his birth, the date of his death. Kasper is unfazed. He is a totally different presence than what I have experienced thus far. The pregnant woman on the train platform was confused; she wasn't even aware of being dead. Kasper knows. Blood drips on the ground in front of him. A crow falls dead on his grave. The birds erupt, making sounds like they are widows crying at a funeral. Run, Jack! Run!

Suddenly it is dusk. The sounds from the crows get louder, constantly interrupting all my tools for staying calm. They fly around us like they are at a prize fight and we are the main event. A migraine beats in my head like my heart beats in my chest. Around us, they screech and dive, making me feel claustrophobic. I step away from the grave.

Don't turn your back on him, Jack!

It is ridiculous of me not to ask him what he wants. Why won't he leave Peter's apartment? My vocal cords are paralyzed. I'm too afraid to speak.

I step away from Kasper, preparing for flight. He stands in place, blood oozing from his wrists. I look down and notice that a drop of his blood has landed on my shoe. I back up, frightened, and trip over a headstone. I have thoughts of hands, arms coming out of graves to grab me. As I leap back to my feet, Kasper is no longer there. I look around for him, but he has vanished. Can they do that? Get in and out of their grave? I try to find my way back to the entrance of the cemetery, but it's a maze, and I find myself standing in front of the Michaels' crypt. Where is he? Don't tell me they're going to show up now! The office is which way? Come on, Jack, keep it together. Confused, I turn around about to lose my shit. The murder of crows escorts me out. They call to me—really, yell at me—as if to say, "You are not wanted here, Jack Kelly. Leave the dead alone!"

Finding my way back to the train is more difficult in the dark. Plus, I am disoriented, crazy. Every freak in the world is heading back into Manhattan. We got your grouchy commuters, drug addicts, drug dealers, pick pockets, crazies, clinical, and other shadows and demons—dead and alive. I want to make them all disappear. Not tonight. The circus is in town.

One poor woman wearing a peacock feather hat appears to be completely out of her mind. She starts berating a woman sitting across from me. "That's my seat!"

At first the other woman is caught off guard. Then she starts arguing back, before realizing it is futile. You cannot argue with crazy.

"You are always stealing from me!" she yells. "That seat is mine!"

The lady with the peacock feathers glares at the woman as if she is going to attack her.

"Miss," I say, talking to the woman being accosted, you can have my seat."

Unfortunately, the woman I think is schizophrenic, which may or may not be true, turns to me. She is a complete Mad Hatter.

"No, that seat has my name on it! Look for yourself!" Then, as an afterthought, she says, "demon."

The woman in the seat gets up and practically runs to the back of the train. The "Mad Hatter" looks over at me, nods, then sits down.

Demon? Well not me, but they are certainly in our midst. You can hear the sound of those creatures. They are in the tunnel or train somewhere. Tap, tap, tap. Several shadows are on my subway car, sitting like typical commuters. One not that far from me looks straight ahead with those beady, yellow eyes darting all over the place. Doesn't anybody see this motherfucker? What about the "Mad Hatter?" Does she see them? The minute the seat next to the shadow opens, I walk over quickly and sit. This seat has my name on it. Fuck, I think, I'm as crazy as the Mad Hatter! I'm in one of those I-don't-give-a-fuck moods. Not after today, coming face to face with Kasper and his bloody wrists.

Could you imagine trying to explain what happened at the cemetery to any normal person? Maybe Mr. David might understand. Dad would want me to go back to the psychiatrist. Sister Elizabeth would likely suggest an exorcist!

I prefer myself in this state. Not the frightened little boy who fell through the floor. These things can't kill me, no matter how often they have tried to scare me to death. Death? Isn't that the final resting place? Heaven? Peace? Why in God's name would I fear death? It's all this "in-between" shit that's hard. Losing people, disappointing people, fear, anxiety, uncertainty.

The "Mad Hatter" gets up and yells something. Maybe she's stuck in the "in-between." We all see a crazy lady; only her every waking moment is stuck in this demon hole. Turning to the shadow, I whisper, "What do you want?"

His eyes turn on me. Did this fucking thing just smirk at me? Oh, hell no! I put my hand into the middle of his chest, only I do not expect to find a heart. I'm not disappointed.

Everything goes silent, still, slow motion. We are on board, yet not entirely on the train. My body is here, but my being walks in the most beautiful winter wonderland. It is cold, the beauty of the snow and its whiteness taking the sting out of the chill. Music plays loudly, one of those old-time sentimental songs my father loves. The songs that remind him of my mother. I'm jerked from that beautiful serenity into my kitchen, where my dad is sobbing, breaking the place up, smashing everything in his way. His loss, pain, and hopelessness are laid out before me.

Now I'm standing across from Kasper. His eyes are glazed over, blood dripping from his wrists. Instantly, the sounds of crashing waves replace that horror show. Within seconds, the sounds of the waves turn into the floor crashing beneath me!

I feel my body hit the ground and explode in pain.

Lying on the wet floor in my own blood and urine, I try to move. "Help…" It is a weak cry … is it mine? I see only darkness but I hear voices, then… a baby's cry?

Back on the train, a moment of clarity. My hand is still in this thing, its eyes rolling in the back of its head as if fighting me. I alter my thought process to focus on those things that live in the tunnels. That skeletal creature. I get hit with every horrifying sight, fear, in this world. Sights of Hitler, the Holocaust. Me? Yes, that's me standing in the yard watching the smoke rise from a concentration camp with the smell from the gas chambers permeating my nostrils. In rapid images, it is me trying to jump aboard the American helicopter in Vietnam as Saigon is falling. The mushroom cloud over Hiroshima, a man stabbing someone, a man being stabbed, a frightened child watching his mother being murdered. Gunfire. A lynching. More and more images. The "Mad Hatter's" mind filled with screaming voices, sending her into total madness.

I'm still aware enough to tell myself to pull out. Take your fucking hand out of this thing!

Too late—I'm on the floor in the boarding house. "Help!" My skull is cracked, blood dripping from my mouth. "Help!" A child's plea. Someone stands over me, praying. "Help!" Someone stands over me with a baseball bat. A woman clutches her throat after being poisoned. Falling to the ground, she crawls toward me on the floor, her eyes bulging from their sockets. "Help…" she screams. A bat coming down. Silence…total darkness. Am I dead?

"That's my seat!" It's the "Mad Hatter!" Once again, she captures everyone's attention on the train, including mine. "It has my name on it!"

It's not clear if she is talking to me or the shadow. I slide my hand from its chest. It is numb, ice cold. I'm having trouble feeling my hand; I try to get my bearings by bringing it to my chest like a tiny baby. "My seat!" she howls again.

Finally, the shadow gets up from the seat and melts onto the train wall with a sucking sound. Creepy. She sits down next to me; it is clear the seat does indeed belong to her. Caressing my frozen hand against my heart, I sit, thankful for her. I must add her to my book of souls.

- - -

I walk down 23rd Street, feeling hung over, the same feeling I had in the hospital when they took me off the morphine and other drugs. Vacant. Hollow. As if my body is vibrating from the inside out, altering my perspective, my view of the world, my reality. I catch sight of myself in a store window. I am that pasty white albino.

Dad is going to be pissed; it's already eight o'clock. I can hear him now: "You should have had the decency to call, Jack." You know he goes back to the night of the fall. "Just having a beer at the corner bar thinking my world is fine."

Still, I decide to stop at Peter's first. He needs to know that Kasper Greenstreet is, well, dead, and that his apartment is haunted. Standing in front of my school, I look up at Peter's apartment window. The shades are drawn.

I've always loved the name Epiphany. In second grade, I did a school report on the name. It is named after the Feast of the Epiphany, which celebrates the three wise men's visit to Jesus. Epiphany can also mean an intuitive grasp of reality; an illuminating discovery, realization, disclosure, or insight; a manifestation of God, deity, or supernatural being; or a sudden, intuitive perception of or insight into the reality or essential meaning which illuminates something.

I like another of its many definitions: "a moment, event or great revelation that changes you or alters your thinking profoundly." My epiphany, obviously, was falling through the floor in some broken-down boarding house, which manifested the supernatural in my everyday existence. Finally, the illumination of my spiritual world, seeing the physical world, as well as the unseen spirits that inhabit it. As in ghosts!

While walking to 2nd Avenue, I run into another ghost. This one speaks; "Kelly!"

Holy shit, it's Brick.

I haven't seen him since the night of my fall. He runs up to me, picks me up in a bear hug, and spins me around. Brick, who led me into that den of iniquity, is also the kid who thought fast enough to save my life. My dad told me Brick ran in front of a police car to get them to stop.

He is with some character I don't know. The kid's stoned. "Thought you moved upstate," I said.

"Yeah, we did," Brick says. "What a fucking bore. My mom and I are back here living with her friend. Mom and her sister could not live together; they were both homicidal maniacs." He laughs. "Besides, I hated it out there in the asshole of nowhere."

Brick is a couple of years older than I am. He's grown a bit since I've seen him and has a little facial hair. "Your dad hates me, Kelly," he says with no judgment.

"My dad doesn't hate anyone."

"You look good, Kelly. A little pale." If you only knew why. "I've been asking around about you."

His friend lights a joint, takes a hit, passes it to Brick. Brick was always a wild child. He used to get older kids to buy him a quart of Colt 45 and started smoking cigarettes at twelve. He takes a long drag, passes it to me.

"Better not—my dad might smell it on me."

The other kid speaks. "This stuff will light you up."

Brick looks at me, winks. "That's his way of saying it's some good shit." Brick takes another toke. "One hit ain't going to kill you."

He offers it again, and this time I take it. We stand in a closed storefront, smoking the joint. "We're on our way to 29th Street Park. Come with us."

29th Street park is filled with drugs.

"I can't."

"Still a good boy, huh, Kelly? I like that about you."

A bus stops at the red light. "That's my bus," Brick announces. They both run and hop on the back of the bus, standing on the bumper. "Hey, if you know anyone who wants to buy some great weed, let me know. I'm living in the projects!" he yells as the bus pulls away. Brick smiles and watches me until the bus disappears up the avenue.

Brick always seems to be running somewhere, to something—the next thing. Maybe I have that wrong. Maybe he's running from something. Guess we all have our private wars. What would Brick think if I told him that my war is with ghosts and demons? Probably tell me I needed more of that pot he smokes. Knowing Brick, he'd want in. "You fighting demons, sounds cool. Let's go kick some demon ass!"

Or not. Everyone has their Achilles' heel. Maybe he can't stop moving because he's afraid of what he'd find if he did.

Peter is awake and happy for the company. "Does your dad know you are here?"

My first thought is to lie. Why lie, Jack? That's so not cool. "No."

"You should call him."

"In a minute. Do you believe in ghosts—spirits?" Peter stares at me. "Good." I say, "Because you have one." Without getting into exact details regarding my cemetery visit, I explain.

Peter figured out some time ago that it wasn't somebody sneaking into his apartment. "It was too weird—it could not be explained by science and reason," he says.

We get honest with each other.

"Susan and Mitch Michaels were long-time tenants in this apartment," I say. "They're dead." I quickly add, "They are connected to an artist named Kasper Greenstreet—also dead."

Peter interrupts. "Kasper Greenstreet? He was big—Warhol type of fame. How do you know all this?"

I can't tell him that I experienced Kasper at the cemetery today. I am still having a hard time processing that; it's just too crazy. "One of your neighbors told me the Michaels lived here for a very long time," I say. "Since they vacated, no one has been able to last longer than the twelve-month lease. In fact, the last couple left within a couple of months after moving in."

Peter nods. "It's been a nightmare. Lost Lee, lost sleep." He looks at me. "Except you, Jack." He takes a minute. "You didn't show up here by accident. You were looking for him—Greenstreet—that first day."

"Yup. You're a lawyer. Can you find some information on him?"

"Yes." He pauses. "Why aren't you afraid, Jack?"

"Who said I'm not afraid?"

I dial my father and anticipate a ration of shit, which to my surprise he doesn't give me. Dad is happy to hear from me. I tell him I stopped at Peter's, but I don't mention Brick. All he says is, "Come home."

Before I do that, Peter and I burn sage throughout the apartment and hang the dream catchers back up. We place religious items such as the cross in the guest bedroom and sprinkle holy water throughout the place. We ask Kasper and the Michaels to leave the apartment, to move on. And pray. We are sincere in our efforts.

Peter insists on walking me home, which I find humorous after the day I've had, but I don't argue; I welcome the company.

KASPER GREENSTREET

The hangover sits on Kasper's head just long enough for him to reach for a beer. The hair of the dog and all that. Although these days, he pretty much stays under the influence. Susan and Mitch have moved him out of the studio apartment and into their guest room. His apartment is strictly for work. And a little play. They are very strong in their parental roles. Kasper is the troubled but talented child. Oh vanity.

Susan entered into a deal with the Guggenheim Museum to rent space for the art exhibition, which will make the show super prestigious. Susan gave the curator at the Guggenheim a taste of the exhibit in her gallery. He was very excited, calling back the same day with a "let's do it!"

Kasper is overwhelmed. After years of begging for a tiny bit of wall space in her gallery, he gets a showing at the fucking Guggenheim! Susan thought her gallery, the original option, was too small. They also talked to Andy Warhol, who offered to host it at the Velvet Underground, but Susan kept saying "this is not 'Pop' art, we don't want to give the impression that it is." Kasper defers to her and Mitch on everything. While living with them, he has never seen two more organized, methodical people in his life, never mind under the same roof.

Mitch came to the apartment after Kasper stayed drunk for two days painting, understandably disturbed by the shape of him, the lack of self-care.

Kasper knows that after years of representing him as a marginal talent, they have never been more excited about an artist or a show. Money is money—who wouldn't want to protect their assets, right? He is attracted to both of them in very different ways, which should make living there a little awkward. Yet, he's not the least bit uncomfortable. The guest room has a pullout couch, and Susan hangs several of Kasper's paintings to make him feel inspired.

Kasper can't seem to paint either of them for the exhibit, though he did render a very pedestrian portrait of Susan. He couldn't find the opposite image, the under belly, if you will, for the dual portrait. Mitch's portrait looked like art class 101.

Susan wants him to do a self-portrait. In the first portrait, Kasper uses the rest of his blood. His decision on the dual portrait is clear: it should be him as a child, skinny in short pants, mismatched socks, uncared for. Since he doesn't have a photo of himself as a child, he goes through old pads to find a sketch of a little boy he drew in Madison Square Park. The kid was playing marbles; he decided to use the kid in his place.

His inspiration leads him to paint shadowy figures all around the kid. They are Kasper's many childhood fears that accompanied him into adulthood. One is the fear of the poor boy with an alcoholic mother and no father. Another distorted shadow represents the little queer boy that he became. Then there is the disturbing shadow, blurred, hazy, the "crazy" he felt growing up, having those same-sex attractions. Only now, in 1973, is the American Psychiatric Association finally thinking about removing it from the list of mental disorders. "Pathological, deviant" is how his drunk and angry mother described him—not to mention how contemptible Kasper felt about himself. There are so many shadowy figures to which he gives life on the canvas… alcohol, drugs, "no talent artist," an inability to truly love someone, to accept their love without soiling the relationship. His abusive childhood, his inner demons leave him with a community of shadows that come to fester in his mind, his soul. Maybe by painting them, by exposing them, he will exorcise them from his life.

But these shadows don't leave. They just get louder.

Susan is his savior. She is taking him, a mediocre talent, and bringing him to the Guggenheim. His joy is quickly replaced with fear of failing, of bombing. The fears rain down on him daily. The closer we get to the opening, the more Kasper misbehaves. Mitch has the thankless job of keeping Kasper from combusting. Staying in bed, he sleeps half the day away. They are two parents who think it best to placate spoiled behavior. At least they know where their child is! The alternative could be Kasper hanging off a bar stool or snorting cocaine.

In all the years he's known Susan and Mitch, Kasper rarely remembers them fighting, he thinks. However, it is a whole new day; they argue incessantly. Most of their disagreements revolve around him. He is the insolent son they cannot agree on. The boorish, petulant child in whom they have invested so much time and money.

Now it must pay off in reputation and finance for everyone. The chance to be in the big time, to be taken seriously, is quickly replaced by Kasper's crippling fear. Of smelling up the art world with clearly his best work. But what if everyone thinks it sucks? Acting out in some sick way is the only way Kasper can relieve himself. Never mind that Susan is putting everything on the line. Her reputation, their money. She has bet the farm on Kasper. Still he takes advantage. Smoking pot incessantly in the room, daring Mitch to challenge him.

Mitch told him he loved him once, Kasper remembers, but never physically—just words. Now with his behavior he pushes Mitch's buttons to the point where he cannot believe he has any affection left for Kasper at all. However, he never loses his cool, which annoys the shit out of Kasper since he lives in a heightened sense of neurosis on a daily basis.

Misery loves company, as they say. But misery is not a place that Mitch likes to visit or will stay for any length of time. Playing Susan and Mitch against one another is so childish. Yet Kasper can't seem to help himself. Still there are good times, moments of enjoyment. Mitch and Kasper like to sit in the garden attached to the building. He reads the newspaper. Kasper sits there smoking cigarettes, drinking coffee, sketching on his pad. There is no longer any talk of love.

On some evenings, Susan and Mitch cook dinner. Kasper sets the table, pours the wine. They are quite happy with one another's company, like old times. The three laugh, talk about the day. News of the world. News of New York. Gossip. Susan mentions that Desiree Diamond's movie is a big hit.

Desiree is getting tremendous publicity, which will help the exhibition and, of course, her portraits.

Sipping his wine, Kasper wonders if Desiree ever thinks about him. Scoffing at his vanity—he mocks himself—like they had some great love affair. Well, they did—he thinks—she is magic. At this moment, Desiree is probably being wooed by some Saudi prince, or underworld figure. Barely remembering who Kasper Greenstreet is.

- - -

Kasper paces around the apartment at three a.m. Another night of unrest. He sits in the dark and feels as if he is being watched or judged, as if there is someone in the room with him. No one is there; it is just his mind playing tricks. He fears he will become the joke of the art world—you know, go back to painting fucking landscapes, you hack.

Susan and Mitch typically take turns getting up when they hear Kasper shuffling around the apartment. The baby they never had? Whose turn is it to feed the kid? Susan usually makes him a hot toddy or a warm brandy and talks to him about anything that will take his mind off the exhibit. Tonight, however, is Mitch's turn. He comes into the room in a tee shirt and boxer shorts, looking exhausted, new parents and all. "Okay," he says, "Let's try something."

Mitch attempts reflexology on Kasper. "I do this on Susan whenever she can't sleep." Which Kasper thinks is…never?

The minute he touches Kasper's feet, Kasper giggles. "No," he says, "Not the feet, I'm too ticklish."

What a fucking girl. Mitch climbs into bed with him. "Let's just try and relax," Mitch says. "We all need to sleep."

His mind goes to places that he knows Mitch's is not going. So, Kasper re-thinks it: Mitch the older brother who crawls in bed with you after you've had a nightmare. It is clear he does not have sex on his mind. He slides his arm around Kasper, his hand cupping his shoulder. Within seconds, his breathing changes. Mitch is sleeping. This won't work, Kasper thinks, pissed that Mitch is asleep. He's trapped; he can't move. Settle down. Kasper. Mitch lays with his arm around Kasper like a baby cradled in its father's arms. He is

Kasper's sleeping pill.

Soon, Kasper is asleep. This becomes the nightly routine. Anything for "art."

The three of them are dressed, but Kasper is paralyzed with fear. Susan heads to the Guggenheim early to make sure any last-minute needs are met. She kisses Mitch; there are no last-minute words, only last-minute glances. They speak volumes. "Make sure you get him there in a timely manner — make sure he's coherent," she finally says.

Once she is gone, they both miss her. "I'm going to smoke a joint," Kasper says, loudly. Mitch nods.

Kasper starts to head out of the apartment. "No, no," Mitch says. "Smoke it here."

"I'm going for a walk."

"Fine," Mitch says. "I'll come with you."

There is something in the air—nerves? It is impossible for Kasper to define. They walk aimlessly as Kasper smokes a joint; Mitch declines.

He must be sharp—take care of the talent! Who will save the day if something goes wrong? Mitch is lost in his thoughts, as is Kasper. Their relationship has changed. The man that I used to meet in the park for lunch, the man who used to profess his love for him, loves him no longer—in fact, Mitch might despise him. Perhaps it was merely an illusion for him, a mid-life crisis. Instead of the cliché of a sports car, or an affair with his young secretary, he pretends to fall in love with a man, an artist, no need for physical contact. Just a distraction?

"What are you thinking?" Kasper asks aloud.

Mitch looks around as if this is the first time in this neighborhood. A neighborhood he has lived in for the past seven years.

"That I should tell you something," he says.

"Tell me what?" That you are in love with me—that after sleeping in bed with me, you want me?

"Desiree Diamond was found dead in her Malibu house this morning."

Desiree Diamond! The "it" girl, the one with the not-so-hidden drug problem. Still, Kasper is shocked. Desiree, the girl dreams are made of— dead. "Is Susan going to pull her portraits from the show?" Kasper asks.

"No."

They stop at the corner bar, not on the corner of any street, which is what Kasper likes about it.

"Cognac."

"Two," Mitch says.

Desiree is on the TV, on the tongues of the customers. Desiree Diamond is dead, and the world is a lonelier place. In the cab ride up to the upper eighties, Mitch reaches over and holds Kasper's hand. The touch is not that of a lover, but a brother. Older brother, Kasper thinks, laughing to himself, which makes it more digestible.

The turnout at the Guggenheim is remarkable. There is plenty of wine. Everyone clambers in front of the portraits of Desiree Diamond. She was the topic of conversation in the bar, on the street, now in the Guggenheim. Desiree will join Marilyn, James Dean, and Sam Cooke as stars too young to die. I hate to say it but I could not buy publicity like this; it is a gift from the gods, Kasper thinks. People praise the work, love the work, take offense at the work. Most importantly, everyone is talking about the work.

Standing in front of his own self-portraits, Kasper feels as if the shadows have moved. Seriously, he doesn't remember painting them the way they are now reflected on the canvas. But who cares—it is a great night! Maybe this painting will become his very own *Portrait of Dorian Gray*. The child in the picture looks tortured; only, in life, Kasper will do and say as he pleases without the least bit of remorse, guilt, or bother.

Susan is much too busy to talk to Kasper, which he takes as a good sign. Everyone is here—celebrities, politicians, Mrs. Hudson Lockjaw, Mr. Hillibrand. They love it or hate it, which is better than apathy. Kasper's self-portraits are the second most discussed. People crowd to examine them. Mitch is talking with his and Susan's beautiful assistant, laughing. She throws her head back in a way that makes Kasper want to slap her. Maybe the sports car is coming.

Kasper watches all the amazing reactions to his work. What he dreamed about. Yet, he spends a good deal of time shadowing Mitch and his assistant like a jealous teenager. Is there something going on here? Is Susan catching this action? People keep interrupting his voyeuristic actions with questions. Questions about Desiree. "Did he know she was in trouble?" "Was the work a vision of her impending death?" "Is the doll box really a coffin?" Yes, he thinks, I saw the track marks on the back of her legs. That's dangerous, don't you agree?

Only, all he says is, "It's too painful to talk about." Never will he utter a word about her, he promises himself.

"What about the shadows in your painting?" "What do they represent? Are they demons?" Fuck! He is on the verge of being the psychic painter. All the rich and famous want him to paint them; they want his interpretation of their life. "Do you see anything around me that you would put in my painting?" people ask.

Kasper finds it fascinating. The painter prophet... or would it be the prophet painter? He is so full of shit that he will play into whatever the critics or buying public want him to be. Mrs. Hudson Lockjaw is not so happy with her portrait, but she is quieted by the rock star standing next to her, gushing over the fact that she has been immortalized. Oh, vanity.

There is plenty of that to go around, and Kasper wears it like a red cape. His immediate and momentary fame earns him an invite from a famous bisexual rock star who invites him back to his place to do a little blow. Chances are the cocaine won't be the only thing that gets blown tonight. It is a surreal feeling, walking around the magnificent Guggenheim with all this talent, money, beauty, and finally being seen. Really seen!

Kasper has spent a good deal of his life being invisible. Here, he is the most visible person in the place. His success tonight has changed the way people react to him, look at him, speak to him. He loves it, wants to bathe in it.

A man stands in front of the painting of Kasper as a child—the one with the shadows. He touches the shadows, brings his hand to his nose, and then smells the painting. It is as if he smells Kasper's blood.

The evening ends with a little press. Kasper is sober enough to be humorous without coming across like a complete twat. "The reviews couldn't be better if we wrote them ourselves," Susan later says.

They have an offer for the paintings of Desiree at least one hundred times greater than anything Kasper has previously received for his work. The money being bandied about is so ridiculous that they are drunk with the thought of it. Offers come in for the painting of Kasper as a child. Susan tells him of one from a very odd man who would like to meet him. Take a number! Susan weeds him out; she says there is something dark about him. Kasper doesn't know what that means, but if Susan doesn't like him, he doesn't either. Requests for interviews from the most prominent newspapers, magazines, morning shows in the country flood them.

They spend the next few days going through the interview requests, portrait requests, and money offers. What Kasper realizes about himself is that he has a gigantic and fragile ego. He makes note of anyone who offers below their means; he will not paint them. Unless they apologize with a much higher fee. Kasper leaves Susan and Mitch to handle the telegrams, phone calls and offers, and heads to his studio apartment to paint. He's had enough of that beautiful little bitch and the way Mitch and her gaze at each other in front of them.

Kasper begins painting boxes. A shoe box, a fancy gift box, a Christmas box. All are his version of Pandora's Box.

Today, we think of Pandora's Box as an idiom. "A present which seems valuable, only in reality it is a curse." The actual story of Pandora herself is from Greek mythology. According to Hesiod, when Prometheus stole fire from heaven, Zeus, the king of the gods, took vengeance by presenting Pandora to Prometheus's brother, Epimetheus. Pandora opened a jar, not a box, left in Epimetheus' care containing sickness, death, and unspecified evils, which were then released into the world. She quickly shut the jar, leaving one thing behind. It is usually translated as hope.

Pouring a Cognac, Kasper thinks of Desiree. What was her Pandora's Box? Fame? Drugs? Drinking and painting are as good as sex. All the boxes have his blood in them. He can't paint without using his blood. He has not shared this with anyone, although Mitch is aware of it since he picked him up from the emergency room the day he slit his wrists. Accidentally! He spends the next two days holed up in his apartment, painting, drinking, smoking pot. Kasper asks his nurse friend to come over and draw blood, so he can paint.

Mitch does not come looking for him anymore.

- - -

For its cover, *Newsweek* uses a silk screen of the portrait of Desiree

Diamond coming out of the TV, "The Death of Venus." Of course, they pay a nice fee. The celebrity Kasper gets from that cover makes him as famous as Warhol. At least for fifteen minutes. The *Newsweek* cover becomes a collector's item, making Kasper's portrait famous all over the world. Honestly, he should have paid them.

Kasper speaks to Susan several times since he moved back to his place, although on occasion he shows up at their apartment when he's haunted. Work seems to be flowing, but sleep is a problem, especially if he's not drunk or stoned out of his mind. On these occasions, he makes his way to 22nd Street, to the guest room. Kasper takes his sleeping pill, and Mitch crawls in bed with him.

No love or sex here. Kasper thinks Mitch is in love with Susan and in lust with their pretty assistant, which makes him a little bitchy when he thinks about it. All those conversations in the park—did they ever really happen? When Mitch is next to him in bed, Kasper wants to ask, "do you still love me at all?" Only, it's obvious he doesn't.

After one such night, Kasper awakens to find Mitch gone from the bed and the apartment. Susan brings coffee into the room, hands him a cup, and gets into bed next to him. "Do you mind when Mitch and I sleep in the same bed?" Kasper asks her.

Susan sips her coffee and smiles. "No. You guys are like brothers." As an afterthought she adds, "He does have a soothing way about him, doesn't he?"

"Why don't you ever come in and sleep with me?" he asks.

Susan smiles. "I sleep with Mitch or I sleep alone. I can't sleep with anybody else." They talk about his new work. She wants to see it. Strike while the fire is hot and all that. "Everyone wants a Kasper Greenstreet," she says, finishing by telling him her mother is not feeling well, and she might be going to Connecticut for a few days.

- - -

New images, dreams, and monsters come to him as he works on the Pandora's Box theme. Why would a good God permit evil in the world? And is it God that permits evil when humankind is given free will? Kasper has no answer; he's never been religious, nor spiritual. In the library, he researches

Pandora, who first appears in literature in the seventh or eighth century. She is supposed to be the first human woman created. He finds linkage to Eve, although he is no historian. Pandora is a myth to build upon; Jewish and Christian theology took it from the Greeks. The reference books also say that other Gods contributed to her creation, not just Hephaestus, which may have muddied the waters. "Too many cooks in the kitchen" in layman's terms.

The mystery: did Pandora know what was in the box when she opened it? Because if she did not know what she was unleashing, then the sin, error, and fault is on the God that placed the evils in the box—not her. He reminds himself it is a myth and to concentrate on painting. He brings the reference books back to the desk and feels the librarian looking down her nose at him. He is a little dirty, paint all over his shirt, hair disheveled; maybe even a smell.

"Are you the artist Kasper Greenstreet?" she asks.

Kasper smiles and gives her a wink and a nod. Fuck, I'm famous!

Each box gets its own evil. One has a demon—a tall creature with a human skeletal body and a horse head whose flesh is partially burnt. He paints it floating inside one of Pandora's boxes, just waiting to be opened. In another box, his blood leaks from the bottom. He does not name any of the evils in the box; each person who comes in contact with a painting will have their own Pandora. Whatever they believe to be in the box will be there. His art takes on a life and monetary reward of its own. He gets enough ass to last a lifetime. Drugs are bountiful; everyone wants to share their shit with him, a famous artist. Maybe he'll paint them?

Everything, even the landscapes that used to sit and sit now sell for a lot of money. Kasper makes a small fortune as an artist in great demand. The fact that he's painting prolifically and selling just as quickly does not hurt his reputation or the value of any of the work. "He is an artist in rarefied air," Susan says.

So, it comes as a stunner when a very wealthy woman, a countess, wants to give the painting back. She outbid everyone for the "child" painting. The woman told her art representative to return it to Susan's gallery, not looking for or wanting compensation.

"She could have easily made money on the resale market. I know that odd man really wanted it," Susan says. "Exorbitant offers are still coming in for the dual portrait work, even though it's all been bought and resides in private collections now."

The countess' representative told Susan, "She doesn't like its energy." It was a complete and total head scratcher. Who gives back a painting worth a quarter of a million dollars? Susan insisted that the representative hold onto the painting until she can have a conversation with the owner, "just to make sure it wasn't stolen or a fraud."

Two days later Susan is summoned to the Plaza Hotel, where the woman kept her waiting for an hour in a penthouse suite. It was no scam. The countess, her lawyer, and the art representative present Susan with the bill of sale and the painting. Even more interesting than those three characters is a tiny man who is the woman's "spiritual adviser." He kept a keen eye on Susan throughout the discussion. This time the countess does the talking. She is much more direct than her representative had been.

"This painting has very bad energy. Very bad!" the countess explains, constantly bringing a handkerchief with some kind of fragrance on it up to her nose. "I did not see or feel it the night we bought the painting, but the moment I hung it up in my home…"

She shakes her head, smelling her handkerchief, as if trying to shake it from her psyche. "I don't want any part of this art, or to be part of its lineage. Give it back to the artist."

Then, in a grand gesture, like Pontius Pilate, she said, "I wash my hands of it!"

Susan knew people like this and had heard stories from other gallery owners. Super rich, super crazy, sometimes super manipulated. Can't buy a house if the front door is not facing north or south. Need to have a spiritualist, a witch doctor, or an energy healer walk through properties with them to see if the vibe is right, the energy is right. Hotel rooms need to be sprinkled with potions before they can rest their heads.

Susan stands up and begins to unwrap the painting. Immediately everyone protests, as if she was about to expose herself—everyone but the lawyer. In her very diplomatic manner, Susan says, "I have to make sure it is the actual painting."

Very slowly she peels the brown paper away from the front of the painting. She confirms the painting is genuine. It's dark, a small boy surrounded by… what? What exactly were these things? Spirits? Bad memories, bad thoughts?

She knew Kasper had been abused as a child, though he never came right out and said it. His behavior and demeanor radiated it. But that is what made art so powerful. It made you feel!

Susan rewraps the painting. "If you would like, I can substitute a piece from the artist. He just finished an amazing collection."

Before Susan can finish the sentence, the little man starts shaking his head. "Madam has been unable to sleep since opening her home to his work. She wants nothing to do with this artist—just take it away."

With that, the wealthy woman leaves the room. Very weird.

Susan takes the painting, the bill of sale, and letter from the lawyer; leaves the Plaza; and hails a cab to her apartment, where Mitch is waiting. "I should have gone with you," he says. "They sound like crazy people."

"They're not crazy, Mitch. They're just rich."

Susan and Mitch begin to look at the painting just as Kasper arrives to inspect it. Mitch opens a bottle of wine. Susan keeps Polaroids of all the work she sells and lays out the five photos she has on this one. Yes, it is definitely Kasper's work. Only something is off—not a big off, but off. It looks like… some of the shadows—images—moved since he originally painted them. They grab magnifying glasses, going through it in detail.

Kasper knows something is different. "Does she want anything?" Kasper asks.

Susan shows him the letter from the lawyer giving it back to him as a gift. "She said it had bad energy," Mitch says, which immediately annoys Susan.

"She actually said bad energy?" Kasper asks, insulted.

Susan tells the story about the spiritualist, the eccentric woman, the lawyer, and the art rep. Soon the three are laughing with the story of high drama—the woman smelling her handkerchief, the little disapproving spiritual guru, how all three of them tried to stop Susan from looking at the painting.

"I tell you I stopped right there," Susan says, laughing. "What if once I pull the paper off it's actually a painting of Mickey Mouse? I'm caught in some peculiar little escapade. How the hell would I escape… get out of the suite?" They all laugh.

"We have ten people in line who will buy that painting," Mitch reminds them. "Should I start vetting? It's worth a lot of money."

Kasper knows he doesn't need to sell it, at least not right now. He never told Mitch and Susan the actual kid in the painting wasn't him, but the kid he sketched in Madison Square Park years ago. In fact, it looks nothing like him as a child.

"Hmm. Still I like it," Kasper says.

"So do I," Susan concurs. "It's thought-provoking."

"Can I keep it here for the time being?"

"Sure." Susan gets up, pours more wine. "You know you can afford a much better place to live—a big loft studio to work in now."

"Some place with security," Mitch adds.

Kasper nods. "All my creative energy is in that little apartment."

Mitch gets up. "If you are going to leave it here, I need to add this painting back to the gallery's insurance." Always the money man, Mitch moves in for a closer look. "These images around the child—were you molested? Is that what they represent?" Susan and Kasper are both surprised by Mitch's sudden lack of a filter.

"Well, yes, that's part of it." Susan and Mitch seem to be waiting for him to continue, so he does. "When I was a kid, around nine, my uncle—my mother's brother—kind of molested me."

"What does that mean—kind of?" Mitch asks, staring at the boy in the painting.

"Well, I didn't object when it was happening."

"That's ridiculous," Susan jumps in. "You were a child. Of course, it's molestation."

"How old was he?" Mitch asks.

"Thirty something."

Silence.

"The reason I say 'kind of' is because, at the time, I thought I was in love with him—and I think I liked it." Kasper looks at the kid in the painting and wonders who he is. Where he is now.

"Until we got caught," Kasper continues. "My uncle blamed me, made it all my fault, telling my mother that I came in while he was napping. Of course, she put all the blame on me!"

"That's atrocious. You were nine!" Susan says.

"I think that is when I started to have trouble sleeping," he says. "Doesn't matter now. Look at me—I'm a famous artist. They're both dead."

Susan wants to hang the painting up in the living room, which becomes an ordeal. She wants Mitch to do it right now. They bicker.

"What, do I look too relaxed?" he says sarcastically.

How odd: this couple that agreed on just about everything, now agrees on very little and is a couple who lives on a steady diet of arguing. Someone must have something on the side. We plow through the wine. Gone are the laughs. The tension finally gets to Kasper, and he excuses himself.

Kasper heads down 3rd Avenue and hits a couple of different bars on his way to the Village. One is totally gay, and one is not, although he's gotten lucky there before. Walking into the Red Light, Green Light, he is no longer the broke gay guy. Now he is a successful artist! Funny how many drinks are bought for him. Now that he doesn't need anyone to buy him drinks, people keep sending them over. Before, he constantly had to make deals when his money ran out. Nobody wanted him to paint them—even for drinks. Now? Everyone wants him to paint them, but they can't afford him. One of life's little peccadilloes. Red Light, Green Light is a gay man's drinking bar, no pulsating music here.

"Cognac, please." Now that he can taste the difference between the good, the bad, and the shit, Remy Martin XO becomes his new favorite. He swirls the cognac a bit, then brings it close to his nose and inhales. It smells better than perfume, with scents of vanilla, nuts, flowers, and a hint of caramel. Counting to ten, he swirls, smells it again. There is actually a name for the succeeding sniff: the "cognac's second nose." Kasper takes a drink, and it smacks when it hits his tongue and palate. Who needs a date when I have this?

The humming of the beer cooler interrupts his moment of joy and brings him back to the sound of those portable fans in his mother's bedroom. She said she needed them to help her sleep, even in the middle of winter. When his Uncle Dan came to live with him, he always needed fans on as well. Kasper thought it odd; still does. Both turned them on high for the hum or squeaking sound.

That was how they got caught, he and his uncle. Uncle Dan put both fans on in his room with the door closed. Neither heard her coming. She beat the daylights out of Kasper, especially when Uncle Dan pretended he had been sleeping. Like Kasper had thought of those acts himself. Guess it was easier to blame Kasper than admit that her brother was a pedophile and she was a monster for looking the other way. Truth is, she hated Kasper's nature. Always rode him about being a sissy, a queer. Now that their "secret" was out, his uncle treated him like a pariah. Except when he wanted to use the boy.

"Kasper." Every tiny hair stands up—one at a time, starting from his lower spine, working its way to the top of his neck. That voice. Uncle Dan. Only it couldn't be.

"Kasper?" came the voice again. All the sounds around him magnify, the clock ticking on the wall, the beer cooler humming, the music bursting from the jukebox. Holding the snifter in his hand, he keeps his head down, trying to get back to reality by way of the aroma from his cognac. With his nose at the mouth of his glass, Kasper feels his body on the stool next to him. This has to be impossible. Uncle Dan is dead—not just to me, but physically. The thought of that allows Kasper to pick his head up and turn to the man sitting next to him at the bar.

He looks so out of place. Waving the bartender over, he says, "I'll have what he's having." My God, it's uncanny. The voice—almost to the note—his uncle's. Kasper can't help but notice how good looking he is, but he belongs in a different movie, not this one. He has this, how can he describe it? other-worldly, Dracula-esque attraction. This is an omen, right?

"How do you know my name?" Kasper asks in a smug famous-artist manner.

"I don't know your name," he says, throwing money on the bar. He sips his drink.

Tilting his head, Kasper waits for him to laugh and say something like "just fucking with you." Only he doesn't. Kasper looks around to see if someone he knows is calling or fucking with him. Everyone is going about their business of drinking.

Kasper goes back to his cognac, his private thoughts. After a minute he says, "What is your name?"

"Kasper." The man reaches out, shakes his hand. "Philip. What do you do, Kasper?"

"Paint."

"Apartments?" Wow, is his ego taking a beating.

"Ah, no. Art."

"An artist. Like Michelangelo?" That's the first thing he says that Kasper likes. Still sounds like his uncle, though. Very disheartening.

Philip doesn't drink much; Kasper drinks too much. They talk about art, what Philip thinks it is, what Kasper thinks it is. Trying hard to impress him, Kasper asks if he has seen his painting of Desiree Diamond on the cover of *Newsweek*.

Philip doesn't seem to know who she is and can't recall the cover art. He does, however, know the magazine. Who is this guy? How the fuck does he not know Desiree Diamond? That should have been the end of it, but Kasper is intrigued, attracted to him, drunk.

"What's the most important thing to you—the smell or the taste?" Philip asks.

Kasper picks up his glass and swirls it around, smells it, then drinks it. "Both," he says.

Philip laughs. There is something incredibly charming about this man. He seduces you on the one hand while pushing you away with the other. "I wasn't talking about the cognac," he says, leaning into Kasper.

"Oh," Kasper says, feeling like a stupid schoolboy.

"Are you a good kisser?" Philip asks but doesn't wait for an answer. "Does your kiss linger on the lips long after you're gone?"

No, but I bet yours does, Kasper thinks. His mind goes to painting a dual portrait of Philip. One as a 1940s movie star, the other as … who? Dracula? Satan? Naked.

Kasper thinks about asking, but before he can, Philip finishes his drink, stands up, and says, "I should go."

"Want company?" Kasper asks, turned on by his dangerous appeal.

Philip smiles. "Sure. Why not." He says it like he's doing Kasper a favor.

Stepping into the cold air, Kasper realizes he is very drunk. Philip leads the way. He's from out of town, so Kasper assumes they are going to his hotel, which Kasper imagines will look like Philip—a sharp boutique, midsize, charming, but very discrete hotel. His mistake is not paying attention to where they walk. Kasper finds himself in the rear of an old tenement building.

"A friend of mine owns this place. I'm helping him sell it," Philip says. "It could be a great artist studio, Kasper."

He opens the back door without a key. Saying Kasper's name brings him back to Uncle Dan, which makes him pause. "You're a broker?" Kasper asks, getting cold feet. The place is run down, deserted. Philip holds the door open for him. "I'm afraid of the dark," he adds, trying to sound calm.

"Oh, there's a light to the left." Philip takes him by the arm.

Kasper knows it is a mistake to not back out now. He smells the fear on Kasper, which he thinks turns Phillip on. He pulls Kasper in close like he's going to kiss him and whispers. "You have to see the place."

Inside, it is pitch black, except for the little light coming through the windows. Philip holds on to Kasper's arm, which in a real hotel would have been hot. Now it reminds Kasper that his first thought was that Philip belonged in a different movie—not this one.

"Is anyone living here?" he asks, his voice unsteady.

"Just us ghosts," Philip says.

"How about a light?"

Philip flicks a switch. A dimly lit yellow bulb lights up a very large kitchen.

"I like what you've done with the place," Kasper says. Philip laughs, which almost makes him—this—what? Normal? Kasper is still spooked.

"Come on, let me show you the place." Philip takes his arm and leads him up a dark staircase. Gently Kasper shakes him off, though up the stairs he goes, knowing it's a mistake.

Kasper stops at the top of the stairs. "I think I hear somebody."

Philip gives him a side glance. His eyes are dead, scary, lustful—only not for sex. Before Kasper has a chance to move, Philip grabs him around the neck and starts beating the hell out of him.

There is blood in his mouth as he fights to escape. But he's not getting away. Philip locks Kasper in a chokehold and drags him into one of the many empty rooms. Fear gives Kasper adrenaline; he fights and elbows Philip's solar plexus. Philip releases, giving him a chance to run. Kasper thinks, this guy wants to kill me! Kasper bounces off a few walls in the dark, feels the loose teeth in his mouth, looking for a place to hide. A match lights a tiny bit of real estate in front of him. What is this place, anyway?

"Kasper. Kasper! This is my foreplay," Philip calls out. "You're my mouse. I'm your cat."

The sound of him moving in the dark keeps Kasper still. "It's sexy, don't you think?" Philip yells.

The mustiness and dampness fills Kasper's nostrils. Sliding into an empty room, Kasper can see that the windows face the street. He tiptoes to the window, tries to open it, only it does not budge. The light from a match turns him back to the door. Philip holds the match, smiling.

Philip looks like he wants to throw the match at Kasper and set him on fire. Kasper charges, but Philip is too quick; he grabs hold of him, kneeing him in the groin. Crumbling to the floor, Kasper crawls. Philip grabs his hair, drags him back into the hallway and down to another room that is completely dark, away from the street. They fight. Raging from all the beatings he has been given at home, on the streets, in the bars, Kasper kicks, punches, scratches, claws in a desperate attempt to get away.

No use. Philip sits on top of him, much stronger than he looks. His hands are around Kasper's neck, cutting off his windpipe. Kasper grabs at his face.

Suddenly, the window slides open. Two men—drug addicts—climb off the fire escape into the dark room. Startled, Philip lets go of Kasper's windpipe.

One of the men sees two bodies on the floor. "What the fuck!" he yells, startled. The other man asks, "They fucking?"

"Help!" Kasper yells. "He's trying to kill me!"

Philip is still on top of him.

"Are they fucking?"

Kasper hits Philip with everything he has, knocking him off. He quickly crawls along the floor to the open window. One of the men sees the blood all over his face and steps aside. "He's a fucking psycho!" Kasper screams.

The man looks at Philip and steps back, frightened, which allows Kasper to climb out the window and make his way down the fire escape, jumping the final four feet to the alley. Paralyzed by fear, Kasper turns, confused. Shadows crawl all over the buildings; the pavement slows his escape. Spitting blood along with a couple of teeth, he drags his leg behind him like Quasimodo.

Half running, half walking up 1st Avenue, Kasper searches for a cab. His nose is bleeding, maybe broken. His face is a mess. No taxi cabs will stop once they see him covered in blood. Don't stop, don't stop, Kasper thinks. He hears some sad, beautiful music from an open window. He half runs, half walks up 1st Avenue like the frightened little mouse Philip said he was. Pedestrians look at him. Stares bring out the shame for picking up a complete stranger in a bar, hoping for sex.

A police car stops and takes Kasper into the emergency room at Bellevue because of all the blood. After cleaning him up, the nurse tells him it is not as bad as it looks, but his nose is broken. Kasper's paranoia reaches an all-time high, and he is paranoid to begin with.

A doctor looks at his injuries. He carries a copy of *Newsweek* with Desiree Diamond on the cover and asks Kasper to sign it. The gesture feeds his vanity and ego, healing his bruises for a brief moment. "I saw your exhibition— fantastic," the doctor says.

"The guy who attacked me was an art critic," Kasper says. The doctor and nurse laugh.

"Do you want to call someone to come get you?" the nurse asks.

"No."

Back in his apartment, Kasper feels frightened and alone. He should have called Susan and Mitch. He sketches a large portrait of Philip while he can still remember him clearly. Thank God for a couple of junkies, he thinks, as he works on Philip's eyes. Cold. Dead. Who knows when they would have found his dead body?

He finishes the sketch by bedtime. Philip looks as wicked as he was by the end of that night. Kasper crawls into bed like the little mouse he feels that he is, hiding under his blankets and art supplies like a child. Falling asleep is easy; staying asleep is elusive. Noises, real or imagined, wake him up. He's disorientated and not just from the intense pain he feels in his body, face, and head. He thinks someone is in the room so he crawls out from under his covers to take a look.

He sees Philip's face, staring at him. "What do you want?" Kasper screams.

Then he realizes it is the sketch of Philip staring at him. He doesn't remember positioning the painting toward the bed. Frantic, he gets out of bed and kicks the easel over, knocking it to the floor. There is nowhere in the room for him to find comfort. So he grabs a blanket and pillow and crawls under his bed.

WHEN THE VEIL BETWEEN THE LIVING AND SPIRIT WORLD IS AT ITS THINNEST

Most people do not like days like this—dark, rainy, moody—but I love them. It looks and feels like evening. I sit in class and watch the clock, waiting for study time. I glance across the street. Peter's shades are open, and his apartment is dark. No signs of Kasper in the apartment since I saw him in the cemetery. Peter wants peace. Me? I want to find out more about Kasper. His art. What drove him to suicide.

We are getting a good old-fashioned rainstorm. The rain beating down on the window pane accompanied by thunder makes for a beautiful orchestral sound. Not to be outdone, lightning makes an appearance, turning an ordinary school day into a wistful afternoon. It puts me at ease. However, I'm aware that not everyone enjoys this type of weather. Some kids are actually freaked out by it.

Lightning illuminates the darkened sky. A girl jumps at the thunder that follows it.

Closing my eyes, I decide to meditate. No homework, no reading, just a little dusting off my mind. I use the sound of the rain to carry me to other places. There is movement around; I can hear and feel my classmates getting books, whispering to each other in soft tones about the lightning and thunder. For me, it is as if I have been covered in a veil. Asleep, but not asleep, in the room, outside in the rain. My God, I am ridiculous! Rain pelts the glass, more of a lullaby than a disturbance. The louder the storm, the deeper inward I go…

It is dark. Brick and I climb through a broken window to get into the abandoned boarding house. Once inside, we pick up broken plaster, throwing it at any window that has glass remaining. The building has a smell—damp, old. We head up what appear to be the backstairs. The sounds of movement close by startle us; we grab one another's arm.

"Rats," Brick says.

Rats alone should make me leave—I hate rats! But I don't turn back. Up the stairs we go. Brick steps away from me on the landing. I remember now that I had the feeling of being watched. We were not alone. Why didn't I leave?

A girl in class gasps as the lightning hits close to the building, followed by loud thunder. It pulls me back into the classroom, but I don't stay long…

- - -

There is a full moon. The moon and light from the street lamps are the only forms of light coming inside the building, so it is dark. Brick and I both break out lighters, but for some reason they don't stay lit, as if some imaginary breath keeps blowing them out. It's raining…wait, is that the present moment? Is the sound of the rain today interfering with my memory of that night? Is it more of an echo?

No, it was wet. Maybe something was leaking inside the building. The walls were wet; the floors were wet. Yes, it must have been raining.

Brick startles me by grabbing hold of my arm. "Fuck! Asshole!" I yell.

He laughs. My heart races. "Let's go in there."

He motions for us to head into a room, which must have been a community room. It is a large living space with the remnants of a big stone fireplace. Brick walks over to the broken stone on the floor, picks up a "piece"

206

and goes into a baseball pitcher's wind up. "The bases are loaded… full count—and the pitch!"

He throws the rock, hitting the frame of the window that separates this room from others in the boarding house. They were called Tuberculosis windows, mandated by a nineteenth-century city law requiring tenements to have cross ventilation. His throw brings the entire window frame crashing to the floor. We jump out of our skin and back out of the room in a hurry.

The feeling of being watched rolls over me like a wave…

At that moment, all four windows inside the classroom slide down. Slamming into the window sill below, they create a loud blast. Everyone in class jumps out of their seats. Except me. Rain pours into the classroom, wetting the kids in the desks closest to the window, of which I am one. Sister Elizabeth barks an order to James Brock and Dan Sullivan. Dan grabs the window pull, immediately closing the first window and locking it. James climbs up onto the window sill, shutting and locking several of the windows manually. I sit motionless, trapped between the present and the past.

A strange, exotic bird lands outside the window. So out of place in the city. Trying to get out of the rain? Or did it escape from somewhere? So unusual.

The thunder and lightning is met with a low noise that begins to rise in the classroom… cicada bugs at night, their otherworldly sound.

The bird flies off. Lights in the room flicker. A few of the kids pant, frightened. I open my eyes to find the room filled with a carousel of shadows jumping on and off the walls. Several kids are visibly scared—can they see them? They look to Sister Elizabeth for guidance. The crackling noise from the thunder joins with the sound of something crawling in or on the walls. The classroom lights up with nearby lightning. The cicada bug sound is deafening—now is the time for prayer.

The lights go off in the room. Sister Elizabeth opens the classroom door and is met with complete darkness in the hall. What little light there is comes from the street. Several of my classmates reach for each other.

Suddenly, a crow crashes into the window, scaring the shit out of everyone in the classroom. I do not move; I know this dream and I've had it before. When was it? It was a meeting in a conference room; I reach for the memory. Jack, that entire life was a dream! So, was it a dream inside a dream? The crow is quickly followed by a pigeon. There is a moment of quiet before an onslaught of birds smash into our school windows. Ten! Twenty! Thirty? There are too many to count.

My classmates are up from their desks and want to flee, but nobody wants to run into the dark hallway. They are trapped in the classroom. Several hide behind desks on the floor. My eyes are heavy, like I am drugged, still I am sure that I am dreaming. This nightmare is mine...

I run past Brick into another room while the cracking sound of the thunder outside the window merges with the cracking sound of the floor giving way under my feet. There is a person on the other side of the room who has been following me, watching me. Our eyes meet; however, before I can see the face clearly, the floor crumples with a loud crash. Flailing helplessly, I fall through space, where people are talking, chanting, screaming. As I bounce off the floor on the lower level, things move all around me. Dead things. Shadows, demons? My pain is electric. I can't feel my body, though I am aware of smells—blood, my own; incense; and rats. Something very large is on the wall.

- - -

The classroom is in total darkness as birds bombard the windows. Where are the sirens? This is an air raid! Wake up, Jack, wake up. The sounds of the slamming birds jolt me into the present.

I realize the birds are in a panic; they are fleeing, not attacking, trying to escape from a force much greater than themselves. As if they are trying to get into our room for safety. It is total pandemonium inside and outside. With nowhere to run, some kids hit the floor, while others get into the coat closet. Sister Elizabeth is pale, holding on to her rosary beads for protection. She is stricken with fear. Birds continue to crash against one another and the windows, also slamming into the side of the building. It's mayhem. The sound of their screeching is amplified to a nerve-wracking level. Shadows are back on the walls, along with distorted carousel music. Classmates hold their ears. I'm not sure if it's strictly because of the birds or all the noises. Demons vomit the fears of my classmates, of Sister Elizabeth, of the people in the buildings all around me. The chorus of nasty, vile shit creates an anxiety level that is making me and everyone else come out of our skin. None of their chants, I realize, articulate any of my own fears. They belong to others, but it leaves me immersed in their anxiety, making me want to flee, to run from the room, from myself. Only I cannot spend the rest of my life running from nightmares that are not my own. But I am paralyzed, which prevents me from taking care of what needs to be done. Which is what? What needs to be done, Jack?

It is real! This is not my dream alone. Everyone around me is experiencing it to various degrees. I force myself to stand and walk toward the window, watching the birds crack the glass before falling to their deaths or erratically away. Looking out the window past their dead carcasses, I see Kasper Greenstreet standing at the window in Apartment 3C, smoking a cigarette. He watches the chaos in our classroom from the comfort of Peter Cairo's apartment. Be careful, Jack, you have fucked with the dead!

The furor created by the frightened birds and loud storm is replaced with eerie silence. Many birds are stuck to the glass, crushed by their own onslaught. The rain has stopped, and lights have come back on. Kasper stares calmly across at me. I run out of the classroom without the thought of asking permission. Taking two steps at a time, I fly down the four flights of stairs and make my way into the main entrance. Kicking the door open, I run out onto the street, where I am stopped in my tracks. Along the sidewalk, in the street, there are dead crows, pigeons, house sparrows, European starlings, and what look like parakeets. What a fucking nightmare! Armageddon! A scene out of a fucking horror movie!

I lose my direction, shocked at the large number of dead birds. My motivation to challenge that fucking ghoul in Peter's apartment has been replaced with horror at this decimation of the birds. Dead birds are laid out in a bloody mess on the stairs, the pavement in front of the school, in the street. Cars stop, unable to get past the pile of destruction. Several people get out to look. No birds are on the sidewalk or have touched the Gramercy Terrace apartment building across the street. This is war!

Sister Elizabeth runs out the front door in a rage, glaring at me, yelling my name. "Jack Kelly! Jack Kelly!" Once on the sidewalk, she breaks as if she has walked into a brick wall. Sickened in much the same way as I am; utter shock replaces the anger, if only for a moment. Sister Elizabeth is horrified by the visual. Immediately following her out of the building is the principal, Sister Thaddeus, office staff and Mrs. Dowd. All are nauseated. One of the office staff begins to vomit.

Sister Elizabeth and I spin in place, literally, turning in circles, looking at the carnage. It is an incredible sight. After a beat, she turns on me. "Mr. Kelly! What do you think you're doing? Running out of my classroom like a maniac! I, for one, have had it with you!"

Oh, God, here we go.

"All of these ungodly incidents are always centering around you! I know all about you—keeping company with people who practice the occult!"

I look at Mrs. Dowd, who immediately looks away. Sister Elizabeth is in full tirade. She has been wanting, waiting to go off on me since I yelled "fuck" out loud in the classroom.

"Yes, Mr. Kelly—do you deny it? Psychics, Tarot card readers? The devil's playmates!"

I want to defend myself, defend my friends, but I know that what happened today is so crazy that I am unsure if or how it can be explained. "I didn't conjure up the birds, Sister, if that's what you are implying," I finally say.

Sister Elizabeth gets right up on me, pointing in my face. "Your behavior is strange. I watched you on the train. You… you were doing something… weird! Today, everyone was frightened but you! You just sat there, calm as could be."

"Well, Sister, you just said I ran out of the class like a maniac."

Oh, boy, once the words were out of my mouth, I wanted them back.

Sister Elizabeth looks like she wants to physically attack me. I step back. Finally, Sister Thaddeus steps in front of her.

"Sister Elizabeth, that's enough. We will talk about this inside."

Sister Elizabeth stares at me with deep animosity. Mrs. Dowd, who might have looked at me with Mr. David in the coffee shop with suspicion, now views me with fear. The office workers no longer look at me like I am the "miracle kid." That is replaced with uneasiness, contempt, and accusation. All of them go inside the school, leaving me standing on the sidewalk in the middle of the dead birds. Except for Sister, Thaddeus. She places her hand on my back.

"Let's go inside."

Sister Elizabeth and I are kept separated. She is brought into Sister Thaddeus's office. The adults need to call authorities regarding the dead birds. There is also conversation on how to release the schoolchildren. Sister Thaddeus wants them sent through the church. Nobody needs to see the carnage on the street. They order me back to my classroom. Sister Thaddeus asks Mrs. Dowd to accompany me.

Immediately she protests. "I should get back to my class. Don't you think, Sister?"

"No. I will have someone else take your class. You get the eighth-grade ready to leave."

It's clear Mrs. Dowd is afraid to be alone with me. Maybe I will put some voodoo curse on her for being such a blabbermouth.

"Is it okay if I run ahead, Sister Thaddeus?" I ask. She nods.

Back in the classroom, I am greeted with lots of unfriendly stares. More foes than friends, but I can count on Peggy and Bobby. "What happened?" Peggy asks.

"What a shit show," I say. "Dead birds all over the street."

James Brock stands up in a combative manner. "You've been very creepy since you fell on your head. All this weird shit surrounds you!"

"And you're an asshole," I respond.

"How about I kick your ass?" he yells.

Bring it, fucker, I think. My peaceful demeanor is now a volcanic explosion ready to be released. I walk right over to him. "How about you try!"

It's on. He punches me in the face. I attack him just as Mrs. Dowd opens the door to the classroom. Of course, the first thing she sees is me leaping on that motherfucker! It is Saturday night at the fights; I give as good as I get. It takes four or five of our classmates to break us up. Mrs. Dowd runs downstairs to get Sister Thaddeus.

A meeting is demanded with my father. It's a surprise to no one, except my father, who I have kept in the dark with just about everything. My dad is ordered to bring Dr. Klein's letter regarding all my tests. They will be disappointed when it shows no seizure activity. Although, I think we are past that now. Sister Elizabeth basically thinks I'm evil. Can you imagine how

211

solidified that thinking would be if she knew I am psychically aware of her three breasts? God, I'm so in over my head. However, I am at war with the spirit haunting the apartment across the street. I find myself in the middle of a supernatural storm and am ill equipped to handle it. Kasper Greenstreet seems to be able to use birds at will. What do I have? What is in my arsenal? White sage?

It gets worse. Animal control is called. So is the press, followed closely by a police presence. Lookie-loos come from everywhere, trying to get down 22nd Street for a better look. Yup, a real shit show. Some of the kids in my class hang around. I'm the only one who wants to get out of here.

Mr. David has already heard about the birds when I get to his apartment. The birds are the story in the city. Not to me.

I start with Kasper Greenstreet. "You guys were right; he's a ghost."

"Who's a ghost, Jack?"

"Kasper Greenstreet."

"Did he speak?" Mr. David asks.

"No. He did however use crows in the cemetery to harass me."

"Similar to today?" Mr. David asks.

"No. Very different than today. Today it wasn't just crows, and today, they were not attacking the school, they were fleeing."

"Fleeing? How do you know?"

"Trust me, I know. He was sending me a message!"

I give Mr. David a laundry list of all the supernatural shit I've been dealing with: the difference between Kasper Greenstreet's energy and the first ghost, the woman on the subway platform.

Then I tell him about the shadows. "On the train coming back from the cemetery, I put my hand in the chest of a shadow."

"What?" he says, alarmed.

"They were all around me, and one kept staring at me. Some lady was causing a scene, so I sat down next to this shadow and stuck my hand in the middle of its chest to see if it had a heart."

Mr. David sighs. "What did it feel like?"

"Freezing. Like ice cold Jell-O. It transferred images to me. Things like war, murder, all the things that have foundations in fear."

"What about today?"

"The shadows came to add to the distress. Like it was an opening."

"Is there an order of power when all of them show up? Spirits, ghosts, shadows, demons?"

"Like a hierarchy?" I ask.

"Yes. Like a hierarchy."

"Instinct tells me they all want something different. Not sure if there is a power structure, but the ghost of Kasper Greenstreet seems the most aggressive, powerful. Much more than the ghosts or shadows I've previously encountered. However, the demon on the train did attack me the day the man died."

"Jack, who's your favorite superhero?"

"Why are we talking about superheros? I'm dealing with fucking spirits—demons!" I say, agitated.

"Just indulge me, Jack."

"Batman—maybe Superman—no Batman."

"That's all this is. Think like a superhero, Jack. These things you're battling are your villains. Supernatural villains but villains just the same." He's reaching, I think; Mr. David has no answer.

He gets up. "I'll be right back."

While he's gone, I wish for some normalcy, to be just another kid worrying about his grades, following box scores. When Mr. David returns, he has an old necklace in his hand. At the end of the chain is an open triangle with a small blue stone held in the middle by three gold wires connecting to each point. He holds it up.

"When I was in my early twenties, I wanted to escape the voices, the fear of the images in my head that were making me different. I traveled around the world trying to quiet them. At a bazaar in Istanbul, this older man called me over. He asked me for my hand; I thought he was going to do a palm reading. Only he held my hand and closed his eyes. When he opened his eyes, he told me to wait. He left for about ten minutes and, when he came back, he had this."

"Can I touch it?"

Mr. David hands it to me and picks up his pad. "Sometimes when people pray, they ask for a circle of angels to protect them. In war, armies try to place blockades to protect a city." He puts a dot on the top of the page, then two more, turning them into a triangle. On the top, he writes "God" and the "Great I Am," on the right corner of the triangle he writes "The Son," on the left triangle he writes the "Holy Spirit."

"The Trinity," I say.

In the middle he writes my name. "There are no spirits, no ghosts, no demons powerful enough to break into the Trinity. That blue stone is cobalt. It represents us — God's children. That is what the man told me while placing this in my hand." Then he looked at me and said, "What God creates is eternal, I love you, as I love myself—go in God's protection. Guilt, fear, evil is not from God. They have no power in his light."

"What did you pay for it?" As soon as I speak, I want to take it back. It's such a dumbass thing to say.

Mr. David laughs; he is not offended. "Not enough. I never doubted myself or what I was here to do since."

I hold it in my hand. "It's yours," he says.

He writes on the pad, tears the paper out, hands it to me. I read the words: "Yugen/yoo gehn, an awareness of the universe that triggers emotional responses too deep and mysterious for words." The phrase is Japanese.

"You understand?" he asks.

"Yes, I think I do. In the chaos, I must unravel their secrets and remember I am from the light."

He places the triangle around my neck. Mr. David hands me a book as I am getting ready to leave his apartment. *The Art of War* by Sun Tzu. "Read this," he says.

I am happy to be back home. However, the horror show at school and birds lying dead all over 22nd Street makes the nightly news, as well as the evening newspapers. If the experience wasn't sensational enough, every news outlet on the planet has put its own spin on it.

"In a scene right out of Alfred Hitchcock's movie *The Birds*, birds from all over the city seem to have attacked a school building on 22nd Street this afternoon." The camera pans Epiphany school as well as the aftermath—dead birds all over the street—fading out on a bird stuck to the front of the school building.

Another channel begins with something a little less dramatic: "Zoologists, meteorologists, and scientists from around the world are weighing in on the unusual flight and tragic end of several flocks of birds that chaotically flew into a Catholic school today." Of course, they, too, show the decimation of the birds. They interview a professor with impressive credentials who believes the event was created by disturbance from the electrical storm. Which created "infrasound-acoustic waves," he says, sending the birds into a confused orbit and then the school building.

The theories multiply by the minute, including aliens from another planet who could only be seen by the birds—and, of course, by the man who filed the report. For others, it was a sign of the end times. Instead of locusts, God sent birds? Since Epiphany is a Catholic school, religious zealots blame the devil, the pope, or the Catholic religion. Every far-fetched and not so far-fetched idea is thrown about. Mass hysteria descends on our little school. Our phone begins to ring incessantly. Faculty members call parents to ask—well, tell them—no one is to talk to the press. Every kook has their own agenda. My favorite is that aliens have planted a source of light in the school that the birds were picking up on.

- - -

While thinking about my conversation with Mr. David, I want to see and talk to Peter. The phone rings. "Hi, Jack, this is Sister Thaddeus. How are you doing this evening?"

"I'm okay, Sister. You?"

"I've been doing a lot of praying, Jack." Pause. "May I speak to your father?"

"Of course," I say, knowing I should have talked to Dad first. My procrastination is going to leave me playing defense.

Watching my father from the other room, it is clear Sister Thaddeus is doing most of the talking. My father says things like, "Yes, very strange."

Dad seems grave when he hangs up the phone. "Apparently there is no school tomorrow due to this incident."

That makes me happy. It will give me a day of respite before going back to deal with the remnants of all that shit.

Over the next twenty-four hours, New Yorkers learn more about which birds inhabit our city. Everyone knows the pigeon, but people have no idea about the Monk parakeet. Why did a bird mainly found in Brooklyn end up on 22nd Street in Manhattan? And how the hell did Monk parakeets find themselves in Brooklyn in the first place? Of course, there are ravens and crows among the dead, along with European starlings, a couple of redtail hawks, house sparrows. A real diverse group shows up in the mix of the dead. People are fascinated.

What captures my imagination is the bird that ends the evening news coverage:

"In an uncanny twist of fate, a mysterious, beautiful Mandarin duck was discovered in Central Park this week. The East Asia duck has made quite a splash due to its vibrant colors and because it is not naturally found in the U.S. A band on the duck's leg indicates it may have escaped from a nearby zoo, only no zoos have reported the duck missing." The Mandarin duck is what landed on the window sill outside my classroom right before the madness started.

The science community states a perfect storm of sights and sounds confused the birds, creating a frenzy of multiple flocks joining together in a catastrophic flight that ended in an accidental but mass suicide. Sounds like bullshit to me; however, no other theories are reasonable enough to alter that conclusion for the news. Ghosts? Aliens? Witches? Demonic forces? Who really believes in any of that shit? At least what sane person would say they do in public?

I know that Kasper Greenstreet conjured up the birds. I believe he killed himself in apartment 3C. I believe he has declared spiritual warfare on me. Me? I'm fucking delusional if I thought a kid with some psychic intuition, white sage, and holy water could make him go away.

I ask Aunt Paula to join us at the school meeting, which my father vetoes at first. After a lot of pleading, he allows her to come, as long as she is there for moral support and is not disruptive.

SISTER ELIZABETH

Sister Elizabeth heard of Jack Kelly long before she ever had him in her classroom. She remembers the moment they were introduced. Sister Thaddeus called them into the community room, visibly upset. One of Epiphany's own had been in a terrible accident. He was in critical condition at Bellevue hospital. Several of the Sisters knew Jack. A couple had taught him along the way; he was in seventh grade. Sister Elizabeth had no memory of the boy before the mention of his name that night. He was a motherless child. Many of the faculty tried to keep an eye on him over the years. The grim news made it appear that he would never make it to her eighth-grade class. However, he became a permanent fixture on the Sisters' prayer chain. All of the nuns followed his dire situation with dedicated prayer time.

His fall happened in an old boarding house that was originally a convent. Several of the older nuns, fixtures in the parish for years, knew the stories real or imagined regarding the place. Many of them were tawdry. There were whispers of nuns practicing witchcraft at the convent and salacious activity at the boarding house.

"What was he doing there at night?" someone asked.

"Boys playing where they don't belong."

Every day, details came to the Sisters of Epiphany, including an account

217

that the boy had been given his last rites. That he had been pronounced dead during a code blue before doctors were able to resuscitate him. Everyone was disturbed, especially Sister Elizabeth, who had once been told by an elderly nun that, when people have near-death experiences, they sometimes return with bad or evil spirits attached to them. There was talk of severe brain damage, of never walking again. Mass was offered for Jack almost daily. Every prayer chain in the tri-state area had the name Jack Kelly on it.

Then the word "miracle" began being repeated in regard to Jack. He was clinically dead and came back. A miracle. They said he would never fully recover, yet was able to walk and return to school. Another miracle. Sister Elizabeth was suspicious of miracles, suspicious of anything returning from the dead.

Sister Thaddeus and Jack Kelly's father sat with Sister Elizabeth, discussing Jack's particular needs. He may need to rest if one of his migraines came on; if need be, he might need to take a painkiller, they concluded. How does one say no to a miracle?

Of course, Sister Elizabeth agreed. She had no idea what to expect when he returned to school, excited to finally meet Jack Kelly.

She remembered his first day back: the conquering hero returning home from war. Everyone was happy to see him. Sister Elizabeth watched him carefully, liking the fact he had no conceit. Almost as an afterthought, she decided to write some notes on Jack Kelly that would follow his progress as he managed his situation. If they were going to give him special treatment, she wanted to make sure he did not take advantage of his privileges.

In her early journaling, she noted his fascination with the building across the street—the Gramercy Terrace. On one particular afternoon, Sister Elizabeth was correcting papers. Jack had fallen asleep during study time. She did not wake him when his classmates left for the day. Sister Elizabeth wrote about the deepness of his nap, how she looked up to find him sitting cross-legged on top of his desk, in a deep trance, eyes wide open. Jack did not notice her and started to curse: "You fucking say it! You fucking pray!"

It frightened her.

Jack began going into the vacant classroom across the way. Sister Elizabeth would check on him. What she found disturbed her. Once Jack was lying prostrate on the floor, he chanted something she did not understand. The list began to grow; Jack also sat at the window, watching the building across the street, focusing on someone in the apartment. Could he be a peeping Tom? Next time she checked on him, Jack was doing what she later discovered were yoga poses in the middle of the classroom. Yoga? Not a Catholic practice, not a Christian practice. A tool of the devil? Migraines?

Meanwhile, Mrs. Dowd had seen Jack in a coffee shop with a known psychic and several other questionable adults. "One of the women was sitting in broad daylight with Tarot cards!" The list kept mounting. One afternoon, Sister Elizabeth was organizing the classroom when she looked out the window. Jack Kelly was in front of the Gramercy Terrace building, looking at the names on the bell. Soon after that, he began working for one of the building's occupants, who turned out to be an Epiphany alumnus. Divorced, no less, after living in California. Sister Elizabeth did not like any of his behavior, making sure she documented everything she saw in the journal, including everything reported to her by Mrs. Dowd or any of Jack's classmates or their parents.

It got worse. The first-class trip of the year turned into an unmitigated disaster. Sister Elizabeth settled in with her group on the subway car, positioning herself so she had a clear view of Jack. She saw him slide up against the window with his back and step onto his seat in the most peculiar manner. He looked like he was under the influence of some drug or something worse, something ominous. In the dimly lit car, Jack savagely grabbed at his own neck like some demon-possessed boy. He was shaking, kicking wildly, and swinging from the top passenger bars like he was in the fight of his life. It frightened her greatly.

Then came the birds. All of the students reacted to the craziness of the storm and paranormal attack, be it in terror or shock. Except Jack. It seemed he was experiencing a completely different event or had some understanding or involvement. She was so shaken she sensed there was something evil in the boy. Was that old nun correct? That something dark had attached itself to Jack when he came back from the dead? She wanted him removed from her classroom, from the school.

- - -

Aunt Paula is waiting for us on 24th Street. She is on time, early in fact. I overheard my Dad tell her the night before: "Don't be late. I'm not waiting for you." She gives me a huge hug, whispering in my ear, "It will be okay." The three of us walk down 2nd Avenue without speaking a word. We are led into the epiphany library by one of the office staff. It is a small room the size of a regular classroom. Sister Thaddeus, Sister Elizabeth, and Father Keenan are sitting at the end of a long table. We sit down across from them, our backs to the door. Are our seats lower than theirs? It feels like our chairs are lower. For some reason, I am glad I wore my school uniform. I'm not sure what to expect but I did not expect Father Keenan, a diocese psychiatrist and priest. An us-against-them vibe fills the room.

"Shall we begin with a prayer, Father Keenan?" Sister Thaddeus asks.

He seems momentarily surprised, then, "Yes, of course, Sister." We all bow our heads. "Lord, when two or more are gathered in your name, you said our prayers will be answered. Guide us through these proceedings."

Proceedings? Isn't he a priest? And a psychiatrist? He really sounds like a lawyer.

Sister Elizabeth opens a notebook in front of her. She begins to read from it. The notebook is essentially a list of everything I've done as she sees it, or anything that involves me in some negative way. They apparently have a game plan, a playbook. Glancing from side to side at my father and Aunt Paula, I get the overwhelming feeling that we are outmatched. Sister Elizabeth references dates and actions, that, I must say, sounded bad.

I begin to smell ammonia. It rifles through my nose, watering my eyes. I am the only one who smells it, and it is oppressive.

She drones on, reading like it is story time. Hell, maybe it is. My father is uncomfortable. Sister Elizabeth mentions Mr. David. "He is a known practitioner of the occult. As are the people Jack and Mr. David were seen with several times at the coffee shop. Tarot readers, fortune tellers, black magic, and the like." This makes Aunt Paula squirm, since it is she who brought me to meet Mr. David.

"Can I say something?" I ask. I'm really bothered by the way those people are being portrayed. Also, the ammonia smell has gotten more obnoxious, if that's possible. I sniff my hands to try and get away from it.

Sister Elizabeth continues as if I didn't utter a word, but Sister Thaddeus says, "You will get your chance, Mr. Kelly." Is that me or my father she's talking to? She looks at him when she speaks.

Sister Elizabeth ramps up the day of the class trip with commentary. "He looked crazed, swinging from the handrail!" That's because I was busy fighting demons! Sister Elizabeth explains about the man dying on the train and how frightfully pale I looked.

My father and aunt both look at me, surprised. Are they disappointed? Neither is aware of or has heard anything about that day in such detail. Previously, I told my father that I had a bad migraine. Sister Elizabeth continues reading from the "Book of Jack" with all my defects and bad behaviors. She starts talking about the prostitute who is actually a transgender woman. This reminds me of the story of Mary Magdalene, who most people think was a prostitute. Nowhere in the Bible does it say she was a prostitute—read it, Sister. Pope Gregory the First gave a sermon in which he equated Mary of Bethany and the anonymous hair-washing woman of sin with Mary Magdalene. Eventually, the woman who committed adultery and was saved by Jesus just before being stoned became part of the Mary Magdalene story. "Let he who is without sin cast the first stone."

I can't help but feel that there are a lot of stones being thrown!

Now she brings up the birds. How poorly I behaved, how poorly I performed in the midst of this chaos. According to her, while James and Daniel were jumping up to help, I sat as if nothing in the world was happening. "Birds were attacking, slamming into the window. You sat." Rephrase. "He sat. Not a care or a worry. As if he was in a trance."

My father leans over and nudges me. "Why didn't you help?"

God, talk about missing the point! They are frying my ass here, Dad! Don't you get what she is saying? That I'm an abomination, defective… unholy?! I stop paying attention to her case against me. What she reads is factually true but spiritually inaccurate. You are religious, not God. "Running from the classroom without permission." Geez, Sister, the house is on fire, and you are worried about the fucking dishes in the sink! I didn't ask your permission to deal with the mayhem — the ghost across the street. Shadows crawl across the walls. NO! Not today! This is not your business—you have no power, no place here. All the power sits across from me, they are the living! They are scarier than you.

My poor aunt is sweating. I touch the triangle representing the Holy Trinity that Mr. David gave me. No spirit, no demon, no entity can break through—we are in the center, protected.

Sister Elizabeth finally stops, and Father Keenan starts. "Jack," he says, like we are friends. "Do you know what a Ouija board is?"

"Yes, Father, I do."

"Have you ever played with a Ouija board?"

"No, Father, I haven't."

"Ever seen one?"

"Maybe in a movie. Never in person."

"These adults you've been seen with claim to be psychic, mediums, Tarot card readers. Do they make you do things?"

"Like what, Father?"

"Ever been involved in a seance?"

"No."

"Have they read your fortune?" I shake my head.

"Did they ever hypnotize you?"

I look at my dad, a rookie mistake. "No, they never did."

Father Keenan does not miss my looking at Dad. "Have you ever been hypnotized?"

"Not by them."

"You're not answering the question, Mr. Kelly," Sister Elizabeth interjects.

"When he was recovering from his fall, a psychiatrist assigned to him put him under hypnosis." Father Keenan waits for my dad to give more information. "It was to help with headaches."

Father Keenan continues. "Mr. David, is he the one who taught you yoga and meditation?"

"Yes."

"Did you know yoga can open the door to other things?"

"Yoga relaxes me. Meditation is a form of prayer."

"Who do you pray to, Jack?"

Aunt Paula jumps in. "What is this?" she says, looking across at me, then at my father. No one answers. "No. What's going on here?" Her voice starts to get screechy.

My father leans in. "Paula."

"No." She looks at him and then across the table. "I'll tell you what this is—it's a witch trial! What exactly are you trying to say here?"

Wow, my typically discombobulated aunt is in the ring, and she has come to fight! Dad is embarrassed by both his relatives; he must see us as clearly unstable.

Sister Thaddeus, ever the diplomat, suggests a break. However, Aunt Paula is not done. "Do you know what this child went through?"

Now I'm embarrassed. Before the fall, all I wanted was to be special. Now I want to be normal, unassuming. "Do you?" She leans in and speaks directly to the three of them. Maybe we don't have a game plan but we do have someone standing up. "So, he didn't get up to shut the damn window. Did James and Dan ever have to fight to breathe, to live?"

My dad stands up, too fast. "Okay that's it! Can we have a minute?"

Sister Thaddeus and Father Keenan stand. Sister Elizabeth doesn't move. Her entire life has prepared her for battle. She is not afraid of us. Sister Thaddeus touches Sister Elizabeth's shoulder and bends down to whisper in her ear. She comes from love; none of this makes her happy.

Once the Sisters and Father Keenan leave the room, my father faces off with Aunt Paula. "You are an observer. You should go."

"This is wrong. I will go because I will never sit here and let them do that to Jack. Do you hear what that woman is saying? The accusations? It's not right!"

"It's okay, Aunt Paula," I say. "Go. I'll fill you in later."

Never in my life have I or will I love that woman more than I do today. The room has lost its ammonia smell. It is replaced by the smell of rosewater.

Aunt Paula leaves. My dad and I use the restroom. When we come back, they are waiting for us.

"Who do you pray to, Jack?" Father Keenan picks up where he left off.

Who do I pray to? Hmm. Who do you pray to? My God is love, not fear. Spirituality comes from the core of the universe. We all tap into it in different ways. You can teach me religion, but if you think for a moment that you can tell me how to seek God, how to communicate with God, how to love God, you could not be more mistaken. Do you think I want these voices in my head? That I want some supernatural being showing up to spoil our class trip or to scare the hell out of my classmates? Do you think I want to be aware of the ghost sitting across the street with some kind of power that I'm not sure how to fight?

They all stare at me, waiting for an answer. Taking into consideration that many of the things I've experienced are thoughts from the middle ages.

"God," I finally say.

"Who do you pray to, Father?"

"Jack, mind your manners," my father corrects me quickly.

"God? That's a broad term, Jack. Does your God have a name? Is it the God you're taught here at school?"

Geez, Aunt Paula is right: this is a fucking witch trial. I touch the triangle around my neck. You would think I pulled a gun or a knife.

"What is that?" Sister Elizabeth demands.

"The Trinity."

"May I have a look at that, Jack?" Father Keenan asks.

Should I let him? Will he give it back? I take it off and slowly hand it to him. He examines it carefully. "It represents the Father, Son, and Holy Spirit," I say.

"How's that?" he asks.

I explain the story as it was explained to me—protection, you are not alone. "What do you need protection from, Jack?" Father Keenan asks.

You! "It's a figure of speech."

"Jack, can we speak to your father?"

"Sure." Only, I don't move.

Father Keenan is losing his patience with me. "Alone."

"If it's me you are going to talk about, why can't I be in the room?"

"This is what I'm talking about," Sister Elizabeth pipes up.

"I'm not being disrespectful." I say. "I stay in the room with all my doctors. It is my life."

They all look to my dad. "We would like to have a conversation with the adults, Jack," Father Keenan states in the most condescending manner.

My father turns to me. "Jack," Dad says.

I get up to leave. "May I have my Trinity?" I ask.

Father Keenan does not want to give it back. "Do you mind if I hold onto it? I've never seen anything like it. I'd like to examine it."

"I mind," I say, putting my hand out. Father Keenan fingers it, looks to my dad to get an override. He doesn't get one. Finally, he hands it back to me.

"Where did you get it?" he asks.

"I stole it." No one is amused but me. "It was a gift," I finally say as I leave the room.

In the hallway, I have some time to think. My father must've thought, "Who was that kid in there?" My father must feel like the parent who came home from work one day to learn his son is on drugs. Only, the way they made me look is that I'm some kind of sorcerer or a witch. Are you, Jack? I close my eyes. What am I going to do about Kasper Greenstreet? That dude is riled; Casper the friendly ghost he is not! As helpful as Mr. David is, the spirits I'm dealing with appear to be above his pay grade. He basically told me that when he said, "I've never experienced anything like this."

I close my eyes and allow myself to remember....

"Happy Birthday to you! Happy Birthday, dear Stevie, happy birthday to you!"

Katherine and I carry breakfast trays as we sing to Stevie on his ninth birthday. Seems like yesterday we were celebrating his first. Mikey, Lilly, and Stevie are sitting in bed, waiting for us to arrive with breakfast. This is our Kelly birthday ritual: breakfast in the bed of whoever's birthday it is.

"We have pancakes with maple syrup, French toast, scrambled eggs," Katherine says, showing everyone the goods.

"There is orange juice, apple juice, and tea," I say, putting the tray down on his desk. All three kids start placing orders. "Pancakes!" "French toast and tea, Dad!"

Happy Birthday balloons float above the bed, and as I pour the tea, I think of the line in a Crosby, Stills and Nash song, "Our house is a very, very, very fine house..."

- - -

"Mr. Kelly, have you no Tarot cards, books on the occult, symbols of any kind? Honestly, I would have liked to study that triangle longer."

Dad sits straight. "Let's cut to the chase, Father, what are we concerned about here?"

"Those people are known to practice the occult—it is not what we teach here at Epiphany," Sister Elizabeth says forcefully.

"Let's not get ahead of ourselves, Sister," Sister Thaddeus interrupts.

"Do you think Jack is dabbling in the occult?" Dad asks skeptically.

Father Keenan speaks. "We want to make sure Jack is not being taken advantage of—that he is not dabbling with things that a Christian boy should not be involved in. Several of these things that people have observed are of great concern. Don't you agree?"

"Well of course," Dad says. Silence. "I've had all the tests done which you requested. No seizures or anything obviously medical."

"That's my point. I'd like to see Jack once a week if that's okay," Father Keenan says.

"As?" Mr. Kelly asks.

"As?"

"As a priest—or as a psychiatrist?"

Father Keenan smiles, nodding his head. "Both. If that's okay with you." As an afterthought, he adds, "And Jack, of course."

Dad looks at them. Aunt Paula was right; this feels like a witch hunt. "And if we don't agree to that?"

Sister Elizabeth responds. "This is a Catholic school, Mr. Kelly."

Father Keenan adds, "We are concerned with Jack, and all our students' spiritual life as well as their well-being." They are thinking about expelling him!

"Let's not get ahead of ourselves," Sister Thaddeus says firmly to Father Keenan and Sister Elizabeth.

Sister Elizabeth and Father Keenan come out of the room first, spoiling my day with my wife and kids.

"Mr. Kelly, let's just give this a try. No one wants Jack to succeed more than I do," Sister Thaddeus says.

"I believe that, Sister, only I get the feeling if we don't give it a try, Jack might be expelled. Not much of a choice."

She doesn't answer immediately. "Not if I can help it, Mr. Kelly."

- - -

Boy, do I get it once we get home. "What the hell are you thinking? Psychics? Mediums? The occult! Talking to prostitutes?"

"I wouldn't call it that."

My father is pissed. I've never seen him this angry at me. "Oh no? What would you call it?" He is in my face now. "Swinging from the bars on a train like a fucking monkey!" I say nothing. "This is going to stop!" he says, pointing in my face. "All this bullshit is going to stop. I want to know who introduced you to Mr. David!"

He waits for an answer, which I am not prepared to give. Finally, I say, "What does it matter who introduced us. He helps me!" The cat is out of the bag and proceeds to run all over the fucking house.

Dad is irate. "Oh, really? He helps you? They want to kick your ass out of school. How exactly is he helping you?"

Bite your tongue, Jack Kelly. Of course, I can't. "Aunt Paula's right; it was a witch trial."

Dad stares at me like he wants to clobber me. "Are you telling me you are a complete innocent here? You weren't standing on the seat in the subway? You didn't yell out 'fuck' in the classroom? You got up and helped when the birds were attacking. You weren't chanting?"

"Not exactly."

"Good. Here is what you are going to do. You are going to see Father Keenan once a week for the time being."

"Why?"

"So, he can…I'll be honest with you—this stuff it's scaring them. Nobody behaves like this, Jack. Why are you hanging out with adults who practice this kind of shit?"

Honestly, I don't have an answer he would like, so I don't speak.

"You will tell me the person who brought you to him, and I want that guy's number!"

"How do you know I didn't seek him out on my own?"

"Was it Peter Cairo?"

I shake my head vehemently. "No. No."

"I can put an end to the job too, so don't try my patience because I haven't any left."

"Fine. I'll see Father Keenan."

"Don't be confused, Jack. That wasn't a request."

A migraine hits. I need to lie down. I take a pill and crawl into bed, tired and defeated. Sleep is a friend that arrives quickly.

- - -

I am falling… Bam! The abruptness of the impact takes all the breath from my lungs. Lying on the floor paralyzed, I feel blood pooling around my head. I gasp for air. Darkness. Someone is calling my name. Brick? "I'm down here!"

Only there is no voice to yell with—I can't move. This is where you die, Jack.

Looking at the collapsed ceiling above me, I see a skeletal horse head with the skeletal body of a deformed human. It crawls through the hole. This creature walks upside down on the ceiling, which freaks me the fuck out. The sounds of people talking and whispering fill the room. I can't make the words out initially, only noises, movements. Shadows circle me. "Give me his thoughts." "Give me his breath!"

None of their mouths move; it is their thoughts I hear. "I want his soul!" barks the creature crawling along the ceiling. Never have I been more panicked. Shadows descend upon me, getting close enough to touch me before a soft voice breaks through the darkness.

"Step away from the boy!"

A light in the form of a woman illuminates the area. An angel? My dead mother? No, she is dressed as a nun. She moves toward me, bringing the light with her.

"Don't listen to that bitch!" "Witch!" "Poisoner!" comes a chorus of voices.

Her light opens a portal to another time and place. We are all in a large kitchen. I sit at the table while my body lies very still on the floor. A very large man, pregnant woman, and two shadows sit at the table. The shadows are wicked and look around, waiting to pounce. The nun is dressed in full habit—a uniform from another time and place. She is brewing something on the stove. The skeletal creature makes its way down the wall. "Watch her, Jack. She's a witch!" cry the shadows, followed by creepy laughter.

Shadows fill the room, jumping on and off the walls. Two more demons crawl through the hole in the ceiling. Clearly, I'm dead. How else can I observe this madness? Surely, this is hell! I witness shadows slide along the floor toward my dead body. The nun's head spins one hundred eighty degrees. "Leave that boy be!" The sound of her neck cracking gives me chills. I have never been more alone. Shadows slide away from my body and jump back on the walls.

The demons crawl down the wall. One of them eyes me. It must be seven or eight feet tall. Another slithers across the floor, getting very close, smelling me. I piss myself. The creature puts its mouth to my ear, speaking in a foreign language. Grabbing the beast by its tail, the nun swings the creature off the wall, shattering its bones around the room. "It can only live off fear. If you don't allow it to seize your fear, it will starve," she whispers.

The nun turns her energy to the remaining demons. "Lay down!" They do as instructed.

"Where am I?" No answer. "Am I dead?" I ask her.

The creatures get back up and snarl like it's feeding time. The shadows begin to run and jump on and off the walls like they are riding a carousel. A disjointed melody begins playing.

"I'll make you some tea," the nun says calmly.

"She's a witch, Jack!" "That's a potion! Don't drink it! She'll poison you!"

My body has not moved since it wet itself. I'm sure it will never move again. The big fat man stands up at the table, exposing himself. The nun's head spins again with the same cracking, chilling sound. I'm not sure of who or what I am more afraid of here… only that I am afraid of everything!

It is freezing. I thought hell was supposed to be hot!

"Sit down and put that away," the nun demands. She speaks to him softly, and he becomes the size of a doll.

"She's a witch!" the shadows yell. "Stand up and whip it out! Show her your dick!"

The nun brings me a cup of tea, ignoring their taunts. "It's very hot, let it sit." Looking up at her, I ask, "Is this hell?"

A choir of voices screeches at me: "It's hell! You're dead!" "Dead, Jackie boy!"

The two shadows at the table begin pounding on it, scaring the pregnant girl. "You belong in hell!" "Don't fight it, boy!" "It's much warmer there!" they scream at me.

The nun grabs hold of the shadow like it is a rag doll and shakes it, then throws it against the wall. Splat! The nun bends down to speak to me. "They feed off your thoughts, your memories, your worries." Only I am so frightened I can't control what I'm feeling, thinking. They run wild. It is too late to catch myself. My father comes to mind. How will he handle my death?

"You're going to hell, Jack, for what you did to your father!" yells the other shadow at the table.

Splat! The nun fires it off the wall. "Witch! Witch!" they yell, jumping on and off the walls. "Drink your tea. It will calm you till they get here," she says, staring into my eyes.

Who? Who is coming?

A stampede of people run through the abandoned boarding house. Voices. "I found him; he's in here."

Firefighters and paramedics race into the kitchen, in the deserted part of the room where my body has landed. The living stand in an empty room in the run-down boarding house. The dead, however, are still in the kitchen, where the battle rages.

The nun stands by me at the table. "Witch!" Shadows jump off the wall in a threatening fashion. "She's a no-good fucking witch!" they yell.

"Go back to your body, Jack," she says firmly. Again, she does not move her lips, but the command is clearly coming from her.

"Isn't the body dead?"

"It is somewhere in the in-between. Now, go back to your body," she says with urgency.

"Am I going to die?" I ask, getting up from the table.

"That's between you and God. Go."

Standing like a baby fawn, I wobble—can't trust my legs. "Can you come?" I beg her. My trust is completely in her now.

"No, I still need more time with these three." The woman at the table has given birth to her baby, which is dead. The man is still as small as a doll. Shadows have circled my motionless body. "We will never let him go!" they yell. "Never!"

I walk like a drunkard, afraid to let go of the table. Stumbling, I call out to the nun. "They'll get me!"

"Yea, though I walk through the valley of the shadow of death, I will fear no evil! For thou art with me!" the nun intones. "Go, Jack. Call on the Holy Spirit to light your way. They will move."

Shadows continue the carousel of jumping on and off the wall. The nun adds. "Don't let them touch you or attach to you."

Hesitating, I move back to the chair, filled with fear. What does that mean, attach to me?

"Pray it with me, Jack," she says firmly. "Yea, though I walk through the valley of the shadow of death, I will fear no evil for Thou art with me…"

I grab hold of the table, taking baby steps toward my body. This is my mountain—my Everest. If I don't get back into my body, I fear I will be lost. "Though I walk through the valley of the shadow of Death I will fear no evil…" My body is in complete darkness as I repeat the lines from Psalm 23 over and over. A light leads me, coming from inside me… my light… God's light!

Shadows recede into the darkness, away from my body. The nun disappears into the astral plane.

Sounds of police sirens float somewhere in or above my head. I can't stay awake. Then the siren is replaced with the ringing of a telephone. Our phone.

I sit up, in my bed, back in my father's apartment.

The memory of what my soul learned while my body dangled between the living and the dead is my road map. The nun. The shadows. The creatures from the subway. All were introduced to me while lying on the floor, fighting for my life in the boarding house. I have learned how to fight them. I must continue to unravel their secrets.

The phone continues to ring. "Jack, can you come over?" It's Peter. He sounds very weird.

"Sure. What's up?"

"Just come over; I'll show you."

I walk quickly to Peter's building, let myself in, make my way to his apartment, and open the door with my key. Peter is sitting at the kitchen table with a folder filled with pictures and articles, mainly about Kasper Greenstreet. A flashlight sits next to the folder.

"Kasper Greenstreet," I say. He hands me a couple of articles and pictures, as well as Kasper's obituary. The article, not his obituary, reports his suicide.

"Looks like he killed himself in this apartment," Peter says.

I read the article as fast as I can; it doesn't actually give an address but does state "a friend's apartment." Makes sense.

"This is going to sound batshit crazy, but I saw him on the street the day I had my accident," Peter says, looking at a photo of Kasper.

I state the obvious. "You know he was already dead, Peter."

"I know."

I see another article of great interest: "A Nun Found Buried Face Down May Have Been A Witch." I pick it up. It reads:

> "Archaeologists made a grisly discovery Tuesday after being called to a construction site by authorities, where they uncovered six skeletons, including a woman buried face down. She is believed to have been a Carmelite nun. Face-down burial was usually reserved for the wicked, and the thought is that the woman was either accused of witchcraft or practiced it. The construction site was once a Carmelite nun convent. The order lived there from 1875 until 1949, when it was turned into a boarding house and later condemned by the city. In addition to the nun's body, they discovered the bones of a stillborn baby; the skull showed evidence of blunt force trauma. Construction was halted on the high-rise co-op."

Now, I know why they kept calling her a witch!

"When did you find this article, Peter? You know that's the place I fell."

"Yes, I do know that. I found the article before I met you, Jack."

"She was no witch," I say.

Peter looks at me intensely, like this just keeps getting more insane. Scared, he gets up from the table and picks up the flashlight. "I need to show you something."

We walk into the guest bedroom; it is freezing. No surprise. This is Kasper Greenstreet. The fucker sent birds for me! Be happy with the chilly room.

"Yes, it's cold again," I say.

"No," Peter says. "It's not the cold. It's this."

He shuts the overhead light off and shines the flashlight around the room. Tattooed onto the wall is a shadow. Fuck, when did they get here? It's still until the flashlight hits it directly. Then it moves.

"Shit, did you see that?" Peter says, frightened. He moves away from the image.

"Yes. It can't hurt you unless you think it can," I say.

Peter looks at me suspiciously; I've never told him anything about them. That I know them. "What?" he asks.

"Peter, I know these things—they're scary, only they can't hurt you unless you think they can."

As if on cue, the shadow slides off the wall, revealing itself. Peter shrieks and drops the flashlight, losing his shit. I step forward. The shadow jumps back on the wall and remains still.

Peter is freaking out. "What the fuck, Jack? Did you bring them here? Did you?"

"No. Your problem was here before you met me. Remember?"

He looks at me. "Yeah, yeah. True." Peter tries to convince himself, only he has a breath of doubt. "Well, what does it want?"

Putting my finger to my lips, I motion for Peter to step out of the room with me. We start to leave the bedroom. Peter steps back and picks up the flashlight off the floor. The bedroom door slams behind him, leaving me outside. Both of us immediately try to open the door. It doesn't budge. Peter is frantic. "Jack! Get me out of here!"

Peter drops to the floor, searching for the flashlight. It is so cold he can see his breath. The overhead light goes off in the room. Peter grabs the flashlight and shines the light on the walls. There are now several shadows on the wall, blowing vapor from the cold temperature in the room at him. On and off the walls the shadows jump, taunting him. Carousel music begins to play as the room spins faster and faster. Peter shines the flashlight around the room, capturing a man standing in the corner smoking a cigarette. It is Kasper

Greenstreet. Peter folds into a fetal position, covering up like a prisoner of war.

I'm still outside the door, trying to get it open with a screwdriver. I know the drill, know what they are putting him through. Finally, I get the door to open. Peter is in the center of the bedroom, cold, alone, cowering.

"Peter." I touch his back. He jerks, looking up embarrassed, manic, speechless. "Let's get you out of here."

In the kitchen, I try to ease his fears like the nun did for me but I'm sure I sound naive. A highly educated man who has been taught that ghosts aren't real is brought to his knees in front of a kid who seems less afraid. How do you tell someone that you have intimate knowledge about such things?

"The easiest and best thing to do is to move out of this apartment like the other two tenants did, Peter. That's what your neighbor told me."

"Why didn't you tell me about this neighbor before?" Agitation replaces Peter's fear.

"Didn't want to spook you. You told me about the strangeness of the place. I just thought…"

"You thought what, Jack? That you would wait until they introduced themselves? Yeah, well, I have money tied up in this place. I can't move back in with Mommy and Daddy. I'm not a kid, Jack."

"Look, Peter, I am on your side. There is no shame in staying with your parents until we figure this out."

"Figure it out? How exactly is a fourteen-year-old boy going to figure this shit out? Did we piss him off lighting sage? Sprinkling holy water?" Peter asks. Is he blaming me? Paranoia is fueling his anger, his fear.

"You saw him the day of your accident…"

"I think I saw him." Peter backtracks, frightened, confused.

"Look, this all started before you and I met. Kasper is unsettled," I say. "That's why he won't leave."

"How do you know these things, Jack?"

"When I fell. No one wanted to tell me that I was clinically dead for a brief time. Only, I knew it somewhere in my soul because I saw things, experienced things that are not of this world."

Peter looks at me with an expression that suggests, "what did I get myself involved in?"

"Now I'm going to go into that room and make those shadows leave," I say. "Kasper Greenstreet is another story. I'm still working on that."

"You're not afraid, Jack?"

"Of course, I'm afraid. With the shadows you have to clear your mind of memories, thoughts. That is what they feed on."

Peter looks down. "What? In that room just now... I felt shame—shame about my divorce. Shame for not being more helpful to my parents after my father's stroke."

I nod. "Stay out of that room, Peter. Find a mantra."

"A mantra?"

"I use parts of Psalm 23 whenever I get conflicted."

Peter nods.

"You can't let them feed off your memories, your thoughts, Peter. It will drive you crazy and empower them."

The room is freezing when I walk in. I close the door behind me. It is as if the room is soundproof — no noise from the street, or apartments. Then I am gang tackled. Shadows storm me, circle me, circle the room. They are all over me. "That nun is a witch, you stupid fucker!" "She poisoned you with that tea." "You abandoned your family!" "Poor Stevie—you let that little boy die!" "Katherine, Katherine, where is beautiful Katherine?" They are relentless.

The shadows continue to accost me. "Alone now, Jack...without the witch to protect you!" They circle me. "You belong to us!" "Let's send him back!"

Fuck this! I grab hold of the first shadow and try to shake it like the nun did, only it is so cold that I burn my hands. Clinging to me, it begins folding, wrapping itself around my arms. Crawling up my skin. It feels like I'm tearing off a limb as I fight to get it off my arm. Finally, I am able to rip it from my body. It makes a retching sound as I peel it back. I fling it against the wall, and it splatters like vomit. My arms are hairless and white. The second shadow is a little easier to handle. It hits the wall and looks like a giant ink spot.

Unfortunately, this brings me to Dr. Melvin's office and the Rorschach test.

They continue to attack. "That doctor thought you were crazy, Jack! That's why they took your family away!" "You kept pretending to be a little boy!" Snickering, sinister laughing. "You have the brain power of a child!"

"That brain injury made you retarded!"

Don't listen. They have it wrong—you thought you were married with three children! These things are liars, manipulators.

Snickering comes from the shadows. "Where's my family? Where's my Katherine?" More mocking.

Yeah, well, I've come to fight! I grab another shadow. Smash, splatter. We are making a mess of Peter's walls. "So, she was a witch? Is that why you mother fuckers were so afraid of her?"

Now who's laughing? Now who's scared? They keep coming with their ineffective chants till they get lower and lower. "You are only scary in the dark—to people who are in the dark!"

Have I become the Mad Hatter? None of this is real. Ah, but they must be—because now Peter sees them! Then there is only quiet. Their splattered imprints on the wall are all that remain. We can paint over those fuckers.

Peter stands in the living room, shaking. He steps back when he sees my ghostly appearance. I know this drill; he sees the black rings under my eyes. "Jack, I should have never let you go in there."

"Do I look that bad?"

Peter nods. "Worse than that night you came into the diner."

I make sure the door to the bedroom is closed. "Yeah, well, I've never felt better."

The funny thing is that that's the truth. I always feel stronger after a row with one of these things. Like a snake that has shed its skin. Lighter, brighter.

Peter is twitching. "Did those things show up that night, too?"

"Yes."

Peter is leery of me now; I can sense it. Like Sister Elizabeth, Mrs. Dowd, all those people from school. My father, if he knew. There is no turning back. I convince him to go to his parents' place.

PETER CAIRO

This is complete madness. A fourteen-year-old boy is walking him to the corner so he can take a taxicab home to his mommy and daddy. Peter is too screwed up to walk. Looking at Jack, he no longer finds the comfort in him that he once did. He spoke about that nun who was buried face down decades ago like he knew her. All this is completely impossible to a sane individual, only none of them are sane. Peter's limp is back. Nerves? It reminds him of the stutter he had as a child, and how it returned in high school, college, and law school when he became overwhelmed with studying. Now he is overwhelmed with his life!

Who is Jack Kelly? Yes, yes, he knows the back story. Peter's father loves him, but…?

"Peter, Peter." Jack is talking to him. "You have to listen to me, Peter."

He nods his head. "Yes of course, I'm listening."

"Don't go into that bedroom without me. You have to trust me on this Peter."

Nodding his head, he can't believe that this kid is telling him what to do in his own apartment. What a coward you are, Peter thinks. His time in the room with those things felt like ten years of therapy. Every emotion he had been harboring came to the surface.

Jack hails a cab for him. Peter and the cab driver get to 19th Street before Peter tells the driver to turn around and bring him back to his apartment. Apparently, he detaches from most things, which is why he is successful at work. Emotion is not needed in law. His marriage didn't break up because she didn't read books or couldn't be alone. It broke up because, well, if he's honest, her needs and wants did not mean anything to him. In fact, they became a bother to him after a while. It wasn't a harmonious breakup like he tells everyone; she wanted half his assets. Being a lawyer, he made sure everything was well hidden. No harmony there.

Back in his apartment, Peter stands outside the bedroom, deciding he will take Jack's advice tonight. His body is hungover. He's tired. Peter climbs into bed and falls into a deep peaceful sleep. When he wakes up, he feels well rested, only it's the middle of the night. 3:13 a.m.

Peter hears voices from inside his apartment. "He's a witch—just like the nun." "A demon." "Masquerading as a kid. If Peter could only see what he really looks like."

He's afraid to move, afraid to let them know that he can hear them. "Always watching this apartment from his classroom."

This is all freaking him out! The floor creaks and the voices go quiet. Shit, they know he is awake. Don't move!

"That kid—Jack Kelly brought all this back with him. He must be stopped."

They are whispering now, making Peter lean in, putting his ear to the door to hear them. "Peter can stop him." Then quickly and louder, "Peter is a coward! A coward! He'll do whatever Jack tells him to do!" "Almost ran home to momma, didn't he?"

Mocking laughter. Peter goes back to bed. The voices are only his own. The things he does understand, he doesn't like. Feelings toward his ex-wife come back, all the grievances. In abundance. His inability to "feel", to "empathize," as Sheila put it. It was a manipulation. He told her that. Especially when he disagreed with her. Which was often. If only she was the kind of wife that could just let him be, it might have lasted.

The end came while she was in Minnesota. He started seeing someone in the office. That's the real reason he came back to New York. Sheila did not want to come back to Los Angeles, didn't think it was healthy for their marriage. "We could start over here, Peter, here or in New York," she said.

"Do you want to do that?"

No, not really. "Do you still love me, Peter?"

"No."

Peter falls back to sleep. An hour later, he wakes up to the sounds of people having a party in his apartment.

The living room is filled with well-dressed people. Very upscale. The apartment is decorated completely different. Artwork hangs on all the walls, an exhibition of some kind. A lovely couple is hosting; He soon realizes that they are the Michaels. The couple who used to live here? Why are they here now? What have they done to his apartment? The party rages all around him and people nod, only no one introduces themselves. They are here to see the art, the artist.

Surely, Peter is dreaming, lucid dreaming maybe, but dreaming nonetheless.

He makes his way around the apartment. One wall is dedicated to a series of paintings titled Pandora's Box. The color is amazing. There is something, not magical exactly, but mystical about them. People are talking all around him. One beautifully dressed woman who smells wonderful starts telling him the artist's story. "Like Pandora's Box, the artist painted something inside. Something that he would reveal only to the person who buys that particular painting a year after the painting is purchased. Tell them how it pertains to their life. But only if they want to know…"

It is hard to believe that these beautiful, vibrant boxes could contain anything evil, but they are titled Pandora's Box. Who would want to know?

The woman joins in Peter's thoughts, as if he'd spoken these words to her. "It could be self-awareness," she says. "We know the scariest thing for most people to face is themselves."

From another wall hangs entirely different paintings. Equally fascinating. The group of art lovers admire them. These paintings come in pairs, portraits of the same person in two entirely different poses, impressions. A famous actress/model who's been dead for a few years. An architect of notoriety. Society people.

"He's a genius, you know."

They are not talking to him, but Peter moves in closer to hear why they think he is a genius. "As well as being extraordinarily talented as an artist, he

239

is psychic. If you look close at the Desiree Diamond study, you can see all the drug symbols."

Peter looks at the painting and does see the drug paraphernalia. Next, he comes to the self-portrait of the artist himself, Kasper Greenstreet. He feels an odd sensation. In the first portrait as a man, an artist, he looks like a modern-day prophet, with lots of gold and red utilized in the painting. However, it is the second portrait that is spellbinding. The artist as a child, surrounded by spirits—those things in the bedroom last night. But wait. Who is he looking at here? The child is familiar to Peter. My God, that child is Jack... isn't it? Jack seems to be captured looking up at something. How the hell can Jack be in Kasper's...

If seeing Jack isn't scary enough, there is a painting of Peter looking very "lawyer-like." Normal. The second canvas of Peter is painted all black, except for his face. Engulfed in darkness. Peter looks from the painting to the person standing next to him; it is Kasper Greenstreet, which shocks him. Stepping back from him, Peter realizes that he is naked in the middle of this party.

Someone points to the blacked-out portrait of Peter. "It's genius. He's not even there—it's like he doesn't really exist."

- - -

Peter opens his eyes to find himself standing in the middle of his living room, naked and alone. The curtains are open, the sunlight shining through the window on his body. Oddly enough, Peter is embarrassed by his own nudity. Bewildered by the dream, he looks around for some relic of the party, the dream. There is none. This fucking haunted apartment! What did those things—the shadows—call Jack? A demon? That Peter wouldn't recognize the true him? Jack in the painting?

KASPER GREENSTREET

Kasper emerges in the early afternoon from under his bed after the best sleep in quite some time. Although the sleep was good, he is still afraid. Kasper is always waiting for something to happen, someone to come. But it is sleep and he is doing it alone, even if it's under the fucking bed. This becomes his nightly routine, crawling under the bed to sleep. He sleeps with a hammer, a flashlight, pillows, blankets, clothes.

Who exactly is he hiding from? The list is long. He knows he is enemy number one, suicidal thoughts that he plays with all day. His fears are only interrupted by his *Pandora Box* paintings — he does them in all shapes and sizes. However, when he puts the brush or pencil down, his thoughts lead him to how much better he thinks he will be dead. That is his goal. Once his need to paint subsides, he will go to the top of the roof and either hang himself or jump. His final art project?

He uses the last of his blood on the newest *Pandora Box* painting. Kasper mixes it with red paint, "Dragon Blood." It makes the box jump off the canvas. By placing the box on an antique table in a large, very grand room, it makes the box appear small. It is meant to create a size distortion. Painting the room in shades of yellow and gray makes the red box color more prominent—you can't take your eyes off of it. His idea is to make it appear as if someone is watching it from afar. Inside the box is a distorted ego, both fun and difficult to paint. It cannot be seen with the viewer's eye. It is the magnifying of one's self, one's worth, one's problems, one's view of the world. All the lies and deceit the ego tells itself. The room's massive crown moldings would be found in a house of great prestige or a public building of much importance. The red box sits, waiting to be opened.

Kasper forces himself to go to the grocery store for some necessary items. It's a massive undertaking. Barely getting through the checkout line with his limited items, he scurries back to his apartment and art—a man with open nerves.

Like a dog in its crate, the tiny space under his bed offers some security from his fears. Kasper crawls on his belly under the bed with an array of shit. It doesn't take long to fall asleep in the mix of old clothes, blankets, small comforts. Kasper has forgotten how to dream, for there is nothing he remembers. The sound of a neighbor hammering wakes him. The noise is persistent. Who the fuck is hammering at this time of night? Kasper realizes the banging is coming from footsteps on the stairs outside his apartment. Judging from the heaviness of his steps, the person is a man. Bang, bang, bang. Looking out from under the bed, he keeps a count with the footsteps. He turns on his flashlight, checks the locks on the door. Somehow in his fright, he did not lock the door.

The man stops outside. Kasper turns the flashlight off.

Time becomes distorted, folding in on itself. He watches the doorknob turn slowly. The door swings slowly open. The creaking sound is excruciatingly loud. Panic! He feels for the hammer, his fear making him impotent. He can't find it among all the shit under the bed. He whimpers. The man's shoes are all he can see as the man steps into the apartment, locking the door behind him. Finally, he locates the hammer, bringing it to his chest. The man walks around the apartment and rummages through things. Steps into the bathroom. Takes a leak. Quiet. Dark.

Then suddenly, Philip looks under the bed as Kasper turns the flashlight on his face. "There's my little mouse," he says, flipping the bed over as he laughs. "Nowhere to hide now, Kasper!"

Swinging the hammer wildly at his head, it lands into the bedsprings, waking Kasper from his nightmare. He does not come out from under the bed the entire day.

- - -

On his fourth night under the bed, there is a knock at the door. He is too busy thinking to answer or call out "who's there?"

A key slides into the dead bolt.

His fear transforms to anger, which he prefers. Mitch opens the door and flips the lights on. Kasper knows it's wrong, but when Mitch passes the bed he reaches out and grabs his ankle. "Kasper, what are you doing under the bed?" Mitch says, like he's saying hello.

Crawling out from under the bed, Kasper drags the blanket and the hammer with him. "How did you know it was me?"

Mitch laughs. "I could see you when I opened the door."

"What?"

Sure enough, there is a clear line of view from the doorway.

"Are you sleeping under the bed?" Mitch asks in a mocking tone, which aggravates Kasper. Mitch stops when he sees his face. "What the fuck happened to your face?"

Kasper gives Mitch the *Reader's Digest* version of the attack. "He tried to rob me." He leaves out the sordid story of Philip luring him to the abandoned boarding house.

Mitch is surprised that Kasper has not called neither him or Susan. Mitch looks him over like he is a doctor. What's all this nonsense, the "we were worried about you" bullshit? Mitch spots the new paintings. "Wow…" His eyes light up as he walks around inspecting them. Kasper is sure he sees dollar signs. "Amazing."

Kasper accepts that Susan and Mitch care about him but mainly because he has become the "goose that has laid the golden eggs."

"I need to talk to Susan about a show—something intimate," Kasper says. "Not like the last one."

"Sure." Mitch picks up the paintings and moves them around the room, which irritates Kasper. "I want my own accountant, lawyer," Kasper blurts out, a little too aggressively.

"Don't trust me anymore?" Mitch is preoccupied with the art.

"It's not that," Kasper says apologetically. Which bothers him. *What is it, then, if it's not that or must he make an enemy of everyone?"* he wonders

"Love this!" Mitch picks up The Red Pandora's Box painting that Kasper completed a couple of days ago. He turns to face him. "Whatever makes you comfortable, Kasper. Susan and I suggested that you buy something. Something with security. You can have statements showing every penny of yours that I handle. I've offered them to you before…"

Mitch brings Kasper up to date on Susan's whereabouts. She is spending a few days with her elderly mother, who has been sick. "Do you want to grab a bite to eat?" he asks.

"Work is calling."

"Susan is going to love the new work."

Kasper smiles. Of course she will. My duality portraits made her— them—a lot of money. Their art gallery has become a powerhouse because of it, making every new artist in town wanting, hoping for Mitch and Susan's gallery to represent their work. After all, look how they nurtured that hack Kasper Greenstreet!

After Susan returns from upstate New York, she comes to the apartment to look at the work. She is alarmed that Kasper is sleeping under the bed. His fear and anxiety levels have decreased quite a bit, but he still loves the comfort it gives him psychologically. No one is going to shame him for sleeping there, not even Susan and Mitch.

Anger is his main emotion. Fortunately, it has the opposite effect on his work, which is vibrant, mystical. Kasper needs to get his nurse to take more blood. Can't make magic without blood.

Susan is talking. She seems amenable to an intimate event. "How about our apartment? I can have our furniture moved out for the weekend. Put it at the gallery. We could use all the wall space. Or is that too small?"

"No, I like that idea."

"This work is just fantastic, Kasper."

It is then that he realizes it is Mitch that annoys him. Not his lovely Susan.

They move the completed paintings around his small apartment, laughing and planning. Kasper asks Susan about her mother; she tells him surgery is in her mother's future. She will have to stay with her mom for a couple of weeks. She takes pictures of the new work with her Polaroid camera, cataloging each one in her usual manner. She is a great list maker.

After they are done, Susan tells Kasper, "I want to pick the paintings up to make sure they are safe. No security here. And Mitch tells me you want your own lawyer, accountant."

Before he has a chance to defend himself, she continues, "You want me to get you some names? Or would you prefer to find your own people?"

"No, if you have names, that would be good."

Kasper loves and trusts Susan. They decide to go to an uptown bistro that is the rage with New York's "art" world. They find a table for Susan and Kasper immediately—it's nice to be famous. All those years of invisibility.

Kasper's anger is unleashing years of rage, disrespect by many of the people in this room. One such bitch slithers over to their table in all her multiple ex-husbands' diamonds. One of the many grand dames of the art world—frankly Kasper prefers Mrs. Hudson Lockjaw to this former Cover girl who is still attractive enough to sleep with whomever she pleases.

"Kasper, how does it feel to be the lion of the art world?" she asks.

What horseshit! But Kasper is not immune to flattery and is willing to drink from that cup every chance he gets.

What a pair Susan and Kasper are. She in all her well-raised, proper manners. Kasper with all the bitchiness of a beautiful actress now being asked to play mommy roles. The two of them need this tonight; it is the first time Kasper has been out from under the bed in quite some time.

They drink champagne sent over by a variety of people, eat caviar, hold court at their corner table, and dish about everyone they know. Except Mitch and the lovely assistant. Those two names will not cross their lips. If Kasper could ever truly love another person, it would be Susan. She is the real deal. Just wonderful. Wouldn't it be a great world if Susan and he could love one another like a husband and wife while having sex with anyone they like? Thoughts of Philip at the boarding house seep into his mind, spoiling his good time and giving him a stomach full of anxiety.

"Do you know a good private eye?" Kasper asks Susan.

"No. Do I need one?"

"Not for you," he laughs.

Kasper has decided to take things into his own hands. Hire a private detective in the hopes of finding this "Philip." Put an end to this boogie man.

She talks him into coming home with her and sleeping in the guest room.

It is a mistake. In there, Mitch has hung up the painting of the little boy with all the shadows surrounding him. Kasper knows it is his creation, but once again, the shadows have repositioned themselves in the painting. Makes him think of the woman who returned the painting. "It has bad energy." Was she picking up similar movement inside the portrait? Of course, none of this is possible…

Mitch is mad when he gets home because Susan never responded to any of his messages from their answering service. Their tension is palpable. As much as Kasper drank, plus the joint he smoked, it doesn't help with sleep. He goes home and crawls under his bed.

JACK

I put Peter in the taxi, knowing he is on the verge of a nervous breakdown.

Suddenly, a shout: "Hey, Kelly, we have to stop meeting like this!" Brick yells from across 2nd Avenue. He is standing on the corner of 23rd Street and 2nd, smoking a cigarette.

Brick jogs across traffic and stops when he gets close. "Kelly, what the fuck?"

I laugh. "Yeah, I'm kind of pale."

"Kind of?" Brick tosses his cigarette into the street. "You make Dracula look like he's been tanning in the south of France." He puts his arm around my shoulder. "You sick?"

I shake my head. "Just a little stressed at school."

"Why? You're smart." Got to love this guy, always good for the ego.

"Nuns and my father are breaking my balls."

"Come walk with me. I have something that will relax you."

It is the first time I've ever smoked hash. Brick is right; I feel good, relaxed. We get as far as 27th Street before I turn back for home. There is a lot in play. Tomorrow I see Father Keenan, which I'm bitter about. I need to check on Peter, visit the mystic crew, get a game plan on how to make a ghost leave. Just run-of-the-mill teenage bullshit.

Sister Elizabeth has nothing to write in her journal today; I make sure of that. I'm on my best behavior. At 1:50 p.m. I grab my books, walk to her desk, and politely ask her if I may be excused to see Father Keenan in the uptown offices of the Archdiocese. However, his agreement with Sister Thaddeus and my father is for him to come to the Epiphany rectory on 21st Street.

He does not keep me waiting. "Monsignor has been kind enough to let us use his office," he says.

I follow him to the office and take note of the place since I've never been there before. The focal point is a large mahogany desk, with two leather chairs directly in front of it and a smaller couch against the wall. There is a large bookshelf and pictures of the pope, as well as other prominent people. A cross and a painting of the Blessed Mother sit on the opposite wall.

Father Keenan sits at the desk and motions for me to take one of the chairs. My mouth wants to say, "shouldn't I lay on the couch?" But why cause trouble?

"Would you like a glass of water?" Father Keenan asks.

"No, thank you."

"Do you know why you are here?"

"Sort of, you are concerned with some of my friends."

He leans in. "Now why does a thirteen-year-old…"

"Fourteen," I interrupt.

"…Fourteen-year-old boy refer to adults in their thirties as 'friends?' Do you have friends your age?" Father Keenan asks.

"Well, because they helped me at a time when I needed people to care. Yes, I do have friends my age."

"Fair enough." He pours himself a glass of water. "Let me know if you change your mind about the water. Do you know what the occult is?"

"Father, I don't practice black magic or witchcraft if that's what you are asking me."

He nods. "Do you know what it is?"

"I do."

"Does this Mr. David, a known psychic, ever read you?"

"No."

"So, you understand what I mean by 'read you?'" I nod my head. It's not the answer he wants. "Then what is it?"

My head throbs. I could use Brick's magic cigarette now.

"Do you believe that seances, Tarot cards, Ouija boards can open the door to another realm, to demons?" he continues.

"No."

"Can you expand on your answer?"

"No, I don't believe that they can open the door. However, I've never been to a seance, played with Tarot cards, or a Ouija board or any of that shit."

Father Keenan does not seem offended by the word "shit." "You like to curse, don't you, Jack?"

That I will cop to. "Yes, as a matter of fact I do."

"Does it make you feel older—like less of a boy?"

"What does that mean?"

"Do your older friends curse around you?"

"Listen, after my fall, the doctor told my dad it was not unusual for patients with head trauma to curse. It's a bad habit, I admit, but I like it. It is a vice of mine."

"Do you have any other vices?"

"Father Keenan, what exactly are you and Sister Elizabeth afraid of? Do you think I talk to the dead or that I practice witchcraft? Too bad it isn't the old days, when you could get away with a good old-fashioned witch hunt. Fucking drown me!"

Father Keenan puts his hands up. "Calm down, Jack. No one is accusing you of being a witch or a sorcerer. At least not me."

We sit in silence, before he asks me if I have any questions for him. There are many, but I am only willing to ask one. "As Catholics, do we believe in ghosts?"

He puts his two fingers to his lips. "Like every religion, we Catholics are made up of a variety of people with different experiences. We do believe in the Trinity and, initially, the Holy Spirit was referred to as the Holy Ghost. Purgatory is the cleansing of a spirit where many ghosts reside. If we look at it that way, then yes, there is at least an acknowledgement of ghosts. It gets tricky when you bring magic into it with the belief you can bring back Napoleon or Cleopatra through a seance or a channeler who claims to have some psychic abilities. That is not meant as a jab."

"No jab taken."

"Is there something behind the question?"

I shake my head. "Just curious."

My visit with Father Keenen leaves me conflicted. I wish I could visit that nun again. I'm feeling like she can guide me. New York is in its final days of fall; winter is making itself known. The chill in the air is clearly telling us to get ready.

- - -

Julia and Mr. Cairo are surprised to see me; it's not my day. I'm surprised that Peter did not show up at his parents' apartment last night. Julia hasn't heard from him in days and is alarmed. I realize that coming here was a mistake. I ask if they need anything from the store, try to smooth everything over. Only it's too late—Julia will call Peter the minute I leave, which is going to place me in a precarious spot.

I let myself into Peter's building. I run into the model, the beautiful woman who always looks like she is posing for a photo. She is at the mailbox and looks up when I come in. "Hey you!"

I turn to face her. "Me?"

"Yes."

She walks toward me. "Is Peter Cairo okay?"

"Well, I haven't seen him today, but I think so. Why?"

The model looks around before whispering. "He was very loud last night in the apartment. Yelling a lot. I saw him in the garden in the middle of the night—he was naked."

"Oh." What do you say to that?

We ride the elevator together. She talks about the strange noise coming from Peter's apartment. We stop in front of 3C, and I wait for her to pass. "If you need me, I am in 3G," she says.

We exchange a glance before she disappears into her apartment.

The chain is on the door. "Peter! Peter!" I call out.

"Who is it?" Peter leers through the cracked door at me. "I'm not really feeling well, Jack."

"Let me in."

He closes the door, removes the chain, and opens it. As I walk into the apartment, it is clear that he's gone sideways. All of his art and mirrors are missing from the walls, replaced by chalk outlines of frames. It is disturbing. He has written notes by hand inside the framed outlines. The guest bedroom door is open. Inside, I see the remains of the shadows splattered on the walls. There is also an image, a painting not by Peter, because it is very professional. It appears to be a man being inhaled by the fog, or possibly a veil closing over him.

Peter has the look of the Mad Hatter in his eyes. I'm scared for him, for me.

"What's going on?" I ask.

"You tell me, Jack, you brought these things back with you."

"Back? Back from where?"

"You know, you know," he says, nodding his head in rapid fashion.

"No. Peter, we talked about this. This apartment was haunted long before you met me."

Peter stands up. "Are you saying you didn't watch this apartment or me from across the street?"

I look across the street to my classroom. Sister Elizabeth is sitting at her desk with her head down. Grading papers? "It wasn't you I was watching. It was him...Kasper Greenstreet." I say.

"Him," Peter sneers.

"Why did you mark up your walls like this?"

Peter puts his face in his hands. "Have to figure this out." He talks more to himself than to me.

"We can figure this out together," I say.

"Can we? Why did you go to my parents' apartment today?"

"I was hoping to see you. You were supposed to go there last night."

"Are you trying to take over my life?" He is combative, crazy. "Possess me?"

Peter jumps up and walks into the kitchen. I follow him. "Come on, Peter. You know me. I'm here to help you!"

He starts making tea. His movements are mechanical.

"Peter, when you moved in here, did you find anything? An object, maybe religious or something that could have been considered occult?"

"Place was vacant, I told you this."

"Storage?"

"Still need to change the lock, never opened it..."

"Why did you go into the bedroom? I thought we decided..."

Peter turns to me in a burst of anger. "Let's get something straight! You don't tell me what to do. Not ever!" We stare at one another. Poor Peter—he's lost his mind.

"Listen, Peter, I'm going in there, because there is something on the wall that wasn't there yesterday."

Peter mumbles more to himself than to me. He yells while I walk through the living room. "There are a lot of things in that room that weren't there yesterday!"

There is something macabre about the painting on his bedroom wall. It is the closing, or burying of a person, or their mind—spirit? That combined with all the splattering of shadows on the wall gives me a sick feeling. Thinking of the nun and her calmness in the way she dealt with evil, I touch the triangle hanging around my neck. "The infinite power, protection of the Trinity," I repeat over and over.

When I come out of the room, Peter is sitting on the couch. His tea and a butcher knife are on the coffee table. "Did you paint that image on the wall, Peter?"

He is startled; I guess he forgot I was here. "No, last night it was there." Peter points to one of his chalk outlines; it is the centerpiece in the living room. It reads, "He is suffocating me."

"What does that mean? Who is suffocating you, Peter?"

He picks up the butcher knife and places the blade on one of his wrists.

"Peter, what are you doing!"

He jumps up from the couch in an attack mode. "You. You are suffocating me. It has to be you! You're the demon!"

I'm shocked. "What?"

Peter leaps at me. I run toward the door and try to open it, but he has put the chain back on the door. He chases me around the kitchen table. I toss chairs to the floor to stop him from getting to me and use the living room and kitchen walls to run around. As he pursues me, he yells obscenities, reminding me of the crazy woman on the train. I know none of this is Peter—he has cracked. Kasper Greenstreet has driven him mad. Now I am in a fight for my life.

"Help! Help me!"

Maybe the model in 3G can hear me. I pick up the centerpiece on the dining room table and fire it at him. It hits him, slows him down, but he does not stop. Round and round the apartment I run. He is tired, clumsy, which is good for me. I toss anything I can find in his way.

- - -

Across the street, Sister Elizabeth gets up from her desk and looks across the street into Peter Cairo's apartment. Horrified, she begins to yell, "Oh my God! Oh my God!" and runs for the classroom door. "Call the police!"

- - -

There is a neighbor at the door who can't get in due to the chain. Peter seems possessed or driven into madness. My words are futile. You cannot reason with a man who is suffocating. Back into the kitchen we go. I toss the garbage can in front of him, and Peter trips, giving me enough time to grab the wall phone. Lifting the handle, I spin to face him and smash the receiver into the side of his head, dropping him to his knees. My second blow is to his hand, and he drops the knife. Then I land another blow to his face and kick the knife across the kitchen. He folds into a fetal position. Sounds of police sirens on the street below. Peter is hurt. I'm sad because I love Peter, but this is not Peter!

Police kick open the door, snapping the chain. Before they have a chance to get fully into the apartment, I bend down to Peter and whisper in his ear. "Let me do all the talking."

The police quickly assume Peter attacked me, which is the correct assumption. "No, no he wasn't attacking me," I say. "Yes, he had a knife, but he was going to cut his wrists. That's why I hit him with the telephone."

They take Peter out; he is crazed and confused about everything. He's babbling about shadows and ghosts. The police look around the apartment.

The chalk marks help me with my story about Peter having a mental breakdown. No one must know he tried to kill me.

"Why are you here?" the lead officer asks.

"I work for him and his parents. You know—chores: picking up things from the cleaners, grocery store, post office and sitting with his dad, who had a stroke." I'm rambling, but it is working. "His dad was a cop—Mr. Cairo? Maybe you know him? He was a detective. His name is Peter, too."

One of the officers is walking around the apartment. I'm worried about what he will think if he goes into the guest room. But it is all crazy, so out of hand. I feel like I am going to places I have to go but should not be.

The officer walks into the guestroom. There is nothing on the walls. No shadows, no painting. Nothing. They have me go over the story a second time, then a third. My lying has gotten so good they believe me. They can ask me the same question a hundred different ways; I answer the same way every time.

"Where are they taking Peter?" I ask.

"Patch him up, then for a psych evaluation," says the lead officer.

The police don't want me to stay in the apartment; they want me to call my father. I show them my keys. I am firm. "I'm here all the time. I work for Mr. Cairo. My dad's at work."

A couple of neighbors gather outside the apartment door, one of them the model. "Yes, he works for Mr. Cairo," she says, vouching for me.

We smooth it out. I promise them I will lock up after I call Peter's parents.

Afterward, the model asks, "Did he try to hurt you?"

"No. Absolutely not. He tried to hurt himself."

She heads back to her apartment. "Thank you," I say, meaning it.

I head straight down to the basement and find the storage unit with a faded decal reading 3C. As if it will magically come off, I pull on the dead bolt. The elevator opens, but no one is there. One of the dryers turns on. Lights blink on and off. Water begins shooting into the washing machines. Still there is no one down here. This does not scare me. What scares me is Peter's condition, the way he chased me around the apartment with a butcher knife.

All the lights in the basement go out. Kasper.

I return to Peter's apartment. Mr. David arrives with Raphael. Within a few minutes, Susie arrives as well. They walk around the apartment, offering any paranormal understanding they have. Raphael, Mr. David, and I set up mirrors around the living room. It reminds me of a carnival fun house. You can't pass one mirror without seeing part of your reflection in another. Susie is walking around, touching all the chalk outlines. Star is the last to arrive. She begins burning incense in each room. Mr. David takes out a spray bottle with holy water and begins to generously spray it around the apartment. Susie starts playing with Tarot cards, dealing them out. Finally, we get in a circle in the living room and pray.

The guest bedroom door slams. We open our eyes—except Mr. David. The Tarot cards blow across the room. One of the cards—the "Ten of Swords"—lands at Susie's feet. The nice smell of the incense is replaced with a foul odor. A dead rat? Backed up toilet?

We go into the guest bedroom, where the majority of paranormal activity has taken place. Nothing is on the wall. The temperature is normal. Mr. David sprays holy water, Star tries more incense, and I hold onto my triangle and pray. Mr. David asks the spirit of Kasper Greenstreet to leave the apartment, to cross over. If only it were that easy, Jack thinks.

When I open my eyes, the earlier images have re-appeared on the walls: splattered shadows, ink spots, the painting Peter believed to be someone suffocating him. The master bedroom door slams as does the bathroom door. Susie fights to breathe.

Finally, she's had enough. "I'll be downstairs."

The rest of us go back to praying. This time Raphael starts having trouble breathing.

"You okay?" Mr. David asks.

"The incense," Raphael replies, but it is more than that. We start again, only his coughing and wheezing keeps him from being of assistance. "I'm going to get some water." He slips out of the room.

Three of us remain. We decide to stop. Mr. David and Star examine the walls, the painting.

From the living room comes Raphael's voice: "What do you want?"

We stand still.

"You must leave." His voice rises, followed by the sounds of breaking glass. I run from the bedroom, followed by Mr. David and Star. Raphael is standing in the living room, staring into space. One of the mirrors has been shattered. Raphael looks at us. "Never seen anything like it!"

None of them want to leave me alone in Peter's apartment, yet they all want to get out. They've had enough. We sweep up the glass and place the remaining mirrors securely in the guest room. Kasper doesn't seem to be affected by anything we've tried. He is a powerful force.

"We are in over our heads," Raphael says, which gives me great pause because he is a warrior. The ink spots hang from the wall. The painting seems to be dream-like; it comes and goes. All the curtains are closed. Before leaving, I make two telephone calls. One is to Julia and Mr. Cairo. The other call is to my Uncle Willy.

Julia has Mr. Cairo ready when I get to their apartment. I'm going with them to Bellevue Hospital in hopes of seeing Peter. Mr. Cairo is in a coat and hat with a blanket wrapped around him. Julia looks thrown together in a long overcoat. Pushing the wheelchair, we head up 1st Avenue to the hospital. The image of the blue blanket sits over Mr. Cairo's head the entire time. Peter is on his mind.

"The hospital wouldn't tell me exactly what happened," Julia says. "Do you know what happened, Jack?"

"I'm not really sure. Peter should be the one to explain."

We walk close together to fend off the chill, an odd little group brought together by a ghost in their son's apartment. My concern—my worry—for Peter is that Kasper has driven him mad.

Bellevue has a reputation for housing "crazy" people. However, in actuality, its history is rich. It is the oldest hospital in the United States, one of many firsts. Bellevue was established as the nation's first nursing school, first children's clinic, and first emergency pavilion. It also created a pavilion for the mentally ill, revolutionary for its time. Unfortunately, with all its many "firsts," the first thing most people associate with Bellevue is that it is a place for "crazy" people.

We sit in the lobby, trying to get information on Peter with hopes of seeing him. After a half hour, a doctor comes out to talk to Julia, Mr. Cairo, and me.

"Peter's doing okay. However, he is not ready to see you," he says to Julia and his dad. Julia is so dejected that my heart breaks for her.

It gets more awkward when the resident follows that up with, "Are you Jack?"

I nod. "Peter would like to see you."

"Is that okay?" I ask Julia and Mr. Cairo.

"Of course," Julia says, putting on a brave face. "Tell him we love him."

When I walk into the room, Peter doesn't look at me. Understandable. He is fragmented, ashamed. He looks around the room, paranoid.

"I'm sorry," he whispers.

I reach across the table and put my hand on his in an attempt to comfort him. Peter is my mentor, an older brother. "I'm not sure exactly what happened, Jack—I mean it was like I was there, but not there…"

"Peter, I know you would never intentionally hurt me."

He cannot hold eye contact. Not to be dramatic, but we have been to war together. There is no one to call, no roto-rooter for ghosts. You can't just talk about it out in the open, or you end up in a place like Bellevue. No disrespect.

"It was the shadows." He looks around after saying it, afraid to be overheard. "They kept at me all night."

"I have them under control."

"What about Greenstreet?"

"That's a little more complicated; I'm working on it. Listen, I need to get in your storage."

"Fine. There's a lock. No key."

"You okay if I break the lock off?"

"Of course."

KASPER GREENSTREET

Susan does just as she says. Their entire apartment's furnishings have been moved to storage for the weekend. Carefully, they plan where each of the paintings will be hung. Mitch and Kasper both think we should take the "self" portrait of me as a child down, since it is not part of the *Pandora's Box* theme. Susan adamantly disagrees. "We want them to see what they missed!"

"She has a point," says Mitch.

She places the paintings against the walls where she wants them hung. The beautiful assistant is on site, trying hard to keep everyone happy. Susan treats her with respect. Does she know? About the affair with the assistant and Mitch? Kasper knows there is!

Mitch hangs the paintings. God forbid he hires someone to do that. Susan switches paintings several times. Mitch is used to it, so he doesn't get upset—this is business. She is very strategic, methodical. Susan keeps walking into the apartment, feeling the natural direction she wants the traffic to flow, setting the mood.

Friday night is the opening. By invitation only. Susan looks amazing. If Mitch is fucking around with their assistant, she will let him see what he is missing! Mitch is Mitch—always in a sport jacket and tie. Their assistant is a beautiful girl who looks wonderful in anything. Why the fuck would you hire her? It doesn't matter how faithful Mitch has been, how confident she is with her marriage, she's playing with fire—messing with the gods.

I'm ridiculous, Kasper thinks; I come looking like the Maharishi dressed in a white shirt with black embroidery. I am a yoga master/psychic painter, he muses. However, he keeps an eye on that girl all night. She is quite a lightning rod. Mitch isn't the only one fluttering around her flame.

The champagne flows, and fancy hors d'oeuvres are passed. The literature says Kasper will explain what is in the box one year after it is purchased, which everyone finds fascinating. Every box—just like every person—has its own secrets. As each potential buyer observes the work, Kasper observes them. What is in their box?

It is theatre. Everyone seems to love it.

A wealthy news anchor with the best ratings in the business sets his sights on the *The Red Pandora's Box* painting. There are no prices on any of the work. If anyone wants to make an offer, Susan will bring them into the master bedroom, the only room with two lovely cushioned chairs and a small table. Middle Eastern music plays throughout the apartment. There is so much wealth and power walking around, admiring Kasper, his work, that he is once again drunk on the attention. A year ago, he was a starving artist—literally!

Susan and Mitch lead buyers one by one into the bedroom, taking offers. Prices are so ridiculous that Susan won't even whisper them.

By 10 p.m., nothing is left. Every painting in the *Pandora's Box* collection has been spoken for. Susan and Mitch have hired two N.Y.P.D. officers to spend the night with the art. The paintings are now worth millions; they can't leave them alone.

- - -

Walking into his studio apartment, Kasper happily crawls under his bed. Never has he felt more himself than when he is under his bed. No fear, no anxiety.

- - -

260

The private detective's hunt for Philip goes nowhere. Not one of the patrons or bartenders remembers seeing him at the bar with Kasper. Kasper's sketch is better than any police sketch artist could have drawn. Philip's face is spot on. Additional information comes in from the private detective. The owner of the building is the Catholic Church; the transaction is being handled through a local broker. They already have a buyer, some big New York developer. No one works there who resembles the man in Kasper's sketch. What a waste of time and money.

Kasper crawls under his bed for a long winter's nap, waiting for his next inspiration. Does he stay with the mystical? Nothing comes. It is very disappointing they cannot find Philip. Perhaps Kasper imagined him…a dream? A shadow? Punishing himself for his narcissistic ways? Starting and stopping several art projects, Kasper drinks to help with…what? Boredom? Inspiration? Nothing clicks. Maybe that's all he had: the two art shows. *Duality* and *Pandora's Box*. Better hold on to some of that money.

The next day, he wanders around New York, looking for something to catch his fancy, inspire him. In search of a friendly face, he stops at the gallery to see Susan and Mitch. The beautiful assistant greets him, and Kasper tries to be nice. She tells him Susan has gone to her mother's in upstate New York again. Her mother needs emergency surgery. "Mitch is in the office," she adds. "Do you want me to get him?"

"No, I know where it is." Mitch is probably counting all the money I've made him, Kasper thinks.

Mitch smiles, happy to see him. Only there are no more invitations for lunch, for coffee. There is a new interest, a new person to help with his mid-life woes. He confirms that Susan has rented a car to drive to her mother's.

"You worried?" Kasper asks.

"Yes, Susan is a horrible driver," Mitch says, making Kasper laugh.

"I was thinking about Susan's mother."

Mitch wants to go over the sales with him. "Or would you rather I talk to your lawyer?"

Kasper is not sure if he's being sarcastic, but he doesn't bite. Kasper is not looking for an argument, just some company. He wishes Susan was here.

Kasper is on top of the world professionally but is swimming upstream in life. Can't seem to paint. He finds himself under the bed sleeping more and more at weird times during the day. At night, he is a vampire. Crawling out from under the bed, he gets dressed, grabs a sketchpad and walks up 2nd Avenue. Hoping to make a last call at one of the many bars along the way, Kasper decides to go to Susan and Mitch's apartment instead.

It is the wee hours of the morning, and the lobby is deserted. Kasper has come many times, drunk or stoned, on the rebound from some affair or a one-night stand that didn't work out. Their apartment is dark; he doesn't turn on any lights. Kasper makes his way in the dark to the guest room, trying not to wake Mitch, but hoping that he does.

Kasper flips on the light switch and immediately wishes he could disappear. Mitch and his beautiful assistant are in a lovers' embrace. Mitch jumps up, "Oh, fuck!"

"Sorry," Kasper says, backing out of the door. Too late—you can't unsee that!

Back in his apartment, Kasper crawls under the bed like a frightened rabbit. Nothing helps. Cognac, a joint, a "lude." Nothing. His hunch is confirmed: Mitch is with the beautiful assistant. It makes things incredibly awkward to catch Mitch that way. Bad, very, very bad. Susan is his best friend, and Mitch is... what? He's not even his sleeping pill anymore.

Kasper spends the next few days doing all the wrong things. Having sex with anybody who will. Too much drinking, too many Quaaludes. Finally, he gets his nurse friend to draw more blood. Ironically the blood helps him settle down and paint. He paints Mitch and the beautiful assistant doing the deed. He calls Susan to see how she is, how her mother's surgery went.

"Can't wait for you to come back to the city," he says, slurring his words.

- - -

Mitch starts screaming. "You fucking told her! You fucking twat! I should kill you!"

"It wasn't me!" Kasper yells back, insulted. "I swear to God. It wasn't me!"

Mitch looks at him in a peculiar manner. "You swear to God? You don't believe in God! I wish that guy would have killed you!"

"You're mad at me because you got caught fucking your assistant. What balls you have!"

"At least I have balls, you fucking twat! Make sure you get your shit out of my apartment. You're dead to me!"

As much as I wanted Susan to know, I did not drop a dime. I try to reason with him, but he is unreasonable. "Mitch…"

He shakes his head. "Do you know what you've done? You're not even man enough to admit it."

- - -

It comes back to Kasper in flashes. Not being able to sleep. Talking on the telephone with Susan. Asking her if she has any suspicions about her beautiful assistant and Mitch. Fuck, Kasper thinks, you drunken idiot—what did you do? Nothing can help him now. Nothing. There aren't enough pills, alcohol, sex partners to undo what's been done. It's been a couple of days since Mitch screamed at him; he is surprised he did not hit him.

- - -

Kasper decides to go to the gallery and beg for his forgiveness.

Kasper has experienced a multitude of feelings over the years while walking into the Michaels Gallery. The first time he brought in some paintings and sketches, no one was interested in his work or in representing him. The gallery door was locked. He tapped on the window.

A good-looking man opened the door. "You're late." Kasper plunged into every bullshit story and apology he could think of.

"You babble," the man interrupted.

"Sorry."

"Don't be. Susan is running late herself. I'm Mitch Michaels."

"Susan's brother?" Kasper asked, hoping. His meaning wasn't lost on Mitch.

He laughed. "Nope, her husband."

Mitch led him into a windowless room, a small meeting room. "Display your work on the table. Susan loves a man with a plan."

"What about you?" Kasper began flirting with him.

263

Mitch smiled. "What about me? Am I a man with a plan, or do I love a man with a plan?"

"Touché, old boy."

They were off to the races, breaking each other's balls every chance they could. Like two kids in the school yard who love each other.

Soon, Susan arrived. Mitch kissed her on the mouth. She is easy to fall in love with, which Kasper does on the spot. It is clear she—they—are throwing Kasper a bone by telling him they will represent him.

Initially, the work does not sell. It is ordinary really, Kasper thinks, knowing he is self-trained, having taken a few classes along the way. Predictable. Susan keeps two of his paintings in the gallery all the time. However, the three start to hang out. They get on very well together, always sharing a few laughs. The Michaels don't use or like Kasper's drug use. Susan sends Mitch around to his studio apartment whenever they haven't heard from him in a week. Already the concerned parents.

After many months of showing the paintings, Susan asks Kasper to stop by the gallery one night. She has to be ending the business relationship, Kasper thinks.

When he arrives, Susan and Mitch have a bottle of champagne waiting. One of the paintings sold!

They work on getting Kasper portrait commissions to pay his rent, which he hates. Kasper balks. Mitch invites him for coffee—alone. They talk about everything, then he tells Kasper he needs to start painting portraits. He is firm. Older brother-like.

Mitch is right of course—it leads to the inspiration for the dual portraits and lots of money and prestige.

Those were the good days. Now Kasper walks into the gallery not knowing if Mitch is going to throw him through a window. The beautiful assistant is out front with a couple. She continues to talk to them as they turn. "Kasper Greenstreet the amazing artist," she says, introducing them. "We love your work," the man says.

"Only we can't find anything of yours available," says the woman.

Stepping away from them, the assistant pulls Kasper aside. "Mitch went up to Susan's mom's. Surgery went well; they should be driving home sometime tomorrow."

Kasper feels like he's stepped into some alternate universe.

As if reading his befuddled mind, she adds, "I spoke to Susan this morning." Daring him to ask her what she already knows…that some time, in a drunken state, Kasper spilled the beans on her and Mitch. Without missing a beat, she says, "This couple has seen your work—they want to commission something. They have money coming out the ass."

Kasper thinks, now that I can paint!

Susan exhibits a couple of new artists on the wall who Kasper has yet to meet. Will they—Susan—still want to represent him? He has broken a code by getting in the middle of a married couple with all their secrets, love, history.

"The mind is a wonderful servant but a terrible master." His master speaks. "Throw yourself off a building Kasper—right now—no one will miss you!"

Later, he spends time drafting his demise. He pulls the blood out of the fridge and paints.

- - -

Snow falls heavily as Kasper stumbles out of the Chinese takeout. It sucks being drunk without good shoes, sliding all over the place. Although why he doesn't have good shoes is beyond him. Dinner is great: wonton soup, shrimp and lobster sauce, fried rice, dumplings, eggrolls. Afterward, he mixes the mustard with his blood from the refrigerator and begins to paint. A man—him?—walking home in the snow, bleeding. Drops of stark red blood desecrate the pure white snow. It makes for a wonderful contrast, as good as anything he has ever done. All because of the magic of his blood.

The problem with an addict, a drunk, a narcissist is they are just so damn unreliable. How did he fuck up Susan and Mitch? He packs up the portrait of the man with open wrists bleeding out in the white snow, deciding he will surprise them, make amends, make an offering. Give them this painting as a gift.

No one is on 2nd Avenue. Snow is falling blizzard-like; Kasper is the only fool slip-sliding up the street. Outside the building, he fears that Mitch changed the locks in anger and he will freeze to death outside their building. Kasper's shame kicks in; he stands outside the apartment door, reviewing his sins. His penance in the hall has sobered him—a little. The key turns the lock, letting him in. They are not home and must have decided to spend another night at Susan's mom's due to the snowstorm. Turning the heat up in the apartment, he leaves the canvas on the dining room table and scribbles a note filled with apologies, asking for forgiveness.

Kasper heads into the bedroom, hoping to sleep. The painting of the child surrounded by shadows stares down at him. The painting once again is different as he looks at it while lying in bed. More movement. The shadows have completely circled the boy, or so it would appear. Once, and what now seems like a long time ago, Kasper imagined that this would become his Dorian Gray. His torments, sorrows, mishaps would fall to the boy in the picture. He mixed his own blood with paint, changing his technique that would reinterpret his skill set, his imagination. No more gardens, trees, flowers. In its place, his vanity painted the souls of people he barely knew. No flattering portraits. Oh, no, it is their inner demons he brings to life, their self-importance, sins, desires.

However, in his cowardice he becomes an imposter, using a child that is not him. A child he saw in a park and borrowed with the hopes of sacrificing his fears and suffering to the boy, as if that were possible. Surrounding the kid with shadows that were Kasper's tormentors and his alone. Hoping for what? That they would go along with him—redefine his past, present, future? Leaving Kasper to his newfound fame and fortune in peace?

The painting's power is in giving Kasper the illusion it is a moveable dream, a feast that is actually a nightmare. Kasper lays in a borrowed bed in an apartment that is not his, and the shadows reclaim him as their own. They move about the painting in front of him with no secrecy, no trick of the eye, no masquerade. Kasper thinks, they have come for me! Mocking and chastising him, they show him Philip walking in the alley next to him. Private eyes may not be able to find him, but the shadows have no problem with his location. It is a coming-out party. One by one, the shadows step from the painting to reveal his many follies, fears, and indecent behavior. They have not only returned the painting to him with its bad energy but his demons as well…

"Don't want his money or any of his work. Just take it back!"

They show him sitting on the floor in his apartment making the telephone call to Susan, saying, "You must get rid of that girl—she is fucking your husband!"

- - -

"Kasper. Oh, Kasper," the voice of Uncle Dan calls from his bedroom. Lying, cheating, they leave nothing unturned. An older, naked woman is mocked with his painting when all she wanted was a flattering portrait to hang over her fireplace. Is that too much to ask for? Is that too much vanity? Apparently, Kasper Greenstreet thinks so. He is the psychic painter, after all.

"Kasper. Kasper," Philip calls. "Come to me, my little mouse!"

Shadows slide off the painting, onto the walls, coming and going as they please.

Finally, Kasper crawls out of bed to look for a sleeping pill. Mitch is not here to rock him to sleep. Shadows show him Mitch putting a pillow over his head.

Rummaging through the medicine cabinet, Kasper finds pills prescribed to Mitch. Mitch? He puts Susan and Kasper to bed and to sleep, only who puts him to sleep—these? Dalmane? Where is the Valium? Whatever the Dalmane are, Kasper takes two. But there are not enough pills to keep the shadows from coming out of the painting with more things they do not want him to forget. Louder and louder, they become… Get up! Get up, Kasper! One more pill will do the trick, and maybe a shot. Getting up to take the painting off the wall, they show their teeth, the faces of the dead. They back Kasper up for daring to try and remove them from the wall, from his psyche. Running across the hall into Susan and Mitch's bed, he tries to hide like a child, the little mouse. Here he can rest, with the smell and dust of Susan and Mitch to keep him company.

But there are no walls, no doors to keep these things out. They sit on the bed while he hides, frightened, under the pillows.

- - -

The ringing phone goes unanswered. It is non-stop and beats like a war drum against his head, intensifying his hangover. He is in Susan and Mitch's bed. He gets up using the walls for support.

Where are they? The buzzer rings. Pulling open the curtains the blanket of white hurts his eyes. He closes the drapes. The ringing stops. Kasper goes on the hunt for aspirin, something to help his crushing skull.

Bang, bang, bang! They're home. Never has he been so happy. But why knock?

He opens the door; it is the beautiful one. Her face is different, red, puffy. The weather? Kasper finds it hard to focus. She is staring. Alarmed? Is something wrong with his face? No, she was expecting to find Mitch. This is all wrong.

"What?"

"You don't know."

Kasper is not in the mood for a game. "Know what?"

"Susan and Mitch were in a horrible car accident. They're dead."

She brushes past him and turns on the television. The news shows the footage, thirteen cars on Route 9 in a huge pile-up, one of the cars theirs. Kasper sobs. Is this what love feels like, or is this shame? I did this, he thinks.

He remembers something, a question he asked: "Are you worried, Mitch?"

"Yes, Susan is a horrible driver."

The beautiful one takes charge. Kasper can't think. He needs a drink. She starts making telephone calls while observing the painting, his note on the dining room table. Kasper rushes over and grabs the note, which makes him cry harder. No one needs to see this. He goes back to bed.

He wakes up at nighttime. The shadows are quiet, but they have taken everything. In the kitchen, Kasper makes coffee and looks for the key to the storage area. It's too late now, but he takes the painting off the wall, wraps it in paper, and carries it to the basement. There is a deadbolt on the door for 3C. He opens it; sticks the child, shadows, dreams, nightmares into the dark storage; and bolts it. Kasper walks to the corner in the snowy street and throws the key into the sewer. He wants to run out in front of traffic, only that would be too easy for him. All is lost.

- - -

The beautiful one handles all of the arrangements. She brings the bodies back to New York. There are whispers as to why the caskets must be closed. Kasper doesn't want to imagine. Mitch died immediately; Susan lingered. He will not leave their apartment and pays the lease in advance so there is time before the landlord calls.

The family wants him to talk at the service, but he is paralyzed. The beautiful one is helpful, amazing even. Susan's mother is too sick to attend. Susan and Mitch have left her well taken care of once the estate is settled. However, that will take time.

The beautiful one approaches him about selling his last painting, the one she admired in the apartment—*Suicide in the Snow*—to the couple he met in the gallery.

"No. That is for Mitch and Susan," he says, knowing just how absurd that sounds.

"There is no access to money," she says. "There are things that need to be done…Kasper, I need your help. We need to take care of Susan's mom. Especially now."

Guilt. His or hers? What the fuck. That painting, money, none of it matters. As she said to him in the gallery that day, the couple "has money coming out the ass!" They are willing to pay a ridiculous amount of cash. This helps immediately. Kasper is too weak to go to the service or gathering at the gallery. It is weeks before he leaves their apartment.

- - -

New York is beautiful with its first snowfall, but when it lingers, it turns to brown slush. The emptiness he feels walking uptown toward the gallery is so deep that it brings all his pain, vanity, and disgust to the surface. He wants to blame the beautiful one, only she stepped up to the plate, retrieved their bodies, handled the memorial, and took care of Susan's mother. Him? He didn't even attend the service.

Apparently the beautiful one is not as amazing as everyone thought. After the service, she takes off with the remainder of the money from the sale of

Kasper's painting, as well as all the cash she is able to get her hands on from the gallery. By all accounts, the memorial was lovely.

Management comes to the door, along with letters from bill collectors. Rent on the gallery is due. Let the courts work it out; he is too tired for such things. Showering is his only task and that he does weekly. Today, he is stronger. Several of Mitch's and Susan's friends have reached out to him. They fill him in on the escapades of "the beautiful one." Apparently, she stole art and money. "The gallery is to be closed if you don't do something, Kasper."

It's a shit show. He needs to see his lawyer and accountant. There is plenty of money to fix everything. Not what I'm good at; Mitch handles money. He has been to his accountant's office once but has never met his lawyer.

In his accountant's office with the lawyer present, Kasper is confused. His head is foggy from all the pot, alcohol, pills, lack of sleep. Therefore, he implores them to repeat the same thing over and over again.

"What do you mean there is no money?" Kasper asks again for the third time.

They exchange glances. "The money has been diverted; small sums were deposited in several accounts for you, but the large amounts that you are owed…"

"The woman?" Kasper asks, referring to the beautiful one.

"No. Mitch Michaels."

Shock? Anger? Kasper feels none of those. Was that his payback for spilling the beans on Mitch's affair? "When?"

More glances. "From the start."

- - -

After getting out of the shower, Kasper looks for deodorant. He came across a straight razor. He immediately cuts his right wrist so deep that the blood shoots across the bathroom and all over the wall. Kasper is an observer, a watcher; he will not take responsibility for murdering himself. Holding the handle in his mouth, he presses against the left wrist with enough force to make that wrist gush as well. Both wrists become rich oil wells.

The razor falls to the floor. Stumbling out of the bathroom, he is making quite a mess; these wounds are deep. Kasper bleeds all over the carpet, the couch. He bounces around the apartment, sacrificing his blood in a ritualistic fashion to cleanse his sins.

It gets hazy from there because there are several things that Kasper can't fully explain. First, he's not sorry he cut his wrist because Mitch and Susan will be home soon. They will save him. Mitch will fix the lies the lawyer and accountant told. Susan will repair his wrists. But he is deluded. They are dead.

While waiting for them to arrive, he falls to his knees and bleeds out onto the living room floor.

- - -

A feeling of lockdown comes over him. Two vibrational forces follow, one a vortex pulling him down into his body, encouraging him to sleep. The other pulls him back to his feet, to the couch. He chooses that; however, a black hole-like energy comes from his body and calls with such force that he has to hold onto the couch. The sounds of a locomotive, a windstorm, encapsulate the apartment. Dreams and visions rapidly fill his mind with such speed that it is hard to decipher what is real, what is imagined.

He holds tight; he will not leave until Susan and Mitch come home, until it is the way it was between them. He looks at his body, the angle in which it fell. Contorted. Kasper wills himself not to return to the body. Waiting for them to return, his body hardens on the floor.

TRANSITION

Movers work in the apartment, removing all the furniture, cleaning. Looks like Kasper has spilled a lot of red paint. They are getting ready for the Pandora's Box showing. Only, Kasper is confused because he doesn't remember Susan and Mitch returning home. He keeps himself busy exploring the building, excited about the show. There are strong vibrational forces coming from somewhere down here. The storage bins? Washers or dryers? Typically, no one is down here; Kasper finds himself floating around. He lays on top of the washers, the dryers, a strong current coursing through his body. The vibrational beat helps him sleep—makes him stronger. On occasion, a housewife or housekeeper is doing laundry. Today, a housekeeper is putting laundry in the dryer, she keeps looking around. Strange, she doesn't speak to Kasper, but she keeps saying, "Is someone there?"

"Yes me! I just came out of the elevator."

Things are changing. Sleeping is no longer a problem. Kasper has started going down to the basement regularly to sleep on the machines. Soothing. There are long periods of time that he cannot account for. His temperament has always been nervous, he doesn't like animals. Never been comfortable with dogs, or cats—never rode a horse. Rats, mice, bugs of any kind make him squeamish. While trying to figure out where exactly the vibrational pull is coming from, two rats reveal themselves. His instinct is to jump, to run;

disgusting varmints. Only he doesn't feel any fear, or disgust. However, the rats are clearly afraid of him! They freeze, their hair puffs out, sides of their bodies cave in, they let out very long, very high-pitched squeals. Yes, they are afraid of me, he thinks—me!

When he walks outside the building, dogs emit a low guttural sound when passing him. Until he looks them in the eye. Then they whimper. There is no fear in his body, only anger, hostility, longing.

He cannot understand what is taking Susan and Mitch so long to get back to the apartment. What he does remember is they are at her mother's house, but on their way home.

When he gets into a taxi on Third Avenue, it is apparent that the driver has some kind of hearing problem, or does not understand the English language. Kasper gives him the address three times, but the asshole turns the wrong way. Leaning in, he barks, "You are a fucking idiot!" He gets out at the next light and walks uptown to the gallery. Something is wrong. There is a sign in the window advertising the space as being available for lease. It is empty. Did Susan or Mitch tell him they were getting a bigger space? Did that stint with the wrist fuck with his memory?

His art sales put them on the map. He's not bragging. Wait. Yes, he is bragging. And where is that girl? What happened to their assistant, the beautiful one? They should have told him if the gallery was to be moved.

More surprises. When he gets back to the apartment, Susan has bought all new furniture. But wait a minute—the exhibit. Vague memories come back to remind him…that's right. It already happened.

It was a beautiful event. All of the Pandora's Box work sold for big money. Also, he remembers the girl with Mitch; they were having an affair.

Strangely, Kasper is never cold. Things are fluid, happening around him with no clear explanation. Like this young couple that showed up today. Moving about the apartment like they live here. Ignoring him. This is unacceptable, it brings out a nefarious attitude in him. Okay, you moved the gallery, but having someone move in without at least a conversation with him? Well, it hits him the wrong way. They will have to go! He turns lights off or on, depending on the situation. Kasper opens doors or closes them. Just enough nonsense for them to pause. Still they ignore him.

Kasper's smoking hits a nerve. She chastises him when he gets home. "I

274

thought you quit smoking," she says.

He looks at her. "I did."

"It smelled like cigarettes the moment I walked in the door."

"It wasn't me."

All the little shit that can upend a relationship. All the little annoyances that can make people second-guess themselves, their partners, scare themselves. Kasper follows her down to the basement to watch her as she does laundry. One by one, he fucks with the washing machines, turning them off, a little trick he has perfected. He goes to the source and runs his hands on the panel, which makes him vibrate. He brings the vibration with him back to the machine and puts his hands on it. Boom, they stop. A couple of times, he has blown fuses when he touches the panel and shut all the lights off.

There are rats and mice hiding in the walls. Kasper frightens them out. It sends the woman into hysterics. She climbs on top of the washing machine, screaming for help.

Kasper starts painting again. He's able to conjure up images on his canvas that help him with the turning of the screws. To make their life uncomfortable, Kasper is a bad itch. He is easier than she is. What a punk! Following him into the staircase, all Kasper has to do is make a light bulb blink or a door stick, and he quickly begins taking the elevator. He plays on their emotions, their fears.

"Why is it so cold in here?" she says, walking around in a sweater.

When he paints, Kasper creates cold bedrooms, spiders and cockroaches in the kitchen, windows that won't open or close. He's learning to play with temperature. First, it's chilly, then it's freezing. Every time the superintendent comes to check the heat, it works fine. The power of the brush!

They must leave!

Something metaphysical is happening with Kasper. After cutting his wrists the second time, his body is not the same; it is better, more powerful. Honestly, he is not fully put together—it sounds ridiculous, but a hologram comes to mind. He's a fucking hologram! Anger and hostility are all he harbors for these people. Their dream apartment quickly becomes a nightmare. They call management. All her complaints make her sound nuts. Sleep deprivation is Kasper's main asset. He keeps disrupting their sleep. One evening while they eat dinner, the man begins to speak about one of the neighbors. It is not completely clear, but it seems like someone died. Where? In the building? Maybe the basement? This knowledge creates an uneasiness in Kasper, which turns into rage. Did something happen to Susan—to Mitch?

Everything is an enigma, wrapped in a mystery. There is only one thing Kasper knows for sure, and that is he has never felt more in control, never had more power. Kasper is not sure how they poached their way into this apartment. Only he will make them leave. It is as if his very being depends on it.

- - -

Somebody by the name of Philip enters Kasper's mind. He is immediately enraged.

- - -

Sitting in the garden late at night is so enjoyable. All the little critters leave at Kasper's command. The temperature is always the same for him. He needs no sweater, no jacket. He smokes until the wee hours of the morning. Listening to the secrets of the occupants gives him energy, fuels his fire. Flashes of a painting of his with these shadows. Maybe Kasper can use them, conjure them up to help him with his deed. Where is it? Susan sold it to some rich woman, only Kasper gets this nagging, pulsating feeling that she gave it back. But why? Everyone wants a Kasper Greenstreet original. How dare her! He is a genius!

Kasper has mastered painting the shadows; it is an unholy alliance. There may have been a time that they were stronger than he is, but not anymore. He is their creator. Nothing is more powerful than him — not here — not in this apartment. Using them very strategically, Kasper works on the male, the shadows playing with his jealous nature and fears of her infidelity. They corner him in the apartment, in the shower. Where is her diaphragm? Why does she need to take that to work? Nothing is better than the shadows to disturb one's peace. She is afraid to go to the basement. "Something is down there." He goes down with her, equally afraid. Frightening the mice, the rats run up the walls. But there are none there when pest control comes.

Everything is in working order. Management has had enough of these two! With all their bellyaches, complaints, letter writing. They fight to get out of the lease. What lease? Susan and Mitch have the lease!

The building super misses Susan and Mitch almost as much as Kasper does, but they will be back soon.

The apartment is empty. Susan is getting it ready for the Pandora's Box show. Very exclusive, only the big money will be invited. It's a great idea using the apartment in an intimate setting. She has some wonderful plans for Kasper.

Feeling the vibrational pull, he goes down to the basement to explore. Several women are doing laundry, two chatting, one reading a book. A powerful gravitational force comes from the storage area. There is also an energy source from the wall, entering the washers and dryers. This is not new to him, only he forgets it from time to time. Standing in front of the storage for 3C, the door appears to be breathing. When Kasper touches it, it stops. Energy drain.

All the women look around. "Did it just get cold?" the book reader asks.

"Yup," another woman says. "Drafty old basement."

He is back to being invisible. Like he was most of his life before he became a prominent artist with the "dual" portraits. He sits on the washing machines; one by one the women leave. He doesn't even have to let the rats out. Curling into a fetal position Kasper sleeps and recharges.

- - -

Upstairs, the apartment is dark. It stays dark for quite some time. Kasper's mind vacillates between whether or not the *Pandora Box* show is about to take place—or already has. He grapples with time or its meaning daily. Especially when he's slept exorbitantly long. What he has come to accept is that time is malleable. Buddha teaching, he believes, holds that asking questions about the origin of the universe, or time, is like "pausing" to find out who made the arrow you were shot with, rather than taking the arrow out of your body. Where is his arrow—in his wrists? Regardless, this time sequence has him perplexed. He does on occasion find himself with missing parts.

In fact, his entire existence has become an anomaly, discontinuity, or suspension of his previous reality. Perhaps it is the near-death experience with the cutting of his wrists that has left him virtually in two places. Doesn't matter because there is nowhere to be, so time is actually on his side…if time exists at all.

Kasper imagines the apartment to be as they left it, before they went to Susan's mother's. He can't remember the reason they went there in the first place. His work is selling, so he must continue to paint. Leaving the apartment is something he does less and less. There's no need really; everything he has is here. Except the keys to that storage—to find out what's making all the noise.

After much mental debate, Kasper decides to take a trip to visit the gallery. But he's perplexed when he arrives. It is no longer a gallery, but a bakery. He must have misplaced the address for the new place. When he gets home, he swears he will never step foot outside again. But an artist with his pedigree must have openings, signings.

- - -

Things just keep folding into one tedious day after another. Until she shows up with all her things.

Her furniture is junk, her art shit. How dare she hang up that garbage in his house! Kasper is offended. Is this the assistant? No, no, she is a squatter. It isn't long before he declares war. He throws everything at this one. She is tough. She doesn't pick up on the little clues. Subtle things like lights, doors, moving small objects, have no impact on this girl.

Her life is quiet; there is no man, or woman, in her bed. She doesn't watch television or listen to music. Boring people are the worst. The girl is shallow, so there is little to use against her. Kasper must find something. He begins to paint the shadows all over the apartment walls. She sees and tries to wash them away. Idiot. When he is not poking her, he spends a lot of time looking out the window, smoking a cigarette. Waiting. Waiting for who, what? Kasper's usual tricks make her fuss, but they are not having the impact he desires. He needs to change his method.

People's rituals are curious. Observing her, Kasper looks for a weakness, a point of entry.

Every night she does the same thing: takes a shower, puts some kind of cold cream on her face, makes a cup of tea, flips through magazines. When she is finished with her tea, she goes back in the bathroom and washes off the cold cream. Kasper moves her items—nothing. There is no fear in the basement; a mouse or visible rat does not have a big impact.

Kasper sits on the bed next to her, watching her sleep. She stirs. He is slowly pulling down the blanket. She sits up, startled. A nightmare? Stranger in the room? Sometimes he lies in bed next to her. This completely creeps her out, making her very fussy. He touches her face, moves her hair. Sitting straight up in bed, they are face to face. She swings wildly. Now she is ruffled. All the little things she now notices. He whispers into her ear, "Get out! Leave this place!"

Her complexion is pale. She stops with the cold cream, the tea. She dreads going to bed at night and stays up later and later. No longer the bright young girl at work, she starts making plans to finish out her lease, go back to whatever place she has come from. Then she disappears.

People keep walking through the apartment, looking around. What are they looking for? The time confusion is happening again, making him think of his art show. Doesn't make sense. None of the paintings are being displayed, so it cannot be his exhibit. Kasper's anger does not make for happy visits. Where the hell is the art?

WHEN WORLDS COLLIDE

Peter Cairo walks through Apartment 3C and leases the apartment immediately without seeing the laundry area, storage, or the garden. The super signs the paperwork before Peter walks through the basement. The apartment's reputation has grown negative over the last few years with disgruntled tenants and their wild imaginings. The suicide, whispered about by long-term tenants, does not help, nor do the strange occurrences being reported. In a city like New York, this apartment is highly desirable. But people walk through and complain about features that at one time were the apartment's selling points. The super heard one couple say, "weird vibes."

Today, however, Peter Cairo wants it on the spot.

- - -

Kasper watches the man standing in front of the storage unit for 3C. For a brief moment, he thinks the man is Mitch. Then he feels angry and hostile when he realizes he is not. Again, the storage for unit 3C vibrates.

- - -

Peter does not notice. Peter pays only half attention to the rest of the tour. He is excited about the apartment.

"This is your storage unit," the super says. Peter looks at the dead bolt lock. "We are having trouble finding the key. The last few tenants never asked for it, but I'm looking."

Peter nods. "I can handle that if it's okay with you."

He loses interest immediately in the basement and laundry area. He will buy everything new and sees no need for storage at the present time. Peter will hire someone to do his laundry, so no reason to give much thought to the number of washers and dryers. He does love the garden area connected to the building and can't wait to show Lee.

With keys in hand, Peter and Lee walk through the apartment. The living room faces 22nd Street and has floor to ceiling windows, creating walls of glass. The apartment is designed to bring the outside in. The two bedroom windows look out over the small garden on the west side of the building.

"Not many apartments like this one in New York," Lee says. "I would love to help you decorate."

- - -

More poachers. Kasper watches as the happy couple floats around apartment 3C making notes, measuring. He is sure they are not here to help with his show. He will get rid of them. These interlopers just make him more powerful.

- - -

The apartment itself is aesthetically perfect. However, Peter begins having difficulty sleeping; a neighbor's cigarette smoke is coming in through the open bedroom window. Its effect on his sleep is immediate. Lee begins sleeping at the apartment less and less. Peter, who never had trouble with sleep, is constantly up and down in the middle of the night. Their romance dissolves.

Everything makes Peter jumpy. He walks around the apartment at night like a zombie. While watching television, the intercom rings.

"Yes?" Static. "Lee?" Nothing.

A few minutes later, the intercom rings again. "Who is this?" he barks into the phone.

Kasper gets a kick out of watching this guy fall apart.

"Nearly all men can stand adversity, but if you want to test a man's character give him power," Abraham Lincoln once said. Kasper liked that quote. It was so different when he was invisible, and then *Duality* made him a king. He remembers feeling powerful for the first time in his life, only that power could not come close to the power he wields now. Kasper Greenstreet, the puppet master! His invisibility gives him immense power that he could use at will.

This is his motherland, the hill he is willing to die on. No one can stay in this apartment. Kasper used this motivation to make a mockery of his enemy—and enjoyed it! He loved watching Peter run up and down from the apartment to the street, looking for...what? Ghosts!

- - -

Peter crosses the street, stands in the entrance of Epiphany so no one can see him. He will be waiting when the person rings his buzzer again. But Peter gets tired of waiting, he enters the garden and sits on the bench next to Kasper.

- - -

Staring deep within his new puppet, Kasper realizes he can invade his dreams! His thoughts! Kasper can't fuck at the moment but can fuck with someone's mind!

Peter's dream is boring, but it gives Kasper enough insight to really have his way with this guy. Kasper left him on the bench while he goes upstairs, turned the sound up on the television, opened the blinds, moved shit around. Afterward, Kasper headed to the basement, turned on the washing machines, crawled on top of them, and went to sleep.

- - -

Peter stumbles to the shower. The mirror tells him all he needed to know; he's coming undone. Groggy from another poor night of sleep, he knows something needed to change. He is floundering.

- - -

Kasper feels great until he's back in the apartment. This fucker is still here. How long had it been since this guy arrived? Kasper's sleep revitalizes him, fuels his hostility. Why are the ones that were so easy to fuck with so difficult to get rid of? Kasper watches Peter shave, momentarily confused. Was this Philip? No. No. This was Peter. Who is Philip? Why does the mere thought of the name Philip conjure up such hate?

- - -

Torrential rain greets Peter as he leaves the apartment building. Looking for a cab is futile. He heads for the subway but is so tired he falls asleep. It takes him a moment to realize the train has traveled several stops past his exit. Getting to his feet, his irritation is only exceeded by weariness. He rushes up the subway stairs into the rain. An empty Yellow cab approaches. Knowing there will be competition for it, he rushes to the corner. For a brief moment, Peter feels like someone is following, possibly trying to catch up to him, maybe beat him to the cab. Looking over his shoulder, he sees a man he knows. No time to stop.

At the corner, a hand touches his back and pushes him into the oncoming taxi as it speeds up the street…

- - -

Kasper no longer questions the effect of the elements. His body temperature regulates itself. He is never cold, hot, or wet. He follows Peter out of the building; the man is dressed for Noah's flood. Morning commuters and students pack the train. Kasper feels an irritation he cannot define and blames Peter. Leaving the apartment drains his power. It makes his anger toward Peter metastasize into rage. Watching him is like throwing gasoline on a bonfire. On the street, Kasper steals bits of energy from any electrical source along the way.

Peter turns to look at him, which confuses Kasper. It is clear Peter sees him. Never before had Peter visually experienced Kasper. Now Peter runs, trying to get away from him. Kasper musters all his energy and aggressively attacks. Unfortunately, he runs into a pedestrian. It is like two worlds colliding, an earthquake, a meteor hitting earth. The explosion of energy propels the man into Peter and Peter into an oncoming taxi.

Kasper is so disoriented from the collision that he wanders aimlessly in the rain, looking for a source of energy to help realign himself. Finding a laundromat, he crawls on the washing machine. Sleep? Dormancy? The abyss? Kasper does not dream, does not remember anything. When he wakes, he is stronger.

Back at the apartment, Kasper no longer remembers that it is Susan and Mitch's place. Time is meaningless. Kasper knows Peter is trying to steal his energy, his apartment. But he will not let him. Since that day in the rain, Peter has not returned. Kasper is able to recover all his energy, all his power. He begins to paint again, remembers only what he wants to. The present is his source of energy. There is no one to disturb him.

And then Peter returns, bringing two people with him. A woman during the day always moving around the apartment unsettling Kasper. And a funny little man at night, a nervous type. Kasper notices a difference in Peter—the way he walks—with a limp. Had it always been there? It doesn't take more than a couple of nights screwing with the "night help" before the man doesn't come back. Her? Just a little longer before nerves get the better of her. Then it's back to Peter and Kasper.

KASPER'S EPIPHANY

Kasper loves the light that comes into the apartment during the morning. It is perfect for painting. He looks out the window, watching the kids from Epiphany head into the building for the start of a new school year. There is lots of commotion in the mornings and afternoons. It gives him something to do, especially in the afternoon while he has a smoke. Watching the older kids in the top-floor classroom becomes his curiosity. What grade is this? Eighth? Ninth? How do Catholics work this?

One of the boys beckons to him like a lighthouse on a dark and foggy night.

This kid sees Kasper. What is with him? He'll admit he's naturally paranoid, only the kid is peculiar. Since his transition, Kasper is much more aware of the differences in people. He is not the same as the rest of the kids, or even the nun. Something is not right with him. Not of this world? People feel Kasper's presence, his effect on them, but he is different. He is across the street, too far away for that. No, he is tuning into Kasper's vibration, his channel. The boy makes Kasper uneasy. He is a threat!

Geez, this boy is intense, the way he stares back at Kasper. Challenging Kasper! Something is not right...

Jack watches as Kasper waits by the window most days now. He always knows when Kasper is looking for him. Is he baiting him? Inviting him? Well, it's working because Kasper is drawn to him, to their game—always hoping he is at school. Kasper's inclination is to go to his apartment and find out what is going on with him.

The kid from Epiphany who is always watching him comes walking up the street. Now this is captivating to him. Focusing in, Kasper gives him a taste of what is to come. However, being this close to this kid, he can see his "Etheric Double" pulsating. Big vibration! Kasper doesn't believe he's a real kid, but he's not a shadow. Is he some kind of... what? Something else going on here. Trouble?

After my interaction with Mr. Greenstreet on the street, as well as my meeting with Mr. David who tells me about all the power I have, I've a newfound set of balls. I'm going to meet Mr. Greenstreet and ask him some questions in person. Today is the day. I slide into the building with the grocery delivery boy. Standing outside Apartment 3C, I hear the sound of footsteps and take a deep breath. The door opens.

"Yes?" A fairly tall man in his mid-thirties holds the door halfway open.

Who is this guy? This is not my guy. This is not the man I watch five days a week who lives in this apartment. "Mr. Green-street?" I stutter.

- - -

So, this kid knows Kasper's name. Has the balls to show up here looking for him. This other clown says, "I don't know who that is." I'm the guy who keeps you up at night, chased your girl away, scared your help from coming back, he thinks—that's me, Kasper Greenstreet! The kid comes into the apartment with a bullshit story. It's funny, now the little prick doesn't see Kasper after watching him all week, at the window smoking, watching him. Guess I don't want him to see me at the moment. Or is he pretending because Peter doesn't see me? The kid has power, not his power, but...

Honestly, Kasper should be more familiar with the neighborhood, only he just started going out again since this kid Jack came around. His last trip in the rain following Peter took a lot out of Kasper. He thought he was gone—but now Jack seems to have rejuvenated him. Jack seems to be able to transition easily from the inside to the outside—need to figure out how he does that. Must be careful of energy loss. One thing I know is Jack's body vibrates at a very different level than anyone. They are easy to follow because of Jack's pulsating light.

- - -

Peter and I arrive at the corner of my street. Several people are walking, one of them Kasper Greenstreet. He is smoking. No surprise there. He stares at us from across the street. "Hey!" I yell, as a bus passes in front of him. When the bus is gone, so is Kasper Greenstreet.

- - -

This game of cat and mouse is keeping Kasper amused. There are two mice he plays with on a regular basis. Peter and Jack. Peter is weaker, easier. The kid is far more beguiling, much more of a foe. Somewhere in the back of Kasper's mind Kasper feels like there was a time when he was the mouse. Only that can't be, Kasper is so powerful.

- - -

Leaving Peter's parents' apartment, I have no thoughts of shadow people or demons, or even Kasper Greenstreet. Birds explode out of the trees after what sounds like a shotgun blast, startling the shit out of me. Within seconds of the bird blast, a mischief of rats and a nest of mice scurry across the walkway in front of me.

- - -

Watching this kid, Jack, jump up on the bench, frightened, reinforces, to Kasper, that he has the upper hand, that he is more powerful. Kasper thinks: looking for me, kid? I'm right here!

Too tired to follow him any longer, Kasper must go back to the apartment to regenerate. Kasper can't stay away from home this long in the future—it is really draining. It ignites Kasper's anger thinking about how long he waited for Jack to come out.

- - -

Kasper can paint anything, only he can't seem to paint the kid—Jack. Capturing his school, his class, the children, is easy, only his image is elusive. It is impossible to capture his vibrational force. Peter is an easy mark. His fears float in front of Kasper like word bubbles in a comic strip. Easy to paint. Must remember not to stay out of the apartment for too long; it leaves him really exhausted. He heads down to the laundry room to revitalize.

The storage unit for 3C continues to have a life of its own. Whatever is inside is trying very hard to get out. Breathing, banging, the sounds drift into the laundry area, waking Kasper up from a well-needed rest. Once again there is confusion with time.

- - -

Holding the address, the man gave me for Kasper Greenstreet in my hand, I look at it repeatedly like it is going to change. I'm going to meet the elusive Kasper Greenstreet. Find out who he is and what he wants!

- - -

Upstairs in the apartment Kasper finds Jack alone, going through Peter's closets, crawling under beds, under sinks, and tapping on walls. What is he looking for? Jack Kelly is the least nervous person who has ever come in the apartment, even when he is alone.

It is a must that Kasper follows this kid in order to discover his motives and weakness, only he is so settled in the apartment. He is powerful there—charged. Leaving to follow Jack is risky.

- - -

Coming out of the subway, I walk through a couple of streets of storefronts. The address leads me to a cemetery. Looking at the address in my hand, it all makes sense. Kasper Greenstreet is dead. How did I miss this? It was a softball pitch. He looks so alive when I see him!

This may be the longest journey Kasper has ever taken, not in physical miles, but in the metaphysical. His body is changing on the train, letting him know that he is no longer able to leave the apartment, his astral plane, without suffering the consequences. He is a freshwater fish in saltwater. But he is determined to follow Jack, to uncover his motive, or a weakness that he can capitalize on. And then destroy him with it.

My instinct is to run. What I am dealing with is myth, hoax, superstition? But when I see it? Meet it? A spirit, a ghost alive and dead at the same time. My soul is not pleased! It is like experiencing the coldest and hottest day of the year within seconds of each other. That is how it feels when a murderous group of crows delivers Kasper Greenstreet to me. His complexion is ash, his wrists reveal his exit wounds, and blood still seeps from them like a slow dripping faucet.

None of the dead come back, but some stay. Kasper Greenstreet has stayed.

Jack leads Kasper to a large field, which he is not prepared for. There are all sorts of mixed vibrational forces coming through the area: electromagnetic waves, kinetic energy, pulsating from stones, from the soil. Kasper is still strong enough to use crows to defend himself. But he is vulnerable. Kasper's reasoning is slow, but he feels this is a showdown. In between are thoughts of Susan and Mitch. The field is an old cow pasture, mixed with lots of stones and half-built caves. Jack's prana is multileveled, his body energy is immersed with that of his soul, creating an array of colors. It is clear to Kasper that he is a general who has made a vast tactical error by following his enemy, rather than making the enemy stay on his soil to fight.

Is it distance? Or is this boy his kryptonite? Kasper's wrists hurt; they leak red paint. The earth in front of them calls his name. "Kasper, come. Kasper, come!"

"Never, never!" Only it is all a foreign language, a code that he does not have the strength to decipher or the patience to figure out.

Kasper realizes he must go.

Jack backs away from him and falls to the ground. It is time to retreat, so he can fight another day. Looking over his shoulder, Kasper watches Jack scramble to his feet. He glows like the sun, pulsating large sounding "Om's."

SPIRITS IN THE NIGHT

Kasper is delighted with Peter Cairo's breakdown, as well as the masterful use of his power by painting dreams and shadows. Peter attacked Jack, almost eliminating his greatest adversary. Only Jack survived by fighting very well, not like a child. He has powers, that one. It was a joke bringing the others here to try and exorcise Kasper out of what belongs to him, this sacred space. This building! It is where he lives beyond the veil. Had them choking on their own incense! The old guy's eyes almost exploded from his head when he revealed himself.

Kasper learned a lot from that day at the old cow pastures. Never will he leave this place again. He does not believe that Jack belongs with those people. He is not one of them. He is not of this earth, only they can't see it, because he is too clever in his disguise.

It is time to paint. Not quite finished with Peter Cairo, Kasper paints him in a straitjacket. He is now housed in a rubber room, so he doesn't hurt himself. Poor fellow. This painting goes up on the living room wall above the couch.

Next, he paints the mystic bunch, starting with Mr. David. A psychic? How dare you come to my land! Your head will explode. Raphael, you are a fallen angel—who can you fight? Shadows fill his apartment, his thoughts, turning him into a fragile old man, afraid of his own shadow. Susie chokes with the never-ending smell of overpowering incense. She goes to bed to the smell, wakes up to the smell. Coughing, wheezing. "But, Doctor, can't you smell it? It's even in your office!" Star has lost her glitter, not that she ever had any. She won't be able to make a decision without going to her Tarot cards. Kasper's mind rages: fuck with me and I will destroy you all!

CHILD'S PLAY

Star cannot get the images out of her head. They are everywhere—the walls of her apartment, elevators, restaurants, bathrooms. The images come from the painting from Peter Cairo's apartment, the one in which creatures are smothering someone. When she goes to her Tarot cards, Star keeps drawing the same six cards. They are the ones no one wants. She must see Mr. David.

Meanwhile, Raphael is afraid to leave his apartment but afraid to be there alone. Talking about the spirit world is one thing, but actually experiencing a ghost, and an unhappy one at that, has rocked him to his core. He returns to his Methodist Church, where he sits for hours at a time, just to avoid those things.

Rinsing her nose with saline, using strong herbs in her cooking and strong perfume on her clothes, will not diminish the smell of burnt sage in her nostrils. It is unbearable! Susie goes to an ear, nose, and throat doctor. He sends her to a neurologist. She can't live this way. No more fucking with the dead.

Mr. David is not seeing clients. His head feels like a radio that will not stop on one station. He is certain it is coming from Kasper Greenstreet. The feeling in that apartment, the evil and hate, was palpable. The spirit has spread his evil like bacteria, infecting anyone who dared interfere with him.

Kasper Greenstreet is firmly planted in Apartment 3C and wants to destroy anything and anyone who challenges him. He is ashamed to say it, but Mr. David wishes he never got himself or his group involved. His only hope is that Jack is stronger and more powerful than Kasper. Somewhere in his soul, he knows this to be true.

Peter takes breakfast with other patients. Looking around, he knows the shadows have taken on other forms. Some are the nurses, one is a doctor, a few of them patients. All of them are keeping him in Bellevue, locked up. Peter begins to hallucinate and attacks a fellow patient. They restrain him in a straitjacket.

JACK

The library is empty, so I have the reference desk and the place to myself. I'm here to find out everything I can about the work of Kasper Greenstreet. The librarian is willing and eager, mentioning to me that he came into the library one time when she first started working here. There were a couple of biographies written after his death; they sat on the table. The librarian tells me she doesn't know how accurate either is.

Most of his work is held with private collectors, leaving books that may have only one or two paintings in them. However, Susan Michaels was very good at documenting the work in her gallery. Her photos are mainly from Polaroid cameras. Unfortunately, most of the books with those pictures are at the New York Public Library at 42nd Street and 5th Avenue, the one with the lions out front.

The librarian calls and speaks to a colleague at the reference desk. As a favor to her, they will help me at the New York Public Library. After I check out the two biographies, she asks, "Why are you so interested in this artist?"

"His work it's haunting, mystical. I need to know more," I say.

The train ride is uneventful and gives me a chance to read parts of Kasper's biography without having to fight my way up town. The less academic book catches my attention. First, Kasper was gay. Second, he was abused for most of his life because of that. Kasper's mother hated her son's homosexuality, thus hating and abusing him. An uncle also molested him.

The walk up the New York Public Library, with its iconic lions sculpted by Edward C. Potter in pink Tennessee marble, never gets old. Although the lions have no official name, I remember hearing once they are known as Patience and Fortitude, given by former Mayor La Guardia during the Great Depression. Those are two things I need in my quest to remove Kasper from Apartment 3C: patience and fortitude. The building is Beaux Arts style, built by the architectural firm Carrere and Hastings on the old Croton Reservoir, also known as the Murray Hill Reservoir. Construction started in 1899, and the library opened on May 23, 1911, with President Taft in attendance. As magnificent as the outside of the building is, its interior is equally remarkable. Before working my way to the reference desk, I float around this magnificent place, forgetting for a moment the reason I am here. Admiring this place would be an understatement. It is like seeing an elephant up close. Awe-inspiring. The first time I was here was on a school trip in third, maybe fourth grade. We all fell silent walking around the building. Not because we were in a library but because we were in this wonderful building with so much beauty and books with words and knowledge most of us would never get a chance to read otherwise.

The building is decorated inside and out with murals and sculpture. Among the outdoor sculptures are the allegorical fountains by Frederick MacMonnies called Truth and Beauty. Truth; "But above all things Truth beareth the Victory." Beauty: "Beauty old yet Eternal voice and Inward word." I glide around as if I am in some beautiful daydream then reach the McGraw Rotunda on the third floor. In this place of words, I can only think of one—wow! The murals by Edward Laning depict the story of the recorded word. Covering the ceiling is the expansive *Promethus brings Fire* mural, the mythic spark of human invention and knowledge. The majestic old-world architecture of the main reading room opens to 52-foot ceilings. The mural of the sky is about the infinite quest to understand the unknown.

Which brings me to finding the reference desk and discovering everything I can about Kasper Greenstreet. The person at the reference desk is a large man with thick glasses. True to his word, he has pulled a variety of books for me to look at and a couple I can check out. His voice does not match his physical stature; it is small, squeaky.

"This is a fantastic look at his work. Landscapes, then of course his *Duality* portraits, followed by his *Pandora's Box* work—with an emphasis on the color red," he says as I stand eagerly.

He picks up a thin little book, examining it like he's not sure how to open it, ludicrous since the man is a librarian.

"Also, this here is a strange little book about a woman, a countess. Apparently, she owned one of his *Duality* paintings and went mad." He looks up at me and smiles. "Of course, she probably was mad to begin with, but it makes for a good story. I skimmed through it; you should take a look."

It takes two trips to the reference desk to gather all the material on Kasper Greenstreet. Starting with the thin little book, I read about the countess who paid a fortune for the *Duality* portrait of Kasper Greenstreet as a kid. Once she brought it home, she and all her people felt the painting had "very bad energy." They returned it to the Michaels Gallery, not wanting a penny in refund, but rather to get rid of it. As the book put it, she went from being a lively woman to a sleepless hag who traveled the world looking for peace. She blamed her torture on the elements in the painting. No photo of that painting is in the book, which makes it more ominous for me.

None of the biographies I pour through make Kasper sound good, nor was his life a walk in the park. So I switch to the large reference books on his paintings, looking for his self-portraits, especially the one of him as a child. Very few of his paintings have ever been resold in the art world. That is why it is so fascinating and why I enjoy looking through the books, viewing his work. Somewhere in this city, in this world, his paintings hang with all their mystery and secrets.

His early work is simple landscape. Peaceful really. Trees, flowers, a lake with a lone rowboat, a pond, waves crashing to the shore. Looking at them, I think I recognize the painting that I saw the night in the gallery when the man from the art gallery gave me the address to the cemetery.

Excited, I moved to the book entirely dedicated to his *Duality* portraits. I open the book slowly, hoping this will be where I find the answer to my Kasper Greenstreet puzzle. These paintings are amazing and disturbing. There is one of a prominent architect, Mr. Ricardo Hillibrand, looking very distinguished. On the following page, his form blends with his prominent architecture, displayed as body parts. Very graphic. It is sexual in a way I can't articulate. I don't think it was meant to be flattering. Then, there is a portrait of an older woman named "Mrs. Hudson Valley Lockjaw." One is flattering, but the other? She's naked in jewels and a vintage mink stole that only covers her neck. Her womanly parts are completely visible, with little dollar signs in areas of her body, coded messages. Is he shaming her body? Or her inner life? It seems to me like the latter.

An entire section is devoted to a famous dead actress, Desiree Diamond. Desiree is drop-dead gorgeous in one portrait, coming out of a television set like *The birth of Venus* coming out of the sea on her shell. I've seen replicas of this painting through the years. I never realized it was a Kasper Greenstreet original. As for the other portrait? Well, it depicts Desiree in paintings of women who are famous for being in well-known paintings—Mona Lisa, etc.—only there is drug paraphernalia in every one. Including "Whistler's Mother!" Desiree died of an overdose on the day the exhibit opened, creating quite a sensation. As a result, Kasper and the entire collection became an instant phenomenon. It created the illusion that he held some mystical powers, some psychic abilities. Wealthy people wanted him to paint them, no matter how ridiculous the commission fee, or how unflattering the portrait. Now that's power.

With great anticipation, I turn the page slowly from the flattering painting of himself to the one of him as a boy. The last painting in this particular book is of a small boy playing with marbles, looking up surrounded by shadows. It looks like me... Creepy... Who the fuck would want this in their living room? Especially since I know what those shadows can do? I'm putting my money on the fact that these images drove the countess mad. Through this information, I discover that the painting disappeared once the countess gave it back. This painting's whereabouts became a mystery to the people who write about such things.

But I think I know exactly where the painting is. In storage, in the basement, a piece of art that by all accounts could be worth close to a half a million dollars today. No, I don't think it's the apartment that Kasper can't move on from. I think the secret is in that painting.

I think of a passage from *The Art of War*, the book Mr. David gave me:

"If you know the enemy and know yourself, you need not fear the result of a hundred battles. If you know yourself but not the enemy, for every victory gained you will also suffer a defeat. If you know neither the enemy nor yourself, you will succumb in every battle."

Know the enemy!

In this collection of books, I still hope to find a reference, another image of the painting of Kasper as a child. Unfortunately, there are none. However, I find the *Pandora's Box* paintings as fascinating as the *Duality* portraits. They are rich in color with their vibrant reds, royal blues, and stunning golds. The history around these is as fascinating as the stories around the *Duality* portraits. People who bought the paintings based on *Pandora's Box* were told that after a year, Kasper would tell them what was inside their box.

Before that happened, Kasper was dead.

I love these paintings. If you take away the crazy stories that come with them, they portray the most beautiful boxes, amazing in color, detail, and scope. Since I'm at the library, I decided to read up on the Pandora's box legend. Things surprise me about the story: first, Pandora's box was a jug, not a box. In addition, the gods set Pandora up, manipulating her with power and cunning. They are really to blame for what was unleashed. But I believe God does not want us to fail. God wants us to have the only thing not released from the box, because Pandora closed the box before it was released.

Hope.

After returning all the books to the reference desk, I realize my guy is gone. It is evening, and I'm going to need a note for school tomorrow. Aunt Paula will help me.

My father is asleep when I get home, and I crawl into bed. Sleep comes easily.

- - -

The kitchen in the boarding house is quiet, except for the nun making some tea. I sit at the table. It is a much more pleasant alternative to falling through the floor. Surely, I am dreaming, another lucid dream, but a dream nonetheless.

"I didn't think I'd see you again," she says, pouring the water into two cups. Looking around, I realize it is just her and I in the kitchen. The room looks as it did when she lived in the convent. Nice. Homey. Warm.

"Am I here because you want to see me?" I ask.

"No."

"Well then, why am I here?"

She does not answer but stands holding her tea.

"Why didn't I fall through the floor? Like I did when I first met you?" I persist.

The nun places her cup on the table and sits nonchalantly, as if we are not time travelers, spirits from vastly different ages. "Well, I think it is because you learned that an entrance to this portal is no longer needed."

We sip our tea while she waits patiently for me to figure out why I've come. "I'm not sure I'm ready," I blurt out.

"You have the fortitude," she says, smiling. "Just remember simple things. Love is greater than fear. Light will always drive out darkness. Hope."

PANDORA'S STORAGE

Uncle Willy waits for me in front of the Gramercy Terrace. While Aunt Paula is always late, Uncle Willy is always early. He gives me the Uncle Willy bear hug while holding a small duffle bag. It is Friday night, so I do not expect to find anyone doing laundry. Flicking the lights on, I bring Uncle Willy to the storage area for Apartment 3C. He takes out a sledgehammer and canned air spray. Within minutes, he breaks the lock open.

I take a deep breath and open the storage door. There is only one thing inside: a painting wrapped in old newspaper.

"I owe you, Uncle Willy," I say. "You don't have to wait. I need to go upstairs."

"You sure? This basement is kind of creepy," he says. He wants to leave.

- - -

Kasper sits at his easel enjoying his work when something releases into the atmosphere, giving him an uneasy feeling. A moment of doubt? A box has been opened—Pandora's box?

- - -

Uncle Willy looks at the covered painting, not the least bit curious of what it is and why I want it. Which, quite frankly, makes things easier for me. Once he is gone, I carefully pull the newspaper back so I can see the painting. It is the one. There is a moment of eerie silence; it is as if I have unleashed something into the atmosphere. Something unholy…

Once upstairs, I let myself into the apartment and put the wrapped painting on the table in the foyer.

Kasper is waiting for me. He is not the Kasper from the cemetery. His complexion is not ashen, nor is blood dripping from his wrists. Kasper looks like the man I've been watching all this time, the man I saw in all the pictures at the library. No one else is coming; it is me alone. I also know that I am all I need.

This is a showdown, a dual, only there are no physical weapons. This is a battle of the souls…much more dangerous.

Kasper steps up, ready to fight—it's time for show-and-tell. He raises his hand as if to announce the presentation is about to begin. A painting appears on the wall—me standing at the window in my classroom, looking across the street, presumably at him.

The walls in the apartment begin to take on scenes from my life. Every wall displays a scene, real or imagined. Me in the hospital with Stevie. Walking down the street with Aunt Paula. Kasper and me in a cow pasture with crows overhead. He is not working in chronological order with his slideshow, which could be a tactic. Or a weakness. Either way, the images have no effect on me. Kasper widens his arms like he is on a cross. His wrists begin to bleed. His eyes roll into the back of his head. He levitates a few feet off the ground. A small earthquake hits inside the apartment, breaking glass from the kitchen cabinets; it falls. The painting on the wall changes to the boarding house. The ground under my feet breaks in the painting; that image is quickly replaced on the wall with one of me falling through space.

"Yes, I was there! So what?" I yell.

The blood from Kasper's wrists shoot across the room, spraying all over me. Kasper paints the walls with shadows, only they will not dare come off the walls. They have no power here! Demons crawl up the building outside the window with their horse heads, skeletal human bodies, and bony tails. Kasper opens the windows without moving to let them in. He is using anything in

304

his arsenal to intimidate me.

They crawl about the apartment, but I remember the nun's warning: "They feed on fear. Show them none, and they will starve!"

My fear is in neon; my heart beats out of my chest. I bind my fear, imprisoning it so it cannot imprison me!

Kasper's mind rages: let's see what this kid does now. They are the lions at the Colosseum getting ready to eat the Christian!

Only none of it will work, Kasper. I am the ringmaster! The demon slayer! Their growls and smells have no power here. I know where they hide. I've beaten them in their underground tunnels. They walk around the living room snarling, dripping with saliva, playing at being fierce, but I command them to "lay down!" They do as they are told.

Kasper thinks: this kid has declawed the things without raising a hand. Perhaps he's one of them!

A vortex starts in the room, tossing everything not nailed down all over the apartment. Walls crack, and glass breaks, scaring the demons. They do not want to stay in this sandbox; this is not their fight, and they are no match for either one of us. The creatures crawl back out the windows while the shadows disappear from the walls. Flying objects make me duck from time to time, only this is a heavyweight fight, and I have Kasper on the ropes.

Making my way to the foyer in the midst of the windstorm, I grab the painting, bringing it into the living room against gale-force winds. Placing the painting on the couch, I remove the newspaper. The room goes quiet. "Kasper, you remember this?"

All the air in the room has been sucked out; it is his dual self-portrait. The painting is very creepy. Shadows are engulfing a child.

"What are you?" he asks.

I do not answer. It is my turn for show-and-tell. While touching the painting, I place my hand on a shadow and watch it slither from the canvas like a snake coming out of a tree. Making its way up the wall, the shadow becomes the image of a man in a bedroom, calling Kasper's name. "Kasper, Kasper." The sound of the man's voice hurts his ears. He is watching a home movie—an unhappy home movie. It is clearly the image of a child and his molester, which makes me pause.

Kasper rattles the apartment, creating a tumultuous wind. However, what he once used for intimidation now represents his confusion. In my mind, there are images of Mr. Cairo in the wheelchair with papers blowing over his head, illustrating his inability to answer a question I asked. This is what I now see in Kasper Greenstreet. Kasper's anger is demonstrated by glass breaking, walls cracking. Which brings me to release another shadow, this pouring from the painting onto the floor. Again, it makes its way up the wall. The shadow becomes Kasper's mother, berating him for being queer. The child is filled with shame, fear, self-loathing.

The unpleasantness of the images makes me sorry for him, makes me want to stop. Only, I know that I cannot take my foot off the pedal because he will never leave if I do. The next shadow to leave the painting shoots directly onto the wall like a giant paintball. Kasper is sitting in Madison Square Park with Mitch in clearly happier times. The rattling stops. More shadows fly from the painting onto the walls. One is the incredible opening of the *Duality* paintings exhibit at the Guggenheim, followed by the cover of Desiree Diamond on *Newsweek*. Kasper's success at the *Pandora's Box* exhibition at Susan and Mitch's apartment is next.

The shadows leave the painting in all sorts of ways, some slithering, some climbing out—bizarre! As the shadows leave the canvas, their suctioning sounds can be heard as they adhere to the walls. The next shadow is of a man named Philip attacking Kasper in the boarding house.

"Are you Philip?" he asks in a fighting tone.

"No."

More of his earthly fears display themselves on the walls. They fly from the painting in rapid orb-like succession, leaving a string of images of Kasper's life throughout the apartment. His final exhibit is provided by the shadows themselves. In the actual painting, the child is no longer surrounded by these things. He physically looks like me, which comes as a shock, a surprise to both of us, but I am prepared for anything.

Being a master at manipulation, Kasper seizes the moment. "That's you!" he screams.

"My likeness, but your shadows," I shout back.

Again, the blood from his wrists squirts at me, this time burning my skin. "You're a demon, Jack Kelly!"

"Even though I walk through the valley of the shadow of death. I will fear no evil for thou art with me!"

The burning pain disappears. "They're your demons, your fears. Not mine. Face them! Own your shit!" I yell. "You hide yourself behind a child. Coward!"

The apartment walls are laid out like a gallery. All of his shadows have their meanings painted and are on display. People, ghosts, or the dust of their memory float through the apartment, observing his life on canvas. I am the curator who must bring this exhibit to an end. One image is of Kasper cutting his wrists, bleeding out, falling about the apartment. The next painting appears on the ceiling. It is of Kasper's body lying in the middle of the apartment six days later. We both look up. It demands our attention.

Suddenly, the body falls from the ceiling to the floor in front of us. It smells like a hundred dead rats, rancid with a sickly-sweet perfume on top of a backed-up sewer. The body is bloated. There is blood on the walls, on the furniture. He crawled for help. We are in the apartment as it was before anyone found the horror scene inside.

Kasper and I both move away from his corpse. "What is that?" he asks. "You."

Kasper is puzzled, looking at his ghostly self, not at the dead body. "Look at me! I am powerful—superhuman! You are a demon! I heard the shadows tell that to your friend, Peter. That is why he attacked you."

"I'm of the living; you are of the dead!"

The apartment is making me ill with its smell of death and misery. Another image appears on the wall, but it does not change the smell or remove the body before us. This painting is of Kasper and me in the cemetery in front of his grave. Again, the apartment shakes.

"Cow pasture," he says, disoriented.

"That's a cemetery," I say firmly.

"Fuck you, demon!"

My body pulsates. "I'm alive, Kasper; I have all the power. You couldn't even go out to Queens without falling apart."

He raises his hands, and the room becomes a wind tunnel. Again, he levitates.

"Parlor tricks. You are stuck in the in-between," I say firmly. "You can't even leave this apartment. When was the last time you were outside? I, Jack

Kelly, can go anywhere I want!"

"With your fat aunt," Kasper hisses at me.

"That's right. With my aunt who loves me. Who loves you? Where are they?"

He glares at me. "I'm not going anywhere—this is my place."

"Actually, this apartment was never yours. It belonged to Susan and Mitch Michaels." Kasper winces. "Only, they don't need it anymore."

I point on the wall to a painting of the Michaels' crypt. Kasper stares at it. "That's their grave. Here's yours!"

An image of the gravestone with the name Kasper Greenstreet appears on the wall. His eyes begin to roll in his head as blood drips from his wrists.

I need to finish this—all this suffering needs to come to an end. "Don't you want to go home?"

His eyes stare straight at me. "I am home."

"No. I mean your real home. This is not home."

"You mean death! The final resting place! Fade to black… why would I want that?"

A painting of Kasper's beautiful red Pandora's box appears on the wall. The one sold at his exhibition to a famous anchorman.

"I'm not talking about your mother's home. Or a place where you hide under the bed. You see that beautiful box, you know the story of Pandora, you painted it. She opened a box, letting out all the evil spirits, sickness, greed. Afraid of what she had done, Pandora shut the box before she had the chance to let out the last thing in the box. Do you know what the final thing is?" I pause for a long moment. "Hope. That's the home I am talking about— hope! You have been waiting for me, standing by the window watching for me. I am your beacon, your light. Open the box, Kasper."

Kasper stands before his corpse looking at the beautiful red box on the wall. "Kasper, it's hope," I say softly.

He closes his eyes as the red box slowly opens. After a beat, Kasper steps into his body like a genie returning to the lamp.

The living room returns to the setting of Peter's beautiful apartment. There are no paintings on the walls, no cracks, and no furniture thrown about. The only sign of Kasper Greenstreet's presence is the little boy in the picture. He is no longer me. It is Kasper Greenstreet as a child, looking up toward something, someone. Hope is on his face.

I need to catch my breath. In the bathroom I put water on my face; it does not help. My complexion is corpse-like, ghostly white, big dark circles under my eyes. The eyes themselves are blood shot and detached. Usually after a supernatural encounter I look like this, but I always feel more powerful. Tonight, I don't; I am muddled, weary. I do a tour of the apartment to make sure Kasper is gone. There is a peacefulness that was never here before. Gone is the ghost of Kasper Greenstreet and the madness of Peter Cairo that much I am certain.

However, looking at the painting, I realize it is now void of the shadows, which in itself is ludicrous. I know that revealing the painting to Kasper may have ended the haunting of apartment 3C, but every nerve, every cell in my body tells me it is the beginning of something else. Something malevolent. Opening this painting has unleashed something wicked and evil, and I fear that all the unclean, unseen spirits heard it, know it. I felt it in the basement and I feel it even more strongly now.

- - -

Leaving the apartment, I walk aimlessly, until I find myself on the street where the abandoned boarding house had been. It is dark, deserted. This is where it all started, and I've come back looking for the spirit of the nun who helped me get back to my body, maybe she can help me get back to Katherine and my kids. Lost in my thoughts in the darkness I walk into a man I didn't see or hear coming. "Sorry." I say, looking up at his face which makes me step back. There is something otherworldly about him, like he is from another time and has stepped into the wrong place. His smile makes my skin crawl; it sets off an alarm in me. "My you look like you just saw a ghost." He says staring deep into my eyes like he is trying to read not my mind, but my soul. I move quickly past him wanting to run, but not wanting to show fear. Oh my God, Philip? The way he spoke, the sound of his voice, the way he said it. "You look like you just saw a ghost…" It was as if he knew that I had just seen a ghost, and he was not talking about himself. Turning back to get another look—he is gone. It is as if he was never here at all, but of course he was; I saw him. He disappeared. Or altered himself in some way. I see a rat make its way into the sewer; it hurries me along. I need to find a way back to Katherine and my kids. But in order to do that I know that something even more sinister is on its way. The painting I now know is not finished with me yet, but it may just be my portal home.

THE

END

BOOK II

THE BOOK OF DEMONS

KEVIN MOORE

PHILIPS

Mr. Philips—Philip—did not always go by that name. Before he was able to shapeshift, he was Seymore Hunter, a good-looking man on the other side of thirty working in a haberdashery before World War II broke out in England. His goal was to leave London for Los Angeles and become a film star. At first, Seymore was more into blackmail than black magic. Then he met Dr. Cecil Dels. Dels was a fancy dresser who became a regular customer and held deep knowledge of numerology, astrology, and Enochian magic. All of this was fascinating to Seymore, but Dr. Dels' involvement in black magic and the occult really made Seymore come alive. Seymore believed in nothing really, other than the magic of sleight of hand. Since he was nine, he was able to lift wallets without ever getting caught. Dels offered a completely different education from anything Seymore had been taught in school or life; he became a sponge. Not because he believed in any of it but because he felt it could be a great tool to make money, especially when he arrived in America.

Dels had invited Seymore to be his guest at the very famous, but hush-hush séance of Alice Walker. Alice was an expat American with a dubious heritage, having been married to an Eastern European count and a German duke. A widow twice over, she resided in London, where her mystique was further enhanced by the many wealthy people who came to her home hoping to contact dead relatives or place spells on enemies. It was all donation-based, but if you wanted to be invited back or needed a reading, your donations would be very well-placed.

Alice Walker did not greet guests when they arrived. Instead, her staff handled it. Drinks were simple in nature—a French 75, sherry, whisky, or a glass of Bordeaux. Guests were directed to the main drawing room and its high ceilings with crown molding, a beautiful large Venetian crystal Chandelier, and white and black marble flooring. Murals covered the walls instead of paintings. The women sat at the end of the couches and chairs, sipping their drinks. The men stood by the stone fireplace, which was lit, even though it was not a cold night.

Seymore felt out of place. He wandered around the parlor, sipping his wine, then made his way back to the entry and the only painting that hung on the walls. It depicted a beautiful woman standing alone in a garden. There was nothing unusual or even special about it until Seymore noticed the woman's shadow. It was not close enough to her body to be her own. Knowing nothing of art, he thought of it as a mistake by the artist.

"It's not a mistake. It's learning how to use shadow energy to your advantage. To do your bidding." The voice was firm, strong, deep. Southern?

Alice Walker. He knew the moment he laid eyes on her his life would change.

She was not tall, but her hair was dark, as were her eyes. Not beautiful but very attractive. Seymore stood there, speechless.

"You're very good looking. As good looking as any movie star." She said it with no smile or hint of flirtation.

"And you…"

She stopped him before he could return the compliment. "Let's join the others. We can get to know each other later."

The party moved into a room in the middle of the house so removed from the living area that you could get lost trying to find it or leave it, which was the idea. On a large round table sat a small bowl of soup, a small glass of sherry, and three candles in the center. There were twelve guests; Seymore learned later that the ideal number was to be divisible by three. A late cancellation allowed Dels to invite him in order to get the number right. Serendipity. Once the doors closed, the room appeared to be soundproof. Alice Walker lit the candles, while the guests were told to place their left hands up and right hands down on those of their neighbors. Seymore watched her intently, looking for tricks or theater. There were none.

It was all very understated until the spirit of Moses began to move through Alice Walker. The energy in the room changed once Moses, through Alice, began to speak. She immediately zeroed in on the couple who had been talking to Dels earlier in the evening. Her voice changed slightly, the accent and speech pattern most notably. Moses-through-Alice began giving very specific insights, conveying information from the man's mother. The private information made him highly emotional. Several others at the table were given minor messages before Alice ended her channeling.

The guests were not encouraged to linger. They left their offerings in a crystal bowl, whispering to one another about how wonderful the evening was. No verbal thanks to Alice was needed, nor expected; their gratitude was reflected in their gift. Seymore looked to Dels, who was meandering in the foyer.

Alice touched Seymore's arm. "A glass of wine?"

She guided Seymore into the large drawing room and poured them both a glass of Bordeaux. "Do you like art, Mr. Hunter?"

"Yes, but my art education is limited." As an afterthought, he added, "Call me Seymore."

She led him to the mural dominating the drawing room. "Would you like me to tell you about the murals?"

"It's beautiful, but may I ask you, why murals?"

Earlier in the evening, Alice had been all business; now she was relaxed, charming. "Why not murals?"

"Well." He paused, trying to choose his words. "I would think a painting would have more value."

"You are talking monetary value."

Of course, Seymore thought, *what other value is there?*

"These are what are known as architectural style or illusionistic images. They were from the Romans—found in Pompeii."

Seymore sipped his wine while looking around the room at the murals. "They are stunning."

"Yes," Alice said, spinning around to view them herself.

She was not acting like a mysterious channeler. He knew women like this—from a distance. They were much smarter than the men in the room but felt they needed to keep a level of gaiety, so they didn't lose their femininity.

"It's to trick the viewer," she said, as if she was reading Seymore's mind.

He took a step back. "What is?"

"The style of painting. It is intended to shift the eye of the observer. They are looking outside at a fountain, or a hillside in the distance, not fully realizing that they are still in a small room."

Seymore stood in front of the mural. There was no fountain outside, no distant landscape. The scene was outside on the patio, the sun was a tarot card, and there was a man—his eyes only white— looking at a beautiful woman with mysterious symbols on her gown.

Seymore finished his wine. "Is he blinded by her beauty?"

"Pour yourself another glass."

Seymore walked to the bar and realized the servers hired by Alice were gone. After pouring the wine, he asked, "Well, is he?"

Alice looked at the painting. "Could be. He's blinded by something." She sat on the couch, joined by Seymore.

"Are these particular murals painted to create a feeling of mysticism?" he asked. She smiled but did not answer. "And the canvas with the shadow? Does all the art set the mood for your guests?"

Alice curled up on the sofa, draping her hand on the back, close to his shoulder. He looked at her and smiled, then picked up her hand, pretending to read her palm.

"What do you see?" she asked.

Seymore caressed her hand. "Unlimited happiness and adventure." He kissed her palm gently. "So soft."

Alice caressed his face in turn. "And what does this unlimited happiness look like?"

He smiled. "It must be discovered."

She gently slid her finger across his lips. They stared intensely into each other's eyes. Seymore leaned in, captivated, then kissed her very slowly, for a long time. She stood and looked at him on the couch, then bent over, her hands holding his face. "I am the first room at the top of the stairs. Come up in ten minutes."

Alice's hands moved slowly from his face, lingering on his neck and shoulders before she left the room. Seymore watched her eagerly.

He jumped to his feet, excited at the feast awaiting him. He paced the room and poured more wine but never drank it. He walked to the fireplace then stood in front of the painting with the shadow, puzzled, sure the shadow had moved. After waiting a moment, he checked his watch and immediately headed for the stairs.

Seymore Hunter could not get enough of Alice. He found himself spending more and more time with her. He quickly grew jealous of the relationship between Alice and Cecil Dels—a very close, very secretive relationship. Although Seymore was her lover, he was the outsider when the three were together. They'd travel to the English countryside, then to Paris, and eventually to Romania. Alice and Dels were in search of mystics; the occult; and more importantly, the fountain of youth. Along the way, she conducted readings, while Dels would offer financial or political tips that were really breadcrumbs to get little pieces of information to help Alice with the readings and perhaps help Dels as a financial advisor back in London. There were always money and contacts to be made, and they always figured out ways to make them.

Meanwhile, Alice laid out small gestures of seduction for Seymore. She gave him little gifts of chocolate, a man's scarf, fancy writing paper, a tiny bottle of cologne. She explained to him about the shadow in the painting, alluding to its magic that she could use to control the shadow to lean in and get information on people who came for readings. In that way, she learned their secrets and their fears. He found much of this to be mad, but Alice did possess insight. He wasn't quite sure what Dels and Alice were after, though. In the beginning, he thought they wanted him for sex, perhaps a ménage à trois. But it never came up. Both were of a certain age and seemingly wanted to turn back time, or at least pause it. The trip to Romania was supposed to uncover an elixir of some sort that would help them do just that.

When they arrived in Romania, a virus was breaking out in Europe and Russia. People were very nervous at how fast and deadly the virus seemed. They began whispering the word "pandemic." Memories of the Spanish flu and the millions killed by it created suspicion of anyone with a cough or a sneeze. If that wasn't enough to worry about, concerns about Germany rearming itself triggered an even higher level of paranoia. People were suspicious of everything and everyone.

None of this seemed to bother Dels or Alice.

The three spent the first night in Romania, having dinner at the Count and Countess Vladimir's house. The Count and Countess were rumored to be decedents of Count Kazikli Voyvoda, who may or may not have been the inspiration for Count Dracula. Seymore found all of it great theater. Everyone was so dramatic. He also found himself in love both with Alice and the excitement she provided.

As he listened, he found himself much more interested in their upcoming trip to Pestera Lilicalor than anything the Count and Countess had to say. Pestera Lilicalor was known as the "Bat Caves." After being very evasive, Alice finally confided in him over drinks in their private suite that they were going with a guide to find a bat species that, when eaten, prevented aging and increased sexual energy. She assured him that he did not need any more sexual energy. "But wouldn't you love to look and feel like you do now for the next twenty years?"

She moved her lips to his ear. "You have to eat the bat while it is still alive in order for it to work, and it needs to be the heart or liver," she whispered.

Seymore could hardly believe his good fortune. This was much more exciting than anything he had done prior to meeting her. He was going from trying to match ties at the men's clothing store to the fountain of youth.

It was a long drive to the caves. As Seymore sat in the front seat with the guide, he noticed Dels had been moving slower all morning; at first, Seymore thought it was because of the early start. However, during the drive, he began noticing a change in Dels' skin and speech. The closer they got to the cave, the more lethargic Dels became. They did not speak about what they knew: Dels was infected with the mysterious virus. Alice wrapped her scarf around her face, moving as far away from him as possible in the back seat. Seymore kept his window down. The guide spoke broken English and spent a good deal of his time smoking cigarettes.

By the time they arrived at the caves, Dels was sweating through his clothes and had fallen into a deep sleep. Neither Alice, Seymore, nor the guide spoke of changing plans and getting him to a doctor. They simply laid him down on the back seat; took the cages, nets, water, flashlights, and other supplies from the trunk of the car; and headed into the caves.

Inside, the interior walls looked like gray granite through the darkness. The damp caves smelled musty, earthy. The guide carried a gun. "Why the gun? Do bats attack?" Seymore asked.

"Other poachers." Through his teeth, a cigarette hanging from his lips, the guide's accent sounded like a bad interpretation of Dracula in a B movie. His voice echoed off the walls of the cave.

Seymore needed to keep his wits and directional aptitude; the gun was making him suspicious. Not to mention Dels being left in the car with a possible killer virus. What if he took their money and left them in the cave to die? There were so many turns and smaller caves into which they kept walking. Not to mention Seymore's anxiety about bats. He went on high alert.

Stepping into another section of the cave, Seymore noticed light from another entrance. "Why didn't we come in that way?"

"Must travel over mountain," the guide replied.

As they walked deeper into the caves, the smell of earth and soil was replaced with the scent of urine and guano. Before Seymore had a chance to ask about it, the guide pointed up. Hundreds of black and brown bats stuck to the ceiling. They made a lot of noise; apparently, bats like to talk, with a language of their own. They even fight over sleeping position, mating partners, and food—and sometimes, just for the fun of it.

Seymore waited for direction as the guide began setting up the cages. Alice watched from a distance with apparently no fear; though, Seymore thought she looked pallid.

The guide took out a long BB gun and another object that looked like a water pistol and began shinning his light onto the wall. It started slowly, like a choreographed dance building into a steady movement. The bats began to move, to make noise. As if to announce the arrival of divinity, they began fluttering around in a frenzy. Slowly, from behind the wall of black bats, an albino bat emerged, glowing in the dark. Its arterial system was completely visible, as was its beating heart. All three gasped at the sheer magic of the creature.

The guide saw an opportunity for an even larger payday. "This is a mystical creature, only in folklore," he said. "Ten times more powerful than the ones we came here for."

He picked up the water gun and pointed it at the bats, handing Seymore and Alice nets.

"Is that water?" Seymore asked.

"No. It is a compound that will paralyze a small mammal. Be ready."

With one blast, the liquid hit the albino bat, as well as several others. One immediately fell directly at their feet, but the albino flew directly at the guide in Kamikaze fashion, followed by an army of bats. Seymore and Alice swung their nets, with Alice catching the albino and Seymore getting a black and brown bat. Within moments, mayhem ensued. The bats did the exact opposite of their typical behavioral response—they attacked! Panicking, Alice and Seymore hurriedly tried to get the bats into the two cages. The plan was for the albino to go in one cage alone, with the others in the second cage. Seymore packed his two bats into the cage quickly.

He turned to find Alice struggling. Immediately, he went to help and found her extremely pale and sweaty. Seymore took the net from her and began working to get the albino bat into the cage. In the process, the bat bit him, but he held onto the magical creature until it was in the cage. Once inside, the bat covered its face and head with its wings.

The guide was covered in bats, spinning and screaming in his native language trying to get them off.

Now very unsteady, Alice grabbed onto Seymore. He took hold of her, as well as the caged albino bat, and began to make his way to the original entrance. There were multiple stops and starts, turning one way and retracing his steps, while trying to hold Alice up. She leaned against the wall, falling to her knees. Seymore tried to help her back to her feet. He then realized that Alice, like Dels, was infected with the virus. She was becoming dead weight. He began to panic, afraid of catching the virus and being stuck in the cave to die.

"Alice! Alice!" he yelled.

She was lost in a high fever and began to mutter. Seymore put the cage down next to her and cradled her head as he looked behind them, hoping for the guide to come and help.

"Feed me the albino bat," Alice said. "It will save me."

Seymore looked at the bat and slowly opened the cage. He needed to steel himself—*but against what? Fear? The virus? From all this madness?*

Carefully, he reached into the cage and took hold of the bat as Alice began to vomit violently and struggle to breathe. She began her death rattle, and then her face went motionless, eyes open, jaw still. She was dead. There was nothing he could do for her now. The albino bat surprised Seymore by biting his hand. It then flew out of the cage, attacking his face. Alice's words echoed in his head: "Feed me the bat; it will save me." In one furious motion, Seymore grabbed the bat and bit deep into its chest, ingesting its heart. He dropped to his knees and held his mouth closed to keep from spilling any of its blood. This was his salvation now, and he needed to eat it all. The albino bat shivered in his hands, then went still and silent.

Getting to his feet, Seymore started to make his way out of the cave until he was hit with seizures. He tried to fight through them, but they rolled through him violently like continuous earthquakes. The cave shook beneath his feet. He fell to the ground in a maddened state, rolling in pain, crawling. Hallucinating. The walls in the cave called his name. He twisted in pain, for how long he didn't know... *hours? Days?* He hoped and prayed to die. "Kill me already," he screamed.

Seymore felt his body being torn apart from the inside out like an intensely primal birth. He screamed in pain; his chest ripped open; his legs shriveled into his body. He reached for his chest but found his arms and hands were now wings.

He fully exploded, metamorphosing into the albino bat. He flew around chaotically, bouncing off walls before disappearing deep into the cave.

The room was dark. Seymore tried to sit, but his head was heavy. He was on a bed, maybe a cot. Still feeling confused, he found the floor with his feet, realizing his hearing was never this good, this clear. Seymore touched a small table with a lamp on it and turned on the light. The cot, table, and lamp were the only furniture in the room. There were no windows, nothing on the walls, and one small door. He could not remember anything but a vague memory of flying. Must have been a dream. Images of feeding on mice, rats, and maybe even a cat flashed before him.

He got to his feet and walked like a newborn fawn to the door. Outside the room was a long hallway; its walls were filled with art. A beautiful chair sat at the center of the blue foyer. It was a complete contrast to the dull room he had left. At the end of the hallway, there was a red door that he presumed led outdoors.

He opened the door. An older couple sat on the porch, surprised to see him. "You're up," the man said.

Seymore nodded his head.

"You've only been getting up at night," the man said.

"I don't mean to be rude, but who are you?"

"I'm Philip Philips. P. Philips. This is my wife, Victoria."

"Where am I?"

"Scotland."

Scotland? How the fuck did I get to Scotland?

JACK KELLY

Study time comes as it always does, but I cannot help myself. I look out the window of my classroom and expect to see Kasper Greenstreet standing with a cigarette in his hands, waiting for me.

Of course, he is not there. He never will be again. *Can a ghost that is presumably the soul of a dead person leave some dust? The spirit leaves a body behind, but are there remnants a ghost leaves behind?*

As hard as I tried to make the ghost of Kasper Greenstreet move on and leave Peter, his apartment, and the physical world, I miss him. *No. Maybe that is the wrong way to phrase it.* My feelings have been misplaced because I have spent the majority of eighth grade watching for him, waiting for him in the afternoon, and then looking for him in the spirit world. Now my days are haunted by the lack of his presence. The apartment is empty. It is a loss. I believe making his spirit move on was my mission, but now I wonder where he went and if there is anything his ghost left behind. *There is the painting…*

Looking at the apartment window, I write on my schoolbook cover: "Pull the shades down at Peter's! Add Kasper to *The Book of Souls*." *The Book of Souls* is a black notebook in which I write the names of people whom I am meant to care for spiritually. It all started with Katherine and my kids.

325

Dr. Melvin, the psychiatrist I was seeing after my fall, insisted that my near-death experience created what he claimed was an imaginary family. He wanted me to stop thinking and talking about them. Get on with my life. Instead, I wrote their names in my notebook so I will never forget them. I refer to it as *The Book of Souls*.

I call Julia, Peter's mother, as soon as I get out of school. I've been working for Peter and his parents for most of the school year. They have become like family to me. She sounds troubled.

"Hello?"

"Julia, it's Jack."

"Jack, thank God you called. Can you come with me to see Peter? Something happened, but I'm not sure what."

Julia Cairo is waiting for me in front of her building, alone. We walk through Stuyvesant Town quietly and then up 1ˢᵗ Avenue to Bellevue Hospital. "I've tried calling, but I can't get any answers." She says breaking the silence.

It is more of the same when we arrive. Neither of us can visit him. Apparently, Peter had a violent outburst. Julia talks to the doctor like she is talking about a son my age, not a grown man. "My Peter hit someone?"

"Yes, I'm afraid he did."

"Well, why can't we see him?" I interrupt. "Maybe he needs us."

The doctor tilts his head like a dog. He is not the same doctor who let me in the last time. His face says *who are you?* "I'm his friend, Jack," I answer without being asked.

"Friend?"

"Yes," Julia says. "Jack is a friend of the family."

"Peter is very agitated," the doctor finally explains. "He is under the belief that some of the staff and patients are wicked—demonic—and that they are spying on him. Out to kill him is the way he phrased it."

Julia puts her hand to her face. "Oh, my God! My God! What is happening to my boy, Doctor?"

"It's still too early to diagnose, but he is showing signs of paranoid schizophrenia."

He is wrong, but I can't explain what has really happened: Kasper Greenstreet's ghost, the shadows, the haunting of apartment 3C. That should be Peter's diagnosis. But if I say it, they will lock us both up.

Julia and I don't speak as we walk back to her apartment. She does, however, hold my hand. She smells of ammonia which is the scent of her fear; of course, Julia smells fine to everyone else. It is just one of my abilities. I can smell some people's fear, anger, emotions. With others, I pick up their aura, their vibration. I can tap into all four of the known intuitions but, of course, not all the time.

There is clairsentience which is clear feeling—picking up the energy in the room. Claircognizant—clear knowing. Those are the moments when you know exactly how to choose. Even if rational reasoning is pointing to B, you know you must choose A. Clairaudience is clear hearing. This can be something as simple as having trouble with a decision and a song comes on the radio and the lyrics provide guidance. The last one, clairvoyance, is known as clear seeing. It can manifest as seeing pictures, images, or symbols. I have that with Peter's father, Mr. Cairo. He had a stroke and can't speak. When I first started working for him and Julia, I picked up symbols over his head. Julia was a red heart, Peter was a blue blanket, and I was a question mark.

We walk through the playground area of Stuyvesant Town. I can feel and perceive her old mental tapes running—Julia sitting on the bench while Peter plays as a little boy. I feel that she is remembering those were the happiest times of her life. The thought of that changes her smell to lemon Pledge.

"It will be all right, Julia," I finally say. "Peter's just going through a rough time."

She nods and puts her hands to her face. "Oh, my God, paranoid schizophrenia? Thank God for you," Julia says before walking into her building.

Afterward, I decide to visit Mr. David.

Mr. David greets me in a bathrobe and slippers, not ready for primetime. It is a far cry from the way he was dressed the first time I met him. He looked more like a businessman than a psychic. It was after my fall, and Aunt Paula took me to see him because of my near-death experience. Of course, we didn't tell my father. Mr. David became my mentor and introduced me to the mystics, who helped me understand my gifts. I have never seen him with one hair out of place—until today. *He is surprised to see me. Apprehensive may be more accurate. I'm here looking for guidance, but who is going to guide him?* Mr. David tells me about the mystic group's troubles. He also explains that he is unable to advise or give readings to any of his clients at this time.

"That day in the apartment has left us pretty fucked up." I've never heard Mr. David use the word "fuck," but honestly, it is a much better description than "in grave shape."

I brought Kasper Greenstreet to life for all of them. Now I feel responsible for their shift, for their lives being upended.

"He's gone," I say, like that will change everything back to the way it was.

Mr. David looks at me.

"He's gone. I made him leave," I say again, waiting for… *what?*

The mystics dabble in the paranormal, but to actually see and meet a ghost—a spirit—especially one as fierce and persistent as Kasper, is like viewing the Earth from the moon. It's not something you can just file away, nor is it what they really wanted. It's not a shape or an image on a photo. They are haunted by it, by shadows, by things that have negatively affected them. Their lives are turned upside down. *No. That's not what they wanted. Not at all.*

Mr. David sits. "How can you be sure?"

"Oh, I'm sure."

He does not ask for details, and I don't give them.

"Maybe we can all get back to normal," I say. "You know, the group?"

Mr. David looks at me. His words say "sure," but his look says something else entirely. Like with Kasper, it will never be as it was.

No one is home when I get to my apartment. Mail in hand, I hold the four envelopes that will decide the next four years of my life. *Should I wait for my dad before I open the letters?* I don't have that kind of patience. *Sorry,*

Mr. La Guardia, sorry, lion. I start with my fourth-choice high school: Power Memorial. If my fourth choice accepts me, that typically means I've done pretty well on the test. I rip open the envelope. *Yes! I'm in!* That's a good sign. Next is Immaculata, my third-choice school; though deep down, this is the school I really want to attend. *Yes! Two for two!* Now comes La Salle. This is tricky because it's my number two. If I had never met Peter, it would have been my number one. It also happens to be a lot of kids' number one choice, so I hope I didn't blow it. They, too, have accepted me.

I look down at the last envelope—Xavier. I'll be proud of myself for getting in, but *do I really want to attend that school?* It's confusing. Quite frankly, it wasn't on my radar until I met Peter. Now it's Xavier, like I am following in his footsteps.

They have put me on the waiting list. Which is both good and bad. My scores are good enough for them to consider me, but it's a passive aggressive way to attend the school that I really want to attend. I can say, "I'm on Xavier's waiting list, but I'm not going to wait."

With Kasper Greenstreet gone, I expect Peter to get better immediately and come home to apartment 3C, his job—his life. But it doesn't work out that way.

Julia, Peter's dad, and I make our trek up 1ˢᵗ Avenue like nomads. I push Mr. Cairo in his wheelchair as the blue blanket representing Peter floats above his head. Julia is bundled up like it's freezing. It's the end of March, and it's going out like a lion. *As for me? I'm happy we are able to see Peter.*

Of course, we do a lot of waiting around. Patience is needed which seems to be the current theme in my life. This time, he wants to see Julia and Mr. Cairo first, which only seems right. While they are visiting, I raid the vending machine. Sitting in the waiting area of the psyche ward, I observe visitors and doctors to see if I pick anything up. *Still playing with fire, huh, Jack?* Then all hell breaks loose. An ambulance arrives with a woman losing her shit. I know this woman. *Jesus, it's the mad hatter from the incident on the subway!* She is screaming every obscenity I know and some I am hearing for the first time. She holds a woman's wig, which she fights fiercely to hold onto.

329

"Fuck you, demon!" she screams.

Is she looking at me? Kasper called me that. Demon. Only, this woman is calling everyone a demon, so I don't take it personally.

I'm out of sorts from all the screaming and "motherfucking demons!" the mad hatter throws around. Being so close to someone drowning in their mental illness makes me feel uneasy, unsure, and a little crazy by the time I finally get to see Peter.

I lean down to hug him. "No touching," the attendant says.

Peter is different today. Calm. More like Peter. "Tell me, did you get into Xavier?" he asks.

"How did you know I got my results?"

Peter smiles. *Yes! Peter is smiling! It's been a long time since I've seen him smile.* "They come the same time every year," he says.

"And you remember that?"

"Of course. It's such a big day."

"Waiting list," I say, embarrassed.

"They put you on the wait list?" He pauses, then nods. "I'll write a letter."

"No, that's okay. You've done so much for me already."

"Jack, it's a great school. Don't you want it?"

"Yeah." Which means *I don't know… maybe not.*

"Don't worry. I'm still a brilliant lawyer," he says with a wink.

"When you coming home?"

"Maybe this week."

"Great."

"I'm going to stay with my parents," he says.

"He's gone, Peter. The apartment is rid of him."

Peter's expression changes like the sky right before a storm. "It's only temporary." He stops making eye contact with me. "I think we are going to move to the Catskills for a few months. Get out of the city for a while."

Leaning in, I speak in a conspiratorial whisper. "Did you hear me? Kasper Greenstreet is gone." His name alone commands major emotions in Peter.

330

"I will never return to that apartment," he says firmly.

Silence. *Nothing is the same. Nothing. I thought I fixed everything.* Some things can't be fixed completely, like Peter and Mr. David's mystic group.

After a few beats, Peter looks at me again. "I was hoping you would help my mother sell or donate the furniture, dishes—I don't really care. Except for a very few personal items, everything else can go. My mother knows what I want to keep."

"Of course, I'll help."

"I'll pay you."

"Peter…" Now it's my turn to look away. *This all sucks. Time for me to go.*

As we get up from the chairs, Peter's smile returns. "This will be good for me, Jack—a new start. I will write an amazing recommendation letter for you. You will be an asset anywhere you go."

I want to say *it won't be good for me. Don't go! Don't move! Don't write a letter.* But "thanks, Peter" is all I can say.

While fighting back tears, I walk with a jubilant Julia back to their apartment. On the way, we run into my friend Brick. "Julia, Mr. Cairo, would you give me a minute? I want to say hello to a friend."

"Hey, I'm Brick. I saved this guy's life," Brick says, introducing himself in his usual grandiose fashion.

Julia doesn't know what to make of him, but she is happy about Peter coming home so nothing can spoil her mood.

I walk a few feet away with Brick before quietly asking, "Listen. Where are you going to be in twenty minutes? I need to get some weed."

After depositing the Cairos in front of their building, I politely refuse the offer to go up to the apartment. Julia and I set up a time to meet and plan the estate sale.

Brick is right where I asked him to be. I buy a dime bag; he lights up a joint rolled in hash oil. Everything's better when you are comfortably numb. The buzz saves me from dealing with my feelings, breaking down, and crying in the middle of 1st Avenue. *You can slay a dragon but you can't handle people leaving? I shake my head.* For the first time in a while, I think of Katherine and my kids, the happily married man I thought I was before I woke up in the hospital to learn I was a teenage boy with head injuries. The doctors who thought I would never walk again. All the physical therapy, the pain, the rope my father ran through the apartment and made me use, clinging to it to get myself to the bathroom. The nights I pissed myself trying. All the people who told me, "We're praying for you." Willing myself to a full physical recovery. Returning to school and hearing the parents and teachers whisper that my recovery was a miracle. My father constantly reiterating "Jack, it's a miracle that you are alive and walking like nothing ever happened."

Only, it didn't feel like a miracle. My first experience with the metaphysical in the subway. All the psychic happenings, picking up people's thoughts, emotions, fears. Seeing spirits and ghosts. The woman who kept throwing herself in front of the train over and over again like she did when she committed suicide. Realizing I could help her. The incredible migraines. The physically painful reminder for my foolish behavior… messing around in a condemned boarding house. Listening to Dr. Melvin insist that Katherine and the kids were imagined, a result of the insult to my brain created by the fall. The tears, my heartache trying to accept that… *I still don't—won't. Which makes me what? As crazy as Peter?*

Now, I want to remember them.

Think, Jack. What can you remember? What do you remember about Katherine? The kids? Think! The last time you saw them…

It is morning; I'm making breakfast… Something happened. A bird got in the house. No, that wasn't the last time. The phones in my office are ringing, exploding; Katherine is calling; one of the kids is sick; a bird hits the office window. No, that happened at school. I can't clear my head, my thoughts. *Remember, Jack. Remember…*

Tears run down my face. *What a mess. I seem to lose everyone.*

It's been a few days since we saw Peter. Now Julia and I are in his apartment getting ready to sell his things. I feel uncomfortable being alone with Julia in Peter's apartment. She has no idea what happened here, what really sent him to Bellevue: a suicide, a haunting, shadows. The strangeness created by a ghost that did not want to leave wreaked havoc on the living who encountered him. He derailed Peter's hope for a new life, his excitement for his girlfriend, for being back in the city he grew up in. Peter had a break-up, then a breakdown, and then almost killed me. I didn't and will never tell Julia how Peter chased me with a butcher knife while locked in the mental chains of madness. She knows nothing about my abilities. The memories I have are transcending—life altering—so it is painful to move on. *I feel hollow. I have no one to turn to—not Katherine, the kids, Peter, or the mystics. Not even Kasper waits for me anymore.*

"What is this?" Julia calls out.

When I walk into the guest bedroom, she is standing in front of the painting. "Oh. Yes, I found that in Peter's storage, left by a previous tenant." *I should have hidden it somewhere.*

"We should contact them. It's a strange painting." Julia says, looking it over. "Wait." She reads the name. "This is a Kasper Greenstreet?"

She knows of him, of his very large moment. "Yes, it is."

Julia looks at me. "It was in Peter's storage bin?"

"Yes."

"No one missed it?" It's a rhetorical question, so I don't answer. "Do you know who Kasper Greenstreet is?" She asks like she wants to educate me.

"...Yes."

"I should think it's worth some money!"

"Yes, I would say so."

Before we can continue, the intercom rings, letting us know potential buyers are here for the estate sale. Three women walk into the apartment. An older couple arrives moments later. They are from the building. Lookie-loos. I'm sure they've heard all the stories about the insanity in this apartment.

The intercom rings again. "Jack, do you think you can go downstairs and put something in the door, so we don't have the constant buzzing?" Julia asks.

When I return, a man is in the apartment. He looks familiar; I think I've seen him before. Something about him seems out of place; no, not out of place—out of time. Like he wandered into the wrong movie. He stands in the guest room, admiring the painting. More than that, he's communing with it, smelling it, touching it. *It's beyond peculiar. It is eerie.*

"That's not for sale!" I blurt out.

He turns to face me. *Yes, I know this guy.* "You are?" he asks in a voice so familiar that it's hypnotic. My mind and blood are racing.

"Jack," I answer.

"All work and no play make Jack a dull boy."

"Who says I don't play?"

"Touché," he says, walking over to me and reaching out to shake my hand. "Philips. I'm Mr. Philips," he says, but I hear *Philip*. "I would love to add this to my collection. I'm an admirer of the painter."

The man is unnerving. There is something very alarming about him. Danger. Evil itself? His hand is icy, then hot. My gifts and abilities alarm me. This is a hunter...

The feeling that someone has walked up behind me is reinforced by the smell of Julia's nervous energy. She distracts me, which makes me unhappy; I do not want to take my eyes and concentration off Philips. I must remember everything about him in detail.

"Nice to meet you, Mr. Philips," I say, "but as I said, it's not for sale."

He looks at me like he is reading me. Trance-like. Trying to figure something out.

Mr. Philips turns and walks back to the painting. He picks it up. *This guy has some fucking balls.* He stands with his back to us. Yet, I feel like he's watching me, which he is; I see his reflection in the bedroom window. His eyes are indeed on me. For a minute, I think he's going to climb out the window with the painting, which is ridiculous, but still, I feel as if he could. *He's so fucking creepy. Draculaesque.*

Turning his head toward me in a wicked manner, Mr. Philips smiles. If he wasn't so odd, you might say he's handsome, but his weirdness dispels that thought. "I can make you an indecent offer."

It is the way he says it that makes Julia gasp, but she says nothing.

I bet you can fucker. I say again, "It's not for sale."

The climate and mood in the room change drastically. It's dark and cold. I wait for him to shake the apartment in much the same way that Kasper Greenstreet did on the night I got him to leave. Only, he turns his back to us and faces the painting, wanting to be alone with it, as if he is trying to absorb the energy in the painting for himself.

I clear my throat. "Anything else?"

Mr. Philips puts the painting back where I had it, turns, walks over to me, and hands me a business card with only his name and telephone number. No address, no title. "If you change your mind—" *and you will* "—and decide to sell, call me." I know that he is speaking, but he is also sending me thoughts, telepathic commands.

Up until this point, he has not acknowledged Julia. Finally, he glances at her. She squeezes my arm. Philips returns his gaze to me and locks eyes with great intensity and power. *Wicked.*

"I've not seen a Kasper Greenstreet for sale in… forever." *You will give it to me!*

Fuck you, asshole; it's not for sale! But wait… that voice.

"As I said, I'm a big fan of Kasper Greenstreet."

I don't really hear his last name, but I know. *Yes, that's it—he is Philip. Now he calls himself Mr. Philips?*

Are you Philip? I want to ask because the anger that man created within Kasper Greenstreet's ghost was explosive. The shadows on the wall that night showed pictures of this man. The shadows let us hear his voice and Kasper's uncle's voice. *I can't and won't forget that moment.*

"Will you excuse me?" Mr. Philip says. *Before I tear off both your heads.*

Apparently, Julia and I are blocking the doorway of the bedroom. "Oh, yes, of course." Julia says, moving quickly. She is frightened but is unsure why.

I step out of the doorway very slowly, never taking my eyes off him. Julia and I exchange looks. We stick our heads out of the bedroom very carefully, watching as he exits the apartment.

"That was spine-chilling," Julia says.

"Yup. Let's get this painting put safely in the closet."

"Thank you, Jack. You handled that beautifully."

At the end of the day, the majority of furniture, dishes, and other goods have been spoken for. Julia is concerned about leaving such a highly valuable painting in the apartment unattended especially after the way Mr. Philips behaved when he saw it. *I don't blame her.* We discuss bringing it to her apartment; however, I'm sure Peter is not going to want anything belonging to Kasper Greenstreet in his parents' apartment. Not now, not when he gets out, not ever.

But Julia doesn't know that. "We should have that conversation with Peter," I say, "since ownership of the painting hasn't been established." Julia looks at me like *what are you, a fucking lawyer?* Maybe she just doesn't like me using "we;" though, a smile appears on her face.

"Good point, but still that painting has to be worth at least $25,000. I would think; although, to be honest, I have no idea," she says.

Take that and multiply by ten, Julia. Of course, I don't say it, afraid she may faint. This painting must possess something powerful within it. I remember reading the book about the countess returning it to Kasper because of its bad energy. *I was a witness to those shadows coming off the canvas! Philips is not just an admirer of the artist. There is something in that painting he needs.*

Rather than leaving it in the closet, we decide to find a better place to hide the painting without damaging it. I pick it up and do a double take. Kasper Greenstreet is still the child, but the shadows have returned. When I pause at the window to get a better look, it seems the painting is shifting back to the original version: a child with several sinister shadows surrounding it. *This shit just won't stop.*

"What is it?" Julia asks.

Not sure what or how much to tell her, I decide to keep my mouth shut. "It's nothing."

We hide the painting between Peter's mattress and box spring, about the only thing that has not sold. It brings us close in a conspiratorial way. Julia makes the bed to make it appear as natural as possible. "I'm sure it will be safe here," she says, proud of herself.

She refuses to let me walk her home. "Such a gentleman, your dad raised you right. But I'm fine, Jack. It's not even seven o'clock."

I leave her on the corner of 2nd Avenue. Every instinct and intuition in my body tells me to go back to Peter's apartment and remove the painting, which I do.

SEYMORE HUNTER

Seymore thought he had contracted the virus, which clouded his memory. *How did he get to Scotland?* He couldn't remember. His last clear memory was of traveling with Alice and Dels to Eastern Europe from London. He let the couple, the Philips, nurse him. *Who names their son Philip when his last name is Philips? Philip Philips? How ridiculous.* Physically, he felt very strong, actually stronger than he ever had. His hearing somehow had changed, too. Whispers sounded as loud as full conversations, even at some distance. He learned to control the intensity of sounds, so they didn't drive him crazy. He hoped all of his memory would come back to him eventually.

The couple told Seymore they had found him on the side of the road one morning like a wounded animal. He was confused, they said, talking about a cave. About friends now dead due to the virus spreading in Russia and Eastern Europe, Romania included. They were happy to inform him that the virus did not spread past those regions. Whatever caused its initial rampage had slowed and was no longer considered deadly, at least not in Scotland or England.

This information relaxed Seymore and helped trigger his memory, starting with the last day in the cave when he lost Dels and Alice to the

337

virus… then finding an albino bat and eating its heart. *Why did he eat the heart? Why did he kill that beautiful creature in such a vicious manner? It was so confusing.* Slowly the memory of that trip filled in, like his other powers. He recalled dining with counts and countesses. Dabbling in the occult. Alice's reason for this trip: eating a bat's heart or liver while it was still breathing so she could remain young and powerful. Then he remembered Alice's last words: "Feed it to me. It will save me."

But they had not been looking for an albino bat; they had no knowledge of such a creature. It was folklore—an amazing find. *Did it now give him something more than extended youth?*

Whispers of Hitler, Germany, and war grew louder as Seymore's mind became as strong as his body. At night he walked, putting his newfound mystical and physical powers together. What he thought a dream due to the virus was, in fact, true. Seymore remembered his body painfully transforming into the albino bat. After struggling at first to fly, he was able to control its wings. Seymore possessed the albino bat's abilities and instincts but with a human brain. He began to experiment. If he killed or even bit another animal, he was able to take on those characteristics later. They had to be alive when he ate a piece of the heart or liver, though.

This began his education and life as a shapeshifter. Seymore spent his nights exploring the Scottish countryside, changing and learning how to use each shifting form for greater and greater use. He had to be careful approaching certain larger animals because of their physical power. When he learned that Philip Philips was a hunter, Seymore asked Philips to teach him to shoot and track an animal.

The man became a mentor in the art of tracking and killing animals for food. They started with ducks and worked their way to larger, more powerful animals, like boars and deer. There was much to learn, and Seymore became a skilled shot.

Knowing that the animals needed to be taken alive, Seymore began to venture out on his own, stray from Philips, or leave him behind completely. He practiced taking an animal down so it was injured and no longer a danger to him. At that point, he was able to eat its heart while it was still beating.

This provided him with the ability to absorb and shape their DNA, to turn the animal's strength and prowess into his own mystical power.

The problem was that he had begun to enjoy the taste of blood and became interested in bigger, more powerful prey, like wolves and bears, which Philips wouldn't hunt. Seymore tried hard to leave Philips at night in order to get to animals one wouldn't serve on a dinner table. One night, he slid out from their private camp as Philips lay sleeping. But Philips had become suspicious after Seymore disappeared the last two times they hunted. Philips thought he heard animal sounds outside the house in the middle of night but only found Seymore returning from one of his many nocturnal walks.

Hearing Seymore leave the tent, Philips waited to see if he had stepped out for a piss. When he didn't return, Philips decided to track him, taking a gun and a flashlight. Philips had seen great growth in Seymore's hunting skills, and his eagerness to learn at first was exciting. But now it was suspicious. Outside the tent, he tracked Seymore's footprints into the woods. He followed his boot tracks deep into the hillside until they came to a stop. Philips shined the light on the ground, spotting footprints a good six feet ahead. *Baffling.* It took Philips multiple starts and stops until he found Seymore's boots and clothes neatly folded and hidden in bushes. *Why on earth would he undress?* Philips took a piece of toilet paper from his pocket and wrapped it on the branch where the clothes and boots were placed. Then he began tracking Seymore's bare footprints, which started a good six feet from where the last boot print was noted. *Did he jump?* Within twenty feet, all of the prints disappeared. This astonished Philips, who began spinning in place. He looked up at the rocks for some sign of Seymore. There was nothing to track; it was as if he flew away.

The sound of a gunshot rang in the far distance. Philips kept climbing toward the top of the ridge. He could hear the sounds of wolves in distress and cautiously moved toward that direction. Within minutes, a pack of wolves moved past him. They were not hunting but appeared to be the prey, which was not possible in the area.

The silence that followed made Philips pause. His heart pounded so loudly in his chest he did not hear a wounded animal in distress or of another animal feeding. Philips stumbled upon Seymore, now bizarrely large, eating the heart of a wolf who was still alive. Philips froze in shock, fear, and disgust until it was too late. The creature stood and smashed Philips to the cold ground, breaking his neck. Seymore took his first taste of a human heart and then assumed Philips' identity as well.

The hunting accident left Philip Philips unidentifiable. By the time Seymore returned to fully human form and led authorities to his friend's body, a multitude of wild animals had fed on it.

Afterward, Seymore stayed with the widow. He began going out into the countryside at night to practice his shapeshifting. He had already killed a menagerie of animals and a human; now, he began to play with the mix. Who would dare fight with a creature that was part wolf and part bear, with the hearing of a rare albino bat and the reasoning power of a human?

All of his memories came back to him while he practiced shapeshifting: how he met Dels at a men's upscale clothing store. His affair with Alice. The scams Alice and Dels perpetrated on people, and the love they all shared for the occult. After learning as much as he could in the countryside, Seymore told the widow he was moving on, using the loss of his great friend and mentor Philip Philips as the reason. He wanted to get back to London to use his new power to make money and prepare for his trip to America.

London had not changed much since his time away. With his newfound abilities, Seymore was able to get in and out of flats and stores, stealing money and anything else he could sell on the black market. His physical appearance, fashion sense, and powers enabled him to collect people that enriched his pockets, as well as his other appetites. The louder the talk of war, the more eager Seymore was to escape to America. His abilities provided him wealth but also created a thirst for more. More violence, more trouble, more wanting to live longer. Perhaps forever.

Seymore also found he couldn't stay away from people who bargained with the Devil—sorcerers, witches, necromancers, spiritualists, mediums, and occultists. He explored all their gifts and powers while never revealing his own. He settled on the necromancer, a being that can live inside and outside of death. Necromancers also have the abilities to communicate with and utilize entities such as ghosts, shadows, and misguided spirits. This became another of his skills, his powers.

Now Seymore had the ability to steal, misappropriate antiquities, and even kill without ever being caught. However, people he swindled began suspecting him of a multitude of sins as did the authorities. Shapeshifting began to change his look slightly over time, presenting him as a man in the wrong picture, the wrong movie, the wrong place.

Seymore was searching for what happened to the painting in Alice Walker's entry, the one with the shadow. He met a sorcerer who was convinced it was an entity you could use for power and possibly a longer life. Seymore remembered Alice stating the same thing about the painting, that she used it to uncover people's secrets, fears, and inner demons. He discovered that the painting had been sent to her family in America once her body was recovered from the cave and the estate settled.

As he planned to leave for America, one item sat on Seymore's mind: Alice Walker's mysterious and possibly powerful painting. His mission was to find the painting with the nefarious shadow. At the start of the summer of 1939, before the war in Europe began, he crossed the *Queen Mary* as one of its last passengers. Three months later, the ship was retrofitted as a troop ship and renamed the *Grey Ghost*.

Seymore had big plans to explore America with all its possibilities. The painting would give him a perfect arsenal of power.

He searched for the better part of two decades but never saw Alice Walker's painting again. He did eventually find documentation—an insurance claim—provided by one of her nieces. The artwork had been destroyed in a fire in 1946.

SEYMORE HUNTER MEETS KASPER GREENSTREET

The *Duality* exhibit of a little-known artist by the name of Kasper Greenstreet was not on Seymore Hunter's radar, alias P. Philips, when a rich female patron of the arts invited him to a showing at the Guggenheim. Philips stood behind a long line of people enamored by the two paintings of the actress Desiree Diamond, who had died earlier that day. Philips could smell the blood; he knew the artist was using it in his work. *Many of the paintings had a mystical look but did any hold real power? Real magic?*

That's when his body began to pulsate. In an area with fewer people, Philips beheld the most amazing painting he had ever seen: the self-portrait of the artist as a child surrounded by three shadows. He moved everyone out of his way and moved close enough to smell it, taste it. Philips felt the energy coming from the painting and knew he had to possess it at any cost. He wanted to be legitimate so he offered every dime he had accumulated or robbed in the bidding process, only to be told he had been outbid. The painting had been sold to some countess.

He knew other ways of getting the painting. Viler, more sinister ways. Before he had a chance, the countess naively returned it to Kasper Greenstreet, overwhelmed by the mystical, dark side of the art without an ability to control its hidden wickedness. Then Philips began following Kasper Greenstreet. He needed to taste his blood, maybe eat his heart. Kasper slipped through his hands due to an interruption by a couple of drug addicts whose bodies were found weeks later. Accidental overdose. The taste of Kasper's blood would always keep him on Philips' radar.

Then Kasper Greenstreet did the unimaginable. He committed suicide. He left the painting and all its power in the hands of some teenage kid and a psychologically damaged adult. None of it mattered now. The painting was close to being his. He could feel it. Young Jack Kelly had powers, but in the end, his power would be no match for Seymore Hunter, aka Philip Philips.

JACK KELLY

School is boring. I've gone from fighting and seeking to understand shadows, demons, and ghosts to trying to figure out what X equals.

I'm no longer able to leave the classroom, even if my head is exploding. These are the terms and conditions we signed off on. No more special treatment for me. I got into more trouble for missing my appointment with Father Keenan than I did for missing two days of school for being sick.

I give Sister Elizabeth nothing to write in her journal today. I'm on my best behavior. At 1:50 p.m., I grab my books, walk to her desk, and politely ask her if I may be excused to see Father Keenan. He works in the uptown offices of the archdiocese. However, his agreement with Sister Thaddeus and my father is for him to come to the Epiphany rectory on 21ˢᵗ Street.

He does not keep me waiting. "Monsignor has been kind enough to let us use his office," he says.

I follow him to the office and take note of the place. It's my first time there. A large mahogany desk occupies the space, with two leather chairs directly in front of it and a smaller couch against the wall. There is a large bookshelf, pictures of the pope and other prominent people, a cross, and a painting of the Blessed Mother on the opposite wall.

Father Keenan sits at the desk and motions for me to sit in one of the chairs. I want to say *shouldn't I lay on the couch? But why cause trouble?*

"Would you like a glass of water?" Father Keenan asks.

"No, thank you."

"Do you know why you are here?"

"Sort of. You are concerned with some of my friends..."

He leans in. "Now why does a thirteen-year-old..."—"Fourteen," I interrupt—"...fourteen-year-old boy refer to adults in their thirties as 'friends?' Do you have friends your own age?"

"Well, because they helped me at a time when I needed people to care. And yes, I do have friends my age."

"Fair enough." He pours himself a glass of water. "Let me know if you change your mind about the water." Father Keenan locks eyes with me. "Do you know what the occult is?"

"Father, I don't practice black magic or witchcraft, if that's what you are asking me."

He nods. "Do you know what it is?"

"I do."

"Does this Mr. David, a known psychic, ever read you?"

"No."

"So, you understand what I mean by 'read you?'" Nodding my head is not the answer he wants. "What does it mean?"

I'm not going to play these bullshit games. I don't give a shit what Father Keenan and the others think about Mr. David. I'm not giving up his friendship or his advice. It may be a moot point now that they are all distancing themselves from me. My head is throbbing. I could use one of Brick's magic cigarettes now.

"Do you believe that séances, Tarot cards, and Ouija boards can open the door to another realm, to demons?" Father Keenan asks.

"No."

"Can you expand on your answer?"

"No, I don't believe that they can open the door. However, I've never been to a séance, played with Tarot cards, a Ouija board, or any of that shit."

Father Keenan does not seem offended by the word. "You like to curse,

346

don't you, Jack?"

That I will cop to. "Yes, as a matter of fact, I do."

"Does it make you feel older—like less of a boy?"

"What does that mean?"

"Do your older friends curse around you?"

"Listen, after my fall, the doctor told my dad it was not unusual for patients with head trauma to curse. It's a bad habit, I admit, but I like it. It is a vice of mine."

"Do you have any other vices?"

"Father Keenan, what exactly are you and Sister Elizabeth afraid of? Do you think I practice witchcraft? I guess in the old days you could get away with a good old-fashioned witch hunt! Drown me! Burn me at the stake!" I deliberately do not say, *fucking drown me.*

Father Keenan puts his hands up. "Calm down, Jack. No one is accusing you of being a witch. At least not me."

We sit in silence, before Father Keenan asks if I have any questions for him. There are many, but I am only willing to ask one: "As Catholics, what is our belief in ghosts?"

He puts his two index fingers to his lips. "Like every religion, we Catholics are made up of a variety of people with different experiences. We do believe in the Trinity and, initially, the Holy Spirit was referred to as the Holy Ghost. Purgatory is the cleansing of a spirit where many spirits and ghosts reside. If we look at it that way, then yes, there is at least an acknowledgement of ghosts. It gets tricky when you bring black magic into it with the belief you can bring back Napoleon or Cleopatra through a séance or a channeler who claims to communicate with such spirits. You have to be careful with the word 'medium'—'psychic.' That is not meant as a jab."

"No jab taken," I say.

"Is there something personal behind your question?"

I shake my head. "Just curious."

My visit leaves me conflicted. *Did Kasper miss the opportunity to go to purgatory for a cleansing? Can I consider what happened between the two of us a cleansing? I wish I could visit that nun again. She—or her spirit—saved me*

347

from the shadows and the demons when I fell through the floor in the boarding house. She taught me how to fight them and go back to my body so I didn't die there. She is a spiritual guide for me; only, I don't know how to get back there.

THE FADING MYSTICS

Mr. David and his group no longer meet. There is no yoga nor meditation sessions. Instead, he plans a meet-up for tea and coffee at our little bohemian coffee shop. I'm sure after the birds crashed into our school, Mrs. Dowd no longer comes here for coffee. She never makes eye contact with me at school anymore, either. It's not likely I will run into her today.

Mr. David has secured a table for us. He is the only one there when I arrive. "I'm not sure Raphael is coming," Mr. David says. "He has gone through a lot of changes."

Mr. David asked me one question on the phone before setting up this group meetup: "Is he still gone?" Then he never mentioned Kasper Greenstreet again. Nor have I.

To our surprise, Raphael is the first to arrive. He tries to put on a carefree face because that is who he typically was; only, it doesn't fit. Raphael is strained, uncomfortable. Susie comes in and orders a tea, then smells its aroma. "It is wonderful to be able to smell again," she says.

We remain silent, waiting for Star; it is an awkward silence. She is the last to arrive. Star acts the same as ever. Everyone is polite and seems very happy to see me. They talk about my next challenge: which high school I will go to.

"Graduation is getting close, Jack," Susie says. "You should be so proud of yourself."

"How is your tea, Jack?" Star asks.

"It's Earl Grey. You want a taste?"

"No, I'm good with the chamomile."

Normally, we would be in deep metaphorical and metaphysical conversation already. Or talking about our group meditation or how powerful the energy is in the circle. Everything has changed. The easy camaraderie is not here, at least not today. *The elephant in the room is sucking out all the air. That elephant is no longer a ghost. It is us.* Kasper Greenstreet is the name we dare not speak, so I never get around to telling them about the final night I had with Kasper. I can't tell them about the painting or Mr. Philips. Mr. David says he will not be doing the yoga and meditation groups, at least for a while. Raphael will be going on a retreat with his church. Star and Susie never mention Tarot, or readings. *It's just all bullshit, really.*

They don't ask about Peter and Bellevue Hospital, either. It is like we are strangers.

Walking home, I am lonely. I love that group. But as Mr. David said to me in private: "Things change. People change. Life doesn't stay the same, and if it did, you would be looking to change it. You are young. Your entire life is in front of you. There will be amazing things to come."

The emptiness I feel is wide and deep. "This too will pass," Mr. David says, his last words to me at the coffee house. I hope this passes quickly because I am uncomfortable with all these emotions.

I resent having to see Father Keenan but I do anyway. I have made commitments to my father, to myself, and to my school. I'm engaging in less lying and am trying to see all perspectives. *Guess it's not really over for Sister Elizabeth and the school since they really didn't know about Kasper Greenstreet and why I was so obsessed with apartment 3C.* Sister Elizabeth's breasts are back on my mind, but something has changed. Watching her from the corner of my eye, I am sure of it.

Father Keenan keeps me waiting. I'm always curious about what he will want to discuss. When he arrives, he ushers me into the office, asking questions. "So, you got your results from the Regents. How did you do?"

"Good."

"Which schools did you apply for?"

"La Salle Academy, Immaculata, Power Memorial, and Xavier."

"I went to La Salle. Why Immaculata?"

"Because it's co-ed."

"Why Xavier? It's one of the more difficult schools to get into. Very expensive."

"Well, Peter Cairo went there; he thought I should try."

"Hmm. Peter Cairo. Shame what's been going on in his life."

Uh oh. Did I just step in it?

When he sees the reaction on my face, Father Keenan doesn't miss a beat. "Can you define your relationship with Peter for me?" *Why is it I'm not afraid of shadows and ghosts, but his questioning terrifies me? I always feel like he wants to trap me.*

"Define?"

"Yes. You are a young man. We heard about the incident in his apartment."

"Incident?" I'm about to plead the fifth.

Father Keenan grows quiet. He looks at me and the papers on his deck, then back at me. *Remember. Patience, Jack. It's a card game.* Father Keenan continues moving papers around like he has all my information right in front of him.

"Yes, the police were called to his apartment. He was chasing you with a knife."

Here I go—time for Pinocchio. I'm about to start lying my ass off. "Knife?"

Father Keenan sits back in his chair. He picks up a paper. "Sister Elizabeth saw you being chased by Peter Cairo from your classroom window. He had a knife. She was one of the people who called the police. The police report said a knife was found at the scene. Two neighbors said they heard you yelling for help."

"No. No. No. I told the police officer that, um, I thought Peter was going to hurt himself." Father Keenan stares at me like the liar I am. He looks again at the paper in front of him, apparently the police report.

"Why were you in an adult male's apartment in the middle of the day? A dangerous adult male? Why would your father let you go there?"

"I work for the Cairos. Peter would never hurt me, not in his right mind..."

"But he's not in his right mind, is he? Isn't that the reason he's in Bellevue's psych ward?" Silence. Then, "Has Peter Cairo ever tried to touch you?"

This is ridiculous. "What?"

"Has Peter Cairo ever touched you?"

"Touched me?"

"Has he ever touched you inappropriately? Told you he loves you?" The buzzing in my head amplifies. "It's okay to tell someone if he asked anything improper of you," Father Keenan adds, thinking he is protecting me.

"Never. Never."

I am offended, but it's just a few months until I graduate, as my dad and Aunt Paula say. If I actually tell the truth, Father Keenan will think I'm nuts. It's easier for him to believe I may have been molested than buying into a ghost story. Or, in this case, a haunting in apartment 3C that caused Peter's breakdown.

"Father, do you have some Tylenol? I'm getting a massive headache."

Father Keenan stands immediately. "Yes, of course. Let me get you some."

While he is out of the room, I look at the police report, which is actually not a police report at all. That's not to say Father Keenan never saw it. He has a lot of connections in this city, and there are police officers and detectives among the parishioners.

When he comes back in the room, I take the Tylenol. It is the one thing I am not lying about. My head feels like it's about to explode.

The session ends, leaving me feeling dirty, confused.

DEMONS BY ANOTHER NAME

Peter is released from Bellevue while I'm at school. He promptly throws a shit fit when Julia talks about bringing the painting to the apartment; my instincts were correct. So much so that Julia surprises me by waiting on the corner for me after school.

"Julia?"

She motions for me to walk with her, aware that we are under the glaring eye of teachers and parents. Julia is sensitive to the stain that the "incident," as Father Keenan called it, has put on the Cairo name; only, she thinks it was a suicide attempt. Not to mention the additional stigma due to Peter's stay in Bellevue. We cross 2nd Avenue, heading east on 22nd Street. "Can you come to my apartment? Peter is home," she says.

"That's great, Julia!" I'm ecstatic about Peter's release.

"You were right; just the mention of bringing the painting to the apartment caused him to act like a lunatic." She pauses, looking to the ground, then up at me. "Sorry, that is a bad choice of words." We walk

353

silently, like spies in the Cold War looking suspiciously at anyone close enough to pick up our conversation. "What's the matter with him? How can a painting he's never seen before make him so crazy?" *Another poor choice of words.*

"Peter just wants to put all this behind him. Anything that reminds him of that apartment. Maybe it has nothing to do with the painting," I lie.

When we get to the apartment, Peter is busy getting his dad situated on the couch after helping him take a shower. "He doesn't need a shower every day, Peter," Julia says.

"He wanted one," Peter says tersely.

It reminds me of one of my father's sayings: "The house is on fire, let's not worry about the dishes in the sink." But I don't say that to Julia. Instead, I whisper, "It's good for Peter to be busy."

I try to change the subject quickly. "Peter! It's so good to see you."

When he is happy with Mr. Cairo's positioning, he turns to me. He smiles, shakes my hand. "Let's go for a walk," he says.

Julia steps forward but immediately changes her direction and heads into the kitchen. "Okay. Enjoy." Her delivery is shaky, not believable.

We descend the staircase to the street. While on the staircase, there is a moment when I wonder if he's going to attack me. *Leftover dust?* Once outside the building, he sort of becomes the Peter I once knew. Smiling at me, he says, "Jack, you have no idea how happy I am to see you outside of that place."

"I feel the same way, Peter."

"I feel like I am waking up from a nightmare." A long pause follows, then he says, "Tell me about the painting."

"You remember I asked you about getting into the storage?"

"Yes."

"Well, I found a Kasper Greenstreet original inside. It was part of the *Duality* series. A self-portrait of him as a kid."

I don't tell Peter the original portrait had me as the kid. I've told no one. That secret will stay with Kasper Greenstreet and me, and Kasper is gone, in the afterlife. I honestly don't think Peter could recover if he knew I was the subject in the painting. I believe that is the reason Kasper and I came together, why I could see him, and why we found one another. That was also why I was the one able to release him from being trapped, earthbound.

Peter looks at me, surprised. "How do you know all this?"

"Well, I knew if I was ever going to get him out of your apartment, I needed to know everything I could about him. So, I spent all day at the main library studying his work and him. All of it was fascinating." He looks at me questioningly, wanting more. "What I found out helped me banish him from your apartment."

We walk a block in silence before he speaks. "How can you be sure he's really gone?"

"Oh, I'm sure. Trust me on that. It was the way he left."

We proceed along the East River. "My mother is being ridiculous, wanting to hang the painting up."

"Peter, she has no idea about what has happened; only we do." After a beat, I ask, "What are you going to do with the painting?"

"Find the owner. The provenance of the painting."

"What does that mean?"

"Well, the reason for provenance is to find out many things. Is it a forgery?"

"Definitely not," I say.

"Well, it needs to be proven. It's important to know if it is a fake, or if it was stolen, looted. Who the original owner was… did they sell it? Is there a chain of ownership? Because if you do that and prove it's true, it makes a big difference in its market value and who it belongs to now."

"Did your mother tell you about Mr. Philips?" I ask.

"Who is that?"

"When we were having the estate sale, a man—a Mr. Philips—came in and wanted to buy it."

"No. She said nothing of that. Where was the painting?"

"I left it out in the open, in the guest bedroom. It was my fault."

We become ourselves again. Peter, the smart lawyer taking an interest in educating me, the little brother—maybe the son—he never had. "I have his card…"

"But?"

I'm hesitant. *Peter just got out of Bellevue. Do I really want to drop Mr. Philips and his scary vibe on him?*

"Peter, when I was doing research, there was a book that the librarian referred to as 'sensationalism.' It said a countess bought the painting for more than $250,000 at the original offering."

Peter is shocked. "What?"

"Yes, but she returned it to the artist and the gallery because it had 'bad energy.'"

Peter looks at me, wanting to be done with Kasper Greenstreet, Mr. Philips, and the painting.

"I don't know if I should tell you this…" I say.

"Jack, I'm good. Seriously. I need to know this shit, even if I never look at the painting or return to the apartment again."

"Well, this book… it said the woman went mad. However, Kasper Greenstreet took the painting back through his gallery representative. I found it in your apartment's storage bin, which at one time was the apartment of Susan and Mitch Michaels, who owned the gallery." Peter's wheels are turning, making me a little anxious. "I'm sure I told you about the Michaels."

"Yes, you told me about them."

"Honestly, I think it was the painting that kept him attached to the apartment, to the building. Not the Michaels." More silence.

We watch the boat traffic on the East River. "Two hundred and fifty thousand dollars… that's crazy!" Peter says.

"Yeah, well that was in 1972. Who knows what it will sell for now? Seven years later."

Peter looks at me intently. "Tell me about the man in the apartment."

"Mr. Philips? He was salivating at the chance of being able to purchase it, but there is something wrong there. He was beyond strange. Very dark. Something…" I stop myself; not sure how fragile Peter still is.

"What are you saying, Jack?"

What AM I saying? The painting seems to have a life of its own. It was the tool that made Kasper move on, the tool that drove him to suicide. I'm not going to go into details; Peter doesn't need to know about the shadows coming out of the painting and attaching to the walls. But he does need to know that there were shadows in the painting itself. This makes him go quiet for a long time.

"Sounds like we shouldn't even think about selling it," Peter says. "I mean if it has some kind of negative—I don't know—power or energy... Do you?"

"No."

"And this Philips? What do you think he wants?"

"I don't think he's an art collector."

Peter goes quiet on me, and I let him. We walk for a long time before finding ourselves back in front of his parent's apartment building. "Oh, I wrote a really great letter to Xavier. Contacted my friend on the board," he says, breaking the silence.

When we go inside, Julia is glum. Her smell is all over the place, the scent of ammonia, body odor. Mr. Cairo has all kinds of things swirling over his head, a full windstorm. I pick up on their dispositions immediately; though, it takes Peter a minute.

"What's wrong, Mom?" he finally asks.

Julia takes a deep breath. "Someone broke into your apartment."

"When?"

"Late last night. They said it looked like a wild animal was let loose, tore the place up." Julia looks at me. "It appears they were looking for something."

"The painting?" Peter asks.

Julia shakes her head. "Gone."

I stop both of them. "No. It's not gone. I have it. After I left you on Sunday, Julia, I went back and took it. I didn't trust that Philips guy."

Julia knows the Kasper Greenstreet painting should be worth some money. Peter understands there is something sinister about the painting. I think it is worth a lot, but it's the shadows that make it priceless to anyone with evil intentions.

Just as I am about to register for Immaculata, my acceptance letter from

Xavier arrives. I'm off the waiting list and on to "Thank you for choosing Xavier. You will be a member of the graduating class of 1983." It seems like a lifetime away. In my bones, I know this is a mistake. I should attend Immaculata, which is really more my speed, but how do you turn down the opportunity to go to Xavier? That's what I keep hearing from Dad, Peter, and everybody else.

Peter does his due diligence in regard to the painting. He refuses to pursue the break-in. The goal at hand is to find out what happened to the estate of Kasper Greenstreet. He wants to make sure that the book's account is true— that the countess returned the picture through legal means, making it Kasper Greenstreet's. He is also looking into the estate of Susan and Mitch Michaels, which may enable us to find the current ownership. According to court records, Kasper's estate has not been settled. The state of New York is still looking for heirs. Also, the numbers are a mess—the accounting does not reflect many assets or much money. *How does an artist who was that famous, selling art for big sticker prices, not have any money?*

Since Kasper did not have a spouse, children, or living parents when he died, it looks like the state of New York will take whatever assets he has unless they find a first cousin or a hidden will. The painting is not noted in the court records. However, the Michaels estate is different. Their wealth was divided between Susan's mother, a nephew, and two of Mitch's nieces. None of that matters to us; we are only after information concerning this painting. Original pictures of the painting will also be massively helpful; however, in all the library books, I only saw one. Peter hires a private investigator, Mr. Cohen, to help locate the relatives.

While all this is going on, Peter and his parents are planning to move out of New York and into a little town along the Hudson River where they can start over. Peter has a little money, as do his parents. I am at the end of my Epiphany career, which after eight years leaves me with mixed emotions. What started out as a miracle—me returning to school after the accident— has dwindled to *thank God we got through the eighth grade!* Several of my classmates think I'm a freak and rightly so. Looking at Sister Elizabeth, I see a running image of the chaos I created. Actually, that is not accurate;

I do not believe I created the man dying on the train, nor did I create the demons, shadows, or birds crashing into our classroom windows. However, I must take ownership of my part in it. If I had never returned to school, none of it would have happened.

Sister Elizabeth and I tolerate each other; though, tolerate is probably the wrong word. I don't have any animosity toward her per se. She is one of the first people about whom I felt a strong premonition. The three breasts and all—of course, I have never seen them myself. But still, I feel strongly that I am accurate in that impression. While watching her from my desk, I do not believe my mission was simply to know that she had three breasts. Something else was at play. However, the events of the school year sidetracked me in my understanding. *I must ask the Holy Spirit for guidance, meditate, use all of my intuition and abilities. If there is something that I was or am supposed to know or do, it will be a shame if I do not at least try.*

Meanwhile, smoking pot seems to be relaxing me to the point where the voices and premonitions have quieted down. Graduation cannot come quickly enough, but before it does, I know that saying goodbye to Peter Cairo and his mom and dad will be by far one of the hardest things I will ever do.

Before it happens, Peter and I meet with the detective. I am Peter's right-hand man, his liaison to a painting he still has not seen. At the present moment, the painting is comfortably sandwiched between the mattress and box spring in Aunt Paula's and Uncle Willy's apartment. Our detective is an interesting man, ex-NYPD. *He wants to know why I am here but is reluctant to come right out and ask.*

Finally, he does. "No offense, but what's with the kid?"

"This is Jack," Peter says. "Everything I know, Jack knows. He actually knows more about the painting and Kasper Greenstreet than I do. I trust him with my life."

Detective Cohen nods but doesn't like it. Peter begins to take us through court documents on the two estates. The Michaels estate is settled. Susan's mother received the bulk of their wealth, plus papers, personal effects, and other items. However, she has passed away, leaving her estate to a cousin.

Kasper's estate planning was messy. At the time of his death, he had just hired a new lawyer and accountant. The state of New York is looking for distant heirs, as well as assets. *Like old artwork sitting around?*

The name of a Candace Kunning comes up, but it appears to be an alias—one of numerous aliases the woman in question used. She was working at the gallery for Susan and Mitch at the time of their death. Apparently, she is a person of interest as she was the last one with access to gallery records. Peter and I will meet next with Kasper's lawyer and accountant. The fact that he includes me in all of this is blowing me away. The detective is here to find the cousin, nephews, nieces, and Candace.

Before we end the meeting, Detective Cohen has an announcement. "Full disclosure," he says. "I worked for Kasper Greenstreet very briefly before he died.

It catches us completely off guard. And I know there are no coincidences. "In what capacity?" Peter asks.

"Typically, I don't divulge my clients or their cases."

Peter, ever the lawyer, is not satisfied. "Well, I need to know if there is a conflict of interest. Besides, your client is dead."

The detective is silent. He weighs the difference between an old case with no money and a new case with money. Money wins. "He hired me to find somebody."

"A relative?" I ask. He shakes his head.

"A friend?" Peter asks.

"No."

My instincts and intuition push me. "Is his last name Philips?"

Cohen's body language and facial expression tell me I have hit his battleship. *Got him.* Peter takes out the business card with Mr. Philips' name on it and hands it to the detective. I've got a copy of the name and number at home.

"Well, yes and no," Detective Cohen says. "Interestingly Kasper only had his first name—Philip, not Philips. Which may have been one of the reasons I couldn't locate him. Although, this could just be a coincidence."

I don't think so, I want to say but stay quiet. "Can you tell us why he had you looking for him? Since we are on the same team now," Peter says.

Detective Cohen looks conflicted. On the one hand, he sits with new clients who prefer him to be tight-lipped about our situation. On the other hand, he wants our trust. His previous client, after all, is dead, and the dead don't talk—at least not anymore. After a certain amount of posturing, Cohen speaks. "My understanding is—was—that this man, Philip, attacked him."

"On the street?" Peter asks.

"You have to understand, Mr. Cairo, Kasper Greenstreet was very cagey about it all. So, he held back details, but I think it was a pick-up that went wrong. This Philip fucked him up pretty good. Really spooked him."

Yes, I did pick this up when the shadows revealed Kasper's fears. Philip made Kasper very irate, fearful, confused, and angry.

Looking at the business card, Cohen states the obvious. "Just a number. No address. How did you come by this Mr. Philips?"

Now it's my turn to be cagey, but Peter chooses full disclosure. "Jack and my mother were handling the sale of all my personal property in the apartment. This guy showed up. He told Jack he wanted to buy the painting," he says.

"Did you advertise the painting?" the detective asks.

"No. Of course not. That's why we're here—to find out the provenance of the painting."

"Maybe we should set up a meeting with this Mr. Philips," Mr. Cohen says.

"Not sure that's a good idea, until we secure provenance," I say.

The detective watches me very carefully. "How old are you?" he asks, clearly not a fan.

"Fourteen."

He looks at me, then at Peter. "Jack is as smart as they come. Plus, he has three balls." Our detective looks at us questioningly.

"Peter's just kidding about the smart part," I say. *No one has ever accused me of having three balls; I like it!*

We leave our detective to find the relatives. We will save Mr. Philips for another day.

361

TURN THE PAGE

I'm struggling with everything: the Cairos' planned move, graduation, my commitment to Xavier, and not seeing Mr. David or the mystics. Old habits die hard. Every day at the same time, I look for Kasper Greenstreet at the window of Peter's apartment. It makes no sense; that part is over. Yet, he lives on in my psyche as I search for records of the painting that brought us together. Peter has rented storage space for the painting. In the meantime, it remains in my Aunt Paula's apartment. Detective Cohen has found Mitch Michaels' two nieces and the nephew fairly easily. Susan Michaels' cousin is somewhere in Brooklyn. It's just a matter of time before he locates her, too.

Uncle Willy brings the painting back to apartment 3C. Peter will not come to the apartment nor look at the painting, which is baffling to me. *Face your fears!* Although that's easier for me to say, since I did not end up in Bellevue's psych ward. Julia and I will pack the painting while Peter makes the arrangements to have it moved with the help of the detective so our expensive piece of art makes it there in one piece. Peter has given us handwritten instructions on how to properly wrap the artwork. Julia and I work well together. She asks in a roundabout way if the Cairos have ever been the topic of conversation in the Parish. "No," I say quickly, not wanting to open that can of worms. Julia doesn't know that they monitor me. She does not know of my required visits with Father Keenan, that Sister Elizabeth does not think highly of me or her son, or that none of them are impressed with my "gifts."

I'm in the end game with apartment 3C and meeting with Father Keenan. My radar regarding Sister Elizabeth tells me there is unfinished business. Not in a bad way but still unfinished. There is something still to be worked out and discovered. A mustard yellow with outer rings of gray radiates around Sister, not from her skin, but her aura. The mystics taught me all about auras, their significance, and what colors represent a person's field of energy. Mr. David also told me to interpret the colors and to use my intuition. "Jack," he said, "you don't need a color chart. If it's telling you something, listen." Most days when I wake up and think about all this shit, I wish it were over. Before meeting with Father Keenan for the last time, I smoke a joint to calm my anxiety.

"Jack. I hear you were accepted to Xavier," Father Keenan says.

I nod. "Yes." *Not sure how he came by this information.*

"That's great news."

He quickly focuses the session on how proud he is of me for turning the ship around. No more talk of witches, spells, who I pray to, or if Peter Cairo is canoodling me. *I don't know what that means because I'm still out here in the water, with new battles to be fought.* He continues the pleasant conversation through questions: What will I do this summer? Will we be going anywhere? The Catskills, the Jersey shore?

Nope, it will be summer in the city for me.

For a fleeting moment, I think about telling Father Keenan the entire story—waking up from the fall, the brain insult, shadows, ghosts, Katherine, the nun in the boarding house once accused of witchcraft helping me get back into my body and teaching me to handle the shadows and the horsehead demons. I just want to get it off my shoulders.

Shit, you must be fucking stoned, Jack!

"Father? Dreams…" Father Keenan stops what he is doing and looks at me. He has started clearing the desk of his possessions; the space, after all, has been borrowed. Our time together is at an end. "Dreams…" I say again. "Never mind." I quickly add.

"No, continue. Dreams…" I have his complete attention.

"Do you think… Well, after my fall when I was out of it—I guess in a coma of sorts—I had a dream that my doctors…" I'm confused and not exactly sure what I want from him. "Forget it."

"Can you tell me what the dream was about?"

I am uncomfortable and squirm in the chair; I'm sorry I mentioned it.

"Do you read the Bible, Jack?"

I don't answer immediately, not sure where he is going with the question. "I mean I've read parts of the Bible," I say somewhat apologetically.

"The point is… the Bible is filled with prophets who had dreams." He leans in. "The verse that comes to mind is Daniel 1:17. 'As for these four young men, God gave them knowledge and skill in all literature and wisdom; and Daniel had understanding in all visions and dreams.' And of course, you have probably heard this one before. Matthew 2:13: 'After they had gone, an angel of the Lord appeared to Joseph in a dream and said: Arise, take the child and his mother and flee to Egypt, and stay there until I tell you, for Herod is going to look for the child to kill him.'"

We sit for a moment, and I feel as if something has been lifted from my shoulders. I see Father Keenan in a different light, a better light.

"Would you be comfortable telling me your dream?"

"It's not a big deal. Just a dream…" I have been so used to keeping secrets that even considering releasing one—no matter how helpful it might be—I find incredibly difficult. He sits for a moment waiting to see if I change my mind about telling him. Initially, I don't.

"I hope our meetings have been of some help to you, Jack," Father Keenan says, bringing our session to an end.

He hands me a business card. *I didn't know priests had business cards. Is this for his services as a priest? Or a psychologist? I guess it's kind of cool.*

"If you ever need spiritual guidance or just want to talk. High school can be very demanding," he says.

"Thank you." I put the card in my pocket.

365

I have the office door open and am ready to leave, but I decide to take a chance. To tell him.

"When I woke up from my fall, I thought I was married with a family. I could remember details about them. The doctors told me it was the injury to my brain that created it. My father said it was a dream."

"And you?"

"Yeah, I guess a dream."

Father Keenan looks at me before adding. "And Daniel could understand visions and dreams. Maybe a dream… maybe a vision of what is still to be."

It is in that moment that I know, for me, it is a new day and that I am thankful for having met Father Keenan. If not for any other reason than what he just said.

At the end of the school year, I can put everything aside to be normal for a moment. I enjoy all the graduation festivities—the dance, the ice cream social, our graduation breakfast, and classroom parties. It's fun. Most of my classmates and I have passed through school together since first grade. I love them. For her part, Sister Elizabeth does her best to neutralize our relationship and not show any hostility she may be harboring from all the crazy shit that happened. I am happy to just be normal for a while.

Three days after graduation, the Cairos leave for the Hudson Valley. All three of them attend my graduation, which really makes me emotional, because I know how awkward they must have felt. *I love Peter!* He hands me an envelope with a hundred-dollar bill in it; though, that's not the reason I love him. I love him because he never treated me like a stupid kid who didn't know anything. He wasn't afraid to say, "You're stronger than me in this area." *What would he have thought if I told him about Katherine and the kids?*

But these are all endings. Endings…

I watch through tears as the movers drive away from Stuyvesant Town, followed by the car with Peter and his parents. They wave and honk the car horn. *It is always harder for the people left behind. I need to concentrate on my new beginning in high school.*

The hot summer in the city heats up. Cohen has located Susan Michaels' cousin in Brooklyn. He asks me to take the train to Brooklyn with him, which I am happy about. I bring the only book I can find in the library with an image of Kasper's self-portrait, which is actually me. This photo is the only one published close to the time of the original sale. We meet at the subway station off 23rd Street and take the subway to 14th Street to get the L line to Brooklyn.

Along the way, Cohen wants to know how I came to know so much about Kasper Greenstreet and his art.

"We found the painting in Peter's storage," I reply. "I decided to find out everything about it and the artist that I could." *He will not get any backstory, just the facts.*

"Who discovered it?"

I could lie, which, quite frankly, I do a lot of the time. Although, I do not consider myself a liar. Only, if he already ran this by Peter, which is possible, it will prove me to be a liar. And he will not trust me. Besides, there is no reason to lie in this instance.

"Me. Peter had me hire someone to get into the storage because management never found the key to the lock."

"How did you start working for Peter?"

What does he want? I'm sick of people asking questions about Peter and me. "He needed someone to run errands for him and his parents. You know his dad was NYPD before his stroke," I say.

"Yes, I did know that…"

"Why did you leave the police force?" I ask, going on the offensive.

Detective Cohen looks at me. *Will he be honest?* "I had a problem with the bottle."

As we settle for our ride, I wonder if any of the shadows or demons will reveal themselves. *Are they gone now? Like Kasper?*

Susan Michaels' cousin, Mrs. Katie Walsh, is not what I expect. She is older, maybe in her late sixties. *It sounds stupid, because people age, but I expected a young person.* She lives in a small apartment not unlike the railroad flat my Dad and I share. It is nowhere near as nice as Peter's Gramercy Terrace apartment. *His old apartment, I should say.* The thought of that hurts. The woman makes us tea and offers a tin of cookies. Mrs. Walsh is very nice, and Cohen is very good with making her feel safe. He shows his private eye badge as well as his retired NYPD badge.

She places the tea down in front of us as she speaks.

"I thought Susan's estate was all settled."

"Oh, it is. We are here on another matter," Cohen says. "We're looking for records from the gallery she owned."

"Or photos of some of the artwork," I interject. "She represented the artists we are interested in. We just need to find out about a certain painting, the year it sold, that kind of stuff."

This woman looks at me as she puts the cookies down. "Who are you in all this?" Mrs. Walsh is not a fragile flower.

I show her my library book. "Working this summer to help pay my tuition for Xavier high school."

It's not a lie. I am still on Peter's payroll, which will pay something toward my tuition.

She keeps standing and leans against the refrigerator. "There was another man who showed up unannounced a couple of days ago, looking for similar information," she says.

"How so?" Detective Cohen asks.

"He wanted information on the gallery and Kasper Greenstreet. He asked if I have records of the people Susan sold Kasper Greenstreet's work to."

Cohen raises his eyebrows. "Did he leave you his name? A card?"

"Didn't give him a chance. He didn't call like you did; he just showed up. Something was not right with that guy."

"Can you tell us what he looked like?" I ask.

"Well, I didn't take the chain off my door. So, my view was limited. Wore a sport coat. He was nice looking, in a shady kind of way; I'll give him that."

The description she gives fits Mr. Philips.

"Do you have any paperwork from the gallery?" I ask.

"Maybe." She continues to assess us with her eyes, her own inner senses. "There are boxes down in the basement. I haven't gone through them personally."

"May we have a look?"

She leads us to the back of the hallway. A little neighbor boy, about six, comes out of his apartment down the hall and runs toward her. He is awkward, a little odd. She unlocks the basement door and flips on a light. All four of us make our way down the ancient staircase. The boy says nothing but makes a humming sound. Not surprisingly, the basement is far from neat. Boxes are piled in the corner, tarps and jars up against the far wall.

"Is that all of them?" Cohen asks hopefully.

"As far as I know. That's what was delivered from the lawyer after my cousin's estate was settled. I'll be upstairs getting my friend here some milk and cookies if you need me."

We divide the boxes. "What exactly are we looking for, Jack? I've never seen the painting."

Yeah, that's a problem. "If you come across any photos of art, give them to me. We want invoices with Kasper Greenstreet's name on them."

"Yeah, I get that," he says.

We spend hours in the basement, going through every box. We find tax records, Susan's mother's medical bills, and a lot of other items, but no photos of art or invoices for the sales of any art. Cohen finally sits on the basement steps, stretching his back. His age is catching up with him.

"We're striking out. What's left?" he asks, as I start attacking the last of the boxes.

"I think just these two."

The first box is not organized but appears to be filled with Polaroid pictures of paintings that hung at the Michaels' gallery. My heart beats faster. Some are random artists, but then I come across Polaroids of the *Duality* portrait and the *Pandora's Box* exhibit. There is the Polaroid of the Desiree Diamond painting—the one of her coming out of the TV like Botticelli's *Birth of Venus*. The next Polaroid is of a famous architect. Kasper painted him using parts from all the architect's famous buildings. I feel like I've hit pay dirt and I get lost in the Polaroid pictures that show these priceless paintings. Kasper painted two portraits—one was of their souls and was not flattering. As I continue to look, I begin to find bills of sale for the paintings themselves. The prices are ridiculous. *Makes me wonder how Kasper Greenstreet could have died broke.*

The last box contains more of Susan's mom's papers and one Manila envelope. I tear it open. Inside is the Holy Grail: the five Polaroid pictures of Kasper's self-portrait as a child and the bill of sale to the Countess Karlotta. For $255,000! There is also another legal document bequeathing the *Duality* self-portrait back to Kasper Greenstreet. It's stated value? $1.

"Oil!" I yell, jolting Cohen from a daydream and his aching back.

I bring everything over to him so he doesn't have to get up. "Peter should be here to interpret all this," he says.

"It's pretty clear," I say. "We can bring it to him."

"That's if the woman lets us leave with anything," he says, unaware of how important the find is.

"Shit, I didn't think of that."

"Don't even think about putting that under your shirt."

"Let's just ask her—beg her," I say, undeterred.

After we return to her apartment, I make an offer. "I can leave the book with you; this way you know we'll return," I say, like that is a proper deal.

Mrs. Walsh picks up the book. "It's a library book."

"Oh, damn." I'm coming off like a dumb shit but I'm just so excited.

"I like the triangle around your neck," she says.

Shit. I grab the pendant, not wanting to give it up. It's from Mr. David and carries so much meaning. But this is too important. We need these pictures and records.

As I start to remove it, she interrupts my action. "What does it mean? The triangle?"

"'The infinite power and protection of the Trinity,' according to the friend who gave it to me."

She stops me. "You keep it. You're young; you may need it."

We all get quiet. She picks up a pad by the telephone and writes down the inventory of the things we want. After a beat, she adds that we have two weeks to return the items or pay her $1,000. Both of us sign her handwritten promissory note, *which means… what? I definitely don't have $1,000, and I'm not sure the detective does, either.*

Behind the woman, the peculiar little boy sits there and stares, not saying a word. *Very odd little kid.*

Cohen grows tired on the train ride home. I'm amped and can't wait to call Peter. We have succeeded in our mission.

"Jack, I want to see the real painting," Cohen says through closed eyes.

"Thought you were napping?"

"Nope. Just resting." After a couple of beats, he adds, "It's probably time to give Mr. Philips a call. Find out exactly what he is up to. Obviously, he wants the same thing we do."

"Don't you think we should run this by Peter?"

"Can't do my job if I have to stop and ask permission every time. I need to make a move."

His point is well-taken, but I know I'll be calling Peter.

As soon as I get home, I telephone Peter and get a busy signal. The other day my dad blasted me for talking to the Cairos so much on the phone. "It's long distance, Jack. It's not cheap." When Peter sends me a check, I offer to pay Dad for the calls; he doesn't accept.

I keep calling until I finally speak to him. Peter has already spoken to our detective. *Guess he did need permission.*

"He's holding the Polaroids and the paperwork," I volunteer.

"Yes, he said he's going to make copies of the bill of sale. He said the other paper is a gift receipt or something to that effect."

"Essentially it gave ownership of the painting back to Kasper," I say.

"Yes, I want to look at it."

"Peter, our detective wants to see the real painting."

"Did he say why?"

"Not really. He also wants to meet with Mr. Philips."

"Yes, he told me."

Silence. "Can you come back to the city?" I ask. A long pause follows. "When we meet Mr. Philips?" I don't want to spook Peter because I do want to meet with Mr. Philips. I also know Mr. Philips is the one who tore up the apartment. "I'm not sure meeting with him is a good idea, but I think we must." I add. "He apparently went out to Brooklyn to see about the painting. And then, of course, there is the break-in at your old apartment."

"Yes, Jack you going back for the painting was brilliant." Peter pauses for a moment. "Jack, when you show Cohen the painting, get the paperwork and the Polaroids from him. You already have a key to my personal P.O. Box; put them in there for now."

Cohen is waiting for me out front at the Chelsea area storage building on W. 23rd Street, where we are keeping the painting. *Should I be suspicious?* He has all the documentation and wants to meet with Mr. Philips, who's hot to buy the painting. Only Peter knows I'm meeting Cohen. *I could end up in the crate, while Cohen ends up with a painting worth a ton of money.* I touch the screwdriver in my pocket for a sense of security despite how false that security might be.

Cohen lets me open the crate while he watches. Together, we carefully take out the painting and unwrap it. Cohen takes a moment to view it, then steps back.

"It's disturbing," he says.

I guess it is, but at the same time, the color is so vibrant, otherworldly. You can't look away.

Cohen hands me the Polaroid pictures. I'm not an art expert but I know, even before I compare the photos, that they will match. The painting itself, though, has undergone a metamorphosis. It has changed drastically from the painting Uncle Willy and I removed from the basement storage that night. The first time I saw the painting, all you could see was a glimpse of the child. A hand, a lock of hair, the marbles. Shadows were engulfing him, smothering him, which I believe is what they did to Kasper during his life.

When I confronted Kasper in the apartment with the painting, the shadows slithered from the canvas like snakes out of a tree. They poured onto the floor, slid up the walls, and eventually shot straight from the painting onto the walls and ceiling. They revealed all of Kasper's fears, his shame, and his humiliation. It gave me the power to set his spirit free. In the end, when Kasper was gone, it became a beautiful painting of him as a child. Hopeful, in fact. In a supernatural way.

After I met Mr. Philips for the first time on the day of the sale at Peter's old apartment, the painting changed again. The outlines of the shadows began to reform. As I look at it now, it has reverted to the original painting, confirmed by the Polaroid pictures in my hands. Physically, the child looks like I did at that age. The psyche, however, is Kasper's. The three shadows sit just as he painted them. This is the reason Philips wants it. The painting is haunted, magical.

A sadness comes over me that I cannot quite define. *What was his intent? Was Kasper driven solely by inspiration or was his hope to exorcise the shadows, demons, and fears from his life by exposing them in his art? Did they take on a life of their own once he painted them? No longer servants of the artist? Did they become masters of his spirit and mind?*

I'm not afraid as I look at the Polaroid pictures. I've experienced this painting at its worst—and its best.

However, Cohen appears to be deeply troubled as he examines the painting carefully. "This sold for $255,000? That's crazy money," he utters, moving back and forth in the storage area, sweat forming on his brow. I pick up that Cohen is conflicted but I'm not sure exactly why. *The image in the painting? The money? His own intentions?*

As we leave, I continue holding the Manila envelope with the photos, original invoice, and documentation returning the ownership of the painting back to Kasper Greenstreet. The countess no longer wants anything to do with it. This is the paper Peter wants; it establishes the chain of ownership.

"Jack."

Detective Cohen motions for me to give him the envelope. I step away from him, prepared to run if need be.

"Peter wants me to place this in his P.O. Box," I say.

"You have the key?" he asks skeptically.

I nod.

"He never mentioned that to me."

"Well, you can call him; those are his instructions."

"Until I hear it from him, Jack, give me back the envelope," Cohen demands.

Everything in me switches to high alert. The blood moves in my veins. I step farther away.

He grows irritated. "Jack." I sense the thought of chasing me enters his head. He knows, however, that running after a fit 14-year-old boy is a losing proposition.

"Call him; call Peter." I continue to back away from him. When he stares me down, I turn and run. *Something is not right.*

Neither of us is aware that we are being watched. Someone has followed us, someone who wants the painting for more than its monetary value.

The P.O. Box that Peter rents is not far from my apartment. I walk there to place the envelope and its contents inside. I've been here before. Peter uses it for items he didn't want sent to the apartment or, now, to the Hudson Valley address. I never ask why.

Alone with Peter's P.O. Box, I am tempted to look at the other items inside. Some I can't help but see without officially prying—his wedding ring and an enclosed envelope with nothing written on it. I feel its contents; it could be money. Carefully, I place the Polaroids in the box. I move things around so they don't bend. Then I notice an open Manila envelope. It's not right, but I look anyway; it is the draft of a handwritten will. Everything is left to his parents—his life insurance policy, investments, and other assets. *As it should be.*

However, he has recently added the Kasper Greenstreet original painting to the will and left it to me.

Summer moves along quickly. Brick and I have rekindled our friendship. My dad is not happy and is very verbal about it. "It's not that I blame him for the fall…" *But of course, he does!* I understand Dad's feelings. He had to place all that fear and anger somewhere while sitting next to my hospital bed, watching me fight for my life. "But when you two are together…" he continues, "that's usually when the trouble starts."

Brick and I are staying out of trouble, but we are smoking a lot of pot. All we do is laugh. There are times when I wish I could tell Brick what the fall created in me—being able to see and hear things that very few people can see or hear, like shadows, spirits, people's fears, thoughts, smells.

My most pressing fear is going to Xavier and dealing with a curriculum that might be over my head in an environment of high-level competition. It is definitely bringing up anxiety in me. Smoking pot seems to comfort me and calm my nerves; only, it also dulls my abilities and intuition. I look over at Brick. *What are his fears?*

Peter wants me to mail the original bill of sale and gifting of the painting to him for his court filing. He has filed under the Abandoned Property Law, referring to property to which the owner has relinquished all rights. "When property is abandoned, the owner gives up the reasonable expectation of privacy concerning it. The person finding the abandoned property is entitled to keep it." That is Peter's legal approach.

"Make copies before you mail them to me. Wait, why don't you come up for a couple of days? Mom and Pop really miss you. You can get out of the city..."

I love the idea. My dad makes several telephone calls with Peter and Julia before the arrangements are finalized. Peter insists on paying for everything.

Grand Central Station is one of the crowns of New York architecture in a city with plenty of architectural marvels to choose from. It was built in the Beaux-Art style in 1913 and has forty-four platforms and sixty-seven tracks. One can happily get lost inside, spending the day admiring all it has to offer. The Vanderbilt food court can accommodate breakfast, lunch, dinner, and cocktails while passengers wait, or just hang out.

The main concourse features an amazing barrel-vaulted ceiling containing a mural of constellations. Apparently, there are astronomical inaccuracies; some stars and constellations appear correctly on the ceiling while others are reversed. Ten globe-shaped chandeliers hang from the constellation-filled ceiling, weighing eight hundred pounds each and holding approximately one hundred and ten light bulbs. Once during a school trip, they were lowered for cleaning. The four-faced brass clock has made its appearance in many movies and television shows. *All amazing!*

While carrying my small suitcase with the Polaroids and documents tucked between my underwear and socks, I feel the presence of someone or something following me. I step into one of the stores and buy a chocolate bar and pretzels for my ride up the Hudson. I look around to see if and what I'm picking up. I can't seem to shake a sense of danger, but no one reveals themselves. *Nothing.* I find my way to Platform 23 and board my train for what becomes a beautiful ride along the Hudson. *I can't wait to see everyone.*

When I arrive at the train station, Peter is waiting for me. We drive to their new house—a small cottage outside of a small town. Julia greets me like I am her grandchild. Long gone is the question mark that used to appear over Mr. Cairo when he sees me. Now, I am greeted with an old fashion Jack in the Box windup toy over his head. Instead of a clown, though, a bear comes out of the box. *Glad it's not a clown; only, I do miss the question mark.*

Peter is so relaxed I barely recognize him. He is a million miles away from the last days of New York—from that Peter. Julia makes dinner while Peter and I ride around on bikes. It is a beautiful, old town with a main street all of two blocks long. I remember Brick telling me once that, when he moved out of New York City, he was bored shitless. But this is nice. Peter and I park the bikes and stroll along Main Street. We grab ice cream, promising neither of us will tell Julia. In the morning, Peter and Julia make breakfast and brew coffee and tea.

After breakfast, Peter wants to see the documents. I unwisely pour everything out of the envelope onto the table—a rather foolish mistake. Julia picks up the Polaroids, looks through them, and hands them to Peter.

He immediately drops the pictures like they have burned his hands. "I don't want that!"

It's hard to get the toothpaste back in the tube once it's been squeezed. What has been seen cannot be unseen. Peter goes into a tailspin. "Why did you give me that?" Peter yells at Julia. "Why are you touching this stuff?" *Is a touch of hysteria returning to his psyche?*

He turns to me. "Why did you bring those pictures here?"

I apologize. It is all I can do. On the one hand, Julia thinks he's being ridiculous and says so; only, she doesn't understand what those shadows did to him, the mess they made of him.

Quickly, I pack the Polaroids into the envelope and hide them in my suitcase. I leave the documents I know he wants and needs on the dining room table. However, Peter has gone sideways. Our once promising weekend is over. He stays locked up in his room all day Saturday. Julia spends the rest of Saturday emptying boxes from their move. They are living in a rural area, which encourages me toward the decision to push Mr. Cairo around the neighborhood in his wheelchair to stay out of both of their ways. There are no sidewalks, but the streets are asphalt.

We begin with a nice leisurely walk. We come along a wooded area with a creek on the opposite side of the road. Very peaceful. Up ahead, there is movement from the woods. *A wolf? Coyote?*

What looks like a large dog trots onto the street. A bunch of question marks appear over Mr. Cairo's head. *They do not represent me.* The animal begins to walk slowly toward us. *It is definitely a wolf.* I stop immediately once it begins to growl. I've heard wolves howl in movies but never like this. It's intimidating.

I hear Mr. Cairo's thoughts. *Back away slowly but don't turn around, Jack. Maintain eye contact.*

There is no image over his head. Just a clear thought. I follow his instructions. The wolf continues to growl and snarl but does not come after us. We back all the way up the street until the wolf fades from sight.

We have a light dinner and then play cards at the table in the backyard. We play Crazy Eights, Blackjack, and Rummy. Mr. Cairo goes to bed early and watches television. Julia and Peter are better, not as agitated, but not as they were when I first arrived.

It is a nice night after a day of tension. Peter is apologetic; the scars left over from Kasper Greenstreet run deep. I make no mention of the wolf encounter, even as several cats appear in the yard, meandering for mice, I guess. Neither Peter nor Julia make mention of them. I assume feral cats and wolves are part of the area's natural habitat.

"Rummy," Peter says, showing us his winning hand.

Julia asks if we want to play a board game. Monopoly? The Game of Life? Peter raises his eyebrows when he suddenly realizes the yard has ten to fifteen cats roaming around. "Mom? Where did all these cats come from?"

Now it's Julia's turn to be surprised. "Let's go in," she says.

"This is not normal?" I ask. I'm sorry I did. Peter looks at me with suspicion.

There are no more games. We all retire for the night. A lone cat sits outside my window, hissing most of the night. I am the last one to fall asleep and the last one to wake. The Cairos are all up having breakfast when I get up. They will be going to church. I ask them to drop me off at the train station; I'm ready to get back to the city.

Brick and I spend our days going to Rye Beach and Coney Island, having a blast. We have begun dating the Taper sisters. Brick is dating the older sister, Annette, while I am dating Ann. They match our ages, fifteen and seventeen. My birthday was July 3rd, but I always wished I had been born on the 4th. The line of the song "Yankee Doodle Dandy" runs through my head: "A real live nephew of my Uncle Sam/Born on the 4th of July."

Brick and I are always riding the subways. Nothing comes out to mess with me anymore. However, the voices are back, some very strong. When I say voices, I mean the thoughts of people or maybe even the voices of their deceased loved ones. *Are they trying to relay a message?* Sometimes, they're too loud, especially when Brick and I are having fun. The marijuana lowers the volume, which is good and bad, because I find myself reaching for a joint at all times of the day. But the good thing is it also helps me with my migraines.

One night, the girls, Brick, and I head out to Coney Island. On the beach, we smoke a joint rolled in hash oil before going on the boardwalk. Our first ride is the Wonderworld, where we have plenty of time for kissing. Next is Spook-a-Rama. Brick sits in his car with Annette. Ann and I share another car. It is a typical boardwalk spook ride, filled with flashing lights and mechanical bogeymen. Ann and I do a lot of kissing. When we kiss, it is always French kissing. She gave me a hickey once, which sent my father into waves of laughter.

"Who gave you the love bite, Jack? When do I get to meet her?"

At some point in the ride, the music and sounds in the haunted house slow down so much it becomes distorted. The ride itself seems to be moving in slow motion. *The weed?* I stop with the kissing and let go of her.

378

A figure seems loose in the darkness. It seems like an illusion, part of the ride, until he sticks his head into our car and calls out my name. The darkness and strobe light alter my facial recognition. It's a man, but I cannot make out his face. I scream, which makes Ann scream. The man is gone as fast as he came, but he leaves with words that sound like "I want it!"

The face I don't know. The voice I do. Mr. Philips.

From time to time, I find myself really missing Peter and Mr. David. They were both my mentors in very different ways. I would not have survived eighth grade without them. Sister Elizabeth comes to my mind more than I would like. I've even had a dream about her. She is walking down 2nd Avenue, her nun's habit blowing gently behind her. I'm running, trying to catch up to her, wanting—no, needing—to tell her something. Some force or wind is holding me back. Nothing comes out of my mouth when I yell to her. I don't know what it means or if it even means anything.

I'm hoping for a call from Peter or Cohen. I'm not sure what we are doing now with the painting or what they want to do. *Is Philips someone we need to speak with? Do we want to get information? And why is he after the same information on the painting? I'm intrigued by him but, at the same time, very leery.*

Peter calls me. We set up a meeting with Mr. Philips for the last week of summer.

Reluctantly, Peter makes the trek back to the city. His parents still keep the apartment in Stuyvesant Town, just in case living away from the city doesn't work out. Plus, there is rent control, and they've been in the apartment for thirty years. How do you give that up? The plan is for Detective Cohen and I to meet Peter at the apartment to go over a few items.

Arriving at the apartment before Cohen, I find Peter very tense, like he was when he saw the Polaroids of the painting during my weekend visit. He doesn't miss the city or any of this drama with Kasper Greenstreet.

"I'm not sure why we are meeting this guy. I have no plans to sell the painting," Peter says the minute I walk in.

I'm a little disappointed because this cloak-and-dagger shit is kind of exciting to me. "Peter, it's your call," I reply.

"Yes, I know, but this detective—Cohen—keeps pressuring me. I should have let all this play out in the legal system." That's where Peter is most comfortable, behind a desk, preparing briefs.

"What do you want to do?" I ask.

"What can I do? Everything is in motion!" He's snappy.

"Peter, we don't have to show up."

"Cohen wants me to meet him alone. He doesn't think you should be there."

"Because?"

"Because you are a kid."

"He didn't mind having me with him when we went out to Brooklyn to meet with Susan Michaels' cousin to look through the paperwork. Which, by the way, I found before bringing him to the storage and showing him the painting. He was okay with all of that."

"Cohen was pissed about you running off with the pictures and documents."

"Did you tell him you needed them?"

"Yes. He still felt you were disrespectful."

"Well, I'm the only one who has met Mr. Philips and knows what he looks like." I say, shrugging my shoulders. "I have to be there."

"You and I know that. Cohen's plan is to wait outside and follow Mr. Philips after we meet with him."

"Wait a minute—Cohen's not going to be in the meeting?" *Suspicious.*

"No. He keeps asking me why I don't want to sell? Get all that money? Of course, he doesn't know what we know about the painting."

"So, he will have no active involvement with this meeting," I say, digesting this new development. "And he wanted you to go alone?"

Peter nods. "Don't let the detective trouble you, Jack. You and I know what you can do; that's all that matters."

With that, he reaffirms that we really are the partners in this, not Cohen, who I do not trust. "Peter, I put the Polaroid pictures back in the P.O. Box. Do you want the keys?"

"No, I want you to hold on to them for me."

The three of us do not travel together to the West Side docks, where the meeting takes place. Peter and I are to meet Mr. Philips at some shithole diner. Cohen is going to be right outside if we need him. Mr. Philips chose the place, which does not equate with his demeanor or physical presence. Our detective will float around, waiting for his chance to follow Mr. Philips when we are done. He has not been able to locate an address on Mr. Philips or his business. Nothing. *This is his chance, but for what?*

Peter wants to take a cab; I suggest walking, hoping the walk will loosen him up. We're running late, so it's a taxi ride.

The diner is set back off the West Side Highway. It looks as out of place as Mr. Philips did that first day I met him in the apartment. As soon as we open the door to the diner, I am hit with a wave, a current, a vibration, a pulsating energy—one of the strangest energies I have ever experienced. It goes through my body, blood, and DNA and leaves me on high alert. Peter does not feel any of this because his own energy is all over the fucking place. *How can he pick up on anything else? I wish he would calm the fuck down and not be so overwhelmed. He is a liability.*

Peter looks around, befuddled. I'm afraid he might break, spill out right here on the floor.

Big red booths are affixed to the walls of the diner, with individual tables in the middle of the room. A long lunch counter sits empty. There are just a few people in the place.

Peter is not sure who we are looking for, so I take control. "This way," I say, heading toward Mr. Philips, who sits at a table.

Mr. Philips is the center of the vortex, the source of the vibration. The pulsating energy is coming from him. He stares straight ahead but not directly at us, trance-like, though aware we are walking toward him. He does not get up from the table to greet us. *There is something completely in-between about this guy. Clearly, he is earthbound, but Vampiresque? If that is even such a fucking thing. Necromancer? Witch? Fucked-up human being?* I can't help cursing inside; for some reason, it is relaxing to me. Keeps me focused. "Don't worry about him cursing, Mr. Kelly. That's not unusual after a head injury!" The doctors had said. Everything comes back to my fall, even my foul language.

"Jack, who also plays," are the first words out of his mouth.

"Mr. Philips."

We lock eyes. It could be viewed as a childish staring contest; only, it is much more than that.

With the risk of sounding like a complete douchebag, I have lived multiple lives since my fall. Battled demons, shadows, and a real live fucking ghost. Yes, I have learned a little about who I am and the people around me.

This man is a danger.

Peter distracts me. It is abundantly clear that the vibration pulsing from this dude has thrown Peter off his newfound peace. His orbit is spinning off course. Mr. Philips and I wait for Peter to speak, but he doesn't. I place my hand on Peter's arm to encourage him, to settle him down.

Mr. Philips sees an opening. He immediately takes advantage. "I was pleasantly surprised to hear from you," he says directly to Peter. "Since Jack here told me the painting was not for sale, I thought the kid was in charge."

Ouch! Peter is mute. Looking over at him, I want to tell him to snap out of it. "Peter," I say softly.

Finally, he finds his voice. "We are exploring our options," he says. "It seems you've been making inquiries with people who cannot actually help you. If you would like to make an offer, or an inquiry, I'm a lawyer. And as you are well aware, I am in possession of the painting, it…" He stumbles over the words. "…will be mine."

Mr. Philips' skin is translucent; the veins in his face, head, and hands are clearly visible. And twitching. I can almost see the blood flow from the outside of his body. *Maybe he is a vampire.* His demeanor changes; I sense a man who can easily commit violence, even murder. Peter is not reading any of this as he continues talking, rambling.

Finally, Peter says, "You seem to have great interest in the painting. May I ask why?"

Mr. Philips looks at Peter like he would like to tear his windpipe out. For a moment, I think he's going to, which makes me feel like a fucking kid. I'm hit with a wave of fear—*how badly am I outmatched?* I slowly handle the fork in front of me, inspecting its tines, because *if this motherfucker makes a move toward Peter, I am prepared to stick it in his eye.*

None of our thoughts escape Mr. Philips. He looks at me just as I've finished that thought. He thinks in moving images, somewhat like Mr. Cairo but on steroids. His gaze switches from Peter to me like he is prepared for hand-to-hand combat. However, it is very clear that this battle is taking place on a spiritual level, not an actual fistfight. Some kind of sorcery here. I become keenly aware that Mr. Philips is a psychic, a magician, an energy vampire. He can steal your thoughts, emotions, and power. He's not a shadow, but... *what?* Certainly an entity like none I've previously experienced or battled.

I must tap into all of it—the shadows, demons, what I learned from Kasper Greenstreet, and what the nun taught me. I must unravel his secret, the source of his power. Most importantly, while in his presence, I must house my thoughts in the injured part of my brain, where they tell me I created Katherine, my kids. My thoughts are untouchable there. I don't want him to see what I'm thinking or feeling at the diner table. I must place them in that untouchable place.

My fear is not for my safety. My fear is that he will destroy someone I love before I've figured out how to fight him. Mr. Philips, like Kasper Greenstreet, knows that Peter is no match. *But me? Kasper thought I was a demon. What does Mr. Philips think? He must know I am the one he must contend with.* I am torn between wanting to protect Peter and getting down and dirty with Mr. Philips. I must be smart and patient. It took me too much time to figure out Kasper. It cost me Mr. David's friendship and resulted in Peter moving away, alienating myself from half my classmates and Sister Elizabeth and led to fighting with my father. I became somewhat of a pariah at Epiphany, the school I love so much. *This time, I must be better prepared. Ready for battle with ghosts, demons, witches, shadowy creatures. And this motherfucker!*

Mr. Philips is sucking the energy from Peter, who has begun to hunch, as if disappearing from his own power. "You may ask me anything you want," Philips finally says. "But I have a question for you. What do you think of the painting, Peter?"

He knows full well Peter has not viewed the painting. *I know that he knows but I'm not sure how exactly.*

Peter's reaction validates his hunch. He freezes. "I… um…"

Mr. Philips stares, his eyes mirroring a weak period in Peter's life: being hauled off to Bellevue. He's not reading Peter's mind, but rather, his biography. Peter doesn't see the mirroring but feels it.

Not good. "Did you see the painting for the first time in the apartment?" I interrupt, trying to deflect whatever spell he is putting on Peter. "Your reaction was intense." Mr. Philips continues staring at Peter. "Did you know Kasper Greenstreet personally?" I ask, trying to disturb the connection. *It's not working.* I touch Peter firmly to arouse him from this spell.

Now Philips looks at me, menace in his eyes and obliteration on his mind. I'm afraid but ready.

Suddenly, napkins, menus, and newspapers begin to blow wildly around the diner. Several chairs blow over from the maelstrom Philips is creating. This does not emerge from confusion or frustration, which is what I've seen over Mr. Cairo's head, nor is it the pure anger of Kasper Greenstreet. This is a combination of rage and power. A dose of *look at what I can do!* Philips' eyes change to the lightest color blue I have ever seen. Mirrors. Only, the image reflecting back at me is that of a powerful warrior. Not some fifteen-year-old boy.

He quickly turns the mirror off. *Is it so I don't see how powerful I am? Or is he toying with me, giving me a false sense of self?*

The black magician's tricks have Peter backing away in his seat. His image in Mr. Philips eyes is that of a mouse, and Peter feels it! The cats scampering around the property on the Hudson reflect in Philips' eyes.

"Afraid of a little wind, Peter? What are you, a mouse?" Mr. Philips asks. *What is this guy? How do I bring this fucker down?*

The witchcraft does not faze other diners. Mr. Philips chose this place for a reason. It hits me that we are in a den of witches, warlocks, and sorcerers and not the good kind.

Philips looks at me with a sly, seductive smile filled with evil intent. Slowly I pull the triangle out from under my shirt saying the words loud enough for him to hear. "The infinite power, protection of the Trinity." *I want Mr. Philips to see and feel the triangle, but I'm not sure why.*

All the chaos and wind stop. He holds his sly smile with great difficulty while looking from me to Peter and back to me.

A long silence follows before he says, "I've seen that thing around your neck before." He is visibly irritated.

"You couldn't have; it's one of a kind," I say dismissively, letting him see that I am lying. Intentionally.

The stare of a hungry lion ready to eat replaces his sly grin. "No, no I've seen it before, somewhere in Turkey. Istanbul?"

Exactly where Mr. David found it. Time to change the subject. "Are you hungry Mr. Philips? Would you recommend the pie at this place?" I ask, knowing full well Peter and I will eat nothing; I say it to inform Philips I can read thoughts as well, pick up on his lion's appetite.

The door to the diner opens and slams several times, startling Peter. He seems to be shrinking in his seat. He's finished. I try and keep myself unfazed by Mr. Philips' parlor tricks.

"Are you planning to make us an offer?" I ask, completely in charge of this side of the table.

It would be great fun to tell him that Kasper threw way more than this little charade at me. But more wind and fireworks follow. Doors open and slam, and chairs are blown around. A fork comes flying toward Peter, which I catch and weaponize.

Mr. Philips is prepared for violence.

Now I understand why Kasper thought I was a demon because typical humans do not pick up on another's energy, do not see their damaged souls. Once you do, it alters the power structure. Kasper didn't understand initially that I was from the light; he was actually looking for the light. Mr. Philips' plan is to extinguish the light!

He looks at me, flashing the image of my girlfriend and I in the haunted house at Coney Island. Then he stands, directing his rant at Peter. "The way I make my inquiries about the possible purchase of art is my affair. Don't ever question me!"

"Okay," Peter says, meekly as a frightened lamb ready for slaughter. He is completely overwhelmed. I'm afraid, too, but I fight not to show it, to reveal anything Philips can use against me.

"You want to sell the painting," Mr. Philips says, like he is ordering it. Or issuing a warning. "Talk. Only, stop being a pussy and leave the boy at home next time."

I don't know exactly what you want, Mr. Philips, with that painting, but I can guess. To unleash those shadows to give you even more black magic.

"I want that painting. And you will want to give it to me eventually!"

Fuck you! Can you read that, Mr. Philips? We will never sell you that painting.

I show him an image of me burning the painting, which alarms him. He looks at me for what I've become to him: enemy number one.

Finally, Mr. Philips leaves through the kitchen. We stay seated till he's gone. An echo moves through the diner. The rest of the patrons—witches, warlocks, magicians—are now keenly aware of the battle looming between us. There is excitement in their vibration.

"What the fuck was that?" Peter says.

Putting my finger to my lips, I motion for him to be quiet. We get up and leave.

On the way back to Stuyvesant Town, we debrief. Peter is a basket case and has decided to take the train back up the Hudson to the safety of his new home. He wants to get out of the city as soon as he can. He wants nothing to do with this voodoo. "Should we just burn that painting, Jack?" he asks.

"We should have done it before you filed all the paperwork," I say. "What if we burn it and it unleashes whatever evil is in the painting?"

Peter is teetering. I hope he is not Bellevue bound. "Yes, yes—you're right. That guy was so eerie. He's not dead, right?" Peter asks. "Because... wow! What's happening?"

"No." I speak confidently, but it's a lie. It's obvious Mr. Philips is into voodoo, black magic, and maybe even has a pact with the devil to keep himself earthbound. *But what is he, exactly? I'm not sure.* He was completely aware of the hoard of cats at Peter's house. He also knew Peter had never

THE BOOK OF DEMONS

seen the painting.

I fix my eyes on Peter. "We need to stay away from him. Make sure he never gets that painting; he only has evil intentions. Playing with some kind of voodoo."

We walk quietly; Peter is shivering, but it is summertime and hot. "Did you see Cohen when we came out of the diner?" he asks.

"No. I thought he was going to follow Mr. Philips."

"Well, I'm going to pay him for his service. Tell him his work with us is done. I need to be finished with all of this, Jack, or it will destroy me."

Back at the apartment, an unsteady Peter pulls his overnight bag together in a hurry.

"I'd like to move the painting to a different storage," I say.

Peter looks at me. "Why?"

"Just a really strong feeling like I had the time I removed it from your old apartment." I don't trust Mr. Philips—or Detective Cohen. "Do you want me to take the train back home with you?"

"No, Jack, I'll be fine. Just have to get out of the city. Triggers too many things for me."

I insist on walking Peter to Grand Central Station to make sure he gets on the train safely. He hugs me tightly before boarding the train. "Jack, it is I who should be protecting you."

I decide to wait until he is safely on the train, looking around to make sure neither Mr. Philips nor Cohen followed us. As Peter gets on the train, I survey the tunnel for horsehead demons and shadows. Nothing. They're from a previous dream; one that has dissipated.

Peter takes a seat and waves as the train slowly pulls out. Through the train car window, I see Mr. Philips on the other side of the platform, standing and watching. Then he's gone. I catch a glimpse of a passenger on the last car—*could it be Mr. Philips?* Across from the track on the platform, another man glides toward the stairs. *Him again?*

My mind is playing tricks on me.

PETER CAIRO

Peter got onto the train feeling shame and fear; all his serenity shattered by this trip to the city. *I'm weak. I can't handle or understand any of these things. Ghosts? Black magic? What I experienced at the Gramercy Terrace sent me to the psych ward.* Peter sees Jack from the window of his train, standing there protectively, like some warrior from a long-lost tribe of angels. This confuses Peter more. Had Peter not lived it clearly, he would think it insane. His stint in Bellevue confirmed the insanity of it all. However, the fact that there are other witnesses— Jack for one—makes his story true. As for Jack's mystic friends? Peter has not met them.

Jack seems to bear no trauma from the incident when Peter chased him around the apartment with a butcher knife. He holds no animosity, no grudge. Incident—the word itself is bullshit, and Peter knows it. *It was a psychotic break. How could he do that to Jack?* Peter loves him like a brother, a son even...

What Peter remembers from that day is he was sitting on the couch when Jack let himself into the apartment. The two spoke, but the words are lost to Peter now. There were things on the walls—shadows, if his memory is correct. They had been there for days. Peter's endless nights of insomnia were followed by days filled with paranoia and delusions. It became a split screen in a movie theater, some madman chasing this kid around the apartment. Paralyzed, Peter had sat on the couch watching, no participation, connection, or way to stop it. He was of no help to this kid. It was as if Peter was... possessed. *Only, now it is as real as this train pulling out of Grand Central Station.*

There were shadows jumping on and off walls, whispering. That guest room was possessed, haunted. Jack seemed to have an answer to their mayhem. He told Peter not to go back into that bedroom. In fact, it was very much like today, with Jack bringing him to the train station. That night he walked Peter to 2nd Avenue, hailed a cab, put him in it, and sent him to his parents' apartment; only, Peter didn't go.

Peter returned to the apartment. The shadows lured him to listen outside the door, speaking lies about Jack, how little they thought of Peter. Trying to get away from the voices, Peter went to bed looking for comfort. It did not come. After just a few hours of sleep, he woke up to find an art show going on in his living room. Kasper Greenstreet was there. *It felt real; it still feels real.* Like Peter had walked in to some other dimension, some alternate reality. Not déjà vu, but a parallel universe. Sliding into crazy. As if that party was happening simultaneously with the present. Stepping into the living room from the master bedroom, it was more surreal than unreal. Kasper's paintings of well-known people, rich people in two different lights—Desiree Diamond among them—lined the walls.

Then Peter came upon a painting of himself. He did not like what it revealed about him. All the time, these people kept saying, "He's genius; he'll paint who you really are." Peter found himself walking through the party naked, through the lobby of the building, the garden. It was as if he had split in two. One was the watcher, one the doer, and Peter was lost somewhere in-between.

Coming back to the city was clearly a mistake. Peter and his parents had found a level of peace in their small little town along the Hudson. Except for the weekend Jack visited, but that was not his fault. Peter knows he is not fully himself yet, but he is beginning to feel settled living with his parents, which at his age seems weird. He knows he must block this from his mind—convince himself it is all temporary and that, eventually, he will move out and find someone to love. Peter and Julia have planted a small herb garden. He's even done a little law work for the local attorney. Together they have been working with Peter's father, making him exercise.

After Jack left that weekend, Julia found coloring books in a box she was emptying. Jack had been using them to work with Peter's dad on improving his writing and dexterity. It was an amazing level of progress. In the beginning, Mr. Cairo could only scribble. Pure scribble in the beginning. Then he made it between the lines, but childish. Finally, he colored some of the most beautiful pictures, with bold colors. Just lovely. Julia and Peter were stunned. She blurted out that Jack had a gift. "He's an old soul in a boy's body." *She's right, but she still has no idea what he truly understands and can do.* Even now as close as they've become, Peter would not dare tell her any of the things that went on in the apartment at Gramercy Terrace. All this occult black magic talk would spook her for sure. Just as it spooks Peter.

When will it end? This painting will legally be his in just a short period of time. He's already insured it. It has to be worth a lot of money, but Jack and Peter believe it should never see the light of day. *What selling it could pay for... a house, college for Jack, even retirement.* However, Peter and Jack both agreed that would be the wrong thing to do.

Who is this Philips that showed up to buy it out of the blue, holding a past connection to Kasper Greenstreet? All that crazy shit in the diner? Witchcraft? Peter knows he needs to distance himself from all this and concentrate fully on getting well.

He closes his eyes and lets the train rock him to sleep.

Peter is back in the Gramercy Terrace apartment on the night of Kasper Greenstreet's art show. There is a man with his back to him, getting ready to pull a beautiful red curtain off one of the paintings on the wall.

"Don't you want to see it?" he asks loudly.

No, I don't think I want to see it. Peter steps back from him, from the painting.

"Yes, you do! You want to see it!" His voice is familiar.

Peter shakes his head slowly then violently, but words will not come. Mr. Philips pulls the curtain away from the painting. "Ta da!" The images in the painting are moving, with Peter in straitjacket, fighting to get free.

Mr. Philips throws back his head and laughs. "Don't you love it? Don't you just love it? It's you!" Mr. Philips turns to face him with a most wicked smile.

Peter's head shakes vehemently, like it's going to explode from his body. The movement transcends the dream, spreads into Peter sitting on the train, waking him from the nightmare. Across is a man who, for a moment, Peter thinks is Philips. He pants, his heart racing with the thought. The man is startled and stares suspiciously at him over his newspaper.

He needs to wash his hands from this entire thing, but how can he? He regrets not having burned the fucking painting the minute Jack described it to him. Now, they must keep it locked away as if it is some living organism with a power all its own. Jack has been true to his word, releasing Kasper Greenstreet's hold on the apartment. In the diner, Jack seemed keenly aware but not overwhelmed by Philips or any of his magic. Or witchcraft. Or whatever the fuck it was. Peter can't help but think this man will undo Jack and that there is nothing he can do about it.

The train rolls into the station. Peter sees his mother sitting on the hood of the car. His dad is patiently waiting in the passenger seat for him. Home.

JACK KELLY

Uncle Willy meets me at the storage unit. We move the painting to a unit closer to Dad's and my apartment. Uncle Willy and I are the only ones who know its new location. I don't even tell Peter because he doesn't want to know. I put the receipt in Peter's P.O. Box just to leave a trail.

It's time for school. My freshman year of high school starts off the way my eighth-grade year ended—messy. Immediately, I feel like an outsider; although, I put myself in the position to feel that way. After two weeks of picking up thoughts and emotions from students and faculty, I've begun smoking pot on the way to school just to quiet the noise. September fades into October without notice. I'm already behind with several assignments. *This passive aggressive bullshit is hurting me, but I don't feel like putting in the work to quiet the voices on my own. Using the tools Mr. David taught me could save some grief in the long run, but smoking a joint is easier, faster. Besides that, I like the buzz.*

Brother Thomas is droning on in my religion class. I'm not sure exactly how long I've mentally stepped away from his lecture. I'm still sitting in class, trying to figure out a way to disappear physically. If I could, I would. Complaining of headaches does not work with the brothers the way it did with Sister Thaddeus and Sister Elizabeth at Epiphany. Even when my headaches get bad, they tell me I need to endure. "Take an Excedrin."

Peter called last night wondering if I'd heard from Detective Cohen. Peter sent him a letter with a check, thanking him for his service and notifying him that his work for us was done. That was several weeks ago.

"The check has not been cashed," Peter says, "and Cohen hasn't returned any of my phone calls. Has he contacted you, Jack?"

"No, he hasn't called me since we went to Brooklyn... wait, no, since we made plans for him to see the painting." A long pause follows. "He never contacted you after following Mr. Philips?" I ask.

"No," Peter says, clearly wanting to be finished with all of this. "Last time we spoke was the day we went to the diner."

A hard knock on the classroom door brings me back. A senior boy I've seen around campus walks in with a note and hands it to Brother Thomas. Brother barely glances at the note before pointing to me. "Kelly, the dean would like to see you." Immediately, I sober up. *"Would like to see you"—does that mean it's optional?*

On the way down the stairs, I imagine that someone has told on me for smoking a joint on the way to school or seen me somewhere taking a hit. I start thinking up a bullshit story. *I'll say it's medicinal, for my headaches. Clearly, it's illegal, so I doubt that's going to fly.* Outside the dean's office, I take a deep breath and get ready to go into the full "poor me" role. I almost died, blah, blah, blah, but even I'm bored with that routine. *Are you a warrior, Jack, or a frightened child? Can I be both?*

When I slowly open the door to his office, I immediately pick up a completely different level of energy in the room. Two men are seated inside, waiting for me. Cops. My mind begins taking mental inventory of the inside of my locker, scanning it in my head... *do I have any pot? Paraphernalia these guys could find?*

"Jack Kelly."

"Yes, sir." *I've been so stupid and careless with this shit like I want to get caught.*

"Come in, Mr. Kelly," the dean says, pointing to a chair. *Don't speak,*

Jack; let them talk first. "These men are detectives," the dean says.

I shake their hands like a proper little gentleman. Detective Gruff shows me a picture of Detective Cohen. "Do you know this man?" he asks.

I look at the two detectives. "Yes. Did something happen?"

"When was the last time you saw him?"

"Is he dead?" I ask, already knowing the truth.

The dean does not like the word "dead" and jumps in with a question of his own. "Shouldn't you be doing this with his father present?"

Detective Gruff continues as if he's deaf to our questions. "Can you tell us the last time you saw him?" he asks again.

"Hmm. It's been a while."

"Can you be more specific?"

I have a bad feeling. "How did he die?" I ask. *I am clearly picking something up.*

"Detective, doesn't he need his father here?" the dean asks again, more firmly.

"Can you tell me how he died?" I repeat.

Finally, the other detective chimes in. "He was found floating in the East River."

Oh shit! "You know he's an ex-cop," I say, like I'm adding value to the investigation.

"Yes, we are aware of that. Now, I would like to know the last time you saw Mr. Cohen."

The dean stops staring at the detectives and puts his attention on me. *This is not the way I want to get on the dean's radar. Have they contacted Peter?*

"Detectives. I really must insist that you do this kind of questioning in the presence of his father!" The dean now says in a commanding way.

No, no. Question me right here, right now! My father doesn't know any of this shit! This is not good. It is one more thing to disappoint my father, another reason for him to be pissed at me.

But the dean has his way.

Soon, my father and I are sitting in the police station, waiting for the detectives to settle in. They have a picture of Mr. Cohen on the desk, the one they showed me at school. They also have several pictures of him after he was pulled out of the East River. I know it's ridiculous, inappropriate even, but I can't help but think of a line from *The Godfather*: "It's a Sicilian message. It means Luca Brasi sleeps with the fishes."

In this case, I believe the message is from Mr. Philips. Sorcerer. Black magician. It's all related; I just know it is. This will set Peter back—maybe lead to another stint in the psych ward.

"What was your relationship with the deceased?" the detective asks, as if we hadn't skipped a beat from the questioning at school.

My father spots the photos of the dead man. "Can you turn those over? He doesn't need to see that."

"Of course. Sorry," says the detective who told me Cohen was dead. Detective Gruff waits for me to answer.

I have him ask the question again. "In what capacity did you know him?"

"He worked for us," I reply.

Peter told me something a long time ago from a lawyer's point of view, something I always try to keep in mind, especially when someone is questioning me. "If you are asked for information, don't elaborate. If someone asks if you know the time, say 'yes.' The question is not, 'can you tell me what time it is?' The question is, 'do you know the time?' 'Yes.' Don't give the time; that's a different question."

The detective looks at my father, who looks at me. "Worked for you, Mr. Kelly?" the detective asks my father.

"No—for Peter and me," I interrupt.

This is going to become a shit show. Peter didn't pick up when I called him after school. I tried him right before Dad and I had to leave for the police station.

"Peter?" The other detective jumps in. "Peter Cairo?"

"Yes." *I'm not sure how much to tell them. Should I play the dopey teenager?*

"Were you paying him, or was Peter Cairo paying him?"

"Peter."

"So, when you say, 'he was working for us,' you mean he was working for Peter Cairo?"

"Okay."

"Okay what?" Gruff is already running out of patience with me.

My father stares at me like I've just landed from another planet.

"Isn't this all semantics?" I ask, as respectfully as possible. "I mean, isn't the important thing here to find out who killed Mr. Cohen?"

All three men—my father and the two detectives—give me that look, which I've seen before from a wide variety of adults. The look that practically screams *you little shit, how dare you talk to me like that!*

"I never said he was murdered," the detective says.

"Well, surely he didn't go for a swim." *Oh fuck, I want those words back.*

"Jack, mind yourself!" my father says firmly and completely out of patience.

I do a quick inventory. First, Peter and I have done nothing wrong. Every step we made has been on the up-and-up. The painting was abandoned; Peter filed a claim with the court. We hired a detective to find relatives who could lead us to photos and paperwork. All legit. Neither one of us asked Cohen to follow Mr. Philips—that was his idea. We didn't get him killed. *I still am deeply sorry and more than a little shocked that he is dead. Scared, even. But we are not responsible.*

I give the detectives three details as politely as possible without elaborating. We went to Brooklyn, just Mr. Cohen and I—that triggers a really bad reaction from my dad. He stomps his feet and shakes his head in total frustration. "Then, we went to a diner to meet a man who was interested in purchasing the painting," I add. "Mr. Cohen waited outside. The last time either one of us saw him was earlier that day."

I leave out Kasper Greenstreet's ghost and the sinister shadows in the painting that possess it, or rather haunt it. I also offer no commentary on the possibility that Mr. Philips, who I think should be the number one suspect, may also be a sorcerer, warlock, or worse. At the very least, he is someone who practices voodoo or some other kind of black magic. *I'm not sure exactly what that fucker is, but he's definitely capable of murder.*

They drill me, asking the same questions over and over in a roundabout way. "Tell us again what was it you were looking for in Brooklyn?" *I guess these men were never interrogated by nuns.*

"Anything that could help us with the provenance of the painting." They stare at me, as does my dad. "Custody of ownership," I add.

"Yes, we know what provenance means. Did you find anything?"

"You should ask Peter that; he is the lawyer. All of this has been filed in the courts."

"We are talking about murder; Cohen didn't accidently fall in the river." My father practically screams it at me, not caring who can hear him.

The severity of that hits me on the way home. Dad gives it to me with both barrels. Well-deserved. "Brooklyn! With some guy who I don't even know."

"Dad, he was an ex-cop; he worked for us."

"Was." He looks at me with that stare only dads can give. "And he worked for Peter, who is going to get an ear full."

Peter cannot survive that. "Dad, please don't."

If my father knew about Peter chasing me with a butcher knife, he would have put Peter in Bellevue by other means.

"Well, I don't think Mr. Cohen's death has anything to do with us," I say. I'm lying but trying to lighten the tension.

"Oh, you don't? What are you and Peter, the fucking Hardy Boys?" It feels like he said that with a hint of jealousy. We walk up 2nd Avenue in silence.

When I finally reach Peter, he is not at all nervous about talking to the cops; although, he is frightened about having to come back to the city.

"Everything is moving through the courts smoothly. Hiring Mr. Cohen was all about due diligence," he says.

Peter is convinced the murderer was some rich philandering husband whose wife hired Cohen to help with a divorce case. Complete denial on his part. My instincts are in contradiction with Peter's thinking because I know Cohen's death has everything to do with Mr. Philips, but I don't want to plant that seed in his head, especially since he has convinced himself otherwise. Peter is very troubled every time he's in the city, and he will not stay overnight.

He eventually gives the detectives information so they can contact the court to see the record. The information Cohen provided us regarding the painting is documented. He also provides them with copies of the checks he paid Cohen, as well as the information on the check that Cohen never cashed. Peter also wants to speak to my dad and apologize for having me dragged into this situation. I remind him it was I who opened Pandora's box.

However, this is all before someone drops a dime on me, revealing all to my father. The police being called to Peter's apartment. The knife. His stay at Bellevue. *It is a disaster.*

My father goes ballistic. "What is wrong with you, Jack?"

"I fell on my head... remember?"

My father looks at me like he wants to beat the shit out of me. Watching Dad struggle to control himself is a struggle for me, too, because I feel like I'm putting him through it. Although, that is not my intention.

"Did I do something to you?"

"What?"

"It's a simple question, Jack, because I don't understand the lying, the disrespectful attitude. Surely I must have done something to you that, in my apparent feebleness as a parent, I am unaware of."

"You just don't understand, Dad."

"Educate me."

"About what?"

"About the police being called to Peter's apartment with a report stating he was chasing you with a knife. That he ended up in Bellevue in the psych ward, which you hid from me. First, the psychic, then the Tarot cards. What exactly is your relationship with Peter? Why would he chase you with a knife?"

My head is splitting open. I try to manage the throbbing and building migraine without using it as an excuse. We stand there in silence. *It's my fault, I fear.* There was a time when Dad and I were never like this, never at a loss for words.

"I didn't forget to tell you. It was... it was deliberate, and it was wrong. The police had it wrong, though," I say softly. *Here I go, Jack the liar, but what am I to do?* You experience this shit and then have to explain it to someone. "He wasn't chasing me. I thought Peter was going to cut his wrists."

There is good and evil, white magic and black magic, angels and demons. *It's all true because I've encountered all of these things personally. So, what I just said, I will not judge myself for, because I love my father and I love Peter.*

"Okay." *Okay?* "Don't lie to me anymore, Jack. I'm on your side."

This makes me feel incredibly guilty. I know he's on my side. I also know I will lie to him again.

Peter and I give the detectives everything we can on Mr. Philips, which honestly is not much. He seemed to materialize from nowhere and has disappeared the same way. We share his number and the diner where we met to discuss the painting. We tell the detectives about Susan's cousin in Brooklyn and how Mr. Philips went out to see her just before Cohen and I. That is all we have on him. That is all we know.

They cannot locate Mr. Philips; it seems he vanished too. His telephone number has been disconnected, which was a telephone service anyway so there was never an address attached to it. According to the detectives, who will not tell me much of anything, the diner is closed. There is nothing, not a trace. *How can you just disappear?*

I take it upon myself to visit the diner. *It's not that I don't believe the detectives, it's just all so strange… but maybe not strange at all.*

It's closed. As I walk around the property, the diner appears to have been closed for years. *How could that be possible? I was just there!* I check the doors, which are locked. There is blackout paper on the windows, so trying to peer in is useless. On my second trip around the exterior, I find a bathroom window that is slightly open. It's too high for me, so I need a boost to climb into the window. I find some wooden crates stacked by the dumpster and use them as a ladder.

It's totally dark inside the diner. I leave the bathroom window wide open for a little light. *Not sure what I am looking to find—a sacrifice? A den of witches sitting around a candle, putting spells on people in the dark?* Feeling my way through the darkness like a blind man, I make my way to the front door. It's locked and needs a key to open it. The glass door is covered in blackout paper, which I peel away, bringing light into the room. I do the same with the windows. Now at least I can move about the diner to get a better view. The kitchen is empty and dirty. There is no cooking equipment. I open cabinets one by one; all of them are bare. I walk in front of a quietly humming freezer.

As soon as I place my hand on the handle, the murmurs begin. Soft chanting voices. I release the handle and turn back to the main dining area to have a look. Silence. No one there. Focusing back on the freezer, I grab the handle. Once again, there is a low murmur. This time, I'm patient. It gets louder.

DETECTIVE COHEN
AND PHILIPS

Cohen watches as Jack and Peter walk to the table so he can get a good look at Philips. He stays outside, waiting to follow him, smoking a cigarette, expecting Philips to come out of the front entrance of the diner. But Mr. Philips leaves through the kitchen. Peter and Jack stay seated at the table until he's gone. There is an echo in the diner. The place is infested with witches, warlocks, and sorcerers and not the good kind. Peter starts to speak, but I motion for him to be quiet.

He is caught off guard when Philips practically runs into him coming out the back door.

Philips stops and stares at Cohen as if he is reading him, which he is, but Cohen is unaware of it.

"Are you looking for me?" Philips asks firmly.

Cohen has been a cop, a private detective, and an addict. He prides himself with his ability to assess people rather quickly, but his read on this guy comes up empty. Well, not exactly empty. It is as if Philips has stepped into a photo in which he doesn't belong.

"Um, yes," Cohen says, motioning for Philips to walk with him. He doesn't move.

"Are you with them?" Philips asks.

The man is cutting right to the chase. Cohen is not sure if he likes this, but it might make doing business easier. "Yes—and no," Cohen says.

"What does that mean?"

Again, Cohen motions for Philips to come and walk with him. Still, he does not move. "I need to talk to you without them seeing us."

They walk along the docks without a word until they are out of view from the diner. "Explain," Philips says.

"I'm a private eye."

"And?"

"And I am technically working for Peter Cairo. I know you are interested in the painting."

Philips shrugs his shoulders. "So?"

"He won't sell it, will he?" Cohen asks.

"You tell me."

Cohen smiles, but the smile leaves his face when he sees the intensity in Philips' eyes. Not intense exactly… more like evil.

"No. He won't sell it," Cohen says flatly.

"Why? I'm willing to offer him a lot of money."

Cohen pauses. This is that line you are not supposed to cross. You are not supposed to betray the people you are working for, especially when it can get someone hurt, but he's done it before as a cop. Cohen was a dirty cop with lots of problems and lots of vices, including his love of cocaine and hookers. Three divorces and a shitload of debt erased whatever moral compass he may have once had. Now he is willing to swindle Peter if it means he can land himself a huge pay day.

"It's the kid, right?" Philips says. It is more a statement than a question. Cohen nods his head.

"He holds power over Peter. Yes?"

Again, Cohen nods.

"How?" Philip asks. Cohen raises his shoulders to indicate he doesn't know. "An invocation? A shadow-field?"

Cohen is afraid, although he is not certain why. He doesn't understand the terms Philips is using.

"You can get me this painting?" Philips says, more a demand than a question.

Cohen does not have the fortitude to walk away from money, but he realizes Philips is dangerous. "If the kid was out of the way, I could definitely get Peter to sell," Cohen suggests.

"Surely you're not suggesting that I kill the boy?" Philips says, licking his lips.

"Of course not." Cohen suddenly wants to run. He feels like a rat or mouse being trapped by a larger animal.

Philips' eyes change to the lightest blue. Cohen sees himself at his worst and feels himself shrink. "How can you get me the painting?" Philips asks. "That is the reason you're here."

"Why do you want the painting so badly?"

"That's my concern. Your concern is how to get it for me."

"The reason I ask is because you might not be able to sell it—at least not in the immediate future," Cohen says.

"Not a worry."

Cohen takes a deep breath. "I know where the painting is stored."

"Do you have the key?"

"No."

"Can you get the key?" When Cohen nods, Philips adds, "You really want to steal the painting from your own client?" Silence. It's out there; no going back now. "How much do you want?" Philips asks.

"The painting is worth at least $255,000."

"I asked you how much you want."

The sky gets ominously dark. Cohen is cold, tired, and now frightened. "Fifty thousand."

Philips reaches out and shakes Cohen's hand. Cohen feels as if there has been a physical exchange—something has been given to him that he does not want, and something has been taken away that he needs.

I let go of the handle. When I release, the images of Philips and Cohen fade away. Quickly, I put my hand back on the handle, but the source is no longer there. I realize the freezer is unplugged, and the humming has stopped. I slowly open the freezer and find a bunch of mouse carcasses. *Disgusting!*

I go through the diner top to bottom, satisfied with the vacancy of the place. I head back to the bathroom. A low hum turns into a loud breathing sound as if the walls are alive. It makes me momentarily dizzy. *Keep moving, Jack. No, this is why you are here.* I refocus, get my head on straight. The sound brings me back into the main section of the diner. I look the place over, expecting to see Philips. Nothing.

Yet, I know that I am not alone. "Show yourself," I state firmly.

I hear Philips' voice very clearly in my head: "I want that painting! I can make you very powerful."

A lie. He will not share power. "Never," I whisper.

Suddenly, a mouse scurries in from the kitchen, followed by a silver cat that pounces on it and tears it to shreds. The pure violence is unsettling, along with the sudden manifestation of both creatures. I remember Philips' words to Peter: "Afraid of a little wind, Peter? What are you, a mouse?"

Taking a breath, I look around. "Just so we're clear, I'm not a fucking mouse!"

I wait for a windstorm but get nothing. Walking back through the diner, I begin to rip the blackout paper from a window. Sunlight pours in. "Mr. Philips? Mr. Philips, can we talk?" I ask as I tear the blackout paper off all the windows. *Let there be light!* "Mr. Philips?"

Nothing. I stand in the middle of the room.

Finally, it's time to go. I use the back of the toilet to climb out the window. My legs dangle behind me as I pull my upper torso through. It is getting dark.

Abruptly, I feel the impact of a cat crashing against me, attacking my leg. "I want that painting!" echoes in surround sound in my head.

With all the force I can muster, I shake the cat off my leg and kick it into the wall. Standing on the top of the toilet, I'm ready for battle. The cat has changed color; it is now black. *Who the fuck is this guy!?* "I'll drown your ass!" I say as the cat hisses at me before running from the room.

As I climb out of the window, I notice someone has removed the crates, forcing me to jump to the ground. *You should be home doing homework instead of chasing these fucking ghouls, Jack.* But I feel compelled that this is my calling, my destiny.

COHEN AND PHILIPS

Cohen leaves Philips on the docks after they exchange telephone numbers and set a time to meet. Cohen finds an employee with drug and money problems at Chelsea Storage—where Jack had stored the painting. Cohen greases the employee's palm with a taste of the money to come and the promise of a bigger payday. Cohen needs another key to storage B21. There is the usual squawking. "It's impossible." Cohen makes him a better offer. The way around this guy's misgivings is through his drug addiction.

Philips keeps Cohen waiting. It is very late when he arrives at Chelsea Storage. Cohen's attitude gives way to Philips' presence, which is powerful, dark, sinister. Otherworldly. It throws Cohen off balance. The building is closed, but Cohen has the right tools and picks the lock. He gives Philips copies of the paperwork and shows him the newly made key to storage B21. Then, he witnesses a literal change in Philips' skin.

B21 is on the second floor. No one is in the building but Cohen and Philips. Philips' temperature has changed, too. He becomes the groom getting ready to see his bride. Cohen is aware of the significant transformation and hands Philips the key. His eyes are on fire as he slides the key into the lock,

slowly turning the handle and opening the door.
The storage unit is empty.

JACK

The Cohen murder case stays cold. I spend a lot of time in the library, not doing homework, but researching shapeshifters. It's all that is on my mind after the incident with the cats at the diner and Peter's house in Hudson Valley. The wolf. The fact that Mr. Philips seems to be out of place, out of time, in the wrong movie. These incidents lead me to entertain this idea.

Shapeshifting appears throughout history, mythology, and folklore. All cultures and tribes have stories about shapeshifting. There is even a name for a person turning into a cat—an Ailuranthrope. Some people think shapeshifting can come from a totem, a spirit, sacred object, or symbol. By the Middle Ages, it was still believed sorcerers, or witches, could shapeshift. *If they could pull it off then, why not now?*

No one can locate Mr. Philips. And, he seemed to appear from nowhere. Even Kasper while alive and his ghost could not identify or find him. But the painting on the wall of Mr. Philips sent Kasper into a maelstrom of emotion. *Mr. Philips is much more powerful than I originally thought. Never underestimate your opponent.*

I find a definition of shapeshifter in an encyclopedia of religion:

"Shapeshifting can be defined as an alteration in form or substance of any animate object. There seems to be no limit to the kind of objects susceptible to such alteration. Examples: plants, animals, humans, and gods." That I find tricky because I believe there is only one God, one source. Shapeshifting can be caused by an external force and can occur for good or evil, for reasons simple or profound. It is not a phenomenon restricted to unsophisticated cultures remote in history and geography. There are elements of shapeshifting in the deepest and even modern spiritual insights of Christianity, Hinduism, and Buddhism. It is found in dominant civilizations and popular modern cultures as well as in major religions.

Angels and demons? Shapeshifters?

Suddenly, the chatter in the library rises to a ridiculously high level. Looking around, I know I'm picking up on the thoughts of the librarian and patrons. Only, there are not nearly enough people here to create such high volume. While trying to stay focused amidst the chaos, I realize the voices are coming from the books. Closing my eyes, I try to equalize the sound and differentiate the words coming at me all at once.

It's overwhelming, like the first time in the subway with my father. I hone in on what the voices from the books are trying to tell me.

Peter and I get good news; he has won the case. The painting now officially belongs to him. He immediately converts that into joint ownership with me.

"Why are you doing that, Peter? It's yours," I say from a pay phone on 19th Street. My father is livid with the entire knife-wielding incident so I can't talk from home anymore. Now I use different pay phones in the city. Peter tells me to call collect, which I do on occasion.

"It's not completely altruistic, Jack," he says. "Like the tenants before me, I would never have opened that storage bin. That was you. However, more importantly, if we can't sell the painting without the other one's approval, we will stick to our word and never sell it."

I'm in agreement, but the truth is we sound bat shit crazy. Here we are, sitting on a painting worth upward of $250,000 that we are promising never to sell.

When talking with him, I'm reminded of something: the more removed Peter is from the city and the supernatural elements that engulfed his life, the better he sounds. He is practicing law again and has never been happier with his parents. Mr. Cairo still can't speak, but his writing is clear enough with his left hand that he is able to communicate his needs and wants without his old frustration. Peter and Julia both credit me with helping him through the use of the coloring books, which improved his left-hand motor skills. *I'll take it, but I'm not sure it's warranted.*

Standing alone in the phone booth, I miss the Cairos daily and deeply. *Maybe it isn't so far-fetched that I created my own family; maybe I always wanted that sort of an intact unit.* Listening to the sound of his voice, I am sure he will never move back to the city, which makes me sad. But I love them, so I must be happy for them. They are where they should be. *Me? I am where I am.*

I walk out of school one afternoon with my head down, knowing it's just a matter of time before shit hits the fan with my failing grades. I don't try to muscle through; I'm just failing, and I don't care. This is a first. Feeling for the joint in my pocket, it takes me a moment to realize the two detectives are waiting for me just outside school property.

I fake a smile. "Detectives."

"Jack."

"What's up?"

"Let's walk," Detective Gruff says as more of a command. "Is there anything you overlooked? Anything you forgot to tell us?"

I shake my head. "Like what?"

"That's what we're asking you."

"Did you find Mr. Philips?" I know they haven't, but I ask anyway.

"Not yet, but we did find out that Mr. Cohen worked on a case years ago, possibly looking for the same guy." They wait for a response, which I don't give. "Not much in his old file."

"Oh?" I say. "That's interesting."

"Yes, he was working for Kasper Greenstreet." The detective lets that resonate within me.

"Kasper Greenstreet..." I repeat. Not with a question mark, but not without one, either.

"The same Kasper Greenstreet that Mr. Cohen was helping you and Peter Cairo track down paperwork for..." Detective Gruff takes a long dramatic pause then continues, "Um... provenance."

I'd love to say *touché*, but I don't dare. "So, you think Mr. Cohen was looking for Mr. Philips years ago?" I ask.

"Maybe. Did he tell you anything?"

"You think that's what I overlooked? That he was looking for Mr. Philips on a previous case?"

"Did he tell you he worked for Kasper Greenstreet, once upon a time?"

A headache is knocking on my door, which makes me pause longer than I need to. "I don't recall if he did, or if he didn't."

"Do you think that would be important?"

"Wait. I'm confused. Which one is more important—that he may have been looking for Mr. Philips or that, once upon a time, he worked briefly for Kasper Greenstreet?" I ask.

"Let me buy you an ice cream," Detective Gruff says as we get to the corner. *I can shake them off here and say I need to go home, but having friends on the police force is always a good idea. Right?*

"I can't. Sorry. I'm lactose intolerant."

"Are you trying to piss me off?" Detective Gruff is losing his patience.

"No, you can buy me a cup of tea. Really, I don't eat ice cream."

Inside, they order coffee while I order tea. "Both—that he was maybe looking for Mr. Philips and that he worked for Kasper Greenstreet," Detective Gruff picks up where he left off. He does ninety-eight percent of the talking.

"If he did tell us that he worked for Kasper Greenstreet—and I'm not sure he told us that—at the time, it wasn't important to me," I tell him.

"Why?"

"Kasper Greenstreet was dead. As for Mr. Philips, if the old file says he was looking for Mr. Philips previously, then it could be important now because of the circumstances. But, again, at the time, we were just looking for Susan Michaels' cousin and paperwork to support Peter's case."

He turns the entirety of his sizeable body to face me. It looks like a posture of intimidation, but I'm not intimidated. "So, you and Peter did not deliberately leave this information out?"

"No. Does the file say he was looking for Mr. Philips? Our Mr. Philips? Same number? Did it give a reason?"

"You should practice law, Jack," the easygoing detective says. "I bet you are the smartest kid in your class." *Is he being sarcastic? He appears to be genuine, but you can't tell with adults sometimes. They like to patronize.*

"Really? Me?"

"You are a very sharp kid," says Detective Gruff, "but you don't have to be such a wise ass."

"Well, I hate to disappoint you, fellows, but I'm flunking most of my classes at the moment." They both seem genuinely surprised. "Did it say why Kasper Greenstreet hired him?"

"A man by the name of Philip tried to kill him. Beat him up pretty bad." *That's the one.* "Philip? Or Mr. Philips?" I ask.

"Only the first name, but damn coincidental, don't you think?"

"God's way of talking to you," I reply nonchalantly.

"What?" asks the easygoing detective.

"A coincidence. It's God's way of talking to you. At least that's my take on it."

"Jack, you know the woman you met in Brooklyn, the cousin, the one with the boxes in the basement?" the easygoing detective asks.

"Yes. Was she able to help you?"

"She seems to have disappeared."

"What?"

"Last time a neighbor saw her, she was heading into the basement. No one has seen her since."

"Did she go visit a relative?" I ask, genuinely concerned.

The easygoing detective shakes his head. "The apartment did not look like anyone was planning on going anywhere. She had lunch waiting for her on the table."

Outside the coffee shop, the detectives urge me to go home and study.

They give me their business cards. "Call us anytime you need to, kid."

My mind is racing. *I guess I'll be heading out to Brooklyn.*

At dinner, I break it to my father that it isn't working out for me at Xavier. "You should expect a phone call from the dean," I say. Surprisingly, he doesn't fight with me or yell, but his disappointment is written all over his face.

Later, I can't sleep. All I do is toss and turn. No amount of meditation or yoga is going to help me sleep.

After I make sure my dad is out for the count, I slide out the kitchen window, down the fire escape, and into the small yard behind our tenement. My first stop is Epiphany School and the Gramercy Terrace apartments. When I arrive, I see no lights from apartment 3C. There is a new tenant in the apartment. I'm sure things are different now that Kasper vacated the premises—no hauntings, no shadows, no sleepless nights.

I stand in front of Epiphany and look at the window of my previous classroom. The birds and their attack come to mind, as well as Sister Elizabeth. Now I understand the reason I picked up on the breast situation: Sister has a lump in one of them, a cancerous lump. *Is this what I needed to understand?* I hold the triangle that hangs from my neck, the one Mr. David gave me. *Do I tell her? Should I tell her?*

From 22nd Street, I head to the 23rd Street subway, where my first encounter with the supernatural happened. The memory of the ghost of that woman throwing herself in front of the train over and over again comes to mind. There is one person waiting on the platform. He looks me over and checks his watch. *Yup, it's late for me to be out wandering by myself,* but I wander anyway. I find myself in front of the site where the old boarding house stood. Looks like construction has restarted. I press my hands on a board, hoping for... *what? To pick up some old energy? To understand why my life changed on this site?* No clarity or answers come.

I make the short subway trip, walk home, unlock the door, and tiptoe into the apartment. My dad is still asleep. As I get ready for bed, I wonder *are we really awake when we think we're dreaming? Or am I dreaming now?*

I sit at the table in the boarding house kitchen. It is nothing like the night when I fell through the floor and almost died here. My injured body does not lie between the world of the living and the dead. No one else is sitting at the table. There are no shadows or demons crawling around me. It is just the nun and I. Her back is to me.

She makes us tea in the kitchen. "You are back?" she asks without turning around.

"Yes."

"Tea?" She does not wait for my answer and pours us each a cup of tea from a scarlet red kettle.

When she turns to face me, I can see she is luminous, like she has swallowed the sun. It radiates from her, lighting and warming the space around us.

Placing the tea down in front of me, she speaks. "May I ask why?"

I'm surprised by the question, even a bit hurt. It makes me sit up and back away, like a wounded child. "Do you not want me to come here?"

The nun places her cup on the table and sits so that we are facing one another. The warmth from her light feels comforting on my face.

She sips her tea and looks at me intently. "It's always up to you."

That's not the answer I want. I wait. *Looking at her for what? Affection? I want her to want me to come, I want her approval, her love.* "But do you not want me to come?" No answer. "I mean I know I can always find you here. Right?"

"Why? Because this is where we met?" she asks.

"Yes."

Drinking her tea is like drinking air. That doesn't make sense, but it does to me.

She is waiting on me. Her eyes are patient; her body relaxed. She knows I am here for a specific reason. "This is just a dream? Right?"

"Does that matter?" she asks.

"I want it to be real."

She smiles at me. *In a motherly way?* "Then it's real."

"Real… okay. I came here because Sister Elizabeth, my last teacher at Epiphany, a nun like you…" She nods. "She has three breasts," I blurt out.

The nun looks at me and smiles. "Did you come here to ask me if all nuns have three breasts?"

Wow, she's being funny. Unexpected. It makes me feel calm and safe. Alive. "No, of course not. It's just that she has a lump in one of them." She nods her head, as if to say *I see.* "I'm not sure it's malignant."

There is a powerful connection between us now. She has saved me from death the first time and now I need her help again to save me from... what? Mr. Philips? The painting? Myself?

I need her strength and her wisdom. We drink our tea in silence. It is not an awkward silence but heartfelt and soothing. I wonder if her tea tastes like air too.

"Earth," she finally says.

"What?" Why does it still surprise me that we do not need words. Everything between us is and always has been telepathic.

Raising her cup. "My tea—it tastes like earth."

"May I taste it?" I ask.

She pushes her cup towards me on the table. "Sure, but it will taste like air to you."

I let that sit with me, not reaching for her cup. "Oh, I see, I think I get it."

The nun smiles. "So, you have a question."

"Yes. Should I tell Sister Elizabeth?"

The nun sips her tea. She is much younger than I originally thought. Her eyes are hazel. Gentle. *She would have been a marvelous mother.* "If I may ask, how did you die?"

"I was murdered." She speaks with no anger or vengeance. I remember that from the article Peter showed me of a nun's bones being found during the excavation.

"Do you know who killed you?" I ask.

"Yes, but none of that matters now."

"Why?"

She looks at me, curious about my questioning. "Why doesn't it matter? Or why did he kill me?"

"Both, I guess."

"Because I have forgiven him. He was ill, and he thought I was a witch."

I look down, then back up, meeting her eyes. They are kind, warm. "But you weren't?"

"Heavens, no. He thought my use of holistic remedies were potions. That I wanted to poison him."

I play with my teacup, hoping I haven't offended her. "What should I do about Sister Elizabeth?"

She folds her hands and seems to be weighing the answer. "What can you do?"

"I could tell her."

She shrugs her shoulders. "So, tell her."

"Well, it's not that easy."

"It never is…"

"Last year, things happened. Very weird events. I think Sister Elizabeth thought I created, or rather, caused them."

She takes her cup and brings it to the sink. When she returns to the table, she stays standing, looking at me. *Challenging me?* But I do not feel threatened or put upon.

"What does any of that have to do with telling her about her cancer?" the nun asks.

"I'm afraid she will react badly, that she'll think I'm some kind of psychic, occultist, or even a witch."

She gives me a reassuring smile. "But you're not a witch or an occultist."

"No, of course not. I'm just a boy."

She tilts her head and looks into my soul. "We both know that you are not just a boy, Jack."

My eyes tear up. *At last, I feel understood for the first time since I woke up in the hospital as just a boy, utterly confused.*

"And why should it matter what someone thinks?" She asks before I can explore those feelings with her. "You know it's not true; your intent is pure. If you are coming from a place of love, then the intention is pure."

"Yes." I nod.

She looks up disturbed. "Did you bring him?" she asks.

"Who?"

I follow her eyes as she looks outside of the kitchen and into the darkness. There, with a soft light on his face, is Mr. Philips. The idea of him being here shocks me.

"I must have because it's my dream, correct?" I ask.

Her attention changes from Mr. Philips back to me. "So, you are dreaming?"

"I'm not sure. Either way, it must be me who brought him. Unless you know him... do you?"

She shakes her head watching him. She is not afraid exactly, but uneasy. We remain silent for a moment. Then I ask, "Is he dead or alive?"

"He just is," she says.

"I don't understand. He is what?"

"He is not like you or like me. He is somewhere in the in-between. In a liminal zone. He occupies space between two worlds. Not living or dead as we know it. He just is..."

I look at the nun and then at Mr. Philips, who fades into the darkness.

"Don't we have to be one or the other? Dead or alive?"

She doesn't answer immediately. She makes me wait. I guess so that I will think about my own question. Finally, she says, "Dead. Alive. Those are just words we create to try and explain things that we don't fully understand when we are having a human experience."

"But you're dead, and I'm alive? Right?"

The nun shrugs her shoulders. "Yet, here we are, talking to one another and having tea," she says.

This makes me feel very funny, not "ha, ha" funny, either. Oddly funny. "Am I dead now?" I ask, barely able to utter the words.

"There is no dead, no living—those are only terms," she replies. "I told you there just is."

My father wakes me, pulling me back to my physical reality as a fifteen-year-old high school student. Getting me up for school seems ridiculous since I know they are going to expel me. I tell him that.

"Well," he says, "you'll go until they actually do it. Right now, it's all in your head."

No, Dad. What's in my head is that there is no dead, no living—there just is...

Dad sets a bowl of oatmeal on the table for me and heads out the door, on his way to work. "Do your best!" he yells.

Putting all my energy and effort into school seems futile, but I decide to try. I make it through the day, but when it's over, I can't get out of the building fast enough. The butterflies cannot escape my stomach, so they make themselves at home. Walking toward Epiphany, I'm counting on Sister Elizabeth to be in the classroom, as she always is on Tuesday afternoon. I quickly move past the front office and hit the stairs two at a time, hoping no one sees or tries to stop me. *I don't want a scene.* My fear is that if I don't do this now, if I don't tell her today, I never will.

The door to the classroom is open, but I knock anyway, not wanting to startle her. Sister Elizabeth looks up from her desk. She cannot conceal her dismay—even trepidation—at the sight of me.

"Mr. Kelly?"

"Good afternoon, Sister, please forgive my interruption."

She motions for me to come in. "Sit if you like." No matter how cordial we try to be, there is too much water under the bridge, as they say. The uneasiness between us is palpable so I decide to cut to the chase.

"Sister Elizabeth, I've been praying about this for a really long time. And, well... as you know, we are taught that God listens, answers..." *I'm not sure if I sound crazy, but I can't stop or I will never say it.* "If I may say, after much prayer, I feel the need—the calling really—to tell you that I believe you need to see a doctor regarding a mass or lump in one of your breasts. I think it it's cancerous."

My stomach feels like it's risen to my esophagus, butterflies and all; I may vomit right here on the floor. The need to curse is pulsating on my tongue like the tic of a person with Tourette syndrome, ready to explode.

Sister doesn't speak. Instead, she stares at me like I've lost my fucking mind. Her humiliation rising like a volcano ready to erupt. I've mortified her in my feeble attempt to warn her, to help her.

"God, Mr. Kelly? God told you to come here and tell me this?" Sister asks incredulously, her head shaking gently side to side. Her eyes studying me. I feel her displeasure.

I step back, planning my escape route.

"Prayer, God, intuition." I'm mumbling now. *This is a mistake.*

"Intuition?" Her discomfort is palpable. Her eyes are filling up with tears. *Jack, what have you done?*

We stare at each other. Both of us lost in who we are and who we are not. Sister takes a moment to compose herself.

Finally, she says. "I'll take it into consideration, Mr. Kelly." Then after a long pause, she says firmly, "You may go."

"You may go?" Wow, lady, *I just told you that you may have cancer. Do you know how hard that was?* I leave the room and run down the stairs; I can't get out of the building fast enough. *Stupid. My decision to see her was stupid.* Sister Elizabeth does not see me as helping; she sees me as something wicked. One thing for sure, I know which nun, of the two that I have visited in the last twenty-four hours, I am guided by. "You may go" rings loudly in my head.

My intent was pure; of that, I am certain.

My next stop is Brooklyn. I can't find the address and certainly can't get it from Cohen. I also decide not to call Peter. He seems to withdraw every time we have a conversation or when our conversation leads to a new piece of information regarding the painting, Kasper Greenstreet, Mr. Philips, or Cohen. I'm pretty sure I can find the building where Susan Michaels' cousin, Mrs. Walsh, lives from memory. While on my way, I keep thinking about how disappointed I am with Sister Elizabeth's reaction. The least I was hoping for was "Okay, I'll look into it."

Then, a reminder comes to me. *Remember, Jack, be of service without being attached to its results. That is something I need to live by because, let's face it, many of the results have not been good.*

SISTER ELIZABETH

*W*hat in God's name is with this kid… *as if Jack Kelly didn't bring enough crazy, supernatural events to my life last school year?*

Sister Elizabeth waits for Jack to leave her classroom and counts to ten before walking into the hall to make sure he is not lurking about. She prays aloud, "Forgive me, Father, but that child upsets me." The sound of Jack running down the stairs and jumping to the landing reassures her that he is gone. Her body shakes. *He must have brought back some evil with him.* All she feels she can do is pray for Jack Kelly.

The school's front doors shut, the sound pulling her back into the classroom. She looks out the window to see him on the sidewalk. There he is, walking toward 3rd Avenue. The feelings he creates within her bring such shame. She does not like the boy. *There is something wicked in him. These feelings, and what he carries inside, cannot possibly come from God!*

Sister Elizabeth shuts the window and looks across the street at the old apartment of Peter Cairo. News of him moving out of the city this summer was whispered about through the parish. It is common knowledge in the convent. *Thank God he is gone. He is another one carrying the devil's influence. He had that full mental breakdown I witnessed; that may be his excuse.* However, she is sure that whatever was going on in that apartment was unholy. It was horrifying seeing Peter Cairo, a grown man, chase Jack around the apartment, wielding a knife. Then Jack lied to Father Keenan, saying it didn't happen. She witnessed it with her own two eyes. *Shameful.*

What was Peter Cairo doing with Jack that would cause him to chase him with a knife? The whole episode still made her feel uneasy.

Another question crossed her mind. *What type of child, or teenager, comes to tell a nun at a religious school that he thinks she has a mass on one of her breasts? Was that some kind of slight or code, wanting me to know that he is aware of my three breasts? How could he know that? Ridiculous.* Yet, there was something about his delivery: "One of your breasts." Like he was aware that there were more than two...

She buries her face in her hands, trying to shut out the world, his comment bringing her shame front and center. *Is this his way of getting back at me? To punish me for how I disciplined him last year after the bird and train incidents? "Incidents" do not describe it well at all—it was demonic!* She thought she was done with Jack Kelly. She decides she should call his father; it's unseemly for a boy to talk to a nun about her breasts. Or to any woman, for that matter.

She has to be on her way. After shutting her binder and lesson plan, she walks slowly down the stairs. The walls fill up with shadows, mocking her, accusing her, shaming her. *I am, after all, a sinner.*

She walks into the convent. Her habit suddenly feels like it weighs a ton so she walks straight to her living quarters and removes it. She then peels off her undergarments until she stands naked. She touches her breasts one at a time; something she has not done since... *the pleasure of my body when I was with Mr. Dillon.*

She shakes off that memory and gives herself a full breast self-exam. On the right breast, there it is—a lump. She checks it over and over again. She feels the lump every time. *When did this happen? Why?*

What Jack said was true.

Once again, her body has betrayed her. She falls into a heap on the floor and begins sobbing.

BROOKLYN

My head is not in the game; I am still upset over Sister Elizabeth. I have shamed her, and in doing so, I feel shame myself. I get off at the wrong stop but manage to jump back on the train before the doors close. While walking into Mrs. Walsh's building, I try to develop a plan. *What am I looking for that the detectives were unable to find?* I'm hoping my intuition tells me.

I knock on her door, but I don't expect anyone to answer. I am not disappointed. After looking around the hallway for prying eyes, I turn the knob; it's locked. Down the hall, the sound of an apartment door opening gets my attention. It's the door for 1A. Out steps the little boy I met the last time I was here.

"Hey," I say as he moves farther into the hallway. "I'm looking for Mrs. Walsh."

He walks a little closer to me. "She's not home."

"What's your name?"

"Michael."

I smile at him. "Oh, like Michael the Archangel?"

"I don't know who that is," Michael says flatly, emotionlessly.

"He's the most powerful angel of them all."

Michael stops in the middle of the hall, watching me. *There is something strange about him, for sure, but I'll bet that's what people say about me.*

"Do you know where she is?" I ask.

He points toward the door of the basement. I walk to the basement door and turn the knob; it's locked. "When did she go down there?" I ask.

Michael shrugs his shoulders.

"Was it today?"

He shakes his head.

"How do you know she's still down there?" I ask.

"I hear the noises at night."

"Noises?"

"Yes." Michael holds his ears.

"The noises are loud?" He nods. I take a deep breath, then ask, "Do you only hear noises at night?"

"Yes, that's when he comes!" Michael says it excitedly, fearfully.

"Who is 'he?'"

Michael's eyes pop. He spreads his hands out, in a menacing way, his arms fully extended, imitating... what? A giant? A monster? He is a peculiar little boy, but the way he immediately stretched his arms out when I asked causes me to believe him.

"Do you have a key?" I ask.

Michael turns and walks back into his apartment. As I stand in the hall, waiting for him, my entire body pulsates. *Is this a warning?* I hold the triangle around my neck and recite the words the man in Turkey used when he sold it to Mr. David: "The infinite power and protection of the Trinity!"

The boy comes back out of his apartment holding a key. He hands it to me. Immediately, I try the lock on the basement door. It doesn't work. I try again, as if by willpower, the lock will turn. No luck.

Michael pulls on my shirt. "It doesn't work," I say, stating the obvious.

"No."

He points to the apartment door. He takes the key out of my hand and unlocks Mrs. Walsh's apartment door but doesn't open it. He turns to me and stares.

"She's not in there," I say. "You said she was in the basement."

"She has the key."

Now I get it. "The basement key is inside her apartment?"

"Yes."

I hear high heels hitting the tiled hallway. The steps stop me from entering Mr. Walsh's apartment. I slide the key out of the lock and put it in my pocket.

"Michael," his mother says firmly in the hallway as she struggles with two grocery bags. She eyes me suspiciously.

Michael walks to his mother. She hands him one of the bags, which he promptly takes into the apartment.

"Who are you?" his mother asks sternly.

"I met your son before when Mr. Cohen and I had tea with Mrs. Walsh," I say, hoping to alleviate her fears. I walk closer to her, so she can see how young I am. I don't want her to feel threatened. "Jack Kelly."

A moment later, Michael returns to the hall from the apartment. "Mrs. Walsh was helping us with paperwork from her cousin's estate," I tell his mother.

She ponders for a moment, then her eyes soften, recalling our last visit. "Oh yeah, I sort of remember her saying something about that." Her posture eases a bit.

"Your son told me that Mrs. Walsh was in the basement," I say.

Her demeanor changes drastically; her body tightens, her eyes widen. She stands firm. It is a fight or flight stance, and she has decided to fight. "Oh, he did? What else did he tell you?"

"Just that Mrs. Walsh was down in the basement. Oh, and something about loud noises."

She stands in front of Michael in a protective manner. *Something isn't right.* "Did I say something wrong?"

"Michael is autistic." She says, but she is thinking *you're a liar.*

"Artistic?" I repeat incorrectly, thinking she means like an artist. "How cool to be a child artist and to know it at such a young age. It must be what

427

makes him so sensitive."

"No. Autistic."

I shake my head. "Oh, I thought you said artistic. Autistic—I don't know what that is."

"Well, it's a lot of things. A wide umbrella. Each child can be very different. There are things we understand about Michael, and things we are still discovering. For one, he's nonverbal…"

It takes me a moment to get my brain around the word. "Nonverbal?"

"He doesn't talk."

Oh, Jesus. Lady, that child was clearly talking to me.

Michael steps to her side. "I talk; she just can't hear me," he says.

How do I recover from this? "Do you hear loud noises at night?" I ask Michael.

She looks down at her son as he covers his ears with his hands. "The noise bothers him. He's very sensitive to noise. Unfortunately, the building has rats," she says.

I stand there like a bobblehead doll on the dashboard of a car, nodding continuously. Finally, I ask, "Have you seen Mrs. Walsh?"

"No one has seen Mrs. Walsh for days," she says. "We saw her go down to the basement a couple of days ago. The police have already been here to check it out. No one has seen her since."

I bend down and look into Michael's eyes. "Thank you."

"I'm going to make dinner. Let's go, Michael." They walk back into their apartment.

"Nice meeting you," I call after her. I count six 'Mississippi's' in the hallway before walking backward to Mrs. Walsh's apartment and sliding inside, all the while thinking *you keep going to places you feel you must go but clearly should not be.*

Inside the apartment, I get a better understanding of what the detectives were talking about. It doesn't look like she was planning on going anywhere. *Why isn't this roped off as a crime scene?* Probably because there really hasn't been a crime, at least that anyone knows about. I pull the nicer detective's business card from my pocket and consider calling him. But I need to look around first and get into that basement.

I start with junk drawers. Everyone has a junk drawer. I check kitchen drawers and cabinets for the keys to the basement. That's where Dad and I keep everything. Not Mrs. Walsh, though. Everything about this apartment is so neat, so organized. I look at the walls, scanning, my eyes finally moving between the kitchen and the living room. There they are, hanging on a hook: the keys. They all appear to be keys to apartments, which make senses, since she is the super of the building. All the keys are of uniform design, but one appears to be a skeleton key.

After removing the keys, I walk to the door and open it a crack. After making sure there is no one in the hall, I quietly make my way out of the apartment. The skeleton key clearly is not the correct key for this door. One by one, I try all of the others; none work.

There must be another entrance. I go back into the apartment and put all the keys back, except the skeleton key.

It is beginning to get dark when I explore the outside of the building. I find a small set of stairs that lead down to the basement's exterior door. I pull out the skeleton key, and it fits!

I try opening the door, but something is blocking it. After a bit of a struggle, I open the door enough to squeeze in. I quickly realize that the items blocking the door are the boxes that Cohen and I went through. I move further into the basement, which is dark and musty. The thought of rats climbing around grosses me out. Carefully, I feel my way in the dark for the staircase. Crawling up the stairs, I am able to find and turn on the basement light.

I unlock the basement door and step out into the hall just to clear my head.

After looking around from the top of the stairs, I head back into the basement, closing the door gently behind me. *What am I looking for? Why am I here? As if my life couldn't get any stranger, it just did today. I'm hearing a mute boy talk.* I shake that off and begin to assess the place. Mrs. Walsh can't be here. The basement is congested with lots of bullshit—boxes, paint cans, an old piano. In the rear of the basement, behind the stairs, an old canvas covers a bunch of items. I look at the boxes again; it is clear that someone has gone through them. I find the box holding the Polaroids of the *Duality* exhibit. I took all of the Polaroids of Kasper's self-portrait with the shadows. They are sitting in Peter's P.O. Box. These photos are scattered, some of them missing. I have a good memory, and there were five Polaroid photos of each painting, just like Kasper's self-portrait. Not anymore.

I rummage through the boxes and find some of the bills of sale, all the while thinking *who else would want these besides me?* Last time I was here, I had asked Cohen, but he said we weren't here for bills of sale, so I left them. Now, after flipping through them, I put them all back inside the envelope and place them outside the basement door, behind a garbage can. I'll take them with me later. They may be useful.

Above, I hear the basement door squeak open. Someone is walking down the stairs.

"Are you down there?" It's Michael.

I walk to the staircase, see him, and motion for him to come down. "Where is your mother?" I ask.

"Cooking. Talking on the phone."

"How come I can hear you?" I ask. Michael shrugs his shoulders. "Can anyone else hear you?"

"Mrs. Walsh."

I nod. "She's not down here," I say.

Michael keeps nodding. "Yes. Yes. Yes," he says, flapping his hands like he is a bird getting ready for takeoff.

"Okay, calm down. Look with me."

Michael and I continue the search of the basement. I come across a sledgehammer; I pick it up and lay it on the stairs. Mrs. Walsh is not here. If she were, we would be hit with the awful smell of her decomposing body. Of course, I don't say that to the little boy. Behind the stairs, I pull the canvas off and toss it onto the floor. The canvas had been covering large and small canning jars, which are lined up in crates. Some are empty, while some are filled with fruit and others with tomatoes. Several very large jars stand against the back wall, jars three feet in height, maybe larger. They are labeled, so it is impossible to see what's in them. Climbing over the smaller jars, I make my way to them. I turn the first jar around. It looks like pickles but has a very weird smell. I clear the smaller jars out of the way so I am better able to get a handle on the bigger jars. The next jar appears to have peaches, but it does not look appetizing.

"It's getting dark," Michael says, an urgency in his voice.

I grab the last jar, struggling to turn it around.

Michael screams. A high-pitched, ear-popping shriek like a wounded animal.

"Oh my God! Oh my God! Holy fucking shit!" I scream aloud, hardly recognizing the sound of my own voice.

Mrs. Walsh is stuffed in the third tall jar. She looks like a medical specimen.

I look over my shoulder at Michael. He is in shock and will not stop his high-pitched screaming. It is creating havoc in my brain to add to the fact I am already freaking the fuck out. *What are you doing, Jack? What is this?*

"He's going to come! He's going to come!" Michael yells between his high-pitched screams.

"Who? Who's coming?"

I bring myself to look at the jar. Mrs. Walsh is curled into a fetal position in some kind of liquid. Her eyes are closed, and strands of hair float by her face like kelp at the bottom of the ocean.

"Oh no, oh no!" Michael starts to give a play-by-play of his emotions between his high-pitched screams, which continue interfering with my thoughts. "Get her out! Get her out!" he screams.

I'm too stunned to do that; clearly, she's dead. *What the fuck am I going to do with her?*

"It's here! It's here!"

I look around frantically, trying to see what he sees. I don't see anything. *The kid is making me a fucking nervous wreck! I need to get him out of the basement, fast, so I can develop a plan.*

I hand him the detective's business card. "Have your mother call this number. Now. Tell the detective where I am! Go!"

He doesn't move. "It's here! It's here!" More high-pitched screams. He stands, pointing.

A rat crawls out of a crack in the wall. *Is this what he's freaking out about? Is this what he thinks is the monster?*

I look back at the jar just as Mrs. Walsh's eyes pop open. "Ohhh, fuck!" I fall backward. *Now it's my turn to scream! She's alive? That's not possible!*

Inside the jar, though, I clearly see Mrs. Walsh mouthing, "Help!"

I try to pick up the jar, but it's too heavy. "Michael, help me!" I say, suddenly starting to panic.

He stands frozen on the staircase. I'm going to have to do this myself. As I begin to roll the jar along the concrete floor, I lose control. It rolls away from me, bouncing off the staircase. Finally, I grab the top of the jar and try to open it. It won't turn. *How the fuck can I get her out of that small opening, anyway?*

Michael has stopped screaming. Now he is pointing; his eyes wide with fear.

I follow his eyes. "Holy Mother of God! What the fuck!" I scream aloud.

The rat is contorting, its frame pulling apart and reforming into some prehistoric…I don't even know what… but some kind of prehistoric fucking animal. This happens as I'm trying to figure out what to do with the jar—*lift it and run?* I pick up the sledgehammer and decide to smash the glass in the hope of setting her free. *A mistake? We'll soon find out.*

Back in the corner, the rat-creature keeps growing, now breaking away from whatever body it has metamorphosed into, reforming again, beginning to metamorphose into something else.

I smash the jar. Mrs. Walsh tumbles out, and I get her onto the canvas cloth. She looks like a gigantic embryo; there is a smell—a sweet smell, but overly sweet—of medicine in the liquid. *Amniotic fluid? Some sorcerer's potion? I really have no idea.* It is all around her; she is slippery and gross to the touch.

Michael lets out another high-pitched scream.

I turn around. The creature is now substantially taller than I am. It is large, nasty, and angry!

I grab Michael and rush him up the stairs to get out of the basement. "Call the name on the card! Tell him I need help!"

Before we make it to the top of the stairs, though, the creature swings its long spiny tail, taking my legs out, as well as breaking several steps in the middle of the staircase. *Fuck, Jack, this is the real demon!* It is already making everything else I've experienced seem like child's play.

The creature flicks its tail at us again. This time, I slam it with the sledgehammer. Which only makes it angrier. "Go, Michael!" I push Michael out the door and into the hallway. "Call for help!"

I turn my attention back to the creature and look at it more closely. It appears to be a Cyclops with a tail. It is more than eight feet tall, maybe as tall as ten feet. Its singular eye sits high in the middle of its forehead—what Mr. David and his mystic friends call the "Third Eye."

The creature grabs my ankle and drags me back to the bottom of the stairs. While bouncing along the staircase, I snatch one of the broken steps and smash it across its head. That stops him for the moment I need to make my escape. It pursues me around the basement, crashing into things, knocking them down, destroying everything in its way.

A flash comes to me: that day in the diner, when the cat tore the mouse to bits. All those dead mice in the freezer. *I am the mouse! I better find a hole I can hide in!*

I hide behind the staircase and watch the creature as it searches for me. I reach around, trying to grab the sledgehammer again. *Jack, this may be the hill you die on. You'd better go out swinging!*

Then it spots me. I club its foot with the sledgehammer. It reaches through the stairs and grabs me by the shirt, then slams my body against the back of the staircase. I hear the crunch of one of my ribs breaking; it takes my breath away. The creature slams me again and again until I've dropped the sledgehammer.

I hang there without much fight or breath left in me; my face caught between two stairs. I reach for the triangle around my neck.

The monster and I look at each other face-to-face, separated by a few inches and broken stairs. I peer into its eye. It is the exact color, with the exact mirroring effect, as I noticed in Philips' eyes. This is all unbelievable. I know he is a shapeshifter, a sorcerer, but this creature, how can it be? What kind of shapeshifting, wizardly shit has he created? Again, his mirroring reflects the image of a warrior back to me.

That gives me instant strength and inspiration. Tearing the medallion from my neck, I plunge one of the triangle points directly into the Cyclops' eye. With all my might, I rip the eye from its socket. The Cyclops loses its grip on me, and I crash to the floor, next to Mrs. Walsh. Now blinded, the creature stumbles around the basement, recklessly bringing everything down in its way and making a horrible yell as it continues swinging wildly.

I feel like we're in the battle of David and Goliath. I crawl along the floor, pick up the sledgehammer, and go to work on him. First, I take out his right knee, then the left. The creature falls but not before landing a lucky slap that sends me flying across the basement.

As I lay on the floor, catching my breath, the Cyclops goes into full retrograde, reverse metamorphosis, turning itself back into the same rat that entered through the crack in the basement and started all of this. Now it is bloodied, with one eye missing.

I quickly get to my knees and crawl along the floor, grabbing a jar and throwing it. I miss my target, and the jar splatters on the wall. The rat bounces around, trying to find its hole. I pick up another jar and fire it across the room. I hit the rat this time, but it still slips inside the wall.

After taking a deep breath, I return to Mrs. Walsh. Her body begins to slowly open, like an accordion that hasn't been played in a very long time. I see my triangle on the floor near the rat hole. I crawl to it, grab it, and put it in my pocket. Fearing some force will drag me into the hole, I back away in a hurry, circling back behind the stairs and next to Mrs. Walsh. She stares blankly at me. Pain shoots through my body.

I close my eyes, hoping someone will come to help us.

When I open my eyes again, the basement is filled with activity, paramedics, and police. It is pandemonium. All the cops and ambulance medics have the same reaction when they see Mrs. Walsh and her crunched up form. "Is she dead?" one asks, spooked. When she opens her eyes, they are alarmed. The woman is clearly catatonic. She can't speak. They try to take vitals. Occasionally, she vomits up some of the amniotic fluid in which she was floating. They rush her out of the building into a waiting ambulance. The look on seasoned responders' faces when they see the damage in the basement, along with my ghostly complexion, is pretty easy to read: *What the fuck happened here?*

They immediately take my vitals and check my eyes. I look like a corpse. It is the same look anytime I have a fierce supernatural experience.

Within moments, Brooklyn police have already begun asking me questions. *Honestly, I don't know how or where to begin.* I feign confusion. How do I describe finding Mrs. Walsh in a jar? A rat turning into a Cyclops? Any answer I give will probably earn me a one-way ticket to Bellevue or another psych ward. *No thank you!*

I notice that the inside stairs are destroyed. The police and paramedic traffic comes and goes through the outside door. After a while, police officers walk me out, giving me a little assistance. My rib is killing me. Paramedics want to take me to the hospital to check the rib and for observation. I'd rather not.

How the hell am I going to explain this to my dad? This shit makes the bird incident look like a day at the park. Then I make a decision. *Nope. I'm not telling him about this. Even if it makes me Pinocchio for the next several days or for as long as is needed.*

We get to the front of the apartment building. "I want to see Michael," I tell the paramedic.

In the hallway, Michael is shaking as he hides behind his mother. She is talking to police.

Several neighbors on the higher floors have come down the stairs— some nosy, some concerned.

I walk over to Michael as he clings to his mother. She looks at me with wariness and shock at my new appearance—the pale skin and darkened eyes. Bending down, I whisper in Michael's ear, "You are going to be okay. That thing is never coming back. You understand me?"

Michael nods. "Besides," I add, "you are like Michael the Archangel. A warrior."

He steps away from his mother and hugs me. It hurts my ribs, but I hug him back, thinking *I need to add Michael and Mrs. Walsh to my Book of Souls.* All the souls that need protection I write in that book. I must come back at some point and check on them, especially because of the other thought on my mind. *You brought this here, Jack—whatever "this" is.*

Detective Gruff and his partner arrive as medical personnel rush Mrs. Walsh into the ambulance. Like everyone else, they are horrified by her condition. Both of them hurry over to me as I continue being examined by the paramedics. They are deeply disturbed by my corpse-like complexion. The Brooklyn police are also circling me.

"Don't let anyone take him anywhere," Detective Gruff barks, leaving me with the more congenial detective.

Immediately, I begin campaigning for them to take me home. "I need to talk to my dad."

The detective walks over to a couple of Brooklyn officers to find out what they know.

Soon, Detective Gruff comes out of the building and walks straight to me. His partner joins us.

"What the hell happened in there? Where was Mrs. Walsh?" he asks, his questions demanding. I close my eyes and begin putting together my own jigsaw puzzle as he follows up with, "Why in God's name did you come to Brooklyn?"

"Alone?" his partner adds.

"Honestly, I can't tell you exactly why I came up here," I reply. "I guess I just needed to see for myself that Mrs. Walsh wasn't just sitting in her apartment having tea. I needed to know what happened to her."

They wait for more of the story. "She wasn't home," I continue, "and I was about to leave when the little boy across the way, Michael, came out of his apartment and told me she was in the basement."

"Told you?" Detective Gruff asks with a sharp stare. "His mother says he doesn't speak."

"Yes, well, he does a lot of pointing."

I wasn't about to elaborate. Michael may be autistic, but he spoke to me and apparently speaks to Mrs. Walsh. "He, Michael, went into his apartment and came out with a key. I thought it was for the basement, but it was for Mrs. Walsh's apartment. We went in and found a basement key for the outside door," I say.

"The kid told you? Or showed you?" Detective Gruff asks, wanting clarification.

"Yes, in his way. Like I said, he does a lot of pointing."

I cannot be completely honest with them. How can I tell the detectives about my vision regarding Cohen and Philips in the diner without them thinking I was insane? Or that the private detective Peter and I had, Cohen, was selling us out? And what about these intuitive abilities that I have? Not to mention that, yes, the apparently nonverbal kid talked to me.

A Brooklyn detective interrupts us. He looks at Detective Gruff. "You guys are out of your jurisdiction."

"Yes, we know that. We are friends of Jack, here for support," Detective Gruff says. I choose to believe him.

The Brooklyn detective holds two pedestrian drawings. The first is of a Cyclops. "The kid drew this." He shows it to the detectives, then to me. I look at it and then give the detective an expression, like *is there a question attached?*

"How did you get that out of him?" asks Detective Gruff.

"His mother asked him to draw what he saw. He can hear. And see."

They all look at me. "He was big, that's true," I say. "Only I'm pretty sure he had two eyes." That gets a laugh. "Not to be too dramatic, but I was fighting for both of our lives and trying to get the kid out of the basement before he got hurt."

"His mother said he came running into the apartment screaming," Detective Gruff says. "She also told us the basement was infested with rats that scared the kid at night."

"If it was a rat that attacked us, Detective, then it was the largest rat I've ever seen. It even walked on two legs," I add, feeling completely in over my head, with no one to turn to for help. Mr. David and the mystics? They crumbled. The nun in the boarding house? *I need her!*

I'm not happy with the fact that I am not supporting Michael's story. I'm making it look like the Cyclops he saw was nothing more than a child's irrational fear. An autistic child at that, whatever comes along with that. Not a proud moment, but who will believe the real story? I convince myself I'm doing it to protect him—and myself.

"How did he escape?" The Brooklyn detective interrupts my internal monologue. "The… whatever it was."

Breathe, Jack, climb that beanstalk, tell your fairytale.

"Not really sure. I'm a little confused because he knocked me around," I say. They are all nodding patiently, but they want an answer. "I think he ran when he heard the sirens."

"Did he run up the stairs?" The Brooklyn detective stares at me. "Into the building?"

"The interior stairs are pretty damaged; could he have made it up those stairs?" counters Detective Gruff.

I think Gruff is throwing me a bone. *Don't lie, Jack, but don't say he crawled into the wall, either.*

"He hit me pretty hard; I was more than a little foggy. But I'm almost positive he did not take the stairs up."

The detective yells to some patrol officers to conduct a full search of the building anyway. He calls over the paramedics and asks if I suffered a concussion in the attack. "Most likely," one of them says.

Great! That's the wave I'm going to ride. Can't remember shit—go with that, Jack.

As I exhale, happy to be off one hook, the Brooklyn detective shows us the second drawing. Although, it is very rough and basic—the scribbles of a young child—it shows clearly enough Mrs. Walsh stuffed in a three-foot jar. It is creepy and accurate.

"What's this?" I ask, the last of my schoolboy innocence on display.

"Thought you could tell us," the Brooklyn detective says.

I stare at Michael's drawing for a long time. His fear is also my fear, a fear we both just lived through and survived—Mrs. Walsh in a pickle jar.

The shock is overwhelming.

Might as well tell them the truth. "Yes, the drawing is accurate. Mrs. Walsh was stuffed in a gigantic pickle jar," I say.

All the detectives stare at me, then at the drawing, their faces registering pure disbelief. Chatter ensues, and then the Brooklyn detective turns to me. "How is that possible? And that she's still alive?"

After the paramedic's finish checking me out, they bring me back to the basement. We walk along the outside of the building to the basement stairs. I look for the envelope with the photos of the *Duality* exhibit, hoping it wasn't confiscated by the police. In the midst of the earlier chaos, the Brooklyn detective is realizing they may have trampled on evidence. I walk slowly, looking for a chance to grab the envelope.

They want me to walk them through the attack from the beginning. Where exactly had I found Mrs. Walsh?

"Can I have a moment?" I ask before we walk back into the basement. The detectives move on ahead, giving me a chance to grab the envelope and stick it under my shirt.

When we arrive, we see the forensics team has arrived on-site to dust for fingerprints and take samples.

"Michael came down the stairs," I begin. "We were looking around the basement. I kept telling him she wasn't down here. Michael started to flap his arms, nodding his head and making noises. All of these jars were covered with that canvas. I started poking around, turned some jars around. He started screaming—it was shocking—and I fell back. That's when we were attacked." I am trying with great difficulty not to lie.

"Was he already in the basement or did he come through the outside door?" the detective asks.

"I don't know. I'm not sure. He was just there all of a sudden. It could have happened either way. Michael was insistent and very distracting."

Again, I feel a tinge of guilt. What do you call it when the truth is not enough? I feel like I am throwing Michael under the bus. A kid who is mute, whose life cannot be easy and will never be easy. *What do I do with all of this?* But I am protecting Michael and myself. We both experienced and witnessed what is rationally not possible, but it is as he has drawn it—a cyclops attacking us and a woman stuffed in a pickle jar. Though, I must tell it in a way they all can believe; I don't make the rules.

The Brooklyn detective wants to know if anybody in the building had a problem with Mrs. Walsh. I know who it is; I know who crawled out of that wall but how do I explain shapeshifting? How do I explain Mr. Philips?

"Can someone get me a fucking aspirin?" I ask while struggling for a way to answer.

The detectives are surprised. By what? That I have a headache? Or that I just said the word 'fuck?' *Give me a break here. First, a mute boy talks to me. Second, I find a woman floating in a large pickle jar. Then, I fight with a Cyclops that is actually… what, a rat? Mr. Philips? Fuck, fuck, fuck!* I start to believe I'm still unconscious from the fall because this is crazier than a make-believe family!

"Can I please have something for my head?" I ask again. "It's about to explode!"

"Let me see if I can get a paramedic."

As the Brooklyn detective leaves, Detective Gruff takes a small bottle of Excedrin from his pocket and hands me two pills. "Go get Jack some water," he says to his partner.

When we are alone, he says, "Look I don't know what the hell happened in here, but you need to be more careful. Stop putting yourself in harm's way."

I nod. "You're right, but on the other hand, we did find Mrs. Walsh."

"Yes… in a jar!" He waits for my reaction. "You saw the shape of that woman. That could have been you. Whoever did that is a psycho and maybe one who plays with the Devil."

Detective Gruff's ability to deliver and understand this bit of information happily surprises me. I think there are people who believe in this—the unseen, the supernatural—and then there are the majority of people who think it's all crazy, imaginary. I would think a detective like Gruff would think people like me are nuts. You know, how everything seems to go back to the insult to my brain. I need someone to believe that we are dealing in the otherworldly. "What happened in there, Jack? Whose story should I believe? Yours? Or the autistic kid's? Because, from the little I've heard about autism, I don't think he knows how to lie."

The detective is correct. It's been a long time since I felt I could tell the truth. I wish it were another way, but it isn't.

"Can you get me home?" I plead, trying to end his inquiry before it gets too far—before I tell him everything. "I'm exhausted, and my father's going to kill me. Maybe it will all come back to me after a good night's sleep."

"Let me see what I can do."

We leave Brooklyn, but I am taken to NYU for observation for a possible concussion as the paramedic suggested. The detectives drive me, which is not protocol, but they come up with a reason that works for Brooklyn PD. Why make this kid's father come out to Brooklyn, especially after he saved a woman's life?

"Not to mention the little kid," Detective Gruff says as he finishes negotiations with Brooklyn PD.

THE HOSPITAL

Dad arrives at the hospital first, followed by Aunt Paula and Uncle Willy, who are both under the influence. They tell me they ran into Brick. Dad is understandably pissed, concerned. He stares at me looking betrayed. "What is it with you, Jack? I don't know what to do with you anymore. It's like you have some kind of death wish." Aunt Paula and Uncle Willy step out of the room.

Detective Gruff becomes my guardian angel. "Mr. Kelly, if I may intrude for just a moment."

Dad spreads his arms and motions with his hands like *please do*. "Sure."

"Don't get me wrong. You have every right to be upset here, but Jack saved a woman's life tonight. And maybe a little boy's as well. If he hadn't gone up there to check on her, she would be dead now. No doubt in my mind. She is in critical condition as we speak. And the..." the detective pauses as if the word he is about to use is not accurate. "...man, who did this to the woman and who attacked the boy—Jack fought him off, for all of their lives."

Dad looks at me with love, but there is also fear in his eyes. A parent may be proud of a child for saving someone, but at the end of the day, they

443

want their own kid home and safely in bed.

"I don't want you to think I'm letting Jack off the hook here. I read him the riot act myself; I told him he should have called me before going to Brooklyn. I told him that there are a lot of bad characters in this world. He didn't run and hide to save himself, and that means something."

"Well, I appreciate that Detective. He... we have had a rough couple of years."

The detective nods his head. "Yes, you have. I know your story." He hands my dad his business card. "Call me if you need anything."

He then turns to me. "Listen to your father; you have a good one."

I could use a joint to calm myself down, but I also know... no more drugs for me. Not even pot. It's been clouding my senses, my abilities. I have to stay alert, ready.

Mr. Philips and I are not finished.

The doctors want to keep me overnight to make sure there is no internal or cranial bleeding. Concern weighs my father down, which makes everything, even the wins, difficult to appreciate.

Finally, Dad and I are alone. "Dad, I'm fine. I feel great. This is just bullshit," I say.

"Well, I'm going to stay."

"No. You're not staying. This is not like the last time. I'm okay; you taught me how to take care of myself. You know all that exercise you made me do after the fall and the rope down the middle of the apartment? It paid off tonight."

He fusses but leaves reluctantly.

Falling asleep is easy but staying asleep is hard. I hear the sound of someone walking slowly down the hall, a telephone ringing, a voice in prayer, a chorus of chants. There is a lot going on, and it's not just in my head. I wake up. The phone must be Dad saying goodnight. I don't pick it up. *Who is praying? Chanting?*

The sound of the footsteps grows louder and louder. There are no lights on in the room or hall. I lay in total darkness.

The noise keeps getting louder. *Damn! The phone won't stop ringing.*

Suddenly, everything goes silent, except the telephone. The footsteps stop. Someone stands outside my room.

The door slowly opens. Pulling myself up, I realize someone is also sitting in the chair next to my bed. The telephone continues to ring.

"Don't let him in, Jack."

I look slowly to my left. The nun from the boarding house sits in the chair next to my bed. My mouth flies open, full of shock. This is the first time she has come to me.

I return my attention to the doorway. A small ray of moonlight reveals Mr. Philips standing there with a deep, nasty cut that oozes in the center of his forehead. The location of the mystical Third Eye… or, for a Cyclops, the only eye.

The phone continues to ring. "Answer it," the nun whispers.

I must still be dreaming, but I do as I'm told. "Hello?"

"Jack? You haven't left yet?"

"Um, no." I'm completely confused, but something in the dream is familiar.

"You had a migraine, right?"

"Katherine?" *Katherine? How is this happening? All the doctors told me it was the brain injury… that I imagined her—my wife—and my kids; the fall created all that. How can she be calling me here in the hospital while I'm still a fifteen-year-old boy?*

"Come home, Jack. I have your dinner in the oven. The kids are waiting for you."

I don't know whether to smile, laugh, or cry. "Oh, Katherine, it's so good to hear your voice."

"Jack, did you have a couple of drinks?" Moment of panic. I remember this. She called me. Stevie is sick.

"No. Just a migraine. Is everyone… is everything okay?" I ask, hesitating on almost every word. *Am I talking to a ghost?*

"Everyone, everything is fine."

I look around the room. No longer am I lying in a hospital bed. Instead, I'm sitting in my office in Los Angeles. It is all coming back to me.

"How's Stevie?"

"Sitting here doing his homework. Want to say hello?"

"Yes!"

Stevie gets on the phone. "Hey, Dad, I'm working on this cross pass in soccer; I want you to help me this weekend."

"You got it. Stevie, how you feeling?"

"I'm great, Dad!"

"How are Lily and Mikey?"

"Everyone is fine, Dad. We are all just sitting here doing homework, waiting for you."

"Great, I'm on my way." I hang up the telephone and head out of the office.

When I walk into my house, everything is just as I left it. The kids are all healthy, and Katherine is moving about happily, as if nothing ever happened. She puts a plate on the table. It's one of my favorites—Chicken Cordon Bleu.

"Did you get the Midrin?" she asks.

"Yes," I lie.

"They delivered the safe. It's in the garage."

I'm trying hard to catch up. It's quite a gap between a fifteen-year-old boy in the hospital and a forty-seven-year old husband and father of three. *Why do I want a safe?*

"Oh. Okay."

"Jack, some guy called today asking about a painting."

"What?" My entire body shakes. I feel like I'm coming out of my skin. *How can I protect my family? This is never ending...*

"He said he was a curator at a small museum downtown that is doing a retrospective on a Kasper Greenstreet. He wanted to see if you might be interested in selling a painting of his that you own?"

I try to answer her but cannot. I feel myself caught in the in-between.

"I must say I laughed," she continues. "Can you imagine us owning a Kasper Greenstreet original? All three of our kids' college educations would be paid for."

446

It feels like a train is running through the middle of my chest. I struggle to blurt it out. "Did he give you his name?"

"Yes. Wait a minute, let me get it…"

My heart is racing. I am no longer there, apparently—or maybe I am, or both, the in-between—

but I can sense Mr. Philips continues moving into my hospital room.

"Seymore Hunter," she says, her voice fading…

I glance away from Katherine and am back to the hospital; I look away from the phone to see the nun firmly blocking the door. She is facing him. Her back is to me, blocking my ability to see Mr. Philips. She is praying with great force in Latin. "Put on the full armor of God so that you can take your stand against the Devil's schemes. For our struggle is not flesh and blood but against the rulers, against the authorities, against the powers of the dark world, and against the spiritual forces of evil in the heavenly realms. Therefore, put on the full armor of God so that when the day of evil comes you may be able to stand your ground…"

I look at my hand, hoping that I'm still holding my fork at the dinner table with Katherine and my kids. Instead, it is holding the telephone receiver, and I am sitting in my hospital bed.

"Seymore Hunter?" I repeat.

Suddenly, the nun is blown back into the chair with incredible power and force. "Don't let him in, Jack!" she yells.

If she can't stop him, how can I?

I get out of bed and walk slowly to the door. Mr. Philips' face is not the same. The hole in the middle of his forehead is now an open, expanding wound, oozing all kinds of secretion. His eyes, however, maintain that icy blue color.

"Seymore Hunter, the painting is not for sale," I say, now realizing that he and Philips are one and the same.

For some reason, reciting that name I'd never heard before prevents him from entering my room, but I know it is a momentary sedative. I close the door in his face.

I turn to the nun. Her voice is urgent, reminding me of our first meeting when I fell through the floor in the boarding house. "Go back to your body. Don't let them attach to you. You must be very careful, Jack. That is pure evil!" Our connection is heart to heart, telepathic. There are no words said aloud.

"Can he hear us?"

"No."

"What can I do?"

"You must find out what he needs in the painting and use it against him," she says. "It's not enough to hide it. He will never stop looking for it until he gets it!"

THE PAINTING

The warehouse is quiet when I arrive. I feel alone and paranoid as I unlock the door to our storage container. While unwrapping the painting, I stare at Kasper Greenstreet's actual child subject. It is clearly me. I see it in an obvious way I never saw the first few times that I viewed the painting. Nothing has moved; the painting has sat in its wrapper just as I left it. I begin to touch the very expensive painting, hoping to understand and even control its mystical elements. I outline the shadows with my fingers, certain these are the things Mr. Philips—Seymore Hunter or whatever his name is—wants. I'm a witness to their power.

I decide to try and command them to move, to step out of the painting. I want to see them in action. The way they were in Kasper's apartment.

"Slide out!"

I step back, waiting for the show to begin. Nothing. "Show yourself. Come dance on the wall."

The sound of an elevator in the distance makes me pause, makes me edgy. I sit in the small storage space, studying the painting, remaining quiet. Again, I trace the shadows and study the painting. I know its magic, its source of power. The silence is deafening. I wait for some kind of explosion.

Nothing. I sit and then meditate. The words of the nun echo in my head: "You must find out what he needs in the painting."

One more time, I ask the shadows to oblige me. "I've seen you in the hospital room, in the subway. I've watched you move, slither from the painting, slide up the walls in Kasper's apartment. Reveal yourself to me."

Again, nothing happens. Surely, they are remaining still because I do not possess the power to make them move. Now I feel ridiculous. I decide to rewrap the painting, but before doing so, I trace the child with my fingers, watching the shadows for any hint of movement.

They are still.

A moment later, though, I feel a sudden current, a movement of energy in my hands. As I step back to view the full painting, I realize the image of the child has moved. He is no longer looking down at the marbles but facing me.

It scares the shit out of me. With it, I can now feel and hear my blood moving through my body. By looking at myself as a child staring back at me, it changes the entire landscape of the image and the painting. It no longer feels like an object of art. It becomes a living, breathing, moving thing. The day at Madison Square Park comes back to me. I remember the marbles, the feeling of being watched. Apparently by Kasper Greenstreet, as the painting shows, but also by something else, other beings or forces. God, for sure. But something else...

"Jack?" I whisper. Who am I whispering to? The image in a painting?

He has some damage. An insult to the brain.

But not on that day. That was long before my fall, my injury. Yet, I still felt something otherworldly.

I place both my hands on the painted image of me, feeling crazy. "I know you moved. Can you help me?" I humbly ask.

"How?" the response comes in the voice of a child.

My heart threatens to jump out of my chest. I look around the room to make sure I am alone. "What are you?" I ask.

"A boy."

"No. You are a boy in a painting," I say.

"Yes, but still a boy," he replies.

"But who—or what—are you?"

"You," he says.

I step back from the painting as far as I can in the small storage space. He now stands tall on the canvas, the marbles at his feet.

This is all demonic to be sure. Everything is making me leery. I gather enough courage to ask, "What should I call you?"

"Jack."

"But who are you? What are you?"

"Yourself." I think I know what he means, but I must be sure.

"You mean… you are me?"

He bends down and picks up a marble, stands tall again, and offers it to me. My brain and body scream to be cautious. The blood in my veins moves like a wild river. It lights me up with a feeling, a sensation, an emotion that I have never felt before. It is as if worlds collide. The living and the dead. The past and the future. For a fleeting moment, I question myself. *Did I bring something evil back with me after the fall when I returned to my body? Did something attach to me?* He stands in place, holding his marble.

"You know, I had—we—had an accident." He looks at me in a peculiar way. "It was after this painting of you—of me."

He again offers the marble to me.

Before I take the marble, I must be sure. "What do you know about these shadows? The shadows in this painting?"

"They've done some bad things."

"Yes, that I know," I say.

"They're not mine," he quickly adds.

"No, I didn't think so; they're not ours," I reach out slowly towards him and pull the marble out of his hand and out of the painting. The feel and the look of the marble in my hand causes me to remember being a boy. I caress its smooth body in my hand while a tear runs down my face.

"Are you stuck in there?" I ask, trying to fight back the tears.

"No."

"Can they hurt you?" The tears keep coming, but I don't know why.

"I told you, the shadows are not mine. They won't be hurting anyone anymore."

I start to wipe away my tears. "How do you know?"

"Because the man who the shadows belonged to is gone," he says.

"Kasper?"

"I'm not sure of his name, but I knew him, and he is gone."

"How can you be sure they won't do bad things again?"

"Because they were lonely and afraid. They were shadow-less, in a sense."

"Are you sure?" I ask.

"How can you be a shadow if the person whose shadow you belong to is gone?"

The boy—the painted boy version of me—makes a good point. "And now, what are they?"

"Now they belong to me!" he says, as though they are innocent little puppies.

He tosses another marble out of the painting. One of the shadows slithers out behind it, picks up the marble, and jumps back into the canvas with the happiness of a dog fetching a bone.

I'm blown away.

After a moment, I sit cross-legged, Sukhasana style. He does the same. We talk about everything that he remembers. The Jack in the painting—Yourself, as he's asked me to call him— reminds me that he—we—heard voices and picked up on different energies long before my fall. He also reminds me that he is not stuck in the painting. He compares it to being in the hand of God, with no fear, pain, or sorrow. However, he is completely aware of all the chaos and sadness that the painting and shadows helped to create. Now, though, he is in complete control of the shadows, which he proves in various ways. He has the shadows move away from him in the painting, giving him space.

The Jack in the painting—Yourself—plays the game "Simon Says." All three shadows follow his instructions. One shadow picks up three marbles and juggles them. Another shadow does a handstand. They are not menacing at all, which is mystifying, because I know what they have done and what they are capable of doing. The shadows are completely at his command. It is a circus but a child's circus. And he shows his control in loving, respectful ways.

It is soothing because I know Yourself is all about love, and he is using this love to teach the shadows that the hauntings will not continue.

I stay with the Jack in the painting well into the night. He reminds me of the many things I have forgotten, along with something that is very urgent and important: the injury to my brain did not bring the supernatural world to me, like I've thought all along. Instead, he says, it was always there for us. We talk about Kasper Greenstreet, the man who created the painting, and the shadows. He tells me how the shadows were able to leave the storage area in the Gramercy Terrace apartment building when Kasper called on them.

Before I leave, I tell him about Mr. Philips/Seymore Hunter, his eagerness to possess the painting, and his wickedness.

"When doing research on Kasper, it was said that he used blood in his paintings," I say. "That it gave him some kind of artistic power, the ability to make magic."

Yourself is aware of Mr. Philips. "There is blood in the painting," he says. "I've seen him smell it, look for it."

"Do you know what in the painting has the blood mixed with it?"

"Yes. Everything." Long pause. "Except for me. The man thinks that's what controls the shadows. The blood," Yourself says.

"And it doesn't?"

"Not anymore. I told you, they belong to me now."

I quickly make a habit of going to the storage unit every day to visit Yourself. On my third visit, we talk again about Mr. Philips/Seymore Hunter and what to do about him. A little later, Yourself tells me not to come back so often, which surprises me and leaves me more than a little sad. Another loss.

"It's not that I don't like seeing you," he says. "It's just the way it should be."

Before I leave, he gets back into his original position—kneeling on one knee, playing with his marbles.

Walking home, I feel a sense of joy and a sense of loss. He asked me not to come back so often which is obviously a loss, but I feel as if I have found myself—my earlier self. My true self. Yourself told me it wasn't the fall that created these so-called abilities that I have; they were there from the beginning. I—we—had these supernatural gifts as a child.

If the fall didn't create my supernatural abilities, it couldn't have created

Katherine and the kids…

My happiness disappears when I think of Philips. He is the one who has the Polaroid pictures; he is the one with the list of people that own the other Kasper Greenstreet paintings. I sense—know—that he wants to find out if the other paintings have any power he can use or if they are just art hanging on collectors' walls.

Mr. Philips has a way of getting into places. And there is nothing in any of the paintings that has power of its own. There is the blood, of course, but blood must be mixed with something evil or mystical, and there is only one painting with that. The self-portrait of Kasper Greenstreet as a child, the one with the shadows. And I am in possession of that painting.

I dread that everything hangs in the balance. Katherine. My kids. The life I know and will know. Philips knows it is I that is keeping the painting from him. Killing me I fear will be his pleasure.

Brick and I walk down 23rd Street, looking for an underground alley to smoke a joint in. The underground alleys are an amazing way to travel without being seen, and we are definitely not looking for attention. We can walk all the way up to 29th Street without coming above ground. Brick lights a joint as soon as we descend the stairs and takes a long hit.

"Do you believe in the supernatural?" I ask.

"You mean like ghosts and shit?" A puzzled look crosses his face.

"Yeah, like ghosts, voodoo, witches."

Brick nods. "You know Miguel's mother practices Santeria? He says she can put spells on people."

He hands me the joint, but I hand it back without taking a hit. "Why, Jack? You seeing ghosts?" he asks.

Philips has me in his sights before I have a chance to pick up on his energy. My loud pulsating energy is easy to find, and Philips follows Brick and I into the underbelly of the tenement buildings.

Everything is moving inside me. My blood races through my veins; it's my warning shot, my alarm, and it tells me all I need to know. We are not alone.

Brick stops in mid-toke. "What is it?"

A cat trails us. I immediately know what that means. I turn around and begin to chase it, but it turns and hisses at me. Two more cats appear.

I'm nervous. "Let's put the joint out and go up to the street." I don't want Brick to get caught in the middle, especially down here.

"You're just paranoid," Brick says. "The pot will relax you; it always does."

"No. I need my wits about me."

At the end of the alley, I see the outline of a large man. My mind races to the thought of Philips turning into a Cyclops, but now we're in an alley, not a basement.

Brick and I start to run. A screeching sea of feral cats greets us. I run right through them as they try to attack my legs. Brick stops, puzzled, before he quickly follows.

Back on 23rd Street, I now see Philips waiting for me. The only pleasure I get in seeing him is the oozing indentation in his Third Eye, which came from me.

"Jack. What's the matter?" Brick yells. "Is this guy bothering you?!" His tone is of a loud, aggressive, threatening teenager.

Mr. Philips does not fear teenage kids, with or without powers. He is a hunter through and through. He lets out a roar and growls at Brick in a chilling, wolf-like manner.

We take off running. He follows us in the many forms he can take on—first, a large rat that appears to have wings growing from its back. It runs along the sidewalk, before it transforms into a raven flying just above us like enemy aircraft. Brick runs down the stairs into the subway. I follow, worried about bringing him into this mess. Brick runs along the platform and jumps on a train that's ready to leave the station. I jump on right behind him.

"What the fuck was that?" Brick screams. His voice is high pitched, hardly recognizable. He is visibly shaken.

Before I have a chance to answer, Philips walks through the subway car, directly at us. His face changes to half-wolf, half-human. A werewolf. He bares his teeth and begins growling in a deep, guttural manner, which scares the shit out of everyone in the car. People fold over themselves and climb on to the seats. Brick and I run. We head through the gangway to the corridor—the area between cars. Philips changes form constantly and uses deep claws to leave scratch marks in his wake, while howling and making other ear-piercing animal sounds.

The lights in the train go off and on.

Brick and I stay ahead of him until we reach the last car. We have nowhere left to go. Brick fights with the rear door, trying like hell to get it open. Philips steps into the car just as Brick breaks the door with the fire extinguisher. We are at the end of the train, which is slowing down as it begins pulling into the station.

"We need to jump!" I yell. "We need to jump!"

We jump onto the tracks. Philips stands at the rear door, letting out a roar that vibrates through the tunnel. His roar brings out the skeletal horse-head creatures, which begin their own guttural howling.

"What the fuck! What the fuck's happening?!" Brick screams, on the verge of a full meltdown.

Philips leaps into the air, changing into what appears to be an albino bat. He then metamorphoses into several different creatures before landing on the tracks as an oversized rat.

I grab Brick's hand. We run along the tracks as a train approaches from the opposite direction. "Brick, stay close to me!" The train horn blasts as we cling to the wall. We vibrate from both the sound and movement of the oncoming train. Brick pisses himself.

After the train passes, one of the skeletal creatures faces us. "You don't know if you are a man or horse, so I'll treat you like a dog!" I yell.

It stops. I grab its tail and swing it with all my might toward the rat. It's not as easy as the nun made it look.

Brick runs down the tracks to the end of a platform and climbs up. He starts to run but turns back to help me up. As I get to my feet, Philips changes from the oversized rat to his own human form except for Medusa-like snakes slithering from his arms. He grabs hold of Brick, stunning him, then wraps himself around Brick's neck, chest, and legs like a serpent. The roaring of another approaching train drowns out Brick's screams for help.

"Please! Please let him go!" I yell. "I have what you want!"

Philips smiles at my weakness as I take out the key to the storage. Not the least bit worried about whatever abilities I may have.

"I'll give you the painting! I know it's the blood and the shadows you want!"

Brick is confused and horrified. Philips dangles him off the platform as the train gets closer and closer. I hold the key up over my head. "Seymore

Hunter! I'll take you there!"

A transit cop has quietly slid along the wall to help us. Philips already is aware of this, and I become aware by watching his reaction. "What the fuck!?" the transit cop yells as he sees all the snakes coming out of Philips' body.

When the train arrives, Philips tosses Brick into a pillar knocking him out. He then grabs hold of the transit officer, tossing him into the oncoming train and to his death.

Before I can react, Philips wraps his serpent arms around my leg, neck, and arm, immobilizing me. There is no escape.

He firmly leads me up the stairs and out of the subway. The snakes tighten their grip as we begin to walk slowly to the storage unit and the painting. While walking down 23rd Street, it feels like we are alone, not surrounded by the mass of people like on any day in Manhattan. They are all around us, yet do not see us.

We arrive at the storage unit. Once inside, he takes the key from my hand and very slowly opens the storage door. *I have failed; all is lost.* I know I will never make it out of the storage unit alive.

Philips shoves me inside and follows me into the cramped area. The painting leans against the wall, just as I left it. Philips' body has returned to its natural state; the Medusa-like serpent arms are now gone, but he is still intimidating.

He gives me an eerie smile. "Unwrap it," he orders.

I do as I am told. His body begins to shine; it is a yellow eerie light. Philips pushes me out of the way and kneels before the painting, then leans in to smell it. Right away, he senses the blood. His licks the painting with his tongue, which is not a normal human tongue.

Smiling, he touches the shadows. "Dance for me," he commands.

They don't move. He smells them again. "You know who I am." He utters it as a statement, not a question. "Come and show me what you can do."

Nothing. He turns to me, his blue eyes piercing and frightening, vengeance on his mind. "What did you do to them that has made them so docile?"

"I didn't do anything."

Philips smacks me into the wall and bares his teeth. *What is with this guy?* Then he turns back to the painting. His face changes colors and shapes.

Demonic, for sure.

"I will kill you here. I will sacrifice you to the power of this painting!" he barks in a multitude of distorted voices, which scares the hell out of me. He turns to face me. "This is where you die, Jack Kelly."

"Mister…" Yourself says from the painting.

Philips turns back to the source of the voice, the painting. Yourself is facing him, which surprises Philips. I can't tell if it is a happy surprise or if he has been caught completely off guard. I know he is here for the shadows and the blood, not this sideshow.

"Want to play marbles?"

While Philips puzzles over the question, Yourself fires a marble at the center of Philips' forehead, where it sticks into the open wound. Philips' natural eyes pop out as he begins to alter his body. Before he gets very far, three shadows grab hold of him and begin to pull him into the painting—the last thing he expected or prepared for. They suck the top half of his body into the painting with a giant gulping sound. In equally spectacular fashion, his legs begin to change into many forms, some that I cannot identify.

Moments later, a vortex seems to open in the painting. With a vile screeching sound, Philips is gone, inhaled by the painting. Smothered between the three shadows.

I sit in place, stunned and in shock. After a bit, I crawl over to the painting. There is a tiny spot of silver hair between the shadows—the last remnant of Philips. The painting returns to the way it was, with Yourself and the marbles in front of him. The shadows stand above, no longer menacing. It becomes clear to me the shadows do belong to the boy in the painting now.

Still, I need to clear something up with Yourself. "You told me you would not let the shadows move when Philips came. You said you wanted him to see they weren't useful." He doesn't answer. "Jack? Yourself?"

I begin to rewrap the painting. Yourself smiles and turns his head ever so slightly. "Don't worry. The man had evil intentions. He was going to hurt you. I couldn't let him do that. Now he can't hurt anyone."

"What about you? Are you stuck with him, with them now?" I ask.

"No. As I said, I'm very happy here. This is my painting, and they belong to me."

I touch his image very gently, and he goes back to his pose. I think of

something I heard once but can't remember from where or who exactly—
school maybe; Mr. David; or Hermes, the herald of the Grecian gods. "As
above so below, as within, so without, as the Universe, so the soul."

HOME

I touch the boy in the portrait, as I always do on the rare occasions I visit with the painting. I hope that he will move, acknowledge my presence. But he doesn't. Nothing has changed in the painting since that day in New York when Yourself outfoxed Mr. Philips/Seymore Hunter and lured him into the canvas.

Katherine and I place the painting into the new safe that has just been delivered, lock it, and get back to our lives.

It is a typical day in the Kelly house, normal as any other any day. Katherine and I have explained to our kids that they must never display or sell the painting. I have not told them everything, but I have told them enough. They understand that not all things are good.

We go about our daily lives like ordinary people. The gifts or abilities that I possessed and used as a child followed me into adulthood, and I can see them developing in my kids. Every once in a while, though, something commands our attention, something that could be considered otherworldly... if you believe in that sort of thing.

THE

END

ABOUT THE AUTHOR

Kevin Moore is the author of *The Book of Souls*, a mystical ghost story, it is his first novel and the first book in the series featuring Jack Kelly and his paranormal abilities. *The Book of Demons* (think Harry Potter meets the Exorcist) is the sequel to *The Book of Souls*. Moore also wrote *Christmas Stories 7 Original Short Stories* which is available everywhere. His play *Conversations From The Sports Arena* was performed at the HBO Theater in Hollywood. He also had his first children's picture book *Me and My Shadow* released in 2021. Moore hopes to continue the Jack Kelly paranormal saga in a third book which he is currently working on. Moore practices Lucid Dreaming which has helped him with his writing. He is a Yogi and an Advanced Reiki Practitioner—most importantly he is Matthew and Madison's father.

Made in the USA
Las Vegas, NV
16 December 2023

82898402R00277